THE
FIRST
DATE
PROPHECY

THE FIRST DATE PROPHECY

KATE AND **DANNY**

TAMBERELLI

KENSINGTON
PUBLISHING CORP.

www.kensingtonbooks.com

To Alfred and Penelope, the happiest twist to our own
Tinder fairy tale.

And to all of the hopeless (and hopeful) romantics out there
still searching: may your dating (mis)adventures bring you
the happiness and love you deserve.

Love yourself first and everything else falls into line. You really have to love yourself to get anything done in this world.
—Lucille Ball

Chapter 1

Lucy

A lonely woman with words but not much else.

"I once ate nothing but chocolate candy for an entire week," I say, smiling in a toothy, bright-eyed, chipper kind of way that I'm hoping just adds to my allure, a heady blend of coquettish oddball charm that whisper-screams *Aren't I so different than every other girl you've dated in this city, so refreshing and unexpected and unabashedly original?*

I am nothing if not mostly unabashed.

It's a fairly tricky, razor-thin line, though, between oddball charm and alarmingly oddball, and I've found myself squarely on both sides before. It's a risk I'm willing to take to end up on the right side, the memorable side, the side that means I am not just a throwaway one-off round of overpriced Brooklyn dive bar cocktails.

"Hershey dark chocolate bars for breakfast," I press forth, raising my highball glass of whiskey in the air, "Butterfingers for lunch, Snickers for dinner, and Ferrero Rocher for dessert the nights I was feeling peckish. And milk. Dear God, *so much* fucking milk."

I deliver this particular anecdote while cruising smoothly on automatic, my timing and inflection the same as it always is, quietly marveling at my ability to make it sound shiny and new, like it has just now occurred to me to share this rarely revealed and coveted piece of myself. Chocolate Week, however, is a Lucy Minninger first-date classic. One of a select, carefully curated list of stories that show my Truest Self. Or at least the Truest Self I'm comfortable revealing to a first date. I often intersperse these performances with absurd hypotheticals—*what if*s and *would you rather*s—designed to start colorful, surprising dialogue.

Sometimes Chocolate Week gets a good laugh. Other times—like this slightly unfortunate moment right now—my date stares silently, sipping his drink faster, ice clinking as the glass drains, not sure what is expected of him next in our conversational volley.

Shit.

Next time, I'll wait until the third round of drinks, *minimum*. Or maybe I'll scrap it altogether. Find a new sparkly tidbit for future suitors. My set could do with some stiff housekeeping, considering how few second dates I've had in the past year.

Five years, if I'm being honest.

My entire post-college adult life, if I'm being more honest.

I would backtrack, but I'm not sure what we'd been talking about before I decided to hurl myself so wholeheartedly down this particular path. The weather, ten degrees too hot for October? How every drink on this predictable menu is at least five dollars too expensive for any self-proclaimed—per the unmissable neon pink sign in the window—*dive*? Did I mull over those topics quietly, or say them out loud? I down the precious last droplets of my nine-year-rum-barrel-aged-ginger-and-lavender-infused Brooklyn Rye and push boldly on, because there's no other way forward but straight through: "You wouldn't believe how angry my body was by the end. Completely enraged."

He puts his glass down, eyes roaming above my head, searching out the waitress. For a refill or for a check, it remains to be seen.

I study him while I have the chance. He's even more handsome than suggested by his profile on HeartThrobs—the online dating app that brought us together, a fateful flip up for *yes, please*—which is about as rare as a full lunar eclipse on Christmas Eve. He'd only had one picture on his profile, always a risk. But a risk I was willing to take in this case, based on both the exceptional cut of his cheekbones and unparalleled depth of his dimples. His bronze tan that only made him appear more statuesque. I usually set my age parameters at a respectable thirty to forty, but I'd taken a temporary hiatus from my senses after too many pinot noirs while crying my way through my one billionth viewing of *You've Got Mail.*

Twenty-three. He is *twenty-three.*

I was seven years old when his mother was changing his first soggy yellow diaper.

"I swear, I was backed up for at least a week."

I gasp. Did I say that? I did. I said that. That detail, while admittedly true, is not an established part of the routine. I'm rarely thrown so easily, at least not after one drink. It must be his age. The unfortunate mental image of those poo-filled diapers.

I was not designed to be a cougar.

He turns his focus back to me, cocks that perfectly coiffed curly head of his as he levels me with dark-lashed minty blue eyes. I'm tempted to ask if he dyes those impossibly black lashes (and if so, would he recommend the salon?), but any thought of comparing lash notes is effectively squashed as he says: "Why would you do that? It sounds . . . disgusting."

"It started as a friendly competition with a college roommate," I say enthusiastically, relieved he's given me the opportunity to elaborate on something other than my bowels. "We'd been drinking chocolate White Russians one Saturday night, watching the new and old Willy Wonka movies back-to-back, and we started debating how long we could survive on chocolate alone. We decided then and there we'd put it to the test. She quit after one day, said her teeth were too sore, but I'd made such a big deal about how easy it would be, I kept at it. Seven days and seventeen hours. Then I caved and started licking the salt from a bag of stale pretzels."

"Wait. You were in *college* when you did this? Having Willy Wonka marathons on a *Saturday* night and living off candy bars?" It's hard to say if the incredulity in his tone is awe precisely, but at the very least, I have his full attention.

"Senior year," I confirm.

"I would have assumed you were, I don't know, *seven*. My senior year was all about Pabst and parties on a Saturday night. Every night, really. That's when I started DJing." His whole demeanor changes with this last word, *DJing*. He is suddenly a peacock roosting at the rickety bar seat across from me, resplendent and dazzling, so pleased with himself you might mistakenly assume he's the only peacock in Brooklyn. I won't be the one to point out that every other man is behind a turntable on HeartThrobs. There are as many peacocks as pigeons in this city of ours. Maybe more.

"Well, D-D-Da—" I stutter and stop, my brain frantically flipping through *D* names, because that much I'm sure of—Danny, Darren, Derek, *Doug*, yes, Doug, I'm certain that's how I entered his contact information into my phone—"Doug, I have to say—"

"*Hashtag*," he says, cutting me off. And as if I'm perhaps in an age bracket not familiar with the term *hashtag*, a Luddite at the elevated age of thirty, he raises both hands and crosses his index and middle fingers to give me a visual aid.

"Hashtag?" I ask, because maybe I do actually need a definition in order to understand why *hashtag* relates to his name. Or any name. Outside of, you know, a social media post.

He nods, those lashes drooping down as if he might be pitying me for needing to ask such an obvious question. "Heart-Throbs wouldn't let me add a character in my name line. I had it in my bio, though. Didn't you see that? It was the first sentence. *Call me Hashtag Disco Douggy, please and thank you in advance.*"

Had I read that? I vaguely recall a string of Greek flag emojis. But I'd remember a detail like this, surely. It's not every day you meet someone who goes by Hashtag. Or has such a great appreciation for disco. But there was the pinot noir. And those dimples. The cheekbones.

"Yes," I lie. "Of course. I *always* read the bios," I lie again. "I just thought it was a . . . joke?" In hindsight, this feels like the wrong thing to say. At least to someone who introduces himself as *Hashtag Disco Douggy* with a straight face. It's maybe one of the more sincere moments I've had on a date recently. (A low bar. But still.)

"It's not a joke." Hashtag shakes his head, lips pursed. Those lips are far too attractive for anyone who insists on being called a pound sign in casual conversation. It's unfair, really.

The waitress appears in my peripheral, orbiting us slowly, taking our temperature. Is this date over? Just getting started?

I'm more pleased than I'd like to be when he uses those hashtagging fingers to signal two more drinks.

"Hashtag Disco Douggy is my brand," he continues matter-of-factly, "a lifestyle, an inspiration, a calling. It's more than just my DJ handle. It's who I am."

"Huh," I say, at a loss for intelligent words.

My phone chooses this prime moment to vibrate in my pocket, and I seize the blessing. "I need to make sure it's not a work emergency," I say, hoping he doesn't ask me to go into more detail about what a *work emergency* might look like for my particular career path. What does my profile say again? *Renaissance Woman and self-made entrepreneur with a specialty in writing and publishing.* Translation: professional Craigslister who does odd jobs to get by, with a part-time gig assisting a demanding YA author who's sold more book copies than Danielle Steel. Perhaps a slight exaggeration. But she's twenty-five and has written three bestsellers, which seems unfair if you ask me. She's cornered the market on her own special brand of quirky, spec-fic rom-coms. I've only written five rom-com manuscripts that haven't sold, but who's counting? (Me. The answer is me. I'm definitely counting.)

The phone vibrates again. I check the screen, and it *is*, in fact, partly work. There's one missed call from my mother that I must have missed while en route to the bar, her weekly check-in to make sure I'm surviving and "thriving." But then there are three new texts from Clementine, my author boss—whose real name is Colleen, though I took an oath my first day never to refer to her as such. An oath I happen to forget on her most demanding days.

I click through to Clementine's messages:

Did Pinky eat anything weird on your walk this morning?

Pinky is Clementine's very small, very ugly affenpinscher.

She just puked all over the sofa, and you saw the price tag on that!!! You didn't let her eat any of your chocolate muffin did you? I saw your wrapper in the trash this morning. (Could you maybe get something besides chocolate next time?)

And lastly:

Can you research a good cleaner for the sofa and pick some up on your way in tomorrow thx

Somehow, the most infuriating bit is the lack of punctuation to go with *thx*, considering those three bestsellers. There's also the triplicate exclamation points, as if I need the emphasis to remember exactly how much money she spent on the couch that I not only ordered, but arranged delivery for, spending an hour on the phone with customer service, and then helped move around her obscenely large living room seven times to achieve her "perfect feng shui" (mispronounced, of course), despite it weighing approximately five tons. I absolutely did *not* give Pinky a crumb of that muffin—for what a muffin costs in Park Slope, I'm eating every last crusty bit.

"So is it?" Doug asks. *Hashtag Disco Douggy*, I mentally correct myself.

"Is it what?" I ask, looking up from my phone, so angry about Clementine that I've forgotten what we were talking about again.

"A work emergency?"

"Oh. Yes. Kind of."

The way his brow wrinkles—or at least, as wrinkled as anything can be on a pristine twenty-three-year-old face—he almost looks concerned. Or maybe just curious, trying to figure out what it means to be a professional Renaissance Woman, assuming he, unlike me, actually read the profile before flipping up.

"What is it?" he asks. "The emergency?"

"I'm not at liberty to say. It's a private matter with a client." That sounds impressively weighty and sophisticated, *not at liberty to say*, and I'm quite pleased with the overall effect. Only someone dabbling in wildly important things lacks that kind of liberty. And technically, I am *not* at liberty to reveal my boss's real name.

The waitress reappears with our drinks, and I stuff my phone in my pocket. Clementine is not the only twenty-something who requires my attention this evening, thank you. Even if my date likes to be called a keyboard character and fancies himself a proper DJ, he does have those delicious dimples. And lips. Etcetera and so forth. And while his black curls are more styled than my hair has ever been outside of senior prom, molded with some kind of shiny product into a perfect tousled sculpture, the overall effect is rather nice in the dim light of the industrial pipe lamp hanging above our heads.

"I didn't mention it in my profile, but I'm thinking about doing a little acting on the side. Just got my mom to take some headshots last week. We'll see, could be cool. People say I have the face for it." He shrugs, smiling in a way that says, *I do have the face, don't I?*

"Oh? Is that so?" I take a long swig of my whiskey. Very long.

Maybe his hair is too shiny after all, unnaturally so.

"Yeah," he continues, not requiring any additional response, thankfully. "She's not a professional photographer, but I think my pics could make a killer portfolio. She could be going places, thanks to me."

"Ah."

I finish my drink as Hashtag Douggy Doodle or Dandy or whatever the hell he likes to be called waxes on about how he's also been told he has perfect fingers for hand modeling, and did I know there's huge demand for foot models, too?

Just as I'm debating my exit strategy, he's flagged the waitress for another round, and even though there's very little of substance that's appealing about him on paper or otherwise, I sip my whiskey and laugh and try again with another Lucy Classic: standing in line during a snowstorm for the red-carpeted grand opening of a fancy new Dairy Queen, and lighting a pineapple on fire because the grocer next door happened to have a good sale, and because the glove warmers I'd brought along were doing nothing helpful. I was the most popular girl in the line that day, carrying my pineapple around to spread warmth to my fellow Blizzard lovers. This time, as I'm delivering my lines, there's actual laughter—because of the whiskey or my charm, it's impossible to say.

When the waitress comes back again, I have the brilliant idea to request the special they've listed at the top of their vintage typewriter-styled (again, not a dive) menu: The Flaming Zombie. I have no idea what it is, or why it's *flaming*, but it's an appropriate follow-up to my story, and it will surely be a memorable bonding activity with this twenty-three-year-old boy-slash-DJ-slash-social-media-character whom I *really* shouldn't care about bonding with. Not only because we'll likely never see each other again, but because I'm thirty and this is not a productive way to find a future partner.

Unfortunately, tragically, I do care.

I care more than I should, and more than I'd ever admit out loud. But I seem to have a chronic, debilitating condition when it comes to romance: I'm most attracted to the people who least deserve it, and am biologically repelled from all the rest. My brain registers *nice* or *easygoing* and converts to *fake* or—perhaps the worst dating sin of all—*boring*.

Where are the men who are equal parts authentically kind *and* interesting?

Surely there are at least a few of them in a city of more than eight million.

"Oh, wow," I say, my mouth dropping open as the waitress makes her way to us with what turns out to be a literally flaming drink, a tall tiki cup topped with a purple haze of fire. "I thought maybe flaming meant heat, like Tabasco sauce. Prairie Fire style."

The waitress carefully sets the goblet down, and Hashtag and I stare, wondering what comes next. Presumably, the flame dies out, leaving a highly potent beverage in its wake.

I think back to my story, holding that glorious pineapple, and—inspired and buoyed by his laughter, his approval—I grab for the drink, holding it up as I yell out, "Free warmth for all!" Unfortunately, in my enthusiasm, I've lifted the glass a smidge too high, the flame licking the tip of one of those highly glossed curls. It lights for a second, just barely, but enough. Any spark lighting any part of your head is *enough*.

Hashtag screams, a shrill, dolphin-like noise that cuts through the crowded bar, standing up as he smacks his hands frantically against his head.

"Shit, shit, shit," I scream back, nearly as shrilly and dolphin-like, dropping the glass on the table, the contents spilling everywhere as I pick up my cup of water and hurl it at Hashtag's face.

Shit, shit, shit, I think, remorsefully, watching as the water drips down his smooth forehead. The flame is gone, thank God. Only a teeny smidge of burnt hair scent lingers in the air.

Hashtag shakes his head, scowling at me. He's running his fingers along his hairline over and over, as if to convince himself it's all still there, it's okay, he has not tarnished his prized locks. That illustrious acting career, courtesy of Mommy's glamour shots, is still within grasp of his "masculine yet elegant" hands.

And then, without a word, he turns and walks away. Out the door.

The waitress hands me the check. I gasp audibly when I see the total.

This truly is the worst dive ever.

The lights are off in the brownstone, so the Myrtles—Estelle and Frank—must already be asleep, or at least up in bed watching reruns of *CSI* on the television that takes up nearly their entire bedroom wall. I'm tempted to call them to avoid being alone, because I'd much rather sit on their cushy velvet couch drinking Frank's latest gin experiment, dissecting the date from beginning to end, making it all feel like one lovely, silly joke, oh what a ridiculous date to add to my collection! He was twenty-three! A DJ! Called himself Hashtag Disco Douggy! I set his hair on fire!

Frank and Estelle will adore this story.

It's exactly the kind of juicy entertainment they crave on a daily basis, and probably the reason they charge me pennies (by Brooklyn's standards) to live in their basement apartment. Money I insist on paying each month, on principle, because I'm an *adult*, even if they'd be happy to let it slide. We've become good friends—yes, best friends even—at least from our mutual slim pickings in this city. Partly by choice, partly by convenience.

I give them color. *Eternal youth*, as Estelle likes to say.

And they give me a home. They *are* home, really. Or at least as much so as the house in Greendale, Pennsylvania where I grew up. If there's something I've learned in the last almost-decade, a true home in New York City is no easy thing to come by.

I check my phone. Eleven o'clock. Frank is enough of a curmudgeon, albeit a mostly loveable one, even after a perfect night of sleep. I'll tell them all the gory details tomorrow morning over Frank's homemade espresso, spit out of a machine that costs more than my monthly rent, and we'll laugh, and I'll undoubtedly feel better than I do right now.

Because tonight, I feel lots of things, none of them good.

Mortified.

Miserable.

Hopeless.

I desperately want to find the spin, the carefree, ha-ha narrative that's my standard mode of processing and transforming shit into gold. I excel at shaking things off, moving onward and upward. But . . . the spin isn't coming to me this time.

It shouldn't feel this bad, should it?

He was a joke, really and truly, and even if things hadn't ended so terribly, I might have come to my senses in the morning. Not initiated any further conversations. But it would be nice to have that decision for myself. To feel like I'm the one with the good judgment.

I slip my key into the garden-level door, double-lock it behind me as I flick on the too-yellow overhead light. It's my mopey substitute sunshine, given I only have two tiny windows in the front, and the rest of my home is burrowed underground. My Spinster Cave, as I don't actually *like* to say, but do anyway for laughs. Frank and Estelle do what they can to add small shreds of cheer—including hanging a handmade SPINSTER CAVE sign from Etsy above the front door—and have invested far more in renovations and appliances than they'll ever recoup in rent. Though no amount of money seems to get rid of the mice that perpetually choose to nest behind my stove, city mice that are too clever for traps or poison. (On the plus side, I suppose I'm never *truly* alone.)

As I change into pajamas and trek the ten steps from my bedroom to the kitchen to put on a kettle for tea, I hear the scribble-scrabble of tiny mouse feet somewhere behind the sink. I sigh and switch on my old radio clock, turn the volume up to drown out the sound.

In the old days, I would immediately fire off every bad date story to Susie and Grace, my best friends from home. We'd been riding on the same life track from Greendale Elementary through Penn State, into the early days of our twenties, when Susie and Grace would steamroll into the big city to visit more weekends than not—duffel bags stuffed with plenty of wardrobe options to accommodate for brunches and museums, dinners and clubs. I had a collection of shiny new city friends then, too, who would join us, other assistants and big dreamers I'd met on various jobs. But New York City is a revolving door. Those friends drifted. And Susie and Grace are both married now, one with a husband, one with a wife, living in expansive homes they actually own, two children and a dog each. We text every few weeks about them bringing the kids up for the Brooklyn Children's Museum, but it seems their schedules are overwhelmingly busy. I visit them when I see my parents, and we try to have a monthly wine and cheese FaceTime, but *dinners and baths and bedtime routines, oh my!*

I don't text them about the Hashtags anymore. I'm selective about what tidbits I share. A carefully curated list of dates. Funny, but not pathetic. It's a narrow border between the two.

Hashtag feels too close to pathetic territory.

The kettle whistles, and I make my tea.

Mug in hand, slippers on, music still blaring, I settle in on my love seat for what, besides a dish session with the Myrtles, is the best distraction on a night like this: HeartThrobs. Hours of flipping up for yes, down for no, waiting and hoping for a good match, for some sense, any kind of sign, that there is more than this for me. More than a string of failed jobs and failed dates, and the constant challenge to make every one of those failures more comedic and less heartbreaking.

I flip for so long, the profiles blur. The movement itself is calming, a rhythmic pattern. More flips down than up, because I refuse to find myself sitting across from an Exclamation Point or a Parentheses or, God forbid, a Question Mark. I have enough of those on my own.

Flip, flip, flip, a long strand of no thanks.

And then: Rudy, 34. Long auburn hair, pale (extra pale, with a smattering of freckles on top) white skin, big brown eyes, bass guitar in hand as he sings into a mic. I pause, squinting at the screen. He looks vaguely familiar. Have we had a first date? Has he served me a latte? Delivered me bagels?

I swipe through his other photos, all fairly standard Heart-Throbs fare—action shots at bars, some wanderlust pics that look to be from Thailand and Italy, a shot of him in a tux with an ex clearly cropped out based on the sliver of cheek pressed against his. There's no bio, just some emojis: Irish and Italian flags, a meatball, and a frothy beer glass. A bro who plays bass and travels and is seemingly very proud of his heritage.

I'm about to flip down, when it strikes me. The familiarity.

Rudy.

Rudy Riziero.

I saw that face on my television screen growing up.

Every Saturday night.

First on *Black Hole Sons*, a weird, trippy show about twin brother aliens who dropped down in their pod into a suburban Jersey yard. Then a kid's comedy variety show, *The Whiz of Riz*. He starred in both with his older brother Rocco—twins on *Black Hole Sons*, but that was fake, a funny shtick because they looked nothing alike. Rudy was redheaded and freckled and stocky; Rocco was dark-haired and tan and gangly—like, when their parents' DNA was doled out, they received the literal opposite genes on offer.

I was just reading about Rocco on the *E!* website—he was picked to play the hero in a new billion-dollar-budget *Space Blasters* movie. And I'm pretty sure he was determined to be 2014's "Sexiest Man Alive" in *People* last year, which is about as illustrious as it gets in Hollywood. But I don't think I've seen anything anywhere about Rudy in over a decade. Huh.

I'm more than mildly curious at this point, as I am about most celebrities, A- through D-list, even F, G, etcetera. (As most New Yorkers are, though we'll take that secret to our graves.) I'm not sure where to place Rudy, given both his nineties and early aughts stardom and his connection to the great Rocco Riziero. Who, shit, come to think of it, stole Rudy's co-star girlfriend at some point. Piper Bell. The brothers' quirky neighbor on *Black Hole Sons*, and also an A-lister now. That tabloid hit was probably the last time I thought about Rudy's existence.

I grab my laptop from the coffee table and search for Rudy online. The top links are all about recent Brooklyn comedy shows. I scan a few event photos, holding my phone up to the computer screen for comparison.

Definitely the same person.

This 2015 version of Rudy looks like . . . he did as a tween/teen in the nineties, but with long hair that's more burnt cinnamon than flaming carrot, and a few more inches added both vertically and horizontally. He's wearing a black T-shirt and black jeans in literally every photo I see, and his overall vibe suggests he's been living out of a rock-and-roll tour van for the last fifteen years. But he's got those gigantic, puddly brown eyes that transport me straight back to my parents' paisley-smothered living room—Saturday nights in pajamas eating Hungry-Man fried chicken, watching Rudy on their little TV screen, usually with Susie and Grace there.

A date with him would be . . . *interesting.*

A date with Rudy—the boy who once made me nearly choke on my fried chicken from laughing so hard. Who just so happens to be the brother of a major Hollywood star, and would be a bright plume to stick out amongst all the gray feathers in my sad little dating cap.

Yes, a date with him would be a story to tell.

Fodder, if nothing else. For my writing. For Frank and Estelle, Susie and Grace.

Just as I go to flip up, a rodent that I very much hope is a large mouse and not a mid-sized rat runs over my bare foot. I scream, clutching my phone to my chest, and as I glance down, I see it—my finger brushing against the screen in a downward trajectory. Before my brain has a chance to alert my fingers to the course change, I flip down.

Delete.

Goodbye.

There's no going back. Not unless you pay extra for the HeartThrobs Ultra experience, which I adamantly do not.

But that was *Rudy.*

Sure, maybe I hadn't actively thought about his existence for years. But I'm thinking about him again now—and missing out on the possibility of meeting him face-to-face is somehow too disappointing to just quietly accept. He'd make for a story, yes. Undoubtedly so. But it's more than that, too. He'd meant something to me once, hadn't he? He'd made me laugh.

Maybe he could mean something to me again now, present tense. Laughter would be nice, and not just at my own expense.

He's a pleasant reminder, too, of a simpler era—when the biggest stressor in life was getting a B in keyboarding or being the only kid in gym class who couldn't do pull-ups for the Presidential Fitness Award. Not bills or failed careers, not evil politicians or climate change. Rudy was like the elusive feeling that buzzed hot through my veins every Friday afternoon as a kid—riding the school bus home, knowing there'd be two days of unadulterated freedom ahead.

Fuck it.

Life is short. And maybe those whiskey drinks are still circulating in my blood.

I click the *Ultra* button.

Thirty dollars for twenty-nine and below, sixty dollars for thirty and above. Is that ageism even legal? I sigh, plugging in my information. Within seconds of subscribing, a text comes in. From my bank. An overdraft. I paid rent this morning, and then those drinks. Clementine is paying me tomorrow, so I hadn't been worried.

Ugh. That damn artisanal whiskey. How did I sink to this level? Paying good money I don't have to *maybe*, if I'm lucky, match with a total stranger?

No going back now, though.

Please be worth it.

I click the new button at the bottom of the HeartThrobs screen: *BACK.*

Rudy, 34.

I sigh in relief as I slowly, purposefully, edge my thumbs upward.

And then I hold my breath, waiting to see the burst of confetti hearts rain down over Rudy's photo, the sign of a mutual HeartThrob.

Instead, I see a new profile. Ethan, 29, a skinny white dude in a muscle tee flashing a peace sign as he crouches next to a massive golden tiger.

We didn't match.

Rudy and I didn't match.

Maybe he hasn't seen me yet?

I scroll to the bottom of his profile, scanning for a detail I should have checked the first time—when he was last logged on.

July 8.

Three months ago.

Chapter 2
Rudy

A lonely man with little beyond his past self.

In a world of juggling odd jobs to pay the bills, the musical ones are always my favorite.

I've schlepped plenty of drywall, grouted tile, power-washed siding, and then headed to a gig just to make sure I did something I was passionate about that day. Regardless of the genre, location, or attire, I'm just happy to perform. I've played jazz in an old folks' home wearing a fedora, rockabilly in front of a bunch of drunk aunts and uncles for an eight-year-old's birthday, a cowbell in a Peruvian avant-garde band in the backyard of a savings and loan bank, and countless pickup gigs to get paid fifty bucks and a couple of drink tickets at venues across the city, sometimes with little to no attendance.

I can shake anything off, as long as I'm playing.

This evening, however, is looking to be quite uncomfortable. Literally.

My friend Brad, who plays what can only be described as experimental weird funky jazz, has roped me into one long set for a whopping hundred dollars to play bass for a private party at a pierogi place in North Brooklyn. It seemed relatively normal, based on his description over the phone. But I didn't ask for specifics. I should have known better. Especially when it comes to Brad.

"Here, try these on. I am sure they will fit," says the owner of Pierozek, the venue hosting the evening, as he hands me a pair of pants. He's a tall, bulky guy. Like a three-quarter-sized André the Giant. He has a big step, and so far I've been amazed by how gracefully he moves around the restaurant. It's a small Brooklyn first floor, so the walking routes are tight. But it's like watching a veteran all-you-can-eat buffet aficionado cut in front of you to grab that last piece of cheesecake without spilling a single drop of their clam chowder.

I hold up the large baggy black pants to get a full sense of what I'm in for. They strongly resemble a look straight out of MC Hammer's vintage collection. And it's not just the pants. Oh, no. I've already been given a long red sash to be used as a belt, and a bright multicolored vest that at first glance appears to be terrifyingly small.

Uniform in hand, I walk over to Brad and say, as delicately as I can muster given the circumstances, "Dude, what the fuck? This was not part of the deal. You told me a button-down and jeans, and I honored that. What's with these getups?"

I glance over to see our flutist Laurie, a sixty-something Black woman, dressed in a traditional-looking blouse that she keeps tugging at around her shoulders, scratching herself. She looks remarkably unhappy but is too nice to say anything. I take in the rest of my costumed bandmates now, too, and they all look quietly aggravated.

Fucking jazz musicians can be too polite sometimes. Mostly due to the scarcity of paying gigs and the fact that this was the path they chose. To play jazz. To make money to live. No one wants to rock the boat. Not even for a hundred bucks.

Brad looks mildly sheepish. Though it has to be said, his usual white hippie dude socks-with-Birkenstocks look, complete with acid-wash jeans and a tie-dye tee, actually makes his costume change welcome. I won't sink so low as to say that to his face, though. I'm not a total monster.

"Yeah, man, I'm sorry. I didn't know, or I didn't *understand*, anyway, what I agreed to. Can you just . . . do it anyway? I'll grease your taste by twenty-five bucks. That work?"

Sold to the highest bidder at a whopping one-hundred-and-twenty-five dollars. I get to play experimental weird funky jazz in traditional Polish garb for a bunch of people eating pierogis on a Tuesday night.

I do have the self-respect to sigh, at least. "You owe me one. I feel like Chris Farley in *Tommy Boy*, the fat guy in a little . . . bright, itchy vest."

Brad doesn't get the reference, clearly, because he asks, "Didn't he die?"

"Yes, Brad. He's dead. Much like my soul in this outfit."

Brad laughs and pats me on the back, a soccer dad sending me to the sidelines.

Once we're all decked out in our traditional Polish folk attire, we're given dinner. You guessed it: pierogis. Puffy dumpling clouds with different types of fillings—meat, spinach, cheese, and potatoes combined in one pierogi, or just meat, or just potatoes, or just cheese. Extremely utilitarian. They don't give us anything else. No kielbasa, no borscht. When I ask for condiments, I'm told, "The clothes you have on are very old and very delicate, so we would like you to keep them as clean as you can."

A troubling statement for two reasons: Has my costume been properly cleaned—or cleaned at all—since the last unsuspecting performer had to put it on? And also, why didn't we get to eat before we put on the clothes? That seems like the logical path, at least for anyone who appreciates a well-seasoned meal. What a topper, being taste-rationed from dinner before playing two hours of music. While wearing an outfit that may or may not have a stranger's body odor steeped into it.

Damn.

This night just keeps on getting better.

Soon after we finish our condiment-free meal, I stand at the bar and sip my complimentary Żyweic beer, waiting for the room to fill in. But after twenty minutes of observing the door, it starts to feel like there's not really a party happening here after all. It appears to just be a regular dinner crowd.

I put down my empty bottle and turn to Brad. "Didn't you say this was a private event?"

"Yeah, man, I did."

I look him in the eyes, grab his head, and turn it toward the door. "Seems like it's a normal Tuesday here. No decorations, unless you count us in this ridiculous gear."

"Okay. Hundred-fifty work for tonight?"

Again with the cash stimulus.

Pride doesn't pay rent, though.

I sigh, leaning against the bar that now has dirty plates with pierogi carcasses strewn everywhere. It's not helping the situation. "Did you really not get any specifics on this gig?"

Brad turns to me and shrugs. "I go where the music takes me and then ask, *who wants a ride?*"

That's the most earnest Brad answer I'm ever going to get. "Fine. But seriously, you need a booking agent to help you with gigs. Next time, we could be playing in a ball pit at McDonald's for the general manager's ten-year sober party, and I do have a bottom line, you know. You'll have to find another bassist."

Brad ignores me and points to the "stage," or what is really the back of the restaurant, right next to the kitchen door.

Wonderful.

On top of the other many humiliations, we're also going to smell like all the food and extras my mouth was not privy to be enjoying.

The lights dim. Showtime. And oh, what a show it will be.

I'm trying hard to tuck myself away—if I can keep subtly edging back, I may even be playing behind the drummer tonight. Whatever it takes to avoid being recognized, because this is not the private event I was hoping for.

And even though it's been well over a decade since I was on TV, it still follows me everywhere. There was a pre-hipster vibe to *Black Hole Sons* that could only be called trailblazing; it defined alt music, absurdist comedy, progressive family values— and used some good old-fashioned sci-fi to create the perfect world for the time. The show ran for five seasons and developed a cult following that's only grown over the years. Brooklyn is hipster ground zero, and fans are everywhere.

Sure enough, I immediately notice at least three people give me the classic double take and check their phones for cross referencing.

This is bad.

The vest I'm wearing is so small on me that it almost looks like I've covered myself with a few dozen candy canes, the earliest Christmas flare ever recorded outside of that store that only sells holiday kitsch all year long. The last thing I need is for pictures of this particular look to float around Reddit. That kind of story lives forever.

I keep getting nods from Brad to take a solo, but I refuse. I can barely keep my eyes on the charts, let alone force my mind to freely wander into some heady, improvisational funk jams. I focus on using the pages of music in front of me like a blindfold. They help me to stop canvassing the room, analyzing who knows and who doesn't. In all likelihood, it's entirely in my head. But as many former child actors will tell you, this kind of thing is a permanent side effect from a childhood in the business.

I'm not ungrateful for the continued attention—I even have a monthly show where all I do is make fun of my former work. *Eclipsed Too Soon* is my way of taking the old stuff and making it new by busting my own balls onstage for fans. I wouldn't do local comedy shows like that, or shake hands and sign shit at a dozen comic-cons every year, if I didn't enjoy the attention. But our culture is so obsessed with "where are they now?" and it doesn't help to have TMZ calling out celebrities who aren't constantly getting high-profile, high-paid gigs, working at Trader Joe's or in HR or whatever it takes to pay the bills instead. Child actors can grow up in a few different ways: they continue working in Hollywood; they decide on their own to pursue more normal roads; or the industry chooses for them when their time is up, and they either move on gracefully, or they find themselves in a Very Bad Place. That doesn't mean anyone should be chastised for trying to survive.

It sucks, to be honest, first-world problems aside.

At long last, the set comes to a close, and I want to get the hell out of Dodge. Ideally through the back of the kitchen. But first I need to get out of this fucking costume, so I move quickly toward the swinging service door to get away from the crowd.

Too late.

A guy approaches who looks to be buzzed, at least based on his glassy eyes and overly confident strut. "Yo, are you Rudy Riziero?"

He cuts right to the chase, at least. There's something to admire about that total lack of bullshit.

"I am indeed."

The guy starts chuckling and then catches himself, clearing his throat. A nervous habit. I see it a lot. "Wow, man, great playing tonight. You probably get this all the time, but what are you up to these days? I see your brother Rocco everywhere! He seems like such a cool dude! I follow him on Insta and love his Michelin-starred restaurant reviews. Classic." He shakes his head, grinning. "How about you, though? Do you play traditional Polish jazz full time?"

I try to laugh it off, because under different circumstances, minus the Rocco adulation, I might have enjoyed that button joke about full-time Polish jazz. Assuming it *was* a joke, that is. Right now, though, I feel extremely uncomfortable, and not just because of the vest currently suffocating crevices in my body I didn't even know existed. "I still do commercials and voice-over work sometimes, and I have a running comedy show at Little Zelda's, along with all sorts of music gigs. I've been playing bass since I was eleven. It was the thing I did in all the green rooms when I wasn't being tutored."

He's already tuned me out.

I can tell from the disingenuous nodding and static smiling. His question about Polish jazz was likely just a vehicle to ask me for a picture, which I almost always indulge. Tonight, however, I will not. At least not until I've stripped off my Polish folk ensemble.

"Sooo, do you think we could maybe take a pic? That would be chill."

Chill. Ugh. This guy keeps getting worse. "After I pack up and get this thing off me, no problem."

Honestly, I'm too kind and generous for my own good.

"Well, I'm late to meet someone, so," he says, as he continues to reach for his phone.

"Aw, that's too bad. Maybe another time."

He looks perplexed.

I'm rarely rude to people. I learned at a young age to always be polite, even when polite was the last thing I wanted to be. Like in college, when a drunk guy asked me one time to sign his left testicle. I didn't, for the record, but I drew a dick on his hand and signed it. I've navigated my entire life without being called out for anything on TMZ or *Where Are They Now?*—no rehab, no drinking, no drugs, no bar fights. That's no easy feat for any child actor.

Tonight, though, I walk away from him without another word, head into the kitchen and the dingy back storage room. I strip the costume off, careful not to ruin the "very old and very delicate" garments.

As I'm heading out with my bass and pedals, I get tapped on the shoulder and turn to see a woman with a five-mile smile.

Oftentimes after a gig, music, comedy, whatever, I discover there's an attendee who wants to get a drink with me. Maybe she thinks I'm cute, or maybe she's trying to relive that sweet adolescent crush. Either way is fine by me. I have very little game, and would never have any dates if it were left to me to initiate.

Tonight, her name is "Sarah, with an H. It's so nice to meet you! This was such a fun surprise—I came in for pierogis, and there you were, jamming out. I was a big fan growing up."

She seems young to have watched the show, at least when it was originally on TV. Maybe twenty-five. Petite and punky, wearing a toddler-sized black leather jacket. Both forearms tatted up in sleeves (no black holes, the mark of the most hardcore *Black Hole Sons* fan, at least not that I can see), a few piercings, a black pixie. She kind of looks like a young Dolores O'Riordan from the Cranberries, which is—obviously—a major plus.

"It's nice to meet you, too," I say, as my mind is telling me to be cool. She checks a lot of my boxes, at least at face value. "I appreciate you coming out tonight."

It's a reflex. The sentence that comes out of my mouth the most when talking to a fan. I sometimes wish my brain and mouth would coordinate with each other better—particularly in this case, since Sarah came here for potato pillows, not for me. I was just a bonus.

"Do you want to get a drink? I bet gigs like these could use a good wind-down hang."

She waits for my response with a smile that gives slight predator vibes. But she's cute in a fun, casual, rock-and-roll kind of way. Seems like a no-brainer.

I smile back. Hopefully not looking too much like prey. "Sure, let's grab a drink. I know a good place." I prefer to know my surroundings, should things go awry. A back-door exit, a big bathroom window. I've had to disappear before, so I like knowing I have an exit strategy.

"Great," she says, confidently, like there was never a chance I'd decline her invitation. It must be nice, having that kind of self-esteem.

We head to Low Down Dirty Dive, a personal favorite of mine that's conveniently close to Pierozek. It's your typical no-frills dive, complete with a sign behind the bar that reads, IF YOU'RE LOOKING FOR DRINKS WITH NAMES THAT DON'T INCLUDE THE BOOZE AND MIXER, THIS PLACE AIN'T FOR YOU. A motto I can stand behind.

I order us a round of Jameson and gingers while Sarah settles into a back booth. When I make my way over, drinks in hand, Sarah launches right in:

"So you really had to wear a dance belt for those weird alien dream sequences?" she asks, eyes wide as she tugs at a dark tuft of her pixie. "The ones where you and Rocco shed your human forms and saw your *true selves*? I read that on Reddit once."

I cringe, partly because I really did hate those belts, partly because she's read about me on Reddit, and partly because she referred to my brother as Rocco instead of his character, Marley. People sometimes seem to think it's interchangeable, our real names and our character names. Rudy/Charlie. Rocco/Marley. Like we're our characters, or vice versa. It's not worth getting into the semantics, though, because none of this is about me. Not really. It's about the shows. The nineties. Nostalgia.

Let's be real, it's about me dealing with this long enough in hopes of hooking up.

"I always hated those scenes because of that disgusting undergarment," I say, trying to make a joke of it, just like I always do in these situations. "I liked to think of it as a glorified jockstrap rather than a terribly invasive and uncomfortable thong. All to keep my 'personal outline' away from children's eyes while in spandex." She giggles, and so I double down, "Honestly, I feel like that dance belt kept kids safe, and so therefore, I'm kind of a superhero of sorts, don't you think?"

Sarah really likes that, apparently, because she grabs my hand and says, "I've always wanted to be with a guy who can talk about thongs and superheroes in the same breath."

Huh. Well. Whatever you say, Sarah-with-an-H.

The night goes on, and we're a few Jameson and gingers deep, the nostalgic anecdotes coming fast and loose, when Sarah says, "I used to have the biggest crush on your brother."

Fuck me, twice in a night? Are Rocco's ears ringing? Is he going to pop out from behind the garbage cans in front of the brownstone later?

"Haven't heard that one before," I say in a potentially condescending tone, but that feels fair here. "What changed? How have I been bestowed with this blessed opportunity to be in a booth tonight with you? Because Rocco's off somewhere exotic shooting right now?"

She laughs and smacks my arm. "C'mon! Rocco was older, more mature. He was the cool, calm, collected Riziero, while you were the wild card. He was the William, you were the Harry." She pauses and grabs my hand again. "It took until college to realize that was the better look, rewatching the VHS tapes with my roommate, who'd never seen the show. Everyone knows now that Harry's the better brother, even if he'll never be king. He's far more interesting. And cuter. God, I love a good ginger."

I smile at that.

Damn it.

I can't help myself, and it makes me angry that I'm not more repulsed by her story.

Sarah smiles back. "My roommate liked you right off the bat and convinced me to switch to team Rudy. I never looked back." She pulls out her phone with great purpose. "You don't mind if we take a selfie for her, do you? She's going to flip out!"

"Not at all," I say as she forcefully presses her cheek against mine, even though I'm starting to seriously question her motives. I try to look happy to be here, with her, but not *too* enthused. The right balance of earnest and cool.

She taps at her phone, presumably sending our photo to her old roommate. When she's satisfied, her prize for the evening securely achieved, she puts her phone down. We stare idly around the bar, and I wonder if now's the time to call it a night.

"More drinks!" Sarah announces, just as I'm about to stage my exit.

One more, I guess. I nod.

She goes up to the bar to order this round. "Cheerio!" she yells in a Cockney accent.

Oof.

I flinch, it's so abrasive. I glance over at Aidan, the bartender, a proud full-blooded Irishman. A friend of mine, at least usually—I have a way with making bartender friends, and could go to any bar in the vicinity and know who's working on any given night. It's a real gift. Right now, though, Aidan's giving me dagger eyes as Sarah says something else too quietly for me to hear. I have no idea what she's doing to irritate him, but I wave my hand to suggest putting whatever it is on my tab.

Aidan turns to Sarah, not bothering to hide his disdain. He's as no-bullshit and no-frills as the drinks he serves. "Sorry, but we don't have Sex on the Beach at this establishment."

Jesus. A *Sex on the Beach*?

Was she trying to joke with him? She looks upset, giving Aiden some distressed hand motioning toward the bar. I'm going to guess not a joke. To be fair, I did neglect to tell Sarah about the sign condemning cutesy nicknamed drinks, but nobody could have predicted the Sex on the Beach. Amongst the other shit on these walls, it's hard to spot, I suppose.

Sarah looks bewildered by Aidan's response, and gets more than a little spunk in her voice as she says, "Well, I see you have vodka, cranberry juice, OJ, and . . . yup, you got schnapps. Can't you put those all together and make two Sex on the Beaches?"

Aidan tries to get my attention again, but like any respectable person sitting alone at a table in a bar, I proceed to stare down at my phone. "I'm saying," he continues, his voice mocking in a way that would ordinarily make me chuckle if it wasn't because of my companion, "we don't make that drink here. Would you like vodka, cranberry, orange juice, and schnapps? I'd be *happy* to make you that."

Sarah doesn't take kindly to this. "Don't talk down to me! I'm trying to be funny, okay? Just make me two Sex on the Beaches so I can go back to the table and get a laugh. And then we'll talk about this awkward conversation and laugh some more."

I don't want to look up, but I can't help myself. I'm a sucker for juicy bar drama, even if I brought it here. And knowing Aidan, I bet he'll win this match and I'll go home alone. He's that good. I watch as he slowly pulls out four glasses. He puts on a godawful fake smile, almost Cheshire Cat wide, while he looks Sarah in the eye and expertly pours all the parts of the Sex on the Beach into separate cups on the bar top.

"Rudy says this is on him. Enjoy."

Damn. This is maybe Aidan's finest moment. Even I'm impressed.

"This is how you treat celebrities?" Sarah is full-blown yelling now, and the handful of late-night stragglers at the bar turn in her direction. I cower lower in my booth. "He was on TV, in case you didn't know, and would've thought that was a funny joke. But you ruined it. My college roommate loved Sex on the Beaches!"

Welp, cat's all the way out of the bag now.

I had a sneaking suspicion this date revolved more around one-upping a friend than wanting to actually hang with me. It's nothing new, though this specific scenario of someone getting fired up over a deconstructed cocktail is a new variation on a theme.

The commotion forces me up to the bar, where Sarah proceeds to look Aidan in the eye as she simultaneously grabs my face and starts kissing me.

"You see," she says in between breaths and sloppy lip sucking, "we came here together, and we're going home together. Who cares if you won't serve me the best drink to make a good joke, he thinks I'm funny already, and that makes you jealous."

Jealous? Wow.

This is never going away. I'll forever pay for this night. Jealousy is the last thing on his mind and solidifies that Sarah is too caught up in a nineties . . . *black hole*. Pun intended.

Aidan laughs, which only makes Sarah angrier.

"Why are you laughing?" she growls. Literally. It's primal. "I can't believe you're going to make me mix these all together. No thanks." She swipes at the four glasses, knocking two over—breaking one, and spilling the other across the bar.

Before Aidan has the chance to eighty-six her, she runs straight out the door on her own steam. Out of fury or embarrassment, it's hard to say. Either way, she's gone.

I sigh. "Sorry, Aidan. Sometimes the superfan energy doesn't present itself right away."

Aidan stares at me blankly. "As much as it pains me to see the alcohol abuse that transpired on this bar, I'm happy it was you so I can threaten to call up TMZ to dish about your special friend."

"Welp, TMZ is always looking for a good child-actor-gone-wrong story, so you can perpetuate the stereotype *and* hype the bar. I'm here to support Low Down Dirty any way I can."

Aidan grabs the Jameson bottle and lines up two shots. We clink, hit the counter with the glasses, and look in each other's eyes while the whiskey goes down. No hard feelings as I pay the tab and head home. I'm relieved Sarah-with-an-H didn't have the power to excommunicate me from one of my most beloved Brooklyn watering holes.

The evening makes for a pretty good story, and I'm looking forward to telling it to my roommates, Matt and Sheeraz. Makes the temporary emotional pain worthwhile. They rely on me for the stories these days, since they're both practically wifed up, if not legally so. Matt's been with his lady Julia for well over a year. And Sheeraz's girlfriend Marguerite, who has a month-to-month lease down the street, is ready to be our new roommate any day now. Sheeraz's family owns the brownstone, so rent is the best deal going in Brooklyn, especially for the Slope. The bachelor pad dream I wish would never end.

"Dudes, you'll never believe what happened at Low Down tonight," I yell out as I toss my gear on the sofa.

No answer.

I walk toward the kitchen. "Sheeraz, Matty? Who orders a Sex on the Beach at Low Down? Absurd!"

Still silent.

Nobody's home, I guess.

They're both probably out with their ladies.

It used to be that Matt—and then Sheeraz, too, after we all shacked up together a few years back—were my automatic plus-ones for any gigs. You wouldn't guess they both crushed it at their steady day jobs with the number of weeknights we closed down a bar. The perk of living in New York City—my favorite part of college never had to end. We had an extra decade before we needed to grow up. And we could feel okay about it, living here. The norm, not the exception.

That decade passed, though. These days, it's a lot of missed connections. And not the fun kind to read about on Craigslist.

Not that I'm bitter or resentful. Because I'm not.

Mostly.

But maybe I do need to go about my dating life differently. Less Sara-with-an-H, and more, I don't know, respectable thirty-something (or thirty-ish) who cares about the future, not the past.

Maybe the answer is at my fingertips. Literally. On my phone.

HeartThrobs.

I haven't logged on in months. I'd downloaded it for fodder, comedy shtick for a show idea that never saw the light of day. HeartThrobs is like stealthily going from person to person at a bar, approving or disapproving of them behind their backs— thumbs up, thumbs down. It's totally bizarre. But it works for people, doesn't it? Lots of people.

I fire it up. Ignore my inbox.

Start fresh.

First up: Stephanie, 29. She has a good smile, but she's so fake-tanned, she's orange, and her first pic is with a white Bengal tiger. Nope. Flip down. I don't understand the fascination with exotic animals, but this site has shown me that there are a *lot* of fans.

Krystal, 32. She's got light brown skin covered in colorful tattoos, definitely a rock-and-roll disciple. I flip up when I see her giving everyone on this app the bird.

I blindly flip down on a few early twenty-somethings next, mostly to prove a point to myself.

Lucy, 30. Long dark brown hair, sharp features, white skin without a hint of spray tan. Nice smile. Sincere, not plastered on. No duck-face pout. Her eyes are a deep green, quite striking. As my very mystically inclined and always wise with her words mother constantly reminds me, "Eyes can tell you everything, if you care to look deeply enough." She did always know when I was lying.

Lucy's bio says she's a whiskey and taco enthusiast, and she loves books and long walks in the woods. Whiskey good, tacos good, books good. Woods are better than a beach in terms of being a total cliché. She also claims to be a "Renaissance Woman and self-made entrepreneur," whatever that means, "with a specialty in writing and publishing." Her dad was a college radio DJ, and she grew up on a steady diet of late seventies post-punk. Intriguing.

I flick through the rest of the photos, none of which appear to have wild animals. There's a cute one of her reading a book with a rocks glass full of whiskey. A few with friends, looking like the life of the party.

Wait. Shit.

Last up, there's a very done-up photo of her, a lot of glossy curls and a short glittery dress. Does this mean she enjoys the finer things in life that don't revolve around sex, drugs, and rock and roll? Back in my early New York City days, when my pockets were still semi-flush with that TV money, I typically obliged a woman with refined tastes. But now, surviving on shows like tonight's means more Coors Original than martinis.

I have to flip for the future, though.

Think beyond my solo nights of tallboys and bodega sandwiches.

Looking past the last picture and the more or less predictable bio—aside from the post-punk dad, anyway—I think flipping up would be the right move. Final decision.

My finger flips up on the screen, and the heart confetti rains down over those green eyes.

It's a match.

Chapter 3

Lucy

She's stuck and she's stalled as she's carried along.

"Do I look adequately enthused? Scale of one to ten, how delighted do I seem? It needs to be a perfect ten."

Clementine is squinting at the latest string of photos in her camera roll, zooming in and scrutinizing every inch of herself, face and hair and hands and legs. Even her feet, the angle of her frilled vintage boots. The galley she's holding in her palms—an early copy of her fourth book, publishing in February, freshly unboxed—seemingly the most important element in a Bookstagram post, is the only part of the picture she doesn't fixate on. I'm not going to be the one to point out that her fingers are covering the *T-h* in the title, *The Cheerleader, the Witch, and the Wardrobe*. The two other *thes* present and accounted for feel like plenty. Her fans will be able to puzzle it out. If I were to point out her finger placement, we'd take a hundred more pictures, and I've taken over six hundred already today.

Six hundred and seventeen, to be exact. The unboxing, the first look, Clementine holding one galley, Clementine holding several galleys, galleys artfully stacked. I'd used her wardrobe change to count pictures, and then to stare again at the match notification in my inbox I'd woken up to this morning.

Rudy.

The overdraft was worth it.

If he messages me, that is. Or if I can think of a suitably enticing message to send him first.

"Definitely a perfect ten," I say, because that's the only right answer. "Maybe an eleven."

She looks up from the screen, frowning. "Eleven isn't an option. It's a maximum of ten."

"Right. Yes. A ten. Your readers will be obsessed."

"You think?" She grins—she's obsessed with their obsession—tossing the phone onto that obscenely expensive sofa of hers. "With the book? Or with me?"

It takes a tremendous amount of restraint not to sigh. "Both. You could be a book model. Even if you weren't an author. People would pay you to hold their books for social media posts."

I'm not paid nearly enough to spin this kind of painfully obsequious praise, but a happy Clementine might make my day end sooner. It's also kind of rewarding to so openly bullshit and not be called on it.

And to be fair, she is annoyingly beautiful. She really could be a book model, if that were an actual line of work. She's like an indie Brooklyn prom queen, gracefully walking that line between bookish nerd glamour and edgy boho chic, with baby-doll big gray eyes, golden tanned skin (courtesy of biweekly visits to Island Breeze Spa), shiny black hair tipped in bright turquoise, and eyebrows that are so perfect I once pulled up a photo of her while at a salon getting threaded. The final product looked nothing like hers, because I'm not graced with her natural arch and delicate bone structure, and I will never admit to anyone that I thought emulating her was either good or possible.

I cannot emulate Clementine, clearly. Not with looks or books or relationships.

I've received three hundred rejections on my various rom-com manuscripts as of last month. Rom-coms are what I read, what I watch, what I breathe, for better and for worse; the only genre that really speaks to me, inspires me. Maybe it's the guaranteed happy ending, the guaranteed sense of hope. But the passes that weren't template all politely suggested there was *too much com, too little rom.* I'm treating myself to a writing (and reading) hiatus, a clean break from words. Temporarily. Or not.

Clementine, of course, sold her first book a week after her agent took her on.

I haven't been in a real relationship since college.

She's had roughly three girlfriends and two boyfriends in the year I've been working for her—with some questionable overlap—and at least five outrageously attractive rebounds.

My phone vibrates in my pocket, and a wave of hope pulses through me. It could be a message from Rudy.

I turn away from Clementine and slip my phone out—*please please please—*

Estelle: Come upstairs when you're back. Frank's been such a miserable old coot today. His new batch of basement gin tastes like sour berries mixed with the liquid that leaks from trash bags on the sidewalk in the summer. For the love of God, don't let him convince you to try it.

"Um. Lucy? Hello? I need you."

I turn back to Clementine, who's eyeing me with the rancor of a teacher finding a student using a phone in the midst of the SATs. Quite a feat, pulling that look off at the tender age of twenty-five, and with turquoise-tipped hair, nonetheless.

"We're not finished. Not even close. We have to get all the books together. And I want some with jackets on, some with jackets off. You'll need to look through the wardrobe for the right accessories." Fuck me. Her towering vintage wardrobe, stuffed with every kind of prop décor conceivable, candles and silk flowers and wreaths and pillows and boas and quill pens and truly the list never ends. "I was thinking we should go out-side for a batch? See what light looks better? Maybe the park. A cute café. We should have too many good ones in reserve, because . . . Lucy? Are you listening?"

I force myself to focus on the positive: Clementine and Pinky are headed to LA at the end of the year to shoot her first book-based movie—because *of fucking course* her debut was not only optioned, but is going into actual production—and she'll be away for two months. Still paying me to water plants, check her email, other less offensive things than this that will help to fund my existence.

And, thanks to Rudy and HeartThrobs Ultra, I need Clementine's payment. Today.

I steel myself and shove my phone in my purse, out of sight.

It's nine o'clock when I'm dismissed.

A perfect October day has become an unacceptably cold October night, and the more fashionable than functional faux leather jacket I threw on this morning does little to buffer me from the wind that's swirling crunchy leaves down Clementine's lantern-lit historic side street.

I usually prefer the forty-five-minute walk home to Crown Heights instead of a subway ride with two transfers, but I've been on my feet ever since the lunch break Clementine gave me eight hours ago. Not really a *break*, more like me inhaling cold three-day-old truffle pizza from her fridge while we scrolled through fifty photos that looked identical to me, but different enough to her to warrant a complex ranking system.

There's an F train pulling in as I descend the steps into the station, always a small miracle. It's not until I'm comfortably situated, the train rolling down the tracks, that I think to check my phone again. I looked as I was leaving Clementine's, but that was at least ten minutes ago. Anything can happen in ten minutes.

And there—a HeartThrobs notification.

A new message.

My stomach twists. I can feel my pulse quicken, my heart beating too fast against my rib cage. My heart is throbbing, *literally*, because it's there, those four letters:

Rudy.

I tap the screen to open it up—*a message, a fucking message!*—and as I sit on that hard blue bench, gripping my phone like it's the Holy Grail, nothing happens.

My phone has no service.

No service.

Wasn't there a citywide initiative to have Wi-Fi on these trains?!

I try refreshing. Nothing happens.

I try again.

I've attempted refreshing approximately twenty times with identical results when the train shudders to a stop. The speaker above me clicks on, and a voice almost entirely muffled by static says: "[indecipherable string of words] SICK PASSENGER [indecipherable string of words] thank you for your patience."

No.

No no no. I am absolutely not okay with being patient. How can patience be expected of me in a time like *this*?

I have a message from a childhood celebrity waiting on my phone! A celebrity who brought a pure, undiluted joy into my formative years.

Fifteen minutes pass. I've taken to staring openly at the other passengers, because there's nothing else left to stare at. I've memorized every slogan for the cleaning service ads plastered above our heads. The catchiest and also most obnoxious: GO GET LEAN WHILE WE DEEP CLEAN with a picture of a smiley-faced person lifting weights at the gym.

I don't wish sickness on anyone, truly. I can say that with a clear conscience. Not even Clementine. (At least not aside from a nasty bout of diarrhea or something similarly innocuous, yet highly unpleasant.) But this sick passenger? They better *actually* be sick, not just lightheaded from a green juice cleanse or blitzed after too many happy hour well drinks.

Twenty minutes.

Thirty.

Will we ever reach the other side of this hell ride?

I should have walked.

Why didn't I walk?

I'm contemplating standing on the bench to see if raising my phone higher wins me a bar of service, when I feel the shudder beneath me, that glorious, life-giving hum of the engine.

We're moving.

I fight the urge to stand and twirl around the pole beside me.

When the train finally pulls in at the station, I'm standing by the door, my nose nearly pressed against the finger-smudged glass, knees bent and ready to lunge. This isn't my stop—it's where I ordinarily transfer—but I can't spend another minute on a train.

The doors open wide and I soar up the stairs, skipping every other step, a daring act of athletic prowess I don't typically possess. I've never flown faster. Higher.

I'm there then, at the surface, clutching my phone, blinking my eyes as I'm bathed in the bright flashing lights of a corner bodega. I take a breath, watch as the blessed bars at the top of my screen fill in, and tap through to the HeartThrobs inbox.

Estelle poses the question out loud for roughly the tenth time in the hour since I arrived:

"When I want to test a psychic, I barge in unannounced, and if they look frightened, I just say, 'weren't you expecting me?' and walk out. Otherwise, if they're cool about the whole thing, I'll stick around. How 'bout you?"

She didn't even reference my HeartThrobs screen this time—she's committed the message to memory.

I swallow the last sip of my martini—made with Hendrick's, not Frank's basement varietal, though he did eagerly try to sell me on it—and lean my head back against their velvet couch that looks like a set piece from *Downton Abbey*.

Rudy started our exchange with a hypothetical. I mean, how utterly perfect. He's speaking my love language. I'm the master of hypotheticals—this should be easy-fucking-peasy. A walk in the proverbial park.

But Rudy's question somehow feels more inscrutable every time I hear it. It doesn't help that Estelle is becoming increasingly tipsy, and with every reading has added her own dramatic flair. On this latest performance, she sounds like the actual psychic, her voice whispery and guttural and entirely un-Estelle-like. She's draped her body across the chaise next to me, wilting over the side like a dying rose in her wine-red silk housecoat.

"What's wrong with your voice?" Frank asks, frowning at Estelle from his puffed throne of a wing chair. He's looking every bit the part of an aging monarch tonight, all six feet of him draped in his own silk housecoat—royal purple, fittingly—with a stack of gold bangles and a Cartier watch shining luminously against his dark brown skin. While he may be lacking a crown, his head is still quite regal, thanks to patches of snow white at his temples, a stark contrast to the rest of his black curls. Estelle claims the white is as real as her nose, which hasn't been real for over a decade. "You sound like a dying unicorn. Maybe less gin and more chamomile?"

"Oh please," she sighs, with great exasperation. "I'm setting the appropriate mood to help us think better. Lucy needs the *perfect* answer. The funniest, most original, most bewitching response a HeartThrobs inbox has ever seen. Her whole *life* might ride on these words. Her whole life!" Estelle's entire body—nearly a foot shorter than Frank's, though what she lacks in size she more than makes up for with might—vibrates as she says this. Platinum curls quiver on top of her head. Her cheeks, usually a shade or two lighter than her white-blond hair, are tinged with hot pink.

"Okay." I hold up my hand to cut her off. "Let's dial it down. While yes, it would be nice to go on a date with Rudy, I think we're setting the bar awfully high. I'm not sure I'd go as far as to say my *whole life* hinges on this. My life is perfectly fine without Rudy."

"Your life is *perfectly fine*?" Estelle asks, bursting out in sharp, bubbly laughter. Frank laughs, too, in his Frank grumbly-guffaw kind of way, grinning like a mildly sinister jack-o'-lantern. He's the only person I've ever met who truly captures the essence of a *guffaw*. Before him, I'd thought *guffaw* was just a weird synonym for a laugh authors used to spice up their vocabulary. But no.

"What's so terrible about my life?" I ask, hotly defensive over what I agree may be a rather pathetic existence, but only I'm allowed to laugh about my personal failings. "I mean, yes, sure, the odd jobs are less than ideal. Clementine is terrible. But she's also a warped kind of inspiration, because someday I *will* write a project that sells."

"Hmm." Frank tilts his head, an excessive furrow in his brow. "Without Rudy, who would be your muse for the great love interest? Every book worth reading needs a dashing suitor. Maybe . . . what was that fellow's name? Colon?"

"Hashtag," Estelle says, her lips curling as she side-eyes her husband. "You really showed your age with that one, *dear.* Everyone who's on social media understands the significance of a hashtag. It's positively vital."

"Well, *dear,* may I remind you that you're only two years younger than me." What exactly that means, age-wise, I'm not certain—early fifties, if I had to guess. Estelle's birthday math can't be trusted, and Frank is forbidden from granting specifics. "And last time I bothered to check, how many followers did you have on that app with the off-centered photos of the potted plants out back and your holiday mug collection? Eight? Nine, after you convinced the pharmacist to add you when you picked up your laxative prescription last week?"

Reminding Estelle of how few followers she has across social media platforms is an offense worse than mocking her festive mugs and her habitual constipation combined.

"Can we get back on topic?" I ask, before this can spiral further out of hand. "I need to respond before someone else beats me to the banter and takes Rudy off the market."

Frank *harrumphs*, folding his arms on top of his robust belly. His word of choice—*robust*—whenever Estelle chooses a less kind descriptor.

I'd say they both look like people who live well, as they do. Two childhood sweethearts from Queens who won millions from a New York Lottery jackpot and immediately up and quit jobs they never loved, bought this brownstone, made a few well-placed investments, and immediately commenced becoming self-proclaimed experts on all of life's finer things. Other than that, they have very little actually in common, except for a shared devotion to me.

"Maybe we should hear the question again?" Estelle asks, looking too eager at the prospect of yet another rendition.

"I think we're set," I say, "but thank you for the offer."

Estelle nods coolly, as if it was beneath her anyway.

"How about another round?" Frank asks, already on his feet. Shiny new loafers, probably hand-delivered from Italy.

"That's the first intelligent thing you've said all night," Estelle says, lifting up her empty Waterford Crystal martini glass for him to fetch. "Don't even think about using your bucket of horse spit in the basement. I'll call nine-one-one for attempted murder."

Frank mutters under his breath as he disappears into the dining room, something about the "dirty rat bastard" who sold him this batch of elderberries. I stare up at the gold-painted tin ceiling, letting my mind drift off.

Psychic, psychic, psychic.

This shouldn't be so hard. It's probably a template question, one that Rudy's been shooting off into HeartThrobs inboxes all day. Which, darn it, only raises the stakes if we're all responding to the same prompt. Is there a right answer? A wrong one?

"Did I ever tell you about the time I went to a psychic?" Estelle asks, sitting up eagerly. I shake my head, hoping I haven't just thrown open the floodgates for a thirty-minute monologue. "It was five months after Frank proposed. The psychic said I had a great love waiting just around the corner, and I'd be wildly happy beyond all dreams if I could be patient. She said I'd know when I found him. I'm not a patient person, of course, so I married old Frankie a month later. I couldn't return my dress, and the invites were out. Who knows, I might've been Mrs. Clooney or Mrs. Washington right now if I'd waited." She shrugs, scowling at a portrait of her and Frank hanging above the white marble fireplace I've never seen them use. They're wearing matching green crushed velvet robes. A harrowing sight.

"Thank you for sharing," I say, just as Frank returns with our martinis on a gemstone-studded wooden tray. He serves Estelle first, because he knows better than to not. I lean over the curved arm of the sofa to pick up my glass, too, and take a long sip. Extra dirty. Very extra. "It actually reminds me," I say, licking the excess olive juice from my lips, "I went to a psychic once, too." I went to a psychic.

I went to a psychic.

"That's it. My phone! I need my phone! Who had it last?"

Estelle looks at Frank, Frank looks at Estelle, their fingers drawn like swords from a hilt as they point at each other.

"I've had it memorized since the first read!" Estelle stands from the chaise, wagging her finger at Frank. "You were the one who had to keep looking at the message. You've never had a brain for memorization! Remember when you tried to learn that monologue from *Braveheart*? Ha! You couldn't get past the first line. And don't get me started on our wedding vows!"

"I know *exactly* what that message said, thank you," Frank says, teeth gritted as he drops the empty drink tray onto the ottoman and starts digging around in his seat cushions. "And for the record, that *Braveheart* monologue was incredibly complex."

"Right. So tell me, then. What did Rudy's note say? Hmm? Word. For. Word."

"Easy, my dear. Too easy. It said: *If I were going to test*—"

"Wrong! *When I want to test*—"

"Stay focused!" I yell, tossing throw pillows from the couch. Ten of them. No couch needs ten throw pillows. "The phone! We've all had it at some point or another. Estelle, you were looking at Rudy's photo from Thailand, asking if Frank and I were in the mood to order some khao pad. And Frank, you were rereading the message to see if the psychic looked more *surprised* or *frightened*. You said the difference was, I quote, 'paramount.'"

"Frightened," Estelle says proudly. "He asked if the psychic was frightened."

"Yes. Right." I accidentally hurl the last of the throw pillows at Estelle's head. "Sorry. Terrible aim. The point is, we've all had the phone, and—"

"I've got it!" Frank screams, lifting the phone triumphantly above his head. "It was on the ottoman under the drink tray!"

I reach up and grab it from his hands, and then sit back down on the sofa to focus. "I need silence," I say, knowing this is a big ask for Estelle and Frank. They settle in on the sofa, too, squishing against me shoulder-to-shoulder, leaning over to see my screen.

My own psychic encounter was twelve years ago—the summer after high school graduation, when Grace found a half-off coupon in the town paper for "The Shining Shannon," who was conveniently located next to Wendy's. Dinner and a show, as cultured a night as one could expect in Greendale.

I channel that memory now, and the answer flows so surely from my fingers, it's almost an out-of-body experience:

Nah, I wouldn't even bother with the testing in the first place. When I was 18, I paid 50 bucks for a tarot reading and the lady ate Doritos and watched TV the whole time she predicted my future. I'd pick an 8 ball every time.

All true. Shining Shannon promised me a great many things that warm summer night: imminently divorcing parents; a great college love; twins before I was twenty-five; and a *published book*. My parents just got back from their thirty-fifth anniversary Alaskan cruise; my college boyfriend dumped me the night before graduation because I was "college fun but too much for real life"; my uterus has never contained one human life, let alone two; and, well . . . no books. I'd been so pleased about that part of Shining Shannon's vision, I was *almost* okay with my parents divorcing.

I read my message again. It feels like a winner. Just one final touch to close out:

✧ ⚫ ✧

"I like it," Estelle says, patting my knee.

Frank nods. "Yep. Me, too."

Their mutual approval is the highest commendation I could receive. The Nobel Prize equivalent for a HeartThrobs message. My vast arsenal of disappointing life stories has come in handy yet again.

I press Send.

We stare down at my phone.

"Now what?" Frank asks. "What happens next?"

"We drink, of course," Estelle says, lifting up her martini. "And we wait."

We waited for about another hour, until Frank was snoring on the chaise and Estelle was scouring Seamless for any Thai restaurant still delivering. I excused myself for the Spinster Cave, drained from the mental gymnastics required to construct a three-sentence response to a stranger who just happened to be on my television screen as a child.

I put my phone down on my old wine barrel nightstand and collapse into bed. My brain is just starting to hum with a pleasant sleepy static when a ping from my phone pulls me back.

Don't check, Lucy. Wait until morning. Be cool. For once in your life, please be cool.

I sit up so fast, the bed frame squeaks, and I hear a mouse startle and scrabble around in the dark. My fingers clutch my phone and swipe to read the message before I consciously decide to ignore my own (quite sage) advice.

Rudy: I like your style.

I laugh. Cackle, more like. A sign that I'm nearing exhaustion-induced hysteria. Can't have that, no, not in this pivotal conversational moment, so I roll from the bed and tug my bathrobe on as I step into the kitchen, stomping to ward off my mouse companion. Tea isn't strong enough for this. I fill my French press with two heaping spoonfuls of coffee and put a kettle of water on the stove, and then I open the freezer door and nestle my face into its frosty depths, letting the cold air prickle my skin and fill my lungs. The water boils, and I step back, my face pleasantly numb and my senses adequately sharpened.

Coffee in one hand, phone in the other, I settle in on the love seat. I will *not* overthink my next message. If we ever meet in person, I won't be able to take an hour in the bathroom stall to rehearse every sentence for optimal wit and charm.

And Rudy is just an ordinary person, after all.

Perhaps an entitled former child star, but ordinary in this decade just the same. Maybe even *worse* than ordinary, given that sort of warped childhood. He's no doubt deluded. A deluded diva. The worst sort of deluded *and* the worst sort of diva.

I take a swig from my mug, the coffee scalding my esophagus before flooding into my empty stomach. I never ate dinner, I realize now. The olives in my martinis were my primary sustenance. Good thing I put a generous pour of heavy cream in my coffee. I take another, more delicate sip and set the mug down as a second message comes through.

Rudy: I agree, I'm on team 8 ball. Also on team Doritos, but only in the privacy of my own home. Never in public. Can't let anyone else see me licking Dorito dust off my fingers. Please tell me there was no finger licking at your reading.

Lucy: If there was, I've blocked it out. Though I do remember the episode of Jerry Springer she had on in the background. A mother and daughter dominatrix team. I couldn't look my mom in the eyes for a week.

Rudy: Oh man. I watched that show with my grandmother when I was a kid. Never saw that episode. I'd remember. Nonna would have needed way too much explaining about what it means to be a dominatrix. May she rest in peace.

Lucy: I watched with my Nan, too! It's basically how I got my sex education.

There's a conversational lull as I stare at my screen, wondering why I thought it was a good idea to bring up sex and mothers in the same anecdote. And grandmothers. Though, technically, the grandmother part is on him.

Rudy: I'm sure it was way more instructive than any high school health class. I thought people only got their periods during a full moon until I was eighteen.

I laugh, spitting out a sip of creamy coffee onto my robe.

Rudy: So um I've actually never admitted that to anyone before. I understand if you delete me from your inbox.

I pause for just a second, and then, my fingers flashing across the screen—

Lucy: I used my own Lisa Frank hot pink unicorn sock as a pad when I got my first period. I was at a classmate's house working on a project, very desperate times.

Lucy: . . . I've also never told anyone that before.

Rudy: Wow. Thank you for sharing that awful story to make me feel better.

Did I really type that? I scroll up to confirm.
Yes. I really did.

Rudy: Are you always up this late?

Lucy: Sometimes . . . I'm trying to write.

A lie, but only a little one. I do try to write some nights, just not these days. And I'm writing messages. I'm not *not* writing.

Rudy: Oh yeah? What do you write?

Lucy: Rom-coms. Heavy on the com. I never seem to get the love part right.

Rudy: Ha. Me neither. I can't write love songs. I'm better at the heartbreak ones.

A red flag? Quite possibly. Yes.

But what's the harm at this stage? We're just chatting. And so far, his grammar and punctuation have been on point. They must have had a good tutor on set.

Tossing any doubts into the draft sweeping in from my tiny windows, I settle farther into the love seat and press forth.

Lucy: So, what was the inspiration behind your (presumably template) question?

Rudy: How long do you have?

Lucy: All the time in the world.

Chapter 4

Rudy

He grows old, never changes, just loops the same song.

I type and send what's probably my hundredth HeartThrobs message of the day:

Rudy: Ah, the damn MTA! They always say they have excellent service at most stations, but they really shit the bed on that promise, don't they?

Lucy, who's just emerged from a long train ride to Manhattan for some vague Saturday evening job duty, is a real spitfire at this HeartThrobs chatting game. Especially when it comes to hypothetical questions. I've never had more hypotheticals posed to me than I have in the last few days. My head's spinning. A weird spin. But a good one. I think?

A new message lands.

Lucy: Would you rather never see anyone in your family again, or flip up on your sixth-grade math teacher for one steamy date night?

Lucy: (As yourself at this age. Nothing illegal getting in your way!)

Um. Mrs. Gardner? *Steamy?*

I guess we had been talking about my Jersey public-school education before the subway service snafu, but still. Quite a leap.

Mrs. Gardner . . . she had a beehive hairdo from the fifties in the nineties, and was the meanest teacher I ever had the displeasure of being taught by in all my years of education. I'd never gotten an F for anything until that woman decided to not like my jokes or my lack of finished assignments. I was basically asking for it, sure, but I was twelve. And I spent so much time working, I needed to be a kid sometimes, too. My parents always worked our schedules out so that we spent roughly half the year in LA—living in a condo, getting tutored on set—and half the year at home in Jersey, our regular, more real lives. Public school felt like the right place to release. Hanging out with kids—*normal* kids. Mrs. Gardner once told my parents in a meeting that I really knew how to stir the pot, and my parents didn't agree. They said I was a kind, obedient child. Mrs. Gardner later told me that "dogs don't shit where they sleep." I'd never heard a teacher say *shit* before.

The moment for deliberation ends with me texting an all-caps **SIGH**, an ellipsis, and then, finally, begrudgingly: **Mrs. Gardner.**

The things I'd do for family.

If the situation turns truly blue and disgusting, though, I might have to think twice. Mom would get saved all of the time. Dad, too . . . unless it's *really* bad. Rocco. Hmm. Rocco. Working through just a few of the grislier hypotheticals, I'd say he gets the axe in all of them. Fans would be upset to lose their A-list Riziero, but his movies would be even bigger hits postmortem. Dad and Mom would make bank.

Jokey hypotheticals aside, it's an unwanted reminder that it still stings. Not just because he's the golden Riziero brother now. But his betrayal. His disloyalty. I recognize, of course, that it's old news, the deep past. But time doesn't change the facts. Doesn't right wrongs.

Moving along . . .

I read back over my answer to Lucy. It sends shivers down my spine, as if those pixelated letters could will it all into being. But my answer was honest.

So honest that I decide to be even more vulnerable.

Rudy: Want to meet up sometime for a drink and food and maybe some more laughs about making out with cruel former teachers?

She *LOLs* and then pauses for a very long sixty-second stretch.

Lucy: Yes. Face to face time is an excellent idea.

She said *yes.*

Oh shit. This just got serious.

Or serious for me, at least. Which isn't saying much, I realize. But still. My first-ever online match brought into the real world. It's kind of a moment.

That moment is fleeting, though, because then my brain immediately cuts to: "Did she recognize me from TV? Is this just another fun novelty dating experience?"

It's unavoidable. I can't *not* ask myself this question. Mentally prepare.

I reread her messages and try to believe I'm just crushing it at the messaging game and, whether or not she knows who I am, I'm doing something right.

Temporary easement of anxiety achieved.

I decide to take the second big leap of the night.

Rudy: Also, can we bring the ultimate buzzkill hypothetical game to texting? It's rough spending most of my day looking at the HeartThrobs screen. Too much pastel.

Lucy: YES. God yes. I thought you'd never ask.

We exchange numbers and immediately continue our conversation in actual texts. Her messages are blue, so we have the same brand of phone. It's already starting off well. I'm always highly suspicious of anyone with green texts.

As we banter along about bands we grew up on to most crucial salad bar items, I'm deep in thought about this next move. How do I stand out from other first dates? I don't want this to be just any old dinner and drinks. I need something more outside the box.

You can do this, Rudy! I did once make a woman an edible arrangement with Slim Jim stems, Tastykake flowers, and Haribo frog gummy leaves. She stuck around for a month, that one. Before she got tired of nights and weekends booked up with gigs. A common breaking point.

I reopen the HeartThrobs app and go back through our conversation, an impressively long thread. I scan through every line, but it's my opening question that gives me the best idea:

We could get a psychic reading together.

That seems mildly unorthodox, but also pretty spot-on for our unusual conversations.

Then it comes to me like a lightning strike—the full plan, the *perfect* plan. There's a great restaurant in Williamsburg that has an actual psychic working on a riser in the middle of the floor. Everyone sees you go up, a real trip. Plus, it's the start of Halloween season, so there should be some spooky vibes to fully set the mood.

It's quite a striking callback, if I do say so myself.

Rudy: How about we do drinks and dinner at Francois Santos? Ever been there?

Lucy: I've never heard of it. But yes! I'm always good with a fresh adventure.

I debate whether or not I mention the psychic. Should I let the cat out of the bag or make it a surprise? Hmm. Maybe if this were an ordinary woman, I'd tell her. Let her be fully prepared. But Lucy? Not ordinary. Not by a long shot.

So. Yup. Decision made. I keep that information to myself and have one hell of a unique first date. Hopefully, she doesn't investigate the restaurant too thoroughly online. I do a quick search, and am thrilled to discover the link to their site takes me to an UNDER CONSTRUCTION page.

Rudy: It's a great place! French and Mexican. You could get some duck and merguez tacos, or a steak au poivre. I'd hope you wouldn't break my bank on the first date with the steak, though.

Speaking of French, it's always a faux pas to bring up money, I do recognize that. But I've had way too many "rich guy from TV" assumption dates, especially when I really did still have some of that TV money—before an overpriced liberal arts education and years of rent wiped out my savings. And there's the "you're Rocco's brother, you must have money, too" fanciful ideas that people still seem to have. So I've developed dating ticks to try to weed out and avoid potential unwanted situations.

When Lucy doesn't respond, I throw my phone down on the couch for some unplugged time. I pick up my bass—*Blondie*, because of her maple neck, my oldest, truest friend—on the other side of the room and start thumping away to clear my fickle brain. Blondie is usually pretty effective when it comes to cutting through any anxious mental bullshit. But she doesn't seem to be doing the trick this time, because I keep thinking about my last text.

The damn steak.

I probably shouldn't have said it. Even if it is a fifty-dollar cut . . .

Maybe it's time to stop utilizing those defense tactics. I'm over thirty, for one. I should be able to judge a date's character and intentions. And to be honest, maybe I use these defenses more as a way to not get close enough to be hurt.

I have dear Rocco to thank for that.

Our co-star Piper had been my girlfriend for over four years. All through high school, the gap year I took to wait for her. Rocco had stayed in LA full-time to keep acting after graduation, but I wanted college. Normalcy. That had always been the plan. Piper's plan, too. She was yessing me at every turn, applying to the same schools, talking about buying a house together near campus. We'd been used to off-and-on long distance over the years, with different shooting schedules and home bases, but now, we'd finally be in the same place, away from LA. When she pulled out for a role in some Disney Santa movie, I was blindsided, and Rocco was the first person I told. He got how devastated I was—he knew exactly how much Piper meant to me. How excited I'd been about our grand plans. But only a few months after I moved east for college—a few months of being in a strange, undefined relationship purgatory—he crept in. On New Year's Eve. 1999. Really kicked off my Y2K with a shitty bang.

But Y2K was great for Rocco; his career was skyrocketing. He became a Hollywood darling, along with Piper, the two of them splashed all over the tabloids—while I resented every ounce of his mediocre talent hidden by a jawline and abs. They had a very public, very tumultuous relationship for the next few years, off and on. She couldn't stand him by the end, begged me to reconsider *us*, but the damage was done.

There was no getting back together with either of them. I knew where I stood. I couldn't top Rocco, could I? Lesser brother and son. Lesser boyfriend. But he sure knew how to use the breakup to tell me she was bad for both of us, and we should just make amends. It felt like someone trying to apologize by telling you they're sorry your feelings are hurt, but not sorry for what they said or did. All surface, no substance.

Deep breaths.

The phone vibrates on the couch, and I prop Blondie against the amp to go check it. The screen's lit up with a new message from Lucy, and I suddenly feel nervous. What if she's canceling on me over the steak?

Lucy: HAHA. Good thing I've always liked burgers more than steaks. But I will order many, many tacos instead.

She's good. Solid deflection.

Rudy: Are you free tomorrow around seven?

Too soon? Too eager?

The response comes in rapid fire this time:

Lucy: It's a date.

This seems like a great way to cap the night. Per George Costanza's sage advice, I always try to end flirty exchanges on a high note. I tell her to sleep well, and she sends a series of emojis that I believe are positive: a pair of hands in the air, a smiley face with a tongue out, a popped champagne bottle, a few stars. Lucy loves emojis as much as she loves hypotheticals. I can't fully explain the verbatim transcription of this particular emoji string, but I try to respond in kind: a moon, some shooting stars, a thumbs-up, and a clown emoji. The clown emoji is an accident, a rogue thumb tap. I leave it, though, to be funny and ridiculous—Lucy seems to like ridiculous—and really, I'm just hoping to pass the millennial test of being emoji literate.

A minute passes with no ellipses on Lucy's end.

I went out on a clown emoji.

Great job, Rudy.

George Costanza wouldn't be impressed by my sign-off. Not that George Costanza should necessarily be anyone's dating role model. He did kill his fiancée with envelope adhesive.

Shit.

I close out of my texts for the evening. Scroll through some local news headlines. I'm about to click on an article about a stray goat roaming the sidewalks of Park Slope when the phone vibrates in my hand with a new text.

Lucy: 😜

A wink. She felt bad for my lack of emoji game, or she has a deep passion for clowns.

Don't respond.

Leave it at that awkward—but seemingly effective—twenty-first century hieroglyphics goodnight.

I plug my phone in and make myself walk away.

The next morning, we three roommates are reuniting at long last for some breakfast jambalaya—an old classic Sunday staple from when we first moved in here together, all of us single and hungover and at our most vulnerable. We'd confess our deepest, darkest drunken mistakes over massive plates of food, usually a surprisingly delicious mishmash of leftovers and slightly funky unused produce and a heavy dose of spices. All tossed together inside what may be the largest wok known to humankind. I'd found it tucked away in one of the house's many closets my first weekend here, like a sweet buried treasure meant just for us and these Sunday meals.

Today's breakfast was Sheeraz's idea, a pleasant surprise, since it's been weeks—maybe months—since our last roommate culinary adventure. I woke up to a group text this morning, a picture of our fridge shelves and a note that said: **Let's do the good work for breakfast, boys.**

My news about the date with Lucy tonight should make for

some lively conversation. Otherwise, these days, our rare Sunday breakfasts together mostly revolve around the sunshiny contentment that comes with longstanding relationships: restaurant and recipe suggestions from the week's date nights, TV shows they're bingeing together, and long-winded stories about searching out the perfect latte on the way to some fun couple's getaway. Stuff like that is perfect talk for the handcuffed. It can be difficult for me to really break into these conversations with any meaningful additions.

I pull on a fresh black tee and jeans and grab my phone, glancing at the screen on my way to the stairs to see . . . *holy shit.*

A text from Rocco.

Rocco: FUUUUUUUUUUUUUUUUUUUUUUUCK, our old favorite burger joint in Playa del Ray closed, Outlaws. The sign with the sleeping cowboy is just a pair of legs and boots now. But how? I know it was on the west side and completely out of the way, but hot damn those burgers were tasty! Hope you're doing ok, brosef.

This feels like such a bizarre extension of an olive branch, I have no clue what to make of it. Sure, it's certainly information I'd like to know, with the countless good times we had at Outlaws. But still. Why text me? Why now? Some baked-in brotherly sixth sense, so he knew how much I was dwelling on his shittiness last night?

Rocco once got a cook at Outlaws to let him work in the kitchen late night as a funny goof. Thing is, though, Rocco wasn't remotely interested in cooking—just snooping for the secret ingredients to a green chile sauce he swore he couldn't live without. He was unsuccessful in his quest that night, but did manage to create a burger later down the road with my help. I flew back from a New Jersey trip a few weeks later with a five-pound roll of Taylor Ham. We brought the goods to Outlaws, and they made special Jersey burgers until the pork roll was gone. What a memory.

I want to respond, but I don't.

My heart says yes, but my brain tells me to hold my position. It's a one-off text about a burger joint. Nothing that will magically heal us.

I walk into the kitchen, still shell-shocked from the unexpected bout of nostalgia, and find Matt and Sheeraz already hard at work prepping. They're in their usual Sunday morning uniforms—Matt wearing a grungy Grateful Dead T-shirt he's had since college, old sweats, vibrant bedhead; Sheeraz in cropped khakis and a sculpted-on Polo, shiny loafers (sans socks), hair combed back in an artful swoop. It's refreshing, the predictability.

There's already quite a spread laid out on the counter: eggs, red peppers, serranos, mushrooms, onions, sweet potatoes, green peas, chicken sausage. A glorious medley soon to be simmering together in that trusty wok.

"Full disclosure," I say, before they even have time to say hello, "I met someone on HeartThrobs, and we're going on a date tonight. Her name is Lucy."

Matt glances over at me with a grin, wagging his finger up and down in a flip motion. He knows what an anti-app dater I am. Everyone does. It's well-documented, with dozens of online videos from various comedy shows. I'm a certified hypocrite now.

I know what'll come next. Their usual pre-date prep, because they understand just how weird and in my head I get about these things. They'll ask worst-case scenario questions—some of which obviously come from their own personal awkward experiences. A questionable method.

Sheeraz takes a minute to wipe his onion tears and then starts right in: "What if you don't like her voice? What if she's into baby talk, or sounds like a total Fran Drescher? Or maybe that whole high-pitched nasally thing does it for you. No judgment." The wiseassery knows no bounds with this guy.

"I talk more to keep her speech to a minimum," I say. "It can backfire, but if you really have a problem with someone's voice, you're not likely to stand a second date. Risk factor is low."

Sheeraz seems pleased enough with my answer and goes back to the onions. I continue to drive the point home anyway, just to establish my expertise in this particular arena. "I've dated a handful of women who probably thought I was the most self-absorbed bragger around, cutting them off so I could listen to the sound of my own perfectly melodic voice." I laugh, and Sheeraz throws an onion ring at my face. "They just took it as me being a typical former child star enamored with himself, I'm sure. Played right into their own expectations. Why not give them what they want?"

Matt, the master of the stove and the kitchen in general, has been busily assembling his counter to have all the ingredients laid out in order of first appearance for the wok. He takes a brief pause from aligning the mushrooms next to the serranos to look up and level me with his smirk. "Oh yes, the voice that informed me and tens of millions of other Americans about the perils of tomato-based products and gastric acid distress."

He's not wrong.

I got paid pretty well for a commercial voiceover job a few years back, some wonder pill for heartburn. It got some great national coverage, which meant a particularly good year for me.

Matt continues: "Speaking of tomato-based products, didn't you walk out mid-date on someone once over the usage of a condiment?"

Ah, yes. A classic Rudy story.

His words instantly transport me right back to Seventh Street Café. A night that started out so nicely, at a bowling alley with a few buckets of beer. "They had a killer tuna melt, and extra crispy steak fries that could sop up a glorious amount of ketchup. But she told me she couldn't stand ketchup, and if we were together, she refused to be around the stuff."

"What a weird thing to feel so strongly about," Sheeraz says as bright flames shoot over his head from the wok, narrowly missing his eyebrows. Too much oil at high heat will do that. This is why Matt's our fearless kitchen leader.

"And you just left?" Matt asks, simultaneously grabbing for a cast-iron pan to help smother the flames.

I stand idly by and stare. I'm the cleanup guy pretty exclusively, and I'm more than fine with that. Too many cooks, etcetera, and also this way, I can't be held responsible if the house burns down. When the fire risk is successfully managed, Matt begins adding his ingredients. The wok becomes a colorful mess of veggies, eggs, meat, and his secret weapon: Old Bay, and a lot of it.

"I got the check," I say, picking up the conversation again, "asked for a to-go box, and dumped a fuck-ton of ketchup on my fries. She freaked out and yelled something about her grandfather and how he invented Pedialyte . . . I don't remember the specifics. But I guess I could have been living large with a keg full of a miracle hangover cure."

"It's only ketchup, dude," Sheeraz states, too aggressively. Perhaps taking some of his flame-induced stress off on me, even if his eyebrows are fully intact. His light brown skin is still flushed with red, from heat or frustration or both. "I mean, I can get behind a flavor choice, sure, but that's a bizarre hill to die on. How are you ever going to find a real partner and leave this brownstone with those weird rules of yours? You know Matt and I are working towards significant other roommates. And that Margs and I have been talking rings and things."

Sure, yes, I realize that Matt and Sheeraz are in serious relationships that will inevitably end in wedding bells or a standard domestic partnership. That much is obvious. But I usually tune out when they start talking details. I'm not there yet, so why listen when I can nod and smile?

"I have my standards," I say, choosing to ignore the rest. "I don't care how cute and funny you are, please keep ketchup prejudices to yourself."

Sheeraz snorts, and I can't tell if it's a laugh or a criticism. I decide to let it go and head to the fridge for beer, tomato juice, and Tajín—micheladas for us all.

The kitchen goes silent other than the simmering sounds coming from the wok.

I'm thinking of potential conversation topics—something I've never had to do with Matt and Sheeraz—when I notice Matt using his fingers to taste test chunks of sausage and peppers. Good thing we've been best friends since he moved to my town in fifth grade, two pasty Irish-Italian kids living on the same block, bonding over our mutual love of Megadeth and Fenders and Kathy Ireland. Otherwise, that behavior would absolutely not fly. It's right up there with licking Dorito dust.

Matt must sense me silently judging, because he stops and wipes his hands on his sweatpants as he turns to me and says, "Didn't you used to suit up early for fake work meetings just to get a clinger to leave?"

Well, we're back to me, I guess. The theme for this Sunday. Slightly annoying, though a bigger part of me is just grateful to be here together in the first place, no matter the subject.

Not to mention I don't think Sheeraz has heard this particular anecdote before. We've known each other for years now—brought together by friends of friends at a Phish show. But we weren't close until this house opened up, and most of my wildest hookup days were in my twenties. The oversupply of missed life stories is endless.

I laugh gamely and turn to him with a serious look. "I was too nice for my own good sometimes. If a woman wanted to stay the night, she either genuinely liked me, or she was a fan looking for a good story—still true, really. It can be hard to discern, because that stage-five superfan flower takes time to fully bloom. Sometimes it requires twenty-four hours for confirmation. But either way, I never wanted to be mean, even if I wasn't feeling the chemistry."

"So you . . . tricked them instead?" Sheeraz asks in a very monotone, very sarcastic way. I can fully sense the criticism in his voice. "Another red flag for Rudy, the city's pickiest dater who will be living with roommates half his age if he's not careful."

I respond in kind, my hackles raised. "First off, it's not bad to be picky. I'm *selective*. And tricked sounds too harsh. I would tell them I freelanced as a consultant, that I'd forgotten an early meeting out in Long Island and had to get up at five-thirty. Or something along those lines."

"Wow," Matt says, nodding thoughtfully, though his *wow* is not one of awe. "Detailed, but also vague enough to input anything that comes up off the top of your head. Insert line here, apply the same rules . . . I get it." Matt had never heard the specifics before, just that I would get up early, put on a proper suit—reserved otherwise for funerals and weddings—and then shoo them out.

"It was a good line," I say. "Worked every time. I'd dress up and then drive them to their subway line, or if I really felt bad, I'd drive them home."

"This boggles my mind. Just be up front!" Sheeraz forces his arms to the sky, like he's questioning God himself why he made such a pathetic, non-confrontational human. "Why did you put yourself through all that? Just to make yourself feel better? Be the good guy? Dates don't always work out, Rudy. People are different. What were you so scared of?"

We're getting extra vulnerable now. I feel a little too put on the spot to enjoy this particular Sunday confession. I'm right back to where I was last night, thinking about my defenses. Why those defenses exist.

I delay responding as I top the micheladas off with some limes.

"I don't know," I say finally, handing them each a drink.

"I guess I kept—*keep*—myself at an arm's length most of the time. Fangirl or not. I've had too many burns, including from my own brother, to make myself too open and available."

This is unusual terrain.

I don't ever talk about the almighty Rocco. Not to them. Not to anyone. But it's true, clearly. Because he's still on my mind. Too much so.

Damn.

That text is messing with my head.

I shrug and take a heavy swig of michelada. "It was easier for me to be nice in the moment. They kept their memories intact, while I Pontius Pilate-d my hands by getting them safely home and feeling like they got something out of the experience that wasn't negative. I usually let there be a little hope, some standard niceties, and then I'd . . . ghost them. For what it's worth, it's been a few years since I used this particular tactic."

Sheeraz and Matt have both stopped what they're doing and are now fully engaged in this oil tanker spill of feelings.

"It was great back in the day, though," I continue, realizing this exercise in emotions has become cathartic, and it feels cleansing getting it out, "before I was doing any monthly shows. Now, if I ghost, I'm too easy to track down."

Sheeraz looks at me and smiles, a pleasant change. "Maybe that's for the best. You can't be a man without owning your feelings, and it's important to be real with people. So, for instance, the date tonight with your dating app . . . date . . ." He met Marguerite in a real-life run-in. As in they literally ran into each other on the street, and she got a bloody nose. He's never accepted the authenticity of an online meet cute. Not that I do, either. Or at least I haven't. So far. "If it isn't going well, don't feel obligated. But don't lie or invent excuses, either. You're a good person, and you're capable of being compassionate and aware of someone else's feelings while still being honest. Just do me that one solid. Okay?"

"I will," I say. And I mostly mean it. I do. I'm thirty-four, and dating like an adult shouldn't feel like such a foreign concept. But I also can't let my guard down, not all the way. "At the very least, I could have some good fodder for this month's show."

Matt looks at me with a pair of deeply judgmental eyes. "Were you listening to anything Sheeraz just said?"

"I know, I know," I say, hands up in surrender, "but I feel less pressure going in if there's the prospect of future laughs in a worst-case scenario date situation. I appreciate the pep talk, though, boys. Really."

And with that, the moment is over.

Our bowls are overflowing with steaming piles of food, and we stuff our faces on the couch as we watch an Anthony Bourdain show. Another key part of the Sunday tradition. We could watch him recite the phone book, then chop it up, stir fry it, ferment it into a spirit, and feed it to some hip foodie who gushes over the culinary experience.

I soak it all in. The food. The show. Our running commentary. This morning was a nice distraction from the online, phone-centric life I've been so accustomed to lately. I needed this in a way I wasn't even aware of until it happened.

Real-life encounters matter.

Tonight will be a real-life encounter.

Will it matter?

Chapter 5
Lucy

These two take a risk, leaping free from their cages.

I'm rarely early for anything—Clementine will attest to this, as she berates me for my failures at punctuality on a weekly basis. But I make an exception for first dates.

My goal is always to be at the chosen venue with at least fifteen minutes to spare. This gives me the opportunity to pick my preferred positioning, ideally with a good view for people watching. I can order myself a drink, so I'm not dependent on him for the first round. And, maybe most importantly, I get to watch my date be the one to awkwardly scan the room for a woman who looks approximately like the one featured in my profile photos, so I can: A, get a good first look at him, and B, see his honest reaction when he spots me. It's like how some people say at weddings they look at the groom first when the bride appears at the end of the aisle, to catch his initial reaction—the unvarnished, instinctual response. It's perhaps less romantic in these circumstances, more to ascertain if there's any initial disappointment or disgust. But similar, nonetheless.

Tonight is no exception, as I step up to Francois Santos

thirty minutes before we're supposed to meet. It's a more nerve-racking first date than most, which requires additional time to settle into my surroundings.

And the surroundings of Francois Santos promise to be a treat, indeed. The outside is already decked out for Halloween: twinkly purple lights and vintage-looking moon and witch and black cat paper cutouts strung along the front window, and carved jack-o'-lanterns with unusually grotesque expressions lining the entrance. It's par for the course here in October; many Brooklynites have a deep, abiding appreciation for their Halloween decor.

I push through the door, delighted to discover the interior is also properly bedecked. Draped dark-purple velvet curtains, more twinkly lights, a big sparkly golden moon hanging from the middle of the room like a disco ball. There's an astonishing amount of burning candles, and I will *absolutely not* come close to touching a single one of them.

In the center of the room, elevated high up on a small stage, is a table—empty now—covered in a black cloth dotted with white stars and surrounded by three wooden chairs. There's a pearly crystal ball, lit up from the inside, on the center of the table, and a star-shaped banner dangling from above that reads *The Great Elvira Gray, Oldest Psychic in New York* in a spindly attempt at calligraphy.

Oh my God.

The restaurant has a *psychic.* Of course it does!

Way to go, Rudy. I'm glad I looked no further than the address online.

I choose a plush leather corner booth and flag down the waitress—Sharlene, a bleached-blond, tired-looking woman in a glow-in-the-dark crystal ball T-shirt—for a non-artisanal whiskey. I drink slowly when it arrives, not wanting to dull my senses for that pivotal first greeting, and am anxiously staring at the door when a text comes through.

Rudy: Ah, so sorry! Got caught up doing a recording for a friend and now the train's delayed at Union Square, so I'm going to be a little late.

No worries, I text back. Just got here. My train was running early for a change. A lie, and one that doesn't even make sense, because an early train still means I was thirty minutes early to the station. I add on: A PSYCHIC OH MY GOD AMAZING!

My phone vibrates with a call, and I almost pick up, assuming it's Rudy elaborating on his timing. But then I see *MOM* and a picture of my mother grinning as she poses with the blueberry pie that won her first place in a Greendale baking contest last year. It was just a small group of bakers, ardent followers of *The Great British Bake Off* (why yes, they *did* call it "The Great Greendale Bake Off"), but I don't think I've ever seen my mom more delighted about anything in my entire life.

I let the call ring out, feeling a small stab of daughterly guilt. But really, does she have a sensor that goes off during my dates? Her timing is uncanny.

She resorts to texting next:

MOM: Hope you're alive!!! Why aren't you calling me back?! I have to tell you all about the scene that old biddy Loretta caused at book club last night. Ha!!

Loretta, our neighbor—two years younger than my mother—is often central to our calls.

Lucy: So sorry, at a book launch tonight!

I fib, yes, because if I say I'm on a date, she'll likely check the Greendale Club calendar for available spring wedding dates.

Lucy: Will call this week! Can't wait to hear about last night!!!

I've achieved my exclamation point quota. This response satisfies her, at least for now.

My phone goes quiet.

No Mom. No Rudy.

A few minutes later, a woman I strongly suspect is *The Great Elvira Gray, Oldest Psychic in New York* slowly ascends the steps leading up to the stage. I'm utterly captivated, as is every customer in the room. She's a bony, fragile thing, wearing a shiny mink stole over a midnight-blue lacy dress that looks like it's been preserved from the Gilded Age. She has a canary-yellow cap with netting draped over flowy white hair, and her hand clasps a long cane topped with what appears to be a wolf-shaped emerald handle. Bright pink rouge dots each paper-white cheek in perfect but aggressively large circles, and her lips are dark wine red.

I do not doubt she's the oldest psychic in New York.

She might very well be the oldest human, period, in the whole damn city.

Rudy is good.

Rudy is so good.

This is already a vast improvement over my Jerry Springer–watching Dorito eater. If I recall correctly, Shining Shannon was wearing a faded Fila T-shirt and holey sweatpants. I would, based on visual effect alone, place far more trust in Elvira's psychic visions.

The first customer approaches the dais a minute later, an older man—though not Elvira old, maybe in his early seventies. I can't hear their conversations, but watching the way Elvira gently sways and dips as she speaks is mesmerizing.

As I stare, lulled by the scene, I deliberate on a pressing conundrum: Do I recognize aloud that I know who Rudy is? That I flipped up fully cognizant of the fact that I've known him—or known *of* him, his existence on planet Earth—since before the DIY unicorn sock maxi pad? Estelle voted yes, better to be up front. Frank voted no, said I'd seem like a "top-notch creeper." On my walk here, I was firmly on team Estelle. Wouldn't most people in our age bracket have watched him on screen? That in and of itself doesn't make me a creep. It means I had refined taste in television shows, and wasn't watching the Disney Channel on Saturday nights.

But what if most of his dates are superfans? What if he avoids them at all costs, and only asked me out because I didn't mention his illustrious past (or illustrious brother, or illustrious ex) in our texting exchanges?

So, yes. The conundrum continues. It'll be a game-time call.

Seven-thirty rolls around with no further updates. I suck at the ice water at the bottom of my drink, deleting the latest unhelpful text from Estelle suggesting that Rudy got caught up in a Tarot card reading in Coney with his first date of the night.

I'm debating the merits of a second drink when the door swooshes open, and a man steps in with a large stickered-up guitar case strapped over his shoulder.

It's undoubtedly him: big doe eyes and long auburn hair up in a messy man bun, pale skin covered in a starry night sky's worth of freckles. He has an orange patch of hair just above and below his lips—not quite a mustache, not quite a beard, but an unusually shaped island of facial hair I've never encountered and thus have no proper name for. Black Docs, black skinny jeans, Buffalo plaid flannel unbuttoned over a black T-shirt— with scratchy white text that is inscrutable at first, but I squint as he comes closer and can make out the name of a bar I've never heard of followed by SATAN IS GREAT, WHISKEY IS SUPER. Interesting sentiment. He's shorter than I would have anticipated, based on nothing but vague memories of his height in relationship to other celebrities in his teen years, seeing as he brushed elbows with literally every person of cultural relevance while on his variety show with Rocco. My height, maybe, but thicker, wider, stronger, like he lifts heavy amps and crushes a Coors all in the same beat.

I've never cared either way in dating about how our chins and shoulders do or don't line up, or who wears bigger clothes. I've dated every body type, every skin color, every hair color, every religion, every kind of person, really. As Frank says, my type is "anyone who can put up with incessant hypotheticals and ridiculous stories." Which is both not true and not exactly wrong. My "type" isn't a neat list of boxes. It's much more ineffable than that. A strange form of alchemy I clearly have yet to fully master.

Rudy sees me then, and his first look is one of pure relief. Most likely because I'm still here waiting, thirty-seven minutes past our scheduled arrival time.

Still, I've had far worse first looks.

He keeps his eyes on me, smiling as he walks across the restaurant. Most people look at the floor during The Walk. Even I'm tempted to look down, because this amount of eye contact is too damn nerve-racking at this early stage in the date. But I stay the course.

"Hey, Lucy," he says as he props his bass against our booth and peels off his flannel, his voice low and heavy, gravelly like a rumbling bear. A happy bear, though—a bear delighting over fresh fish or a cute cub.

"Hiyah, Rudy!" Jesus. *Hiyah,* like I'm some piggy-tailed girl from a fifties sitcom, and my next exclamation will be *golly gee*, then maybe a *holy smokes* for good measure.

To Rudy's credit, his cringe lasts for all of a second, then he smiles again as he drops down into the booth across from me. Though he is—or was—an actor, which makes it more challenging to determine what's real polite versus fake polite. A potential quandary. "So sorry I'm late. A friend asked last-minute if I'd record a bass line for him, and I didn't know he was a mad perfectionist who would keep me locked in the studio for hours."

"Totally fine," I say, and then I giggle. I fucking *giggle*. "I had a whiskey and observed the evening's entertainment." I point at *The Great Elvira Gray, Oldest Psychic in New York* as if he might have missed her and the glowing crystal ball on his way in.

"She's a fun surprise, right? I've never had a reading here, but friends swear by her. It seemed like the perfect first date. How do you feel about going up there? Excited? Terrified?"

"I feel . . ." Like I'm forgetting basic adjectives.

Get it together, Lucy.

I'm never this verbally incapable on dates. Perhaps it's knowing that I'm being weighed against the likes of Piper Bell and other wildly funny, attractive, successful people he's surely done much more than rub *elbows* with over the years. Or maybe just the sheer fact that I once saw his face on a TV screen and in *Tiger Beat* and *Teen* and now here he is, an actual human being sitting across from me, not made of pixels or ink. I've seen a few reality "stars" on the sidewalk, and once stood in line at Duane Reade behind someone I'm 85% certain was Paul Rudd, but that's a paltry list after nearly a decade of living in New York. And I was never expected to converse with any of them. (I did try, once, with a contestant from *The Bachelorette*; it's an embarrassing story, involving street meat and pepper spray, and will never join the ranks of Lucy Classics.)

"We need drinks," I manage to say, and my hands, which seem to have a will of their own, start flapping in the air for the waitress like a pigeon taking flight from a stoop. "Have you had a Prairie Fire?" An autopilot line; I've started many bar conversations with this question.

Rudy shakes his head.

"Perfect. They're a great ice breaker. Really bring the heat."

I give Sharlene our order, Rudy looking mildly puzzled but still pleasant.

"You're sweaty," I hear myself saying then, completely aghast. He *does* look sweaty, it's true. He clearly booked it from the train. Which is endearing, really. He cared enough to shave a few seconds off his arrival time. Me pointing out his sweat is decidedly less endearing.

"Uh. Yeah. I guess I am," he says, looking down with a frown at his sweat-stained T-shirt, tugging it away from his skin to vent. He grabs for his flannel and gives his dewy face an aggressive pat down.

I laugh. "Very resourceful."

Rudy's hand freezes mid face-swipe. "Sorry. That was caveman of me, wasn't it? I'll freshen up in the bathroom with some cold water."

"No need!" I say, grinning in a way I suspect looks equal parts delighted and demonic as I pick up a glass of water that went untouched alongside my whiskey. "I have water right here."

He shakes his head. "It's okay, I'll just—"

I don't *throw* the water in his face necessarily, but I thrust it forward with such gusto that the end result is identical. The entirety of my glass ends up in Rudy's hair, on his face, dribbling down his scruffy chin onto his shirt, and oh, God. This was record time, wasn't it? Hashtag survived a few hours before calamity struck.

Rudy's mouth is frozen in an O, and he's watching the *plink, plink, plink* of water as it streams from his hair to the table.

"I am. So. Sorry."

He shakes his head, making the *plink*s faster and more numerous. "It's okay."

"I can be a bit . . . overzealous. That's maybe too kind a word for it. It's the nerves."

"Don't be nervous." Rudy himself looks deeply nervous as he says this, and I wonder if it's occurring to him just now that perhaps I'm *overzealous* because I'm a rabid *Black Hole Sons* superfan.

And that's that, I'm siding with Frank.

Honesty does not feel like the best policy at this point in the evening.

Sharlene returns then, setting down our Prairie Fires, tequila shots with a strong dose of Tabasco sauce. She gives Rudy and his wet . . . everything a slow nod of appraisal before asking, "Will you be ordering food, too?"

Are we still dining together? I look to Rudy for the answer. Hoping.

"Uhh." His hands tug at his collar, wringing out a few more drips.

"How about I give you a minute," Sharlene says, edging a few steps back.

"No. No, I mean, *yes*," Rudy says, nodding—too effusively, like he's working extra hard to convince all of us of his eagerness. "We'll be ordering food. That is, if you're hungry, Lucy?"

"Of course." I sigh inwardly with relief. This hasn't been enough time to adequately assess potential chemistry. It's not enough of a story yet, either.

"Good." Rudy gives a final hearty nod. "Great. That's decided, then."

"I put my steak eating pants on," I say, giving him an emphatic wink. I'm not typically a winker, but for some reason, it felt like an appropriate gesture here. I have instant regrets.

Sharlene leaves us with menus, and we sit for a moment quietly staring at the pages in front of us. I'm not actually reading a single word, as I'm instead still trying to picture just how ghastly that wink must have been.

"I thought you didn't like steak?" Rudy asks, looking up from the menu.

"Oh. It was a joke." I laugh loudly. "That's why I twitched my eye. I won't really order the steak. Not that you have to pay for whatever I do order," I say in a rush. "I'm not expecting that. When I reach for my wallet, it's a real reach."

"Er. Got it. So, no steak."

"Should we toast?" I move the conversation along, reaching for my Prairie Fire.

Rudy picks up his shot glass and sniffs, his nose crinkling. "Smells . . . interesting."

I lift my glass, and clink it—ever so gently, to avoid further catastrophe—against Rudy's. "To this Sunday night adventure. And to *Great Elvira Gray, Oldest Psychic in New York*, and the wonders of the future she'll soon reveal to us."

Rudy taps his glass against the table, and I do, too, in case that's an essential toast ritual I've been missing out on all these years, and then I drain the glass, the heat of the tequila and the Tabasco tracing a warm line from my tongue to my belly.

"That was—" Rudy starts, and then sputters out in a coughing fit.

"Too much?" I ask. I should have suggested a pickleback instead. Or maybe steered clear of shots altogether, seeing as I'm *thirty* and attempting to have a respectable date experience. Shots are for twenty-somethings and Saturday nights and sweaty, sticky dance floors; they're the leading cause of regrettable one-night stands.

"Not my favorite drink, no. But it was an . . . experience? So, er, thank you. For expanding my horizons." He smiles.

My God, he's polite. Shockingly so, given the whole *deluded diva* prediction. So far, he appears to be both less deluded and less diva than a certain twenty-three-year-old aspiring DJ/hand model/actor. It's a miracle, really, that someone could pass through the most fragile, volatile years of their lives being chewed up and spit out by the Hollywood machine, and yet still become a normal, stable adult.

I myself am barely a normal, stable adult, and my childhood was *relentlessly* normal and stable. My mom was an elementary school nurse, my dad a pediatric dentist. We said *God is great, God is good* every evening before eating our homemade (except for Saturday's Hungry-Man) dinner. Their great passions included the PTA and couple's tennis and antiquing.

Rudy is still busy smiling. Looking so damn *affable*.

The epitome of affable. I cannot imagine a greater degree of affability in a human being.

My brain clicks and whirs, the inevitable questions now fully taking flight:

Is he *too* polite? Is that possible? Too much politeness?

Do I repel from polite because it so rarely seems authentic?

What is my problem? *Is* it *my* problem?

Or his? Theirs?

Be cool, Lucy. We're only fifteen minutes deep. *Take a breath.*

I smile back.

We continue to sit in silence, pretending to study our menus again, and I force my mind to shift gears, running through my full catalog of stories and hypotheticals. Despite the fact I have at least ten dates' worth of material catalogued, nothing feels right. I want something new for Rudy, something fresh. I want to feel in the moment, less rehearsed. More . . . myself.

Who am I to judge his authenticity?

How can I judge his politeness when I'm incapable of even basic conversation?

"Maybe this would be smoother if we keep texting," I suggest, only partly joking.

We've spent nearly a week bantering effortlessly over text. How is it that now, in person, even though we are the same two humans with the same two brains, we can't think of a single thing to say?

Rudy tilts his head, considering, and then he reaches for his back pocket and slips out his phone. He furrows his brow as he taps at the screen. The tip of his tongue pokes out between his lips, like he is deep in concentration.

A minute passes. Two.

He's either typing an essay, letting me down politely and at great length, or he's doing the good old type-type-delete-type-delete that is usually my way. Though it hasn't been, not with Rudy. I've been type-type-type-send with him.

Rudy looks up just as my phone pings in my purse. I reach for it, bracing myself.

Rudy: Why don't we grab another drink and go meet Elvira? I've heard there can be a line later in the evening. I don't know about you, but I'm not leaving until I know my cause and date of death.

I laugh, and then text back:

Lucy: I don't think psychics reveal those specifics. But yes. Stellar plan otherwise.

Rudy heads over to the bar, where Sharlene seems to be taking five chatting with some regulars, and comes back a few minutes later with two highball glasses of margarita.

"You didn't have to get more tequila," I say, standing to meet him.

"This night is an adventure, right? I don't drink tequila, I don't get psychic readings, I don't really online date. If I'm stepping outside my comfort zone, might as well be all in."

"You don't online date?"

"You caught me on my first week of actually using Heart-Throbs. I had no clue what I was doing, to be honest. Do you use it much?"

Constantly, for years, and go on first dates every week.

"Eh. Only sometimes."

"Well, aren't we lucky, then? I guess we're meant to be on this date."

I nod coolly and lick salt off the rim, and then start walking toward Elvira. She's alone right now, her hands gripping the crystal ball as she stares blankly into the glowing center.

We step up to the stage. Elvira doesn't seem to notice at first, she's so fixated on whatever vision she's seeing in that ball. Is she really seeing anything? What is there to view when there are no customers? Her own future? Or just the battery-charged bulb at the bottom?

"Madame Elvira?" My voice sounds unusually timid. I don't necessarily believe in any psychic powers, but Elvira has a presence. I won't argue that. It's her advanced age, or the eclectic outfit, the white hair that dips down below the seat of her chair. All of the above.

"Just call me Elvira, please," she says, not looking up. Her voice is rustling dry leaves and ringing church bells in the same breath, the combination so perfectly *psychic* it's as if she were classically trained in the art of selling bullshit predictions.

"Elvira," I repeat. "Shall we . . . ?"

She nods as she extends an arm in welcome. "Step up to Elvira's Ball of Truth."

I hear Rudy muffle a chuckle behind me, and kick back with my heeled bootie, catching him in the shin. He gasps in my ear.

"Thank you. We're honored." The words spill out on instinct. I feel like I'm back at my parents' church, accepting communion from our pastor, who always seemed to me to be ten years older than God. (By that count, Elvira is at least twenty years older than God.) It's the same energy, the same sense that I must obey. Or else.

Not that I really think the Great Elvira can predict my future, let alone control it.

But still, why take any chances?

I step up first, and Rudy follows. We settle into the two chairs across from Elvira.

"My name is Lucy," I start, "and this—"

Elvira waves me off with a hand covered in vibrant green-blue veins. "You don't need to speak. I know what I need to know. The important things."

She looks up then, and I'm fairly certain I gasp out loud. Unless it's Rudy. Or we gasp in unison. Because her dramatically protruding eyes are such a light, faded blue—bleached by a century of sunlight—they're nearly invisible rims. It's like staring into two solid white eyeballs with small black pupils in the center. I reach over and slip my fingers around Rudy's palm and squeeze—which is maybe a bit forward of me, considering we've only just met, and the date hasn't exactly been smoldering with romance yet. But I do it on instinct, and having his hand in mine provides a surprising amount of comfort.

He squeezes back.

"Uh, sorry, yes," I nod, forcing my focus back to Elvira.

She blinks a few times, her eyes roving from me to Rudy, Rudy to me. Though I don't have any real baseline for comparison, she looks a bit . . . *unwell*. She has beads of perspiration along her hairline, and her breath is raspy, short. There's a glass of water on the table, and if I wasn't so intimidated, I would hand it to her—being sure to do so more delicately this time.

I'm not sure how long her assessment will take, or where I'm supposed to look in the meantime. I study the ball, the tablecloth, my margarita, Rudy's Docs, occasionally chancing eye contact with Elvira, feeling a spark of something like hot static every time I do.

Five minutes pass. Maybe ten. My margarita glass is somehow empty.

I squeeze Rudy's hand harder. She's lingering on us more so than other customers, isn't she? There's more scrutiny. More intensity. Like those round, bulging eyeballs are somehow seeing through our layers of skin and tissue and arteries, cutting straight to the core, the heart, the *soul*.

What does my soul look like, I wonder?

I've only gone to church for weddings, funerals, Christmas,

and Easter (a *Chreaster*, as my mom likes to remind me) since high school. That must leave some kind of blemish. Though I'm not sure that soul—the Bible-thumping, Jesus-worshipping kind—is the same as the souls Elvira deals in.

Not that Elvira deals in any souls, because readings are a sham.

Right?

Lucy?

"Hmm, very interesting, the pair of you," Elvira finally says, and the deep timber of her voice is so unexpected after the long silence, my entire body stiffens. I feel it in Rudy, too, the rigid grip of his hand.

I want to ask what's so interesting about us, but I know better than to interrupt.

"I can see that this," her eyes flick from me to Rudy, "is very new."

I nod.

"No need to nod."

I start to nod again, and stop myself just before my chin dips.

"There's something very powerful at work here. Something, dare I say, *destined*." She drags this word out, *destined*, for at least five seconds. As I said, masterful. She's giving me tingly prickles down my neck. "I don't use that word lightly. I believe in free will. What I read is only the result of that free will. But the two of you prove to be stronger together than alone. From the very beginning, I know that to be true. I've met many couples in my day, foretold many unions, many paths, but this—you two, together—may be the most incredible bond I've witnessed yet."

She closes her eyes, and it's a relief, to have at least a brief reprieve from that gaze.

Rudy and I turn to each other, brows raised, and then quickly look back to her, not wanting to be caught in any illicit behavior.

But she keeps her eyes closed. She starts her sway, her arms and shoulders and neck and head undulating side to side, like there's a sleepy, swoony song playing that only she can hear.

I almost want to laugh—because everything about this moment is feeling increasingly batshit bizarre—but of course I wouldn't dare.

"You both seek great success." Her voice is louder now. Somehow even throatier, like a full-body echo chamber. "You *live* for that success. It rules your dreams. Your *nightmares.*"

The sway becomes faster. Much faster. Her arms flail out around her sides, the rhythm from before broken as they move in opposing directions, up, down, down, up. She continues speaking—faster now, too, everything is fast—in a trance-like state:

A lonely woman with words but not much else,
A lonely man with little beyond his past self.
She's stuck and she's stalled as she's carried along,
He grows old, never changes, just loops the same song.
These two take a risk, leaping free from their cages,
The good and the bad, oh it's all for the ages!
The bread that you break, the seeds that you sow,
Light stages, fill pages, with all that you know.
You dream and you work and life still takes a bite,
You laugh and you sing and yet oh what a fright!
The greenest of pastures, the fire, the ice;
Seek out your friends wisely, forever play nice.
The fruits of your labor, first sour now sweet,
A delicate union of skin, flesh, and meat.
Under the stars, become one with the moon
As gravity tugs you from Earth oh so soon.
A family rift swallows all who are near—
Beware a clean slate when there's nothing to clear.
A beginning, an ending, may be one and the same,
Long will you prosper if you treasure my name.

She pauses this odd proclamation—not a song, not quite spoken word, but rhythmic and intoned, chant-like—and takes a deep, shuddery breath.

I feel dizzy and disoriented and enormously relieved that whatever just happened has ended, and—

"What you need to know—what I, Elvira, am here to tell you," she's yelling now—*genuinely* yelling, and I don't need to look to know the whole room must be staring—"is that you will only find success if you share it with one another. Alone, you are nothing. But together . . ." Her mouth is stretched and contorted, those wine-red lips a shriveled, puckered ring, and her eyelids are flickering, *trembling.*

She breaks off, and I lean in, still wholly sucked into whatever the hell is happening here on this star-spangled dais.

"TOGETHER," she starts again, louder still, "TO-GETHER YOU WILL . . ."

Her eyes flutter open, and she's staring straight at me with such a burning intensity, I wonder vaguely if maybe she sees more deeply into me, the real Lucy Minninger, than anyone ever has in my entire life, and then—

Elvira lets out a great, heaving gasp. She keels over, her head knocking into the crystal ball, which then thuds sideways against the table.

The crystal ball rolls, crashes onto the floor. A bomb of glass shards erupts.

I lunge forward along with Rudy, my empty glass slipping from my hand. It smashes against the table, sending more glass shards flying, landing like glitter on Elvira's head.

She doesn't move, though. Doesn't flinch.

Because the Great Elvira is dead.

Chapter 6
Rudy

The good and the bad, oh it's all for the ages!

That gasp.

Oh, God.

I've heard the term *death rattle* before, but never really understood what it meant.

Not until now.

And it was loud. I'm talking Maria-Sharapova-tennis-backhand loud.

The patrons closest to the stage start freaking out—which makes the fringe patrons freak out next. Within sixty seconds, the whole place is spiraling into chaos.

Elvira lies outstretched on her own table. One arm pointing toward my left foot, the other covering her face in what immediately and inappropriately strikes me as a bad, local-theater style of acting. An over-the-top "woe is me" vibe.

It's hard to look.

It's harder to look away.

I reach over to check Elvira's pulse. Just to be certain.

Lucy—who's been a statue up until now—screams bloody murder, stopping me in my tracks. "You can't touch a dead body!"

Now the entire restaurant knows what happened, if there was any lingering question. I feel a wave of embarrassment come over me—a strange sensation to feel while looking at a corpse, but Lucy just ensured that we're the center of everyone's attention.

"We have to know for sure," I say through gritted teeth. And then I reach out again for Elvira's wrist before Lucy can stop me.

Nothing.

I stick my fingers under her nose and elicit another violent shriek from Lucy.

"I'm checking to see if she's breathing!"

Lucy goes quiet. "And?" Her voice cracks.

"She's not."

"Oh."

I extend my hand out to her, but she just stares down at it, unblinking, her eyes glassy.

"You touched a dead person with that hand," she says.

I go to grab her hand anyway, and she starts screaming again.

How is this real life? Why am I here? Why am I with Lucy?

I should have known better. I mean . . . those hypotheticals. Who asks those kinds of twisted questions? Who?!

Lucy. That's who, apparently. *My date.*

Everyone continues to stare at us on our perch raised above the middle of the room. I can feel the eyes, all of them, on me and Lucy. On the fucking *dead body.* I got used to having people's eyes on me at a very young age. It was a normal part of life. But nothing about this right here is normal.

Lucy continues to scream, which drives other people to scream. There's lots of screaming, shrieking, shouting all around me, and here I am, still trying to hold Lucy's hand. But she's just shaking her head, pointing at Elvira's frozen face.

Elvira died with her eyes wide open, those beady pupils directed straight at Lucy.

Lucy seems entranced, almost. Like she's become possessed from their staring match.

I have to do something, anything, to break the spell. Get this train moving along so we can at some point get the hell out of here.

I take a page from Lucy's book, picking up a water glass from the table—a glass that somehow managed to survive both the crystal ball and the corpse—and toss the contents in Lucy's face. In all my thirty-four years' worth of bar fights and dive rock shows, I've never gotten to dump a glass of water on someone.

It's rewarding, I have to admit.

Lucy chokes mid-scream, her mouth open so wide it almost seems impossible her jaw hasn't detached. After catching her breath, she looks at me—*really* looks at me. Wherever she went, she's back now. Which would be good, if non-possessed Lucy didn't freak me out, too.

"I was stuck in a tunnel between my brain and her eyes, Rudy! I was paralyzed and all I could do was scream and scream and scream. I was screaming, right? I think it was my voice." She glances around worriedly. "My God, did I make a scene?"

I nod. "You sure did. Now can we please get off this platform?" Lucy follows me across the stage, and I lean in to say more quietly, "You don't have any drugs on you, right?"

Lucy looks confused for a few seconds, then mildly offended. "Uh. No. I don't do drugs. Why?" She presses up against my chest as we try to shuffle over to the stairs without grazing Elvira's fingertips.

"I was at a murder mystery dinner once where the victim died of natural causes, but the person who found the corpse had some pills and became a prime suspect until they did a toxicology report. I was that suspect, so this hits too close to home. I had to ask."

She laughs through her frown. "That sounds like a terrible murder mystery dinner. It's not even a murder. Did you have to wear a costume?"

"Nope. I got to wear my own clothes. I guess I naturally dress like a druggie." I clap my hands together once and then open them wide, like a magician at the end of a trick. "Sorry. That was weird. I'm just trying to help you calm down a little so we can find somewhere other than this awful stage to hold up while we wait."

We reach the bottom of the stairs, where there's a sizable huddle of concerned diners and waitstaff in their crystal ball tees. There's also Sam the Manager, according to his name tag, a scrawny white guy who's seemingly allowed to wear a normal shirt that doesn't glow in the dark.

Sam approaches me, frantic-looking, a thick line of perspiration beading on his forehead. "Is she okay? Oh my God, *oh my God*, I told the owners that she was too old and we shouldn't make her go up all those steps. What did you two do?"

There's a hint of accusation in his tone that I'm definitely not okay with. She died on his dime, not mine. "Nothing! We were just getting a reading, and she dropped dead!"

"Well," Lucy chimes in, "she *was* moving and swaying a lot before . . ." She pauses, looking anxiously back up at the stage. Elvira's lifeless form. "Before it happened. I've never seen a psychic so committed to the bit, not even in the movies, and then she just . . . well . . . *died*."

Sam is visibly losing his shit, the sweat by now practically running down him in sheets. He's sweatier than I was upon arrival, and that's saying something. He runs up the stairs, trips a couple of steps from the top, and on his way down, his hand hits Elvira's chair. In the space of about five very long seconds, her body tilts, leans, and slips off the side of the table, falling squarely on top of Sam's overextended arm. Pinning him.

He's screaming now, Lucy's—of course—screaming again, the whole huddle is screaming.

I'm silent in the middle of the chaos. Frozen in a real fight-or-flight kind of moment.

I could stick around and help. Or . . .

"Let's leave," I say, taking Lucy's hand—gently, not wanting to further set her off. This time, she lets me.

"Won't we look guilty?"

"Nah. We can wait outside until the cops get here. Talk to them then. I need to get out of here. Away from this." I motion toward Sam, still pinned, still screaming, even though he could easily lift her spindly arm. I doubt the rigor mortis has fully set in. "This place is nuts. Plus, if I'm being honest with you, I don't want to get recognized."

Lucy glances up at me with a disarmingly mischievous look and says, quietly, thank God, "Hey! Aren't you from that alien show that was so big in the nineties?"

Right. So she does know.

It's pretty good timing, I must say, even if it does make my skin crawl a bit.

She interlaces her fingers with mine, and we bolt for the door.

As we're running, I hear Sam yell out from behind us: "She had so much life left to live!" An interesting, albeit highly inaccurate, proclamation about the Great Elvira.

Cold night air hits us as we step out onto the sidewalk, a refreshing jolt after everything that's happened. We make it across the street just as a police car rolls up to the curb. It parks directly in front of us.

"Should we get this out of the way?" I say, pulling Lucy to a stop. She nods, and we approach a pair of cops who look like complete opposites: one young, portly Black male officer, and an older, six-foot-tall, jacked-up white female officer who reminds me of Brigitte Nielsen. I'm nervous to even look her in the eye, despite our innocence.

We introduce ourselves, and Lucy launches into her account of the evening. But she can't get through a full sentence without sniffling and crying, her voice cracking on every syllable. It's painful to watch, and the cops are trying to speed her along at every turn, glancing pointedly toward the restaurant.

I squeeze her hand—we never stopped holding hands, I realize—and turn toward Brigitte. "She was giving our reading when it happened. She was old. Like, was in gym class with Moses old. No offense to her. She died doing what she loved, I think. Giving a first date a real punch up. We'll never forget her, that's for sure."

Brigitte continues writing in her little book for a moment, then nods at us in dismissal. I wave goodbye with my free hand, just as Sam pops his head out of the restaurant door, arms waving in distress. Then I tug Lucy along the sidewalk to get us the hell away from this place.

So long, Francois Santos.

Not even those merguez tacos are enough to make me ever come back.

Whiskey seems like the only appropriate response to the spectacle just witnessed, so we post up at a bar down the street.

Lucy keeps mumbling fragments of Elvira's words on a loop under her breath:

"She's stuck and she's stalled . . . these two take a risk . . . fire and ice, beware a clean slate . . . hmm, what else? Fruits and skin, flesh and meat . . ."

I zone out, picking at the free popcorn that came with my drink. I'm beginning to feel like I'm in a little over my head.

Or more like way over my head.

I mean, this was a *night*. A very interesting, fodder-filled night. One for a half-hour special kind of night. Not Lucy's fault, of course, any of it. I think she's funny—an eccentric, outside-the-box kind of funny—and objectively attractive. I could see us having a good time over too many drinks. But it's hard being immediately thrown together into this kind of intensely serious situation, seeing someone so close up, so raw, so soon. There was no time to ease in, just *poof*, *dead body*, and now I can see clearly that we handle trauma very differently.

It's a strange night with a strange woman, a meeting from a strange app that brings strangers together. And now I'm not sure what I'm supposed to do with that stranger. What happens for us next. If anything should happen.

I turn back to Lucy, and she's still muttering to herself, "Bread that you bake, seeds that you make," staring into the empty bottom of her whiskey glass. There were so many words, most of them nonsensical, they're already blurry in my mind. The only real standouts for me:

A lonely man with little beyond his past self . . .

Which, fuck that hurts. And—

Alone, you are nothing. Together, together you will . . .

We will *what*?

Did we somehow break the veil with our undeniable greatness? The knowledge about our combined strength was too much, too powerful—more than Elvira's frail, worldly frame could handle? What could possibly happen that was so amazing from an app algorithm that shoved us together for some French-Mexican food with a little psychic activity on the side?

"What the fuck do you think she meant by any of that?" I break down and ask, trying to get on par with her brain. No easy task, I suspect.

Lucy comes back to earth, putting down her glass. "What did you say?"

The double shot of whiskey may have been a bad idea. At least without more sustenance than popcorn.

"I asked what you thought she meant. You've been trying to remember her words since we got to the bar. Any luck deciphering her code?"

Lucy pins me with those shockingly big green eyes. "It's obvious, isn't it?"

I shake my head. "Uh. No? Not really?"

She gives a pitying look, pats my hand. "We have to do something together. If we ever want to actually succeed. That's what she was saying."

This answer just frustrates me more. Because *together* could mean anything. We could go take a piss in the individual stalls of the bathrooms here, side by side, *together*.

I snap a bit, because, you know, this whole night. "Like, bake a cake together? Write a hit song together? Open a Friendly's franchise together? Start our own dating app together?" I pause and take a deep breath, trying to get control of myself. Put my mom's meditation drills into good use. She used to make me meditate after a long day on set—part of why I turned out so "mentally healthy," she says. *This isn't Lucy's fault.* "Sorry. I don't mean to take any of this out on you. You don't deserve that. I'm just saying that *together* could mean absolutely anything, if you even believe in her at all. She could have been deceiving us for the sake of a good show, and probably would have died in that moment no matter what, with or without us. I mean, she was in gym class with Moses, for Christ's sake." I recycle the same description I used with the cops, because it's the most fitting way to capture just how old Elvira really was. And because my brain is too fried to think of anything better.

Lucy's lips turn up slightly, even if it's the second time she's hearing the line. I make a mental note of it, for when the right comedy moment comes up.

Though is it wrong to use any of this for laughs? A woman died, on one hand. But on the other, it's also kind of comedy gold. Based on my self-deprecating style of comedy and penchant for finding humor in tragic life moments, these thoughts and correlations pop out involuntarily. I should probably try to suppress them this time, though. For the sake of my present company, and out of respect for what's just transpired. Or really, you know, *expired*.

Nope, stop, Rudy.

"So," she says, "you don't believe that she was really read-ing our future? You don't think what she saw about us was so intense that she got caught up in the veil and . . . was trapped permanently on the other side?"

"I don't know what to think. Truth be told, I'm the son of a self-proclaimed Irish witch. A *mystic*. Red hair, brown eyes—it's an old superstition. But my mom did know everything bad Rocco and I did, always. She knew if we smoked, drank, stole candy from the grocery store when we were kids. All of it. Every damn time."

Lucy scrunches her nose, creating two defined lines that show off her sharp cheekbones. "That sounds like she just had a good nose for trouble, and you and your brother were sloppy."

I guess I didn't spell it out well enough. "It wasn't only when we were living together. And we were not sloppy. We were ex-tremely stealthy, but she somehow knew anyway and would point at the places where we hid bottles, pipes, nudie mags, other unmentionables. If we had a stash, she knew about it. It happened, too, when we were in separate places. When I was in college, I'd get detailed emails about the stuff she was hearing and seeing about me. Most of it was spot-on. Like eighty-eight percent or so. Total B plus."

Lucy is squinting at me in a tilted, lopsided kind of way. Yep, we definitely need some proper dinner. "So again," she says, "your mom knew you were partying, and she would make vague but logical assumptions so you'd think she had a sixth sense? To scare you into good behavior? I like your mom, she's got moxie!"

I can't help but laugh at that. Besides, I love my mom, but I don't necessarily believe in the psychic energy. I do, however, respect the craft and know better than to just pass it off as phony. Though that doesn't mean I'm ready to stake my entire future around a reading.

My love life.

My career.

I wouldn't admit this out loud, ever, but I've always expected the "love at first sight" storybook kind of moment. It was that way with Piper, even if I was still just a kid. One locked-eyes instant that changes the trajectory of my whole life. Elvira is a story, but not necessarily a part of that story. And Lucy is stirring up feelings, sure, but I'm not convinced it's *that* feeling.

Or maybe there are just too many feelings right now fighting for space.

I don't know.

I have no answers.

Lucy returns to silently staring at the bottom of her whiskey glass. Is she questioning everything, too? Wondering why me, why her, why *us*?

She comes alive again a few minutes later, those already large eyes doubling in size. It's like her brain had been running a cleanup program and deleted all the excess gigs of trash. "So, you have a comedy show you're worried about keeping afloat, right?" Sure, I might have mentioned the show—vaguely, since we didn't acknowledge my past until tonight—in a text or two. The pressure to draw in new people. Her way of saying it feels especially blunt, though. "Of course she wouldn't have known that, or anything else about you. Even if she had kids, they'd be full-fledged AARP cardmembers at this point. Not your demographic, so perhaps a point in favor of her authenticity. Maybe the *together* talk was about me helping with your show?"

I must look less than enthused to hear a friendly stranger trying to tell me how to do my job, because Lucy pauses, like she knows she's stepped over a line.

"I'm not sure what she was suggesting, but I do know I have the show under control," I say, trying to keep my tone level. I'm not sure how successful I am. "And if numbers drop, I'll just invite new guests who have illustrious pasts, show their clips, too, and razz them. It could go on forever, like *America's Funniest Home Videos*. Many guests, same shtick."

She frowns and stares off at the bar.

Well, if there's anything here to blow, I'm blowing it.

Maybe love at first sight is a load of bullshit.

Maybe there's a good reason I'm always single.

Even if our first meeting wasn't what I envisioned, she has a kind of charm that is undeniably unique. I can't quite tell what the whole package is yet, but if I keep my walls up, I won't have the opportunity to find out.

And what if Elvira *was* on to something?

Shit.

My head is spinning like the girl's did in *The Exorcist*, and it's not because of the whiskey.

I try again, determined to do better. "Like I said, I may not always believe, but I do respect the craft. What are things you're lacking in your own life? Maybe that'll help us figure it out. You said you work with authors, and mentioned writing, too?"

She looks at me straight on. "All I've ever wanted was to be a published author, from the time I could first read books and realized that somewhere, at some point in time, someone wrote those words. Created those worlds." She sighs, and I take a pretend sip from my empty glass, avoiding eye contact. We've gone below the surface now. And I can totally relate—that's how I feel about music, or a good show. "No one likes my stories, though. I'm not even sure I like my stories. So instead, I'm a thirty-year-old errand girl. A Craigslister extraordinaire who's done every odd job this city has to offer—minus anything involving nudity, and there's a surprising number of jobs that require you to expose your bits. Anyway. I also assist an actual author who's young and whiny and annoyingly brilliant. Too brilliant for her own good. Too beautiful, too."

I take a moment to process this. Our conversations hadn't been this real or honest yet, not tonight, not in texts. Our exchanges were almost exclusively funny quips, verbal wordplay to see who could one-up the other's jokes. This is a new side of

Lucy. I appreciate the candor, and her trust in me to feel this comfortable. I'm envious of that.

Lucy continues, "I have five manuscripts written and nowhere left to take them. I've been rejected all around town. I'd ask Clementine for advice, but she'd just hand me the poo bags to take her dog for a walk."

I stop her before she continues farther down this sad, tipsy path. "The truth is, tonight I was looking for a memorable interaction with someone, and I'd say this date . . . exceeded expectations. And you should know, I usually bail after the first dead psychic. But not with you."

Lucy smiles, maybe her first real one of the night. It's a good smile, warm and cheery. The effect is unexpectedly spellbinding.

A tap on my shoulder brings me back, and I spin around.

It's Sharlene, from Francois Santos, still in her glow-in-the-dark crystal ball tee. She already wasn't the youngest waitress there, but in this dim bar light, and after what happened, she's looking extra withered. The bartender slides a whiskey towards her. A regular, I guess.

"Ah, we meet again." She nods at us, then downs the shot. "Thanks for leaving your card at the bar—I closed it out and added twenty percent gratuity. You can go claim it anytime."

"Shit," I say, "sorry we left like that. It was, uh, a little overwhelming to watch someone die. I'd actually feel like a sociopath if I tried to settle up after what we witnessed."

Sharlene doesn't seem to care either way—she's already moved on. She sits down next to Lucy and places both hands evenly on the bar, leaning in close.

"Listen. I've worked at that place for fifteen years. Seen it all. Elvira was the real deal. I mean, we're all human, so she wasn't one hundred percent, but she did have a knack for seeing relationships. I can personally attest to a handful of very successful marriages that started with an Elvira date. I don't want to brag here, since I served them and all, but one pair became an A-list celebrity couple you might know . . . I'll give you a hint, their mashup name starts with a B."

"Are you fucking with us?" Lucy asks, squinting over at Sharlene. "Because we've already been through a lot tonight. You're filling our heads with wild ideas, and our heads are plenty filled without your help."

Sharlene rests her hand on Lucy's back. "Filled with what? Did she say the two of you were . . . destined?"

My stomach drops. If she is, in fact, messing with us, she's a terrible person.

"She did use that term," I say. "Was that one of her go-to moves? Get the kids to think about their future?"

"Well, she was a psychic in the middle of a Brooklyn hipster restaurant . . . so yes, she didn't want to make anyone feel like it couldn't be their night. She was encouraging in her way. But she only said 'destined' if it was the real deal."

"You've got to be shitting me," Lucy says a little too loudly, causing a few people at the bar to stare down at us.

"Nope, no shitting. It's not all rosy, though. I know more 'destined' couples that flamed out into the worst breakups of their lives. I mean, it was odd to have these strangers come back and tell us about their personal misfortunes. But the misfortunes were just so . . . *epic*. And they wanted to talk about it with people who understood. Back at the source. I respect that."

I take the rest of my beer and guzzle it down. Sharlene just keeps laying it on us. I'm good at spotting a bullshitter—their small smirks, feeding you what you want to hear or what you fear in order to control your brain. It's a director's tool to get the performance they want. And it works. It's time-tested. Sharlene is not bullshitting. She's speaking with an earnestness that might be missed if you weren't from the East Coast.

"I'm not trying to scare you. Just giving a heads-up. I never saw her act like that, all the swaying and yelling. So, my advice? I would listen to what she said. Fight for that destiny. I was

'destined' once, too. Me and my ex. We . . . didn't end well."
Her eyes go all misty, and she looks down at the floor. "Anyway, I gotta get home."

With that, she throws a twenty down and leaves. A true service industry professional.

Well, shit.

I have so many more questions.

Lucy is silent for longer than what seems to be her usual, looking tired and spent from all that's transpired. I don't have words, either. We stare blankly at each other, surely thinking the same thing.

Should we take this seriously?

Would we be a wild success, or a flaming failure?

Lucy waves the bartender over as she grabs for her purse. I can't just have her pay for the drinks, not after this whole night was my grand idea. No dinner, just some stale popcorn.

"I insist," she says, cutting me off at the pass. "You got my Prairie Fire, and my margarita."

The margarita glass that ended up in shards coating Elvira's lifeless body.

I shake my head to clear the image. "How about some late-night dumplings? You get the whiskey, I'll take care of the food."

Lucy seems to consider this as she pulls bills from her wallet. "I've never said no to dumplings before, but honestly? I think I need to get home. This whole night has made me extremely tired. And extremely not hungry."

"Yeah, I'm beat, too. But I got the drinks. Really."

She nods, stuffing the money back in her bag. I'm not sure who leads then, but we hug.

It feels . . . okay.

There's a brief pause after we both pull away, an enormous *what the hell happens next* elephant filling the space between us.

Lucy goes first. "I know this was a deeply weird night, but

I'm glad if it had to happen, it happened with you. Why don't we take a breather, process, and reconvene in a few days? Talk about what to do next, if we do anything at all?"

How could I say no?

And like she said, it's just a talk. Maybe after some proper food and good sleep, the idea of believing anything Elvira said will feel even more absurd.

Probably. Likely.

"Sure," I say. "Send me a location and time, and I'll be there. But no psychics allowed."

Chapter 7
Lucy

The bread that you break, the seeds that you sow.

"Welcome to my humble Spinster Cave," I say, gesturing grandly to Rudy as I step back from the door to welcome him inside.

He looks anxious and uncertain, both hands fiddling with the fraying strap of his messenger bag, like my doorstep is not high on the list of places he'd like to be. Not top ten. Maybe not top hundred. He also looks rumpled and exhausted—red-eyed and paler than before, freckles even more freckly, hair tangled up into a bun—like he hasn't done much sleeping since our date. Neither have I, which is why my apartment is the cleanest it's ever been, including the professional deep clean that cost more than a month of my rent. (Courtesy of the Myrtles.) I Cloroxed my refrigerator shelves. At four this morning. Because every time I close my eyes, I see Elvira, those large, nearly colorless eyes staring, unblinking, her red lips gaping. *Gasping.* I replay her words—what I can remember of them—try to process frame by frame. And I wonder if there's anything we could have done differently. If we could have saved her somehow.

He's *here*, though. Rudy's here.

Her words meant something to him, too.

Her death meant something.

"Spinster Cave?" he asks, raising his bushy dark left eyebrow. His eyebrows are almost black, a contrast against the pinkish-red tones. The Italian side fighting through the Irish.

I point to the engraved sign above my head. "Yes. I'm the spinster, naturally. And this is my lair. The natural light is scarce, the rodents are plentiful, but the rent is cheap, and my landlords are like a second set of parents. Don't mention that to them, though, if you meet. They have a false sense of their youthfulness."

"Got it," he says, and we stand there for a few more seconds before he nods and steps across the threshold. I glance at the basket of shoes next to the door, and he nods in understanding, slips his off. He's wearing black socks with hot-pink polka dots. I smile approvingly, and then lead the way to the living room, fighting down my nerves.

I'd been the one to suggest he come *here*, even though there are roughly a hundred cafés and bars and restaurants we could have gone to within a three-block radius. But something about this conversation—*everything* about it, really—feels too intimate for public consumption. I don't need any rabid nineties' fans tuning in. We're talking about our fates, after all. Our *destinies*. That's pretty private shit. And besides, I do my best thinking in this tiny hole.

But it's been a long time since any man other than Frank or the exterminator stepped foot inside these walls. A very long time. Some first dates, some bad decisions. I've changed my ways in the past few years, because the Spinster Cave is cursed:

Any man who enters never returns.

This is a different kind of visit, though. More of a meeting than a date.

Hopefully the curse will not apply.

"Can I get you something to drink? Water? Seltzer?" I

glance back at the clock on my nightstand. Quarter past noon. "Whiskey, gin, mezcal?"

Rudy shrugs off his jacket, tosses it on the arm of the love seat. "Depends. What kind of seltzer are we talking about?"

I side-eye him on my way over to the pristine fridge. The outside of the door has also been scrubbed clean, and I tossed all of last year's Christmas cards from Greendale of toddlers smiling on hay bales, tree stumps, snow mounds. The next wave will be coming soon enough. "I should have known. You're one of those types."

"If you mean someone who distinguishes between good seltzer and mediocre seltzer, then yes. I'm one of *those*, I'm afraid. I like my seltzer zesty and zippy. It's all about the bubble size and ratio."

He's trying to keep a straight and serious face as he says this, but I see his lips tugging up. Thank God. Men in Brooklyn— maybe men in general, though I've met very few specimens outside of New York in the past eight years—have far too many idiosyncratic tastes and strong opinions about things that don't require much in the way of opinions, let alone strong ones.

"I'm mostly kidding," he says. "Though if you say Polar, we'll be friends forever."

I open the fridge door, smiling. "Then I guess we're destined by the stars." I pull out a can of Polar for each of us and kick the door shut, turning toward Rudy. "Not that we need a reminder of that. It's why you're here, isn't it?"

"Destined by the stars," he repeats, moving over as far as he can to the edge of the love seat. I sit down next to him, handing him a can. It's a tight fit side by side, thighs touching, seeing as it's a *love seat*, not a sofa. Why pay double the price for a sofa, though, when I'm the only one who sits on it? And why call half a sofa a love seat instead of, I don't know, a *half sofa*? It feels cruel to all of us loveless but practical furniture buyers.

He pops the can, takes a swig. "Is that what you think, after

time to mull? Are we . . . destined to be together? Or not necessarily *together* together, that is, but to do something grand and
life-altering?"

I've of course thought about this question a lot since Elvira's
death. It's all I've thought about, really. Do I believe in the
power of Elvira? Do I believe in psychics, period? I certainly
didn't after Shining Shannon's string of failed prophecies. And
I haven't considered the question of psychic energy once in the
years after that first underwhelming experience. The Wendy's
cheeseburger combo I ate after the reading was the more rewarding part of our night on the town.

But Elvira. She felt different. The whole moment felt different.

Heavy. Thick. Charged.

A lonely woman with words but not much else . . .

I'm not sure I completely believe what she said to be true,
but I also don't *not* believe. While vague enough, some of it
felt . . . a little on the nose.

"Maybe?" I say, turning to look at Rudy. He's watching me
closely—not just because we're literally very close physically,
but like he's cataloguing every line and curve of my face. It
makes the tips of my ears burn. "On one hand, I'm not someone who reads horoscopes or cares about astrological signs or
rubs crystals before bed. But on the other . . . *damn*, Elvira
was convincing, wasn't she? Even before she keeled over.
Though a mid-reading death does add a certain gravitas. Sub-
par psychics of the world, take note. Maybe I'll call up my
Dorito-eater."

Rudy smiles, but it feels flat. Of course it's flat, because *a
woman died.*

"Sorry," I say, looking down at the unopened can in my
hands. "I joke when I'm nervous. It's a bad habit. My Heart-
Throbs profile should have more disclaimers."

"Hey, I get it. Trust me." Rudy nudges me gently with his

elbow. "I'm the king of inappropriate and poorly timed jokes. Part of a long history of overactive defense mechanisms."

That feels uncannily relatable—*a long history of overactive defense mechanisms.*

"You just so happened to find yourself the queen." I flip the top of my can open, lift it up to clink against his. "Cheers to not being fully functional adults, even in our thirties."

He clinks back in solidarity. "That's why we live in this city, isn't it? Easier to fit in. We'd stick out like sore thumbs in suburbia."

I nod as I take a few sips of seltzer. I am most definitely a very sore thumb in Greendale. Even with Susie and Grace these days.

"Anyway," I continue, looking up to meet his eyes, "it's not remotely funny that Elvira died. I'm still trying to process seeing my first corpse, at least outside of a funeral setting. Trying to figure out what it means, if it means anything at all. Because as much as I'm not a believer, there's a part of me that wonders. What if what Sharlene said about 'destined' is true, and it wasn't just the same script Elvira used on every new couple who climbed up on that stage? And if there's any chance at all she had some kind of *vision* about us . . . do we at least try to see it through? If our two paths are either a celebrity couple mashup name or some kind of epic devastation, I'm picking the mashup every time. Except . . . darn it. *Ludy* and *Rucy* are both pretty mediocre options."

Rudy cringes. "Yep. Not happening. Another question, though: if being together means we either win big or fail big, what happens if we don't try at all? Does that still put us in the fail big category?"

"Damn. I didn't even think about that. Are there two potential fates, or three?"

Rudy rubs the small patch of orange hair under his bottom lip, deep in thought. "Are you the kind of person who makes long lists before any big life decisions? Weighing pros and cons?"

I'm taking another sip of seltzer as he asks, and I laugh so hard a few stray bubbles catch in my nose. "If I was that organized and efficient, do you really think I'd be thirty years old and paying rent with Craigslist money? C'mon, Rudy."

Rudy laughs, too, and it's a great laugh, round and rolling. The first time I've heard him laugh for real, not just to be polite. It feels well-earned, especially considering who he is. *I made a comedian laugh.* "In case you're wondering based on my random gigs, I'm not a list person, either."

"So where does that leave us? A coin flip?" I dig my hand around the edge of the seat cushion for stray pennies before remembering I vacuumed the love seat last night. "Or no, oh my God, I know! A Magic Eight Ball. My first message to you was a sign."

"Hmm. That's an idea. But if we believe in signs, that's a mark in Elvira's favor, no?"

"Shit. Good point."

A loud, enthusiastic knock comes from the door. Followed immediately by another even louder, more enthusiastic knock.

"Luce! Are you there, Luce? It's me. Frank."

I hear some muted grumbles and feet shuffling, and then, "We got bagels and lox from Bagel House and they *accidentally* doubled the order. Do you want any?" Estelle, yelling through the door. "If Frank eats all this lox, he'll be complaining about bloat for the next week."

I sigh. "My landlords. Looks like you'll be meeting them sooner than anticipated."

Rudy shrugs. "No big deal. It's not like it's your real parents. And besides, she said bagels and lox, so . . ." He shrugs again. "Wouldn't want good ol' Frank to get the bloat, after all."

"So you're altruistic," I say, pushing myself up to stand. "And you're not even asking up front if the bagels are kettle-boiled."

"You underestimate me if you think I don't already know that Bagel House makes bagels the only acceptable way."

I laugh as I walk over to the door, opening it just as Estelle's fist is poised to bang.

"Oh! Hello!" She turns that fist into a twirly princess wave, her professionally curled and dyed eyelashes fluttering as her eyes dart behind me to Rudy. She's been spending all of her ample free time watching Rocco Riziero movies these last few days. "I didn't realize you weren't alone, Lucy."

"Yeah. You're always alone," Frank adds. He points to the sign above our heads. "That's why it's called the Spinster Cave."

Frank guffaws, as he does. Estelle titters, another strange but true variation on a laugh.

I hear a proper chuckle from behind me and turn to give Rudy a daggery glare. "You don't get to laugh about me being a spinster. Far too soon."

"I like this man already!" Frank declares, sweeping into the room like it's his. Which, technically, it is.

"You're right, and I'm sorry," Rudy says, frowning, and it looks like he actually means it. "I only laughed because I'm always alone, too. I can relate. What's the male equivalent of a spinster? Bachelor doesn't feel quite right. Too positive."

"Bachelor does sound very positive, doesn't it," Frank says, side-eyeing Estelle. "I quite like the ring of it myself."

"That's the whole problem." I grab the brown bag of food from Frank's hand and stomp the fifteen feet between the door and the kitchen to drop it on the counter. "There isn't a male equivalent. Only women are judged if they choose the single life."

"Well, I wouldn't say you're *choosing* it." Estelle tilts her head thoughtfully, one freshly French-manicured finger tapping at her chin. "More like it's been choosing you."

"I'm not going to make the mistake of laughing at that," Rudy says, smiling pleasantly.

"Thank you for the food," I say, gritting my teeth. "That was very thoughtful of you."

"Of course, dear. It's our most rewarding duty in life, making sure you're fed and comfortable." Estelle flashes me a saccharine smile before turning to Rudy. "Now, did you want to introduce us to your new friend . . . ?"

I return the smile, upping the sugar content twofold. "Certainly. Rudy, these are my utterly delightful landlords, Estelle and Frank. To be honest, they've already heard all about you and HeartThrobs and our unfortunate date. They know you're a Riziero, and Estelle has quite the schoolgirl crush on Rocco."

Estelle gasps. "I do not!"

"I caught you watching that damn pirate movie he's in three times in the last two days," Frank says, frowning. "I missed the end of *Wheel of Fortune* because of it."

"Not the whole movie! Just that very pivotal moment at the beach. The musical score in that scene is so moving. And the water, it's so blue!"

"Ah, yes. I see. How convenient that so much skin is exposed next to the blue water."

Estelle and Frank continue bickering, and Rudy observes quietly, eyebrows raised. I mouth *I'm sorry*, and he shrugs back. He's a big shrugger, Rudy. Like everything is just fine and dandy. A-okay. No worries. It's both vaguely annoying and highly enviable.

After a few minutes of this—listening as they compare recent *Wheel of Fortune* and then *The Price Is Right* victories—I manage to usher them out of the apartment, nearly closing the door on Estelle's nose as she turns back to say, "Pleasure to meet you, Rudy! I hope the cave's curse doesn't strike again!"

I shut the door loudly, lock it for added precaution. "Don't ask. There's not a real curse. Elvira's prophecy is the only true supernatural dilemma in my life, I promise."

"That's a relief. I'm not sure I could handle a curse *and* a prophecy. The curse might negate the good of the prophecy."

"I'm sorry—they're a lot, I know. But they mean well. Mostly."

"Nothing to apologize for. They seem like real characters,

but that keeps life interesting. Plus, they delivered us bagels and lox. I can forgive most things for a good New York bagel."

I laugh. "Good to know. So . . . are you hungry now?"

"Starving. I usually have breakfast around noon, so this is perfect timing."

"Noon? That's like frat boy college life."

"Yeah, I know." He rubs his belly thoughtfully. "It's a bad habit from too many late-night gigs. My body's internal clock never syncs up with the sun. But I assure you, I was never a frat boy. My college didn't even have frats. It didn't have grades, either. Total hippie-dippy school."

"That *is* reassuring. I would've been pissed if Elvira paired me off with a frat boy."

I walk to the kitchen and open the brown bag, pulling out two Everything bagels and plastic tubs of lox and capers and cream cheese. Just the scent of the peppery Everything medley is enough to make me swoon. We're quiet as I pull out plates and smear cream cheese onto the bagels, layer on thick slices of lox. Frank and Estelle's unexpected drop-in derailed my thoughts:

Elvira. The prophecy. What the hell happens next.

"So," Rudy says, as I hand over his plate and shuffle back in next to him on the love seat. He pauses to take a long sniff of Everything magic. "Where were we? We both suck at list-making. A Magic Eight Ball will only confuse things."

"Right. Though I feel like whatever our plan, it's an all-or-nothing scenario. We decide Elvira was just an overzealous eccentric—may she rest in peace—and move on with our lives . . . or we decide she was a real VIP on the other side of the veil, and go all in to find out what our great success will be. Cross our fingers we don't go up in flames along the way." I realize, as I hear myself say this out loud, that I very much do *not* want to just move on. That would make the curse true again, because this would be our first and last bagel date to-

gether. The thought makes me sad, sadder than it should probably, and I take an exceptionally large bite of bagel to soothe
myself.

"Hmm." Rudy takes a big bite, too, closes his eyes as he
chews. "*Damn*. Bagel House." He swallows, grinning, and
turns to look at me. "Okay. That's a start. Let's walk through it.
What would it mean to *go all in*? What would that look like?"

"Well, her . . . *riddle* . . . referenced work and family and
friends." I put my plate down, balance it on my knees. "She said
something like: *the sweet fruits of your labor will be a union of
flesh and meat.* Which, to be honest, makes very little fucking
sense. I wish I'd thought to record her, because it's all starting
to jumble in my head. But my takeaway? We go in deep. Way
deeper than any jaded single New Yorker would usually choose
to go in a year, maybe ever. Get to know one another as well
as possible—the people we love, the random jobs we do to survive, our *eclectic* skill sets we've built up over the years."

"Uh-huh." Rudy looks down at his plate. "But if we do that,
are we actually . . . together? You know, as in dating? A couple?
Because that's a hard thing to just make believe about. You can't
force genuine feelings."

Force.

I feel my ears burn again, not for a pleasant reason this time.
Clearly, Rudy feels zero chemistry. And really, it's not like I'm
swooning all over the place—the Everything scent has a more
visceral effect on me. But a true human-induced swoon can
take time. Rudy's funny enough, presumably with some good
life stories up his sleeve. Creative and musical. Handsome in
a comfortable, unexpected, original kind of way. Not objectively cookie-cutter hot, like Rocco. And that's a good thing.
He seems kind, but potentially, hopefully not in a fake way.

Who knows what more time together could do?

"I don't think we can *force* anything," I say. "That wouldn't
work."

Rudy cringes. "Sorry. That didn't sound great. I just mean that usually deciding to be in a relationship is a longer-term process. It doesn't happen overnight."

"I agree. And if we're being honest—and it feels like honesty is the only way ahead here—I haven't been in a serious relationship since college. So I wouldn't even know how to effectively make believe. I'm out of practice."

He drops his bagel mid-bite. "Same. Wow. We really are a pair of Brooklyn misfits."

"Elvira sniffed us out. Maybe that's why she assumed we were so well aligned."

We're silent for a few minutes, both of us chewing our bagels.

"Alright," Rudy says finally, resting his empty plate on the love seat arm. "How about this? We don't make any formal decisions about coupledom, but we keep . . . hanging out. We give each other mini tours of our lives. I take you on jobs, you take me. We start there. Keep it simple. Then, if we both feel up to it, we meet friends. Family comes in later. My mom would break out the ancestral china plates if I brought a woman home for Sunday dinner. Can't have that just yet."

I nod slowly as I take this idea in. "It sounds kind of like what I imagine dating is outside of New York. You go on a few dates, feel it out before deciding what to do. You don't just disappear because you have a thousand other equal or better options in your HeartThrobs inbox. It feels . . . quaint. Vintage. I like it." I do. I really do.

"Yeah?"

"Yeah."

"Cool. So, we made a decision then? Or a non-decision, but still a kind of decision in its own right. Which already seems like a pretty wild accomplishment for two anti-listers who suck at making real-life adult choices."

"Maybe that's proof Elvira was onto something."

"Maybe." He doesn't look totally convinced, but neither am I.

That's why we'll take it nice and slow. One "date" at a time.

"Let's promise to be open and real with one another," he says. "If it's not feeling right for either of us, it's okay to bail. We'll know we tried, and Elvira was likely more batshit than VIP."

"I can do open and real. That feels . . . refreshing."

"Right?"

"And if nothing else," I add, "even if we don't find success together, we'll both have a good story to tell our married friends back home. I call it: *The Great Elvira Challenge.*"

"The Great Elvira Challenge." Rudy nods in approval. "A good name for a good story."

No. Not just good. Or even very good.

A fucking *great* story.

As long as we don't implode altogether along the way.

Chapter 8
Rudy

Light stages, fill pages, with all that you know.

"So the show is basically just you making fun of your past?" Lucy asks, spinning around to take in Little Zelda's and all of its divey understated cool. "That seems entertaining and soul-crushing at the same time. I commend the ability to mock yourself like that."

Lucy has me pegged.

My monthly gig I've been running since January, *Eclipsed Too Soon*, is a look back at the work I did as a child actor, a video-heavy show that confronts the ins and outs of my past in front of a room filled with strangers. Tonight will be the usual sea of scruffy beards and flannels and nineties-inspired tees—grunge bands, sketch comedy acts like *The State* and *Mr. Show*, the occasional vintage No Fear. And of course, *Black Hole Sons* and *Whiz of Riz* hats and shirts and hoodies, the shows that made most of the people in the audience come out to see me laugh at myself for ninety minutes.

Nostalgia is powerful—and lucrative, it turns out. Just enough so to get by in New York.

Eclipsed Too Soon is the perfect gig to demonstrate for Lucy how my comedic brain functions. To show her my style of humor, and how I create behind the scenes, in real time. TV magic captured all of my most embarrassing milestones, from the tender ages of five to eighteen, for the world to see—my voice cracking like a sick yodeler who didn't take the cough drop; emergency makeup for face-mauling pimples; a unibrow my castmates said Frida Kahlo would have envied. And a plethora of other horrific things that most kids experience within the confines of their own family and friend groups. Clips like these are the backbone of my show.

Sometimes I think about how it'd be fun to show new footage of "current Rudy," but then I remember how the handful of indie flicks and web series pilots I've shot over the years have never seen the light of day, other than a couple of trailers. What a sad way to remind people of just how far I've fallen from the Hollywood scene.

Because it's not that I've never tried . . . it just seems like I'm either doing passion projects for people that don't pan out, or submitting tapes for a good role with no real follow-up interest. I *do* miss the acting biz—some parts of it, at least. I miss the challenge, the thrill of becoming someone else, temporarily at least. Being one part of a larger story. Making art that speaks to so many people, brings meaning, joy, a distraction from real life. I miss the camaraderie of a set, too, being immersed in a crew of new people for a short time, summer camp style. The hijinks. One of my favorites, the clothespin joke, where you write a word on a clothespin—usually a crude adolescent one, "dingleberry" being my standard pick—and try to stick it to a crew member's clothing without them noticing. A total classic. Yeah, I miss all of that. Instead, I get to hang my hat on the acid reflux commercial that was out half a decade ago.

Anyway. Tonight. My show. Lucy.

If we're going to create something special and be successful together like Elvira prophesied, Lucy has to appreciate my adolescent comedic sensibilities. My comedy isn't for everyone. I doubt Lucy's is, either. But I can't tell yet where that puts us together on the humor spectrum. Two off-brand humors don't necessarily mean a perfect pair.

She's here early to see the setup and get situated. It's a weird date, since I'll be doing most of my talking to the audience. But everything about this is weird. And I can at least set her up with a bar tab and a prime viewing spot for the evening.

"It's so cool to be behind the scenes of a show," Lucy says, standing in the middle of the dance floor as rows of chairs are being set up around her. I'm up onstage, half watching her, half fiddling with my laptop, where a clip that I'm showing tonight is running video but not audio.

"John," I yell out to the sound tech, "do you need another HDMI cable? I've never seen it run without . . . oh, my bad. I had the video muted." The audio blares through the PA system at a decibel level that makes every person in the building stop what they're doing and stare angrily up at John. "Sorry, that was on me."

Lucy spins and gives me a goofy *what happened?* face, complete with hands on cheeks.

Am I nervous because she's here? Maybe a little. If this were just a shadowing session for a money-making project, I wouldn't think twice. But this feels way more high stakes.

"I think that's all I need to check, John, thanks." He rolls his eyes in typical audio engineer fashion. They're a surly bunch.

Lucy approaches the stage and leans in toward me. I bend down to meet her, reaching out to give her a hand in getting up.

Our faces are suddenly close, so close, our eyes locked. Lucy's eyes are intensely green in the stage lighting. A sunny Irish green.

I blink, and the moment ends. Lucy's arms are raised, and I grab her wrists and lift her up.

"There are stairs on either side, for future reference."

Lucy nods, a slow grin softening those sharp cheekbones, dimples flashing. "A next time, huh? You better be funny! I don't leave my cave for just anything, you know."

"Well, I can't promise, since comedy is subjective, but I did set you up at the best bar seat in the house. A clear view, and your own tab. The VIP rollout. Hopefully it gives me some bonus points if the comedy part sucks."

"You won't suck. We haven't spent that much time together, but I can sense how funny you are. I have faith."

"Yeah?"

"Yeah."

Her faith only makes me more nervous. "Okay, well. They open doors in ten minutes, so I need to go backstage to keep the magic alive for the patrons. You want them to await your arrival."

I place my hand on her back to bid her farewell—and immediately wonder if that was too much. What are the boundaries here? I take my hand away and step back. "I'll see you after the show. I know where you're sitting and will be checking on your laughter levels. And I've been in the business long enough to tell real laughter from fake." I squint at her and waggle my eyebrows.

"Promise, no faking it. Like I said, I have faith. But I'm all about that authenticity. This research is serious business. So get up there and break a leg." She shakes her head. "Actually, nope, don't do that. Nobody wants paramedics here. No more nine-one-one dates for us, please."

"Truth." I say, trying to wrap it up and get backstage. I don't want to be rude, but I have a routine that needs to be followed.

Maybe I am *slightly* superstitious.

In the green room, I have three beers, headphones, and note cards. Before the show starts, two beers must disappear, and I need to listen to "Air on the G String" by Bach seven times. It's ritual. Playing that piece on loop seven times resets my brain, washes away any anxiety or uncertainty about the show ahead. It's never failed me. Tonight, I add another round for good measure and, let's be honest here, for Lucy's presence.

The note cards are already written and memorized, but I study them anyway. It immerses me in the show I'm about to perform. I check the crowd attendance from the stage door, and a decent amount of people are out there. Less than last time, but still a solid size for a good show. I do one round of deep breaths and give the thumbs-up to John. I see that Lucy has bellied up to the bar, talking to Carole, the bartender. I've always been a big admirer of Carole; she kind of looks like me in female form (plus twenty good years or so), a short, round, freckled redhead, a Philly girl at heart, even though she's been in Brooklyn for decades now. She's made of tough stuff, to put it mildly.

Whatever Lucy's saying right now, she's making Carole laugh pretty hard. As a hardened veteran who's seen comedy six nights a week for most of her adult life, I always judge my performance based on getting even a few laughs out of Carole. Lucy seems to be doing it with such ease. Maybe that's a good sign for the night?

A good sign for us doing some kind of comedy work together?

Before I can mull this further, the lights go down, the intro plays, and I walk up to the mic to a nice round of applause. Lucy's clapping and yelling the loudest. By far. She lets out an effusive round of catcalling, and I grin at her through the haze of stage lights.

I run through the standard opening and then move into my redhead eighties villain shtick, where I let the audience in on a dark red secret about redheads playing creepy and/or annoying bullies. (See: *A Christmas Story*, *Children of the Corn*, *Problem Child*, etc.) From there, I whip out my old fake teeth I used when I was losing my baby teeth but needed to audition with a full set—which coincides nicely with my stint as the LEGO maniac. Always a fan favorite.

"Yes, indeed, kids, I was one of the Zack-the-LEGO-Maniacs, but I was the only one with that particular ginger mullet and denim vest." I point to the projector screen behind me to really emphasize the mullet, the long strands of red hair fanning down my neck like Raggedy Andy. "We all lived on an island together, our own little Island of Misfit Toys. Most kids were stranded there, but if you've got a very successful brother in the biz, he can get you out."

The crowd *loves* the brother talk.

Tonight and every night. They eat it up.

I don't ordinarily like to acknowledge Rocco's existence, at least not in my personal time. But I pull it out in public for a good cause. His stock is always high, and if I can use that to better myself, I feel like I'm pulling one over on him. A mild catharsis. The show brings fans—and also friends of fans who were coerced into coming along. Once they figure out my brother Rocco was involved, they gobble it up, too. Maybe it's the fact we're brothers in real life who also had two TV shows together. And then for our third act, a very public, very messy emancipation from one another after a co-star love triangle. Whatever. All I know is that a few solid references to the great Rocco Riziero makes for a happier crowd. Anything for laughs and rent money, right?

Well, anything with one exception.

I don't talk about *her*. Never.

And certainly not with Lucy in attendance. No dating jokes tonight, period.

I check in on Lucy a fair amount, and she's been laughing pretty consistently. She's actually been a huge asset—her laughter is honest, contagious, and *loud*. Giving me a lot to go on, and making the crowd laugh more, too. Carole is laughing more than I've ever witnessed at one of my shows.

Maybe I need Lucy here every month if I want to keep my numbers up.

The show rolls along, and suddenly, we're at the big finish, a scene from *Black Hole Sons*. The clip is great, a real brother moment where Marley is explaining why he's so grateful to be Charlie's twin. The moment has been hotly speculated about among fans for years, and although the details are common knowledge (there's even a Wiki page), it apparently never gets better than when the person in the story tells the facts himself. Rocco might be above this kind of fandom these days, but I'm certainly not.

I let the video play for a few moments, and then pause on the pivotal frame. "Now, I know most of you are wondering what actually happened in this scene, and I'm happy to confirm that Rocco *did* fart silently, and he caught it with his hand right . . . there." I stretch my arm out and push the mic as far as I can to reach the screen and scratch around Rocco's hands, providing evidence for the silly truth I've just dropped on the audience. "See? Right there! He grabs the fart and then, in an effortless show of true fake TV emotion, he brings his hands around my head to embrace me in a hug. All the while he just wanted me to catch a whiff. Good ol' Rocco. And it was such a great take, they kept it! And I get to relive it, here tonight, just for you. It smelled like a Frito pie, which is why I haven't had one since. But the ones here at Little Zelda's are excellent, I'm told. Goodnight, and thanks for coming out! Make sure you tip Carole and the rest of the staff well for all their great work behind the bar."

The stage lights dim, and I bow out to rowdy applause.

Lucy's first show in the books.

My voice, vibe, and brand were fully on display for her to take in tonight. I'm curious to know what she thought. Curious to see if she's still interested in Elvira's grand plan for us.

Back in the green room, I text her to meet me by the sound booth in fifteen minutes; then, I head out to mingle with the crowd. I've always been down to hang with fans and answer questions. It's not like I'm Shia LaBeouf or anything. I'm not

Rocco. And to be honest, they're all mostly good people I might strike up conversations with, anyway. It's the kind of person who connected with a weird show like *Black Hole Sons* in the first place. A cool band of misfits. Why not sprinkle a little bit of magic dust in the form of some casual Q&A after the show?

I've heard every question there is. Every.

Tonight's questions come as no surprise:

"How long did it take you to get into the alien dream sequence costumes?"

This particular question pops up every few months. An easy one. "Five hours start to finish when you count the makeup, too. Game Boy helped to pass the time. And the prop department made me a giant carrot dangler, but instead of a carrot, it dangled a magnifying glass, so I could read a book from far away. Yes, an intern turned the pages. The sweet life, amirite?"

Cue laughter.

"Did you get cast first, or Rocco?"

Always a Rocco question. "We auditioned together, and I think that's what sold us as a team. We were lucky to be taken on as a package deal." I keep it positive. And it's true. We *were* a dynamite pair. I was every bit as good as he was, back then—he wasn't always the superior Riziero.

The fan circle huddled around me is all eagerly tuned in.

"Have you met a lot of people with the black hole tattoo?"

Usually when this question pops up, the person asking reaches their forearm out to display the tattoo, a look of great pride on their face. Tonight's no exception. The ironically mustached dude who asked is rolling up his Buffalo plaid flannel to show me his own fresh-looking black hole.

"Yeah, man. Awesome. I've got so many pictures of black holes on my phone, I should make a coffee-table book that's cut in the shape of the tat. It would be hard to put away anywhere with normal books, but it'd sure look rad."

Murmurs of agreement.

"Did you really have to wear a dance belt for those weird alien dreams?"

Blindsided.

Staring at me with a deadpan look is Sarah-with-an-H.

Shit.

Of course she came.

Some people have no boundaries. Or they might just be unhinged. Sarah is likely both types. And the last thing I want right now is for Lucy to catch wind of her. I'll look like a desperate fool who only dates groupies.

I try to maintain composure, as I'm around about ten other people who are hanging on my every word. *Don't make this awkward, Rudy.* Be classy.

I plaster on a smile and say, "I always hated those scenes because of that disgusting undergarment. I liked to think of it as a glorified jockstrap rather than a terribly invasive and uncomfortable thong. All to keep my 'personal outline' away from children's eyes while in spandex. Kind of made me feel like superhero, really."

Everyone laughs. Except for Sarah, that is.

Because she just caught on that what I said to her in private is actually one of my go-to responses. She's not special. I can see her stewing. Her attempt to restrike up conversation has proved futile. I take a few steps back as I thank the crowd and tell them to come back for my next show, easing into my exit. I feel Sarah's eyes pinned on me as she realizes this was probably not directed at her.

She tails me as I head for the sound booth. I don't have to look back to confirm. It's a sixth sense. Every celebrity, no matter how minor, develops it.

I can see Lucy waiting. Not even on her phone, just watching. A wry smile on her lips.

Damn.

I give Lucy a look that screams: "Stalker trailing me, please help!" At least that's what I hope I'm conveying. But before I can make it to the booth, Sarah taps me on the shoulder. I begrudgingly stop and turn around.

"Hey, Rudy. Funny show tonight. I just wanted to say that I wish you'd picked any other bar than the one we went to. I was only trying to be funny, and that jackass bartender ruined it for us. I feel like we were having such an awesome night until he came along."

I take a deep breath. Kill 'em with kindness, right? "Yeah, I'm sorry it didn't work out, but I appreciate you coming tonight and hope you had a nice time."

Before Sarah has a chance to respond, I turn back toward Lucy. She's walked over from the booth and is now getting a close-up viewing of this tense exchange. Without saying a word, she grabs my hand and pulls me to her side.

Sarah apparently takes this as an invitation to really try to rattle me, because she says: "One more question. I didn't want to ask in such a big group, but this feels intimate enough. How would I rank?"

"Uh. Rank? What do you mean?" It feels way too hot in here, like I'm still baking under the stage lights.

"You know what I mean. On our *date*."

"Was that a date, though, really? Or just an after-show drink?" Honestly, I wish I could be less polite. Why the fuck can't I be less polite? A person like Sarah needs a more direct message. No frills. Unlike her drink of choice.

"It was *definitely* a date." Sarah narrows her eyes and glances pointedly at Lucy. "And I was asking about how I ranked against the other people you've kissed. Was I close to Piper?" She doesn't wait for an answer, just keeps hurtling on. "I just want to be in the top five. I watched that scene from Piper's movie *Candy's Crush* dozens of times—I know it was hot. Top five. Totally. Bye."

Sarah about-faces, gives the finger, and stomps away.

Wow.

A unique woman, that one.

Lucy watches Sarah go, and then slowly turns to me. She looks shocked. And I imagine Lucy has a high shock tolerance. "What was that? *Who* was that? How are you so nice to people? *Why* are you so nice to people? Do you pick up groupies often?" There's no pause for breath between questions.

"That was her feeble attempt to get me to feel bad after a post-show drink that went epically wrong. Her name is Sarah. With-an-H, as she likes to clarify. I had to learn to be polite to fans over the years—part of the price entertainers pay, if we want to have a career built off of people adoring us. And no, it doesn't happen that often, because I don't *often* take home bona fide groupies. Unless I'm feeling particularly down and out about myself. We're all human, right?"

Lucy looks like she's regretting asking those questions as funny throwaway lines, questions I answered honestly. Too honestly, maybe.

"I have to settle up, then we can get out of here," I say, trying to alleviate any potential awkwardness. Better to just move on with our night. I take a step back.

Lucy puts her hand on my wrist. "Hey. I'm not judging you for Sandra-with-a-bitchface. It must be incredibly hard to date if you have some fame, past or present. And even harder to be that kind to people. I'm sorry if I overstepped, grabbing your hand. If it was too possessive. I was just trying to help. I didn't know the backstory, though. It wasn't my place."

"It's fine. Really." I make a quick pivot, hopefully without sounding like I'm brushing her off. "How about I take you to the best late-night taco place by my apartment? We can crack a beer and munch on the stoop."

Lucy smiles. "That sounds nice. How's their al pastor?"

The kind of question only a true taco connoisseur would ask.

"I like the way you think. They make my favorite al pastor

around. Smaller chunks of pineapple, so you never get hung up on the fruitiness."

"Go! Collect your money! I need this taco. *Now.*"

"Oh my God, these are ridiculous," Lucy says as some porky goodness spills out the back of her corn tortilla and onto the stoop.

I gasp. "No! Ten second rule. I'll eat it off the stoop if you don't."

Lucy takes my dare seriously. She swipes the meat off the step, dunks it in the salsa verde, and away it goes into her mouth.

"Respect. Also," I say, because I'd been thinking about our conversation the whole walk home, "I respect and appreciate what you said at Little Zelda's. About Sarah. *Sandra.*" I chuckle. "It's nice to know someone understands. I get weird talking about it sometimes. It's not . . . easy."

Lucy looks back at me with those wide-open eyes, and I know she meant what she said. She's not judging. Her eyes really do tell me more than actual words convey. It's like staring deep into a fountain of truth. I bet she would be horrible at poker.

"And if I'm being completely honest," she says, "I grabbed your hand because I wanted to. Igniting Sally-with-a-rash was just an added bonus."

I burst out laughing. "I can assure you, I never got close enough to know whether or not she had one. It's a good thing, too, given she clearly exceeds my superfan limits. I was having one of those nights, when I met her. The moody single blues. But I should have never taken her up on those drinks. She ordered a Sex on the Beach. At a dive bar."

She winces. "Shit."

"Yeah."

It hits me now, the other part of what Lucy said.

I grabbed your hand because I wanted to.

I'm pretty sure I'm blushing, and I'm grateful Lucy's so pre-occupied with her taco.

More stuffing falls out, this time onto her tray, as she takes a bite. "I took a cooking class once from a woman born and raised in Mexico City. She said you have to pinch the top center of the taco to eat it properly. I try my hardest, but I usually fail."

I grab my al pastor taco and back the butt of the tortilla against my palm. "See, if you block the back with your hand, the innards can't pop out." As I'm saying this, the al pastor juice starts running out of my palm and down my sleeve. It was a stupid joke. I have immediate regrets.

"I *hate* that feeling. Makes me want to tear my clothes off." Lucy grabs a napkin and tugs up my sweatshirt sleeve. She rubs the napkin over the mess, down my wrist to my elbow. "Looks like you got lucky, only a little al pastor juice on your hoodie. A subtle perfume of pineapple pork. Kind of sexy, actually."

I'm watching her hand, the napkin rubbing slow circles on my skin. It's maybe the most domestic thing anyone's done for me in a long time.

She drops the crumpled napkin on the stoop, trailing her hand down my arm until her palm brushes against mine.

I lace my fingers around hers and squeeze. She squeezes back.

We sit on the stoop for a while, hand in hand, sipping our beers. Enjoying each other without saying another word.

See what a fun show, a little jealousy, and some delicious tacos can do?

Chapter 9

Lucy

You dream and you work and life still takes a bite.

"So, let me get this straight." Rudy pauses to take a sip from his tall paper cup of foamy matcha. My favorite caffeinated beverage, and his first cup ever—courtesy of me, to kick off our inaugural Craigslist adventure together. "This guy Rhett is paying you to let Pinky run around in a pen with his dog? Why? It feels, I don't know . . . highly suspect."

I booked this particular job before I knew Rudy would be tagging along; it was perfectly timed with a three-day dog-sitting stint while Clementine was in LA for film pre-production-related things. A win-win, two paying jobs in one.

"There are lots of lonely people in this city." I stop walking as we approach the dog run and motion for Rudy to stop, too. I don't want Rhett to be uncomfortable about an uninvited plus one. "Not every lonely person is a serial killer."

"I realize that. I mean, I'm lonely. You're lonely. But that doesn't mean we pay people to hang out with us. That's a different kind of low."

"Oh, really? You've never paid for a woman's drink for the sake of her company? What about that nice young woman from your show . . . Sarah-with-an-H, was it? Or Sally-with-a-rash? I can't seem to recall."

"Ha. Not the same."

"Isn't it? Also, you're assuming I haven't killed anyone . . ." I flash him a wolfy grin and then turn to survey the humans lining the edge of the fenced-in dog run.

The Craigslist post had been straightforward: *Looking for a 30-something woman in Park Slope with a dog to accompany me and my dog at the Washington Park Dog Run. I'm a friendly 30-something man, looking for conversation/companionship. Will pay well for 30 minutes.*

There had been, I admit, a small, annoying voice niggling at me as I responded to the post, telling me perhaps it was *too* good to be true, because why would any kind, well-adjusted man pay for half an hour of a dog-walking companion? And not just *pay*, but a hundred dollars. A hundred! I've done far weirder and more questionable jobs for less, and walking Pinky in a public place in the bright light of morning seemed low risk. There was a photo exchange—a prerequisite for Rhett—and his showed an average-looking white guy wearing an NYU sweatshirt and jeans and Adidas sandal slides with yellow striped socks. Though I suppose plenty of axe murderers might not, at first glimpse, give off murder-y vibes, and that socks and slides combo was less than ideal, in hindsight. Heinous, really.

But we're here now, aren't we? And it's a perfect Brooklyn October day, bright orange leaves and clear blue sky and crisp air that smells fresher than it does every other month of the year. October air has its own scent, even here. Especially here, maybe. The essence of hope and promise that's always so tangible in the New York City air is sharper than ever. Extra alive. It's air that makes you believe all things are possible.

I'll be fine. No—better than fine.

Besides, Rudy will be watching from a safe but stealthy distance, and there are at least a handful of other dog walkers around to hear me should I need to scream for my life.

"Okay," I say, reining Pinky in from what looks to be a pigeon corpse on the edge of the sidewalk. "We're heading over, and you stay here by this bench. Be discreet, but also close enough to observe. Not just in case things go awry, but to see me on the job. Jot down some notes on your phone."

I start walking, tugging Pinky along behind me.

"Lucy, are you sure you—"

I wave Rudy off without turning back around, lift my chin up, and straighten my shoulders. Random Craigslist jobs are not for the faint of heart. That's important for Rudy to understand as part of Lucy Minninger 101.

There's a handful of dogs—rather big ones, actually—already in the pen, running and chasing and barking, all very animatedly. Clementine would most likely (definitely) not approve of this level of socialization. She keeps Pinky on a very short leash. Literally. I've never seen such a short strap. Pinky's constantly stepping on my feet. But surely this will be good for her! A little canine companionship might be a mood enhancer. And Pinky's mood is always in need of enhancement.

"Bertha?" A rumbly male voice that sounds at least ten inches too close to my ear makes me drop my phone onto the cement next to the pen.

I bend over to pick up the phone, cursing as Pinky snaps at my ankles—her predictable show of displeasure in some instances, and misplaced affection in others. Always displeasure when it comes to me. As I straighten back up, I glance around, for Bertha, and for the stranger yelling in my ear. Except it turns out the man is not actually a stranger, it's Rhett, and I recall now that *I* am, in fact, Bertha. I prefer not to use my real name if I can avoid it, and rarely use the same fake name twice.

This morning, I'm Bertha, and so I stand, giving my best merrily-at-your-service grin. I imagine it looks something like a cross between a used car salesman and a rabid chipmunk. "Hiya, Rhett. Nice to meet you, and—you're Bob, I presume?" I wave down at the large, floofy black poodle who's currently yanking the leash taut in a desperate attempt to join his peers in the pen. He's at first glance roughly ten times the size of Pinky, and the idea of them fenced in together is, I must admit, rather harrowing. Perhaps I should have asked Rhett for more details about Pinky's playmate.

Clementine would slay for me for this. Maybe the job *was* too good to be true.

"Pinky's been a bit off today," I start, "so maybe she should stick with—"

"*RHETT?*" A shrill female voice cuts me off.

Rhett, Bob, Pinky, and I spin in the same direction. The woman I assume to be the source of the scream—based on her inflamed, scowling face—looks in her thirties; white; attractive, I suppose, in a generic, hipster kind of way; blunt-cut hair and leather jacket and flowy cropped linen pants, a French bulldog sitting calmly at her heeled booties.

"Oh, hello, Beatrice," Rhett says coolly, taking three steps closer to me. That's exactly three steps closer than I'd like him to be. "I didn't expect to see you here."

The way he says it suggests that he *absolutely* expected to see her here, and that all is going according to plan. Beatrice has now turned her alarmingly fierce gaze to me.

"Who's this?" she snarls.

"A new friend," Rhett says, leaning in until his shoulder brushes mine.

Hell. No.

This is very far from what I signed up for. While I'm not opposed to an acting gig (I once pretended to be the long-dead daughter of a nice old lady for a day, and we baked and knitted and played Parcheesi), I am very much opposed to not being in the know about said acting gig.

"Lucy?"

I turn to see Rudy standing just behind me, concern etched into every inch of his handsome freckled face. In the chaos of

Rhett and Bob and Beatrice, I'd almost forgotten I had backup. It's a wave of relief, seeing him.

"Lucy?" Rhett shakes his head. "That's Bertha."

"What's going on?" Rudy ignores him, looking from me to Beatrice, back to me.

"I suspect I was hired for an acting gig without being notified," I say, frowning at Rhett. "Maybe to make a certain ex jealous?"

"Not true!" Rhett yells, too loudly. Bob does not take kindly to his owner's discontent, and gives one sharp, assertive yip as he snaps his snout in my direction.

"Get away from her!" Rudy lurches in front of me, a generous blockade.

Bob snaps again, affronted at this invasion to his personal space, and then goes straight for the jugular—or in this case, Rudy's slip-on Vans sneaker. He chomps down on the toe line and shakes his rounded pompadour of curls, tugging to free the shoe.

"My foot!" Rudy yells, flailing. "His fangs are in my foot!"

"Bob does not have fangs!" Beatrice yells back. "How dare you! He's not a monster! *You* are the monster!"

I scoop Pinky up before she can join in—especially as I'm not sure whose side she would take. "Do something!" I shout to Rhett, who's watching this play out in a state of mild panic.

"Bob, my sweet boy," he coos, "it's okay. Daddy is okay. Daddy and Mommy are *both* okay. Leave the bad man's sneaker alone." At this, fortunately, Bob releases his grip, giving the shoe one last mournful look before sitting down and licking his paw.

Rhett and Beatrice nearly trip over themselves in their rush to comfort Bob, petting his fluff, checking his teeth, reminding him that he is a *very, very good boy*.

"Oh my God, Rudy, are you okay?" I ask, shouldering Pinky in one arm and offering my other to steady Rudy as he bends down to take off his shoe, and then his sock—both of which have two small punctures straight through the material. His skin, luckily, has just two tiny indents. No blood.

"See?" Beatrice grimaces, looking down at Rudy's naked toes, as if she's witnessing something obscene. "Bob was only playing. He has a fondness for sneakers. It can't be helped."

"Besides," Rhett chimes in, "you scared him, jumping in front of us like that. He thought you were going to attack!"

"So, was he playing, or protecting you?" I ask, ignoring Pinky's sticky breath in my ear. I shuffle her to the other shoulder. "Just so we're clear."

"Both," Beatrice and Rhett say at the same time. They turn to one another with slow spreading smiles.

"You called me *Mommy*," she says wistfully.

My God, I may gag.

"Of course." Rhett clears his throat. His voice has turned simpery. "You'll always be Bob's Mommy."

"Yeah?"

"Bob misses you. Daddy does, too."

It somehow manages to get even more disgusting.

There's a dramatic, loaded pause, their two bodies leaning in, closer.

Closer still.

It's a gruesome wreck.

I cannot for the life of me look away.

"This is disgusting," Rudy interjects. *Yes, Rudy, Yes!* After the encounter with Sarah-with-an-H, it's refreshing to see him speaking his truth. Reassurance that fan treatment doesn't necessarily spill into all real-world encounters. "Reuniting because your dog bit a stranger, and because you're both too horrible to apologize. I suppose you two really might be perfect for one another."

It takes great restraint to not actually pump my fist in the air.

"Maybe we are perfect for one another," Beatrice says, grabbing for Rhett's hand.

"No maybe about it." Rhett pulls her in, wraps his other hand around her waist.

The two go moony-eyed, sauntering off without another word, dogs trailing behind.

"What just happened?" Rudy asks, tugging his sock and shoe back on.

I set Pinky down on the sidewalk. "We were reminded of how many terrible people there are in this world. And that terrible attracts terrible."

"I think I've dated a Beatrice or two."

"I've definitely known a Rhett in my day. It was entertaining, though, hearing you call them out. I saw a new side to you."

"Yeah? It felt pretty good, actually."

We're quiet for a minute, watching the dogs fly around the pen. Pinky yips a few times, then hides behind my legs.

"I'm sorry we won't be making any money this morning," I say, turning to face him. "I was going to split the earnings down the middle."

"No worries. I didn't get rabies, so we're all good."

"We do have a second part to this workday, if you're up for it?"

Rudy winces. Any reasonable person would pass. "Will there be other Craigslist canines? I'm pretty fond of these sneakers. My toes, too, for that matter."

I shake my head. "Just you, me, and Pinky. It involves sitting around Clementine's empty apartment, forging her signature."

One bushy eyebrow lifts up dramatically. "Forgery, eh?" He grins. "I can get behind a little illicit activity. I'm in."

"Explain to me again why you're signing five thousand title pages as Clementine Carter?" Rudy flicks his finger at the messy stack of papers on the coffee table in front of us, and then leans back into Clementine's (puke-stain free, thanks to my scrubbing skills) couch.

"She's off in LA for some big important film talks. They're shooting her first book in January. Her publisher needs these tomorrow, so here I am, the ever dutiful, underpaid intern." I drop my Sharpie and flex my right hand. "I'm probably better at doing her signature than she is at this point. Deliveries, checks, contracts."

"And her publisher has no idea they're being conned?"

"Nah. But they wouldn't care. As long as her fans don't find out Clementine's molecules never graced this paper, it only matters that they have everything signed by the deadline."

"Ah."

"Ah?"

"Nothing." He stares up at the crown molding on the ceiling, the best part of a historic Park Slope brownstone.

"I realize you're still learning about me, but I hope you recognize I'm nothing if not candid."

"You're right. I was just wondering . . . why you do this job, I guess. I'm getting the sense you're not a fan of Clementine, as an author or human. And if you're not getting paid well, why not take your chances on other jobs?"

A fair question. My brain poses it on a regular basis. But it's easier to ignore myself than to ignore Rudy, and ignoring is my favored approach.

I shrug. "It's steady work. I like having one predictable paycheck, scrappy as it may be."

That's part of it, anyway.

"That's all there is to it?"

Ugh. Damn you, Rudy, and your uncanny knack for reading the room. Maybe it's an actor thing. I detest it. But also adore it. It's nice to be seen.

"I guess I like that I have a foot in the publishing door, even if it's a long way from the lobby to the top floor. I know someone who is not only published, but a *bestseller*. And as much as I might not adore that someone, it feels better than not knowing anyone who's published. It's not necessarily logical, but it makes me feel like I've gotten somewhere in almost a decade of living in this city. A shitty somewhere feels better than a nowhere."

I feel deeply sad, saying this. Hearing it out loud.

How long is too long to have the same improbable dream?

What else is there for a thirty-year-old former English major and *Craigslist extraordinaire* with a patchy history of short-term office jobs?

"That makes sense," Rudy says quietly, and now he's looking at me, not the ceiling. "I hope it pays off. Doing the grunt work. Making connections. Maybe someday, Clementine will get one of your manuscripts into the right hands."

"She doesn't know I write. I tried to mention it once, making small talk while we did a photo shoot, and she cut me off. Started talking about how her new hair streaks matched the title color. How we had to find the best light to call attention to it. Par for the course, any time I dare to mention something not pertaining to her books, her brand, her brilliance, or her dog."

Rudy doesn't say anything to that, and I turn back to the pages, pick up the pen. I'm about thirty more sheets in with, oh, a good 4,500 to go, when he speaks up. "Let's leave some Easter eggs for her fans."

"Easter eggs?" I look up from the latest page, where I've scribbled a loopy C, some squiggles, another C, a few more squiggles. The whole thing takes roughly two seconds. "What are you suggesting here? That we doodle a tiny dick and balls? Maybe find a way to incorporate an artful f-u-c-k somewhere in the elegant vines surrounding the title?"

"While, yes, a dick and balls doodle did come to mind, I also don't want to get you fired. Not unless you want to be. I was thinking more along the lines of a personalized note with a misspelled word or two. What's something you word lovers find especially egregious? Maybe a—what's it called? Homophone? Yeah. A homophone mistake."

I tap the pen against my lip as I consider. "So you're suggesting we confuse an *its* with an *it-apostrophe-s*, or a *your* with a *you-apostrophe-r-e*? I suppose that's tame enough. While still being hugely mortifying. No self-respecting author, bestselling or otherwise, would ever make a public-facing error of those proportions."

"Exactly. To be honest, I've never proofread texts more than I do with you. I'm terrified of messing up."

"Really?"

"Really."

"That's kind of adorable." Very adorable, actually. He cares that much about my opinion. "But just so you know, we're past the point of me judging you for that. You aced the grammar test before our first date. Everyone is allowed some typos every now and again. Even I've been known to have a homophone error. Once in a blue moon, but still."

"Phew." Rudy pretends to wipe sweat from his brow. "I can't tell you what a relief it is to hear that."

I grin, and he does, too. His eyes are the smiliest I've ever seen. The equivalent of a full toothy smile in eyeball form.

Who knew smiley eyes could be so . . . sexy? I usually go for mysterious eyes, apathetic eyes, eyes that require more winning over.

Rudy's eyes are clear and open, and *damn*, if that isn't making me warm all over.

"So-o?" he says after a minute, "what do you think? How about: *I hope you enjoy you-apostrophe-r-e read*? Adequately shameful, but not as overtly problematic as a scruffy scrotum."

"I think it's . . . perfect." I put pen to paper and write it out, and my God, is it deeply satisfying to see that *you're* in black and white under Clementine's name. "I feel such a rush right now." I flip the page onto the finished pile, start signing a fresh sheet.

"Look at us," Rudy says, leaning in to admire my handiwork. I breathe in deep, soap and mint and a dab of something spicy I can't place. "Making quite the team."

"Uh-huh." I breathe in again, hopefully subtly, and double down on my task. Two sheets down, onto the third. Maybe I'll do ten special title pages. Maybe fifty. "I'd chalk this round of the Great Elvira Challenge down as a wild success. Unless it's canceled out by Bob?"

Rudy shakes his head, his hair brushing against my cheek. "Nah. That was a learning experience. A reminder that there are terrible people in this world, and we've both had the unfortunate experience of dating some of them. But you're decidedly not terrible. And neither am I. So, win-win, no blood lost."

"Let's toast to that," I say, enjoying another few seconds of his nearness before I put down my latest page and stand up.

"Here?"

"I know where Clementine keeps her Johnnie Walker. *Blue Label.*"

"Hot damn."

Hot damn, indeed.

Maybe we *do* make quite the team.

Maybe Elvira really was onto something.

Chapter 10
Rudy

You laugh and you sing and yet oh what a fright!

I'd heard the saying "never meet your idols" many times over the years.

But I'd also had the pleasure of working with more than a few idols on television and movie sets, and never had a bad experience.

So, when I got an email from an old producer friend a while back to audition for one of my idols, Ronny Boyd—an early punk rock icon from New York City whose band Cable became *the* musicians' band—I didn't hesitate. Little did I know I would get the gig, tour the world, and see just how much trouble a sixty-something-year-old rocker could get into.

It was a lot. A lot of trouble.

Bailing him out of jail, driving two hundred miles in the wrong direction for needles he left in the hotel, hiding drugs in my gear for him, the list goes on. The last time I saw him, he got carted away in an ambulance after drunkenly falling off stage and cracking his head open. He left the touring circuit after that. Needed to "sober up and regroup." That was three years ago.

When I got an email from Ronny last month asking if I'd

play a Halloween show in Brooklyn, I was taken aback. I'd sworn I would never go back to him—saved him as "Nope Boyd" in my phone. But there was something highly unexpected in his email: an apology.

Rudy, I wanted to also let you know I'm sober now and have tried to atone for my past ways. I put you in some tight spots, and it wasn't fair to assume your life was less important than mine. I'm truly sorry, and would be happy to have you play this gig. I can offer you a thousand dollars for the night.

A grand?
Fuck. That complicated things.
It would be the most I'd ever been paid for a music gig.
How could I say no?
I might have some pride, sure—but not that much.

"The band is Cable, have you heard of them?" I ask, searching for a specific distortion pedal as Lucy watches me flounder around my living room.

I've got a studio recording gig with a friend this afternoon, but Lucy and I grabbed some lattes down the street just to, well . . . hang out, I guess. Not an official Great Elvira Challenge project. I'm not even sure how it happened. We both needed caffeine, because we'd stayed up too late texting about our favorite *Curb Your Enthusiasm* moments—too many good ones. So, here we are, at my place. Hanging out with no clear agenda.

"Wait, *that* is the Halloween show tomorrow? At Brooklyn Trade? I *loved* Cable! It was one of my dad's favorite bands back in the day. He used to spin them on his radio show all the time. 'Hear No Evil, See It All' was always one of my favorites. That and 'Winter Moon'."

Lucy knows Ronny Boyd? That's great!

Well. Kind of.

Less great considering what a scumbag he is. Or, at least, *former* scumbag.

"Awesome, tomorrow will be a fun date then," I say as I pack up my bass. The missing pedal magically appears in my gig bag. "It's sold out, but I can add anyone you want to bring along to the list. I need to get there early for sound check, but then I'll be free to hang out with you right up until I go onstage."

Lucy looks excited, her cheeks flushed as she says, "My dad's going to be so jealous that I get to hang with Ronny Boyd. From *Cable*. He. Will. Freak. You think he'd let me take a picture?"

"He's been known to take more pictures with ladies than gentlemen, so you have that going for you. But he can be a real kook. Kind of . . . unpredictable." I almost add that besides being *unpredictable*, he was also chauvinistic, rude, and lewd in my experiences with attractive women approaching him. But I don't. I want to give Ronny the benefit of the doubt. And also preserve Lucy's nostalgic appreciation, if possible.

"I might go do some record shopping to find a vinyl copy of *Winter Moon* for him to sign as a consolation prize for my dad. I mean, he *raised* me on this music." She shakes her head, looking dazed and awed. Ugh. "Good thing you didn't have a photo of him on your HeartThrobs profile, or you'd have to be questioning my motives for flipping up. Rightfully so."

Shit. All I want to do right now is throw Ronny under the bus and tell Lucy how much he messed up my musical confidence. Made me an errand boy, and almost got me arrested for possessing things that weren't even mine.

"I think I can get him to sign that," I say instead. "Leave it to me."

She beams at me like I handed her a winning lottery ticket. Or a platter of al pastor tacos. It feels pretty good, to be honest, even if I also feel gross for encouraging her Ronny enthusiasm.

"So I can invite Estelle and Frank? We've been together

every Halloween since I moved into the cave, and I felt guilty about ditching them. They won't know Cable, but they love a good reason to dress up. This is a show that encourages costumes, right?"

"Sure. Just tell Frank not to flask up with that bathtub gin, okay? No blacking out." Lucy laughs, even though I'm only partly joking. His basement concoctions sound lethal. "As far as costumes, it's Halloween, right? You do you. I'm dressing up as a washed-up nineties star."

Lucy frowns. "Excuse me. You are not washed-up. Your costume is nineties star trying to camouflage himself in a sea of Brooklyn hipster superfans."

I had a feeling Lucy was a Halloween person. Me? Not so much. I'm not the biggest fan of dressing up. But when it's mandatory for a paycheck, I resort to comfortable costumes that make me feel like I'm not a spectacle. All of them revolving around my old-school Adidas tracksuits: a Beastie Boy, an eighties mafia foot soldier, an Italian soccer player in warm-up gear.

Rocco used to ride my ass hard for not being more "Halloweenie." He once convinced me to dress up as a clown to play a prank on one of his buddies who was terrified of them—it was all a sham, though, to get me in a costume for a Halloween party. My fault for not connecting things sooner, but also the calendar's for having Halloween land on a Tuesday. Those weekend-before-Halloween parties are harder to track. What a fucker, my brother. Burns me to think about how good he got me, and how much fun we ended up having at that party, clown costume and all. Burns me to know I'm thinking about Rocco, period. I've been doing it more lately, too much—I blame that stupid Outlaws text.

Back to tracksuits: I have a few different colors, so tomorrow will be the black one. A safe choice, because I don't want to piss off Ronny if he isn't interested in Halloween shtick.

Lucy and I head outside together, our shoulders and arms

bumping all the way to the subway station. When we say good-bye for our different trains, she gives me the biggest hug yet.

I've never seen a more put-together Ronny Boyd.

His typical frazzled hair, what's left of it anyway, is now neat and parted back with some gel. His usually chalky white skin has more color in it, looks more alive. He traded in his smokes for a vape pen, and his backstage bottle of Jim Beam is now a jug of Arnold Palmer. He's quieter. More reserved. Seems like the booze really was the X factor for him. Or the Nyquil and Adderall. Either way, I'm pleasantly surprised. The sound check was our only rehearsal, but it was solid. Ronny's playing is as good as ever, and it'll be a personal treat for me to play some of the songs Lucy loves with the man who wrote them.

I head out of the green room for the stage door, where I'm greeted by a trio of hot sauces.

Literally.

Lucy, Frank, and Estelle are wearing matching red pants and shirts with different hot sauce labels, and knit hats for their respective hot sauce tops. Lucy must be partial to Tapatío. Estelle enjoys Texas Pete's. Frank, however, has me stumped. His shirt has three X's on it and flames that resemble what I suspect Guy Fieri's bathroom walls must look like.

"Whoa! What a fiery bunch!"

Lucy laughs, but the Myrtles seem less impressed with my punning.

"Frank, I've never seen that kind of hot sauce before. What is it?"

Frank looks only too eager to explain. "It's a very expensive, *very* rare hot sauce from Costa Rica. Effin en Fuego. The greatest hot sauce around, and I've had many fine sauces. Damn near impossible to find in the States. There might be some animal product involved that the FDA is too lazy to check out. Anyway, it's the best." He nods authoritatively.

"I hope I get to try it someday."

"We'll see. You have to prove your mettle first."

"Er. Right." I pass out the wristbands then, and lead them to the rickety old balcony that serves as the VIP "lounge," which feels like too generous of a word. But it'll be less chaotic up here than on the floor. As we pass coat check, Estelle tosses her jacket at Frank.

"Check your keychain, too, Frankie. Remember when you were at that Alice in Chains show, and lost your keys because you insisted on moshing?" She turns to me, rolling her eyes expansively. I have questions—lots of them—about why they were at an Alice in Chains show in the first place, but I bite my tongue. "We were *two hours* away."

"Yes, Estelle. You certainly remind me often enough. And I convinced a friend of a friend to drive us back to the apartment to get the spare, and then back to the parking lot, all for a nominal fee." He turns to me, grumbling. "Turned out to be one of the worst car rides of our lives, between the speeding ticket and the peeing in a bottle. And the feet smell."

Estelle chimes back in, "I'll never forget that smell as long as I live!"

Lucy and I silently observe.

It's like an old TV sitcom with these two. I can see why Lucy enjoys their company.

As Frank checks their goods, Ronny Boyd walks by on his phone. He waves at me but keeps moving. Lucy looks starstruck, her eyes as gigantic as I've ever seen them. She turns to me, mouthing: "Holy shit!"

I reach out for her hand. "I promise, I'll get you that signature. When he's in the right headspace."

"I believe in your ways of coercing a gruff old rocker," Lucy says, lacing her fingers around mine. "Maybe even a selfie, if he's feeling extra indulgent."

We head toward the bar to post up before all the stools disappear.

Because there are a *lot* of people in Brooklyn Trade right now, a wide range of ages represented—even young hipster kids who must have grown up with good parents who liked this music. Or they all had a few Cable songs pop up on their Spotify Discover Weekly. Either way, I can see why Ronny is able to offer me a grand. That and I assume he's probably pissed off every other bass player in the city. Once you drunk-abuse everyone you've ever played with, that pool really shrinks. Sometimes you have to fall from grace and be out of the spotlight for a while to get back in.

I can relate, at least when it comes to losing the spotlight. Rocco once told me that if I left LA for college, I'd never be able to come back to the biz. It cut deep, when he said it. Like the only way to succeed was to follow him.

But he was wrong. Because there's more than one way. I went to school, then built my own brand of the biz here in New York. Sure, it's not making me rich or famous, but it's mine—a life on my own terms. I've been back to California for a potpourri of creative endeavors in the last decade, too, music gigs and comedy stuff mostly. I can tolerate it better in my older age, at least in smaller doses. Who's to say I couldn't make it back in LA one of these days if I really wanted it? I could find a new manager, ramp up my auditions.

Just look at Ronny: he blacked out every night and burned every bridge he could find. But he made it back to his dream biz, too. He's here, tonight. We both are.

After securing some bar seats, we kick off the night with a round of martinis on Frank.

And then another.

I drink the second one slowly—I need to keep myself neat for the show.

We've been having some lively conversations involving Lucy's hypotheticals with our bartender Georgia, a tall Black woman with an afro and cat-eye glasses who ignores other patrons as Frank continues to grease her a five spot for every drink on the tab. It's a pro tip I've never used, mostly because the beer I order is typically five bucks or less.

"Let me get this straight." Georgia squints at Lucy from across the bar. "Only eat escargot for an entire year, or eat one baby toe? And I have to somehow *find* the baby toe on my own?"

Lucy smiles, all her teeth bared. "Yup. What do you do?"

"This is some seriously twisted shit." Georgia shakes her head. "I love it." She's quiet for a moment, staring up at the ceiling, deep in thought. But her concentration is interrupted by a man who's obviously seen the bar bias, and has now physically inserted himself between Frank and me to get Georgia's attention. He looks like the typical Ronnie superfan: middle-aged white dude in a vintage Cable tee at least a size too small, black dress pants he probably wore straight from his day job at an accounting firm, fresh Chucks I'd bet he's breaking in tonight.

"Eat the toe," he says enthusiastically, "and wash it down with a fine Carlsberg beer. Oh, I see you have that on tap! One of those, please."

"Excuse me," Georgia says, snapping back to attention, "that was my question to answer. You clearly didn't hear the whole thing. You know, the part about *finding* your own baby toe."

The man shakes his head. "Damn, that's cold-blooded! Changes everything. I thought it was like eating chicken from the store. It just showed up as is, ready to eat. I couldn't harm anything except for a roach or rat. Not that I have an infestation problem . . ."

Georgia laughs, then turns away to start doing her job again.

I point at Lucy's forehead. "No one would ever guess that under this lovely face, there's such a warped brain. You hide it disarmingly well with those beautiful green eyes."

Lucy blushes and gives me a big smile.

It's a good one, her smile. So good.

A Carlsberg is bestowed upon our new friend by Georgia, and Frank picks it up. "Slick move, pal. I'm Frank. Nice to meet you. Were you looking for the beer or the conversation?"

"Noel, thanks. And both. Truth be told, I've tried to chat with her at the last three concerts, and have yet to even get an order in. She's a tough cookie to crack. Or so I thought, but then I saw how much fun she was having with you four. I figured this was my shot."

Frank takes him in by the shoulder. "You're on the right track. Stick with us, kiddo, and we'll do what we can to assist. But choose your words wisely. It's all about the banter."

Lucy leans in and whispers something in my ear. The first band is raging, so a whisper won't cut it.

"Speak louder!"

Lucy, in turn, responds very loudly, over an unfortunately timed lull in the song: "Last three concerts? Are we enabling? Is he a stalker?"

Everyone in the near vicinity overhears. Including Noel. And Georgia, who's just rejoined the conversation.

Noel turns an incredible shade of red. The most vibrant red I've ever seen on human skin.

Georgia doesn't skip a beat. "I've thought about it, and I would have to do escargot for a year, goddamn it. I couldn't bear to take a toe off of a baby. I won't do it!"

Lucy opens her mouth to respond, but Noel's quicker. "If you wanted to eat a toe to dine freely otherwise, I'd find you one. My family's from Wisconsin. Lots of unfortunate frostbite accidents up there. Might not have to snip the toe, just snap gently and get a nice, clean break."

Even Lucy looks shook.

It's a Larry David–level of awkward kind of moment, with Georgia—all of us, really—trying to decide if he's joking or not. This is New York. There are all types.

Georgia and Noel stare into each other's eyes for a long, loaded moment.

I break first. The awkwardness is too much. "That's dedication," I say, "to go all the way to Wisconsin for a frozen baby toe. Could you bring back some cheese curds and New Glarus, too?"

Georgia breaks her stare and turns to me. "New Glarus? I love that brewery! One of my friends went to UW and used to sneak cases back in her car."

Noel perks up at this. "Your friend was breaking the law, because New Glarus isn't supposed to leave the state. Though to be fair, I drive back after every holiday with a few cases. Look, what if I don't get you that toe, and instead I bring you back some bubbly contraband?"

Frank and Estelle are both nodding approvingly, sipping the dregs of their martinis, as Noel and Georgia continue to animatedly chat.

Lucy leans in close and says, at a more appropriate volume, "Way to go. You totally paved his way."

"It was your hypotheticals that brought her to us in the first place, so I'd say it was a joint effort. Though if he ends up nabbing anyone's toes, it was all you. And Frank."

Lucy laughs, taking my hand again. "I'm thoroughly enjoying our time together, you know. It's a real treat."

"Feeling's mutual."

The opening act yells their closer into the mic: "This is our last song; thanks to Ronny Boyd for having us, and happy Halloween!"

My cue to get backstage.

"I need to go, but I hope you have fun. I'll be looking for you!"

Before I even realize what my mouth is aiming for, I lean in for a kiss. Our eyes lock. My lips are just about to make contact with her lips, full and red and slightly parted, so close I can already taste them, when it hits me—*fuck fuck fuck, what am I doing?* Instead of completely backtracking, I veer to the right, enough so to just miss the edge of her lip. A quick peck to the side of her chin.

Her chin. I kissed her *chin*.

I avert my eyes and turn away, my cheeks flaming hot.

"What the hell kind of grandma peck was that?" I mumble as I walk off, not letting myself turn back to catch Lucy's expression.

I don't know why my body did what it did, except that it just felt natural. Total autopilot.

Damn it. No time to dwell now, though. Not with a show to play.

Ronny is pacing around the green room when I get there. "I was worried you left or got too drunk. You're not too drunk, are you?"

I'm gently buzzed, maybe, but definitely not drunk. "I'm good, promise. There's a solid crowd down there. It'll be a fun show."

"How about the chicks? I saw you talking to a spicy little hot sauce. She your girlfriend?"

I bristle—*chicks, spicy little hot sauce*—but grit my teeth and shrug. "Not my girlfriend. Just hanging out. She's actually a big fan of yours. I told her you'd sign a copy of *Winter Moon* for her superfan dad, maybe take a picture with her, too."

Ronny smiles. "That can be arranged, sure. But you should run down there and make her your girlfriend before I lure her away from you. If she's any kind of true fan, that is."

Disturbing.

Especially because I know him well enough to understand he's probably half serious. Or all serious, for that matter.

I pull out Lucy's record—newly acquired yesterday, and passed on to me this morning during another latte run—from my bag and hand it over. Ignoring him is typically the best policy. "Thanks. It'll mean a lot to her."

Ronny rubs his finger along the top of the record, admiring the faded photo of himself on the cover.

So many years, not many hits afterwards.

He signs and holds it out to me. "Hope your lady's dad enjoys it. Don't say I never did anything for you. I look forward to meeting her and taking a selfie or whatever."

I, on the other hand, do not look forward to that moment.

The green light goes on, saving me from a response.

Ronny flashes me his canned smile as we head down the stairs to the stage, like a pushy stage mom reminding me to be entertaining. Part of his routine.

We hit the stage to a packed crowd. All the pierogi gigs in the world feel worth it for a night like this. Ronny starts his classic riff from "Hear No Evil, See It All," and we're off—and sounding better than ever. Sobriety has really worked for his playing. I'm glad I said yes to this show, against all odds. Glad that Lucy's out there in the audience.

Wherever the Great Elvira is right now, I hope she's glad, too.

The set goes by like a supersonic jet. We're at the big closer, "Winter Moon," when I finally catch sight of Lucy, alone without Frank and Estelle. I'm glad she's solo—selfishly, these are the kinds of moments you're looking for as a musician. Perhaps my second favorite thing about playing, other than the music itself.

Lucy stands out in the crowd for obvious bright-red shirt reasons, but it's more than that. Her smile is the more intimate kind—usually reserved for the phone screen, when you gaze at a text that brings a tingling feeling up the back of your neck. There's the piercing eye contact, too. Lucy's watching me, and I'm watching her, and it suddenly feels like it's just the two of us in this massive hall.

We connect.

I bite my lip.

She bites hers.

I do a silly shimmy with my bass, sliding back and forth in my slip-on Vans.

She shimmies right back with her air bass, complete with some amazingly exaggerated windmill arms.

It's palpable—this connection. All martinis and the rock show aside, I'm feeling much closer to Lucy, and it zaps me with an electric buzz. She gets a glimpse, too, of what my screen sees when we text. It's one hell of a feeling.

Ronny chooses this moment for an unannounced solo and pushes me off to the side. He starts making puppy eyes at Lucy, swiveling his hips with his guitar. Lucy looks into it at first, smiling at least—though a different kind of smile, not our private one—but then gets swallowed up by a bunch of dudes air guitaring in circles around her as they follow Ronny's lead.

I start playing the chorus of the song and the drummer follows, forcing Ronny to rush back to his mic. He gives me brutal side-eye as we finish the set, and all through the encore, too.

Once we officially wrap up, Ronny stays on my heels as I head backstage, unleashing as we step inside the green room. "You always follow the singer! I don't care how far out I go. I've played that song for over thirty years, and I can do whatever the fuck I want."

He continues his ranting until a knock comes at the door.

"Rudy?" Lucy.

Shit. Quite the moment for her to witness.

"The performers are in here," Ronny spits out. "We need privacy."

"I'm sorry. I shouldn't have gone off your path. It's your show." I'm not actually sorry, but I don't want to be stiffed that fat paycheck, so I revert to the lowly pissant asking for forgiveness. I hate it. But, bills. "Can I let my friends in now?"

"Fine. But if they're wasted, they have to go."

I open the door, and Frank seems to be the only truly inebriated one of the group—he makes a mad dash for the remaining green room snacks Ronny insists on for every show, part of his rider. Slim Jims, Pringles, Double Stuf Oreos. His taste buds are as shitty as the rest of his personality—clearly, nothing's changed about him, after all. I delicately suggest to Estelle that they should pick up their coats before another Alice in Chains incident. She storms out, Frank trailing like a leashed kid in her grip, Slim Jim dangling from his mouth.

Ronny strolls over to Lucy with wide eyes and wider arms. They hug, awkwardly. Lucy pats his back, looking uncertain about where to put her hands. He seems cozy enough, though, hands snug around her waist.

"Hello there," he says—letting go of her, thank God— "Rudy's pretty friend who's a big fan of my work. I played that solo in 'Winter Moon' just for you."

Lucy looks taken aback. "Why, thank you, Mr. Boyd! My dad was obsessed, and I was happily indoctrinated. Could we maybe take a picture together?"

Ronny looks at me, and then at Lucy. He grins. "As long as it's just the two of us."

Lucy turns to me, and I shrug. "If that's okay with Lucy."

She nods, and Ronny moves in even closer. Way too fucking close. He's pressing his cheek against hers for this photo like they're besties.

Someone from the venue arrives for the payout, and Ronny's manager, Phil—a hulking second-generation Puerto Rican born and raised on the Lower East Side—settles up the night as the selfie photo shoot continues. Phil used to be a bouncer at Studio 54, and has a seemingly infinite collection of stories from that disco era. I did kind of miss the cliché "And you'll never guess who I caught snorting cocaine" anecdotes. He's in the middle of telling one now as he's paying me out. It was a local politician, the mayor, in fact, and I'm double-checking Phil's counting skills when Lucy yells from behind me:

"That's incredibly disrespectful. The *Kama Sutra*? Let me remind you, Ronny, you are fucking *old*. And while I may be a fan of your music, that doesn't mean I'm a fan of your penis.

You probably couldn't Kama Sutra anyone anyway without a little blue pill to assist." Damn. I think she's finished, but then, "And your breath smells awful. You should look into a proper flossing regimen. Perhaps a Waterpik. I've heard they work wonders."

Silence.

The sound of metal clanging onstage.

Silence again.

Ronny is speechless.

I don't think he's ever been spoken to like that. Not in decades of performing.

To be honest, I've always wanted to bring up his oral hygiene.

It's a good thing I've already settled up and don't have to wait around this terribly awkward green room. Ronny's still stunned from Lucy's verbal assault, but he manages a terse, "Tapatío sucks," as I grab my gear and we make our exit.

We head out the back door—both of us too stunned to speak, too—to find Frank and Estelle waiting in their Uber SUV.

"C'mon, Luce," Estelle yells, head hanging out the window, "these hot sauces need to get back in the cupboard. The Effin en Fuego has gone rancid!"

Lucy asks for one minute, and then pulls me aside.

"I'm sorry," I say first, "about Ronny. What a bastard. I was hoping he'd changed his ways. That was naïve of me. I should have spoken up. Called him out."

"It's fine." She shakes her head. "Telling off that old creep was *deeply* rewarding, I promise—I love giving a good dose of brutal honesty. I'm just happy I got to watch you in your zone. Your playing is so . . . passionate. You have a real gift."

"Yeah? I'm glad you were here—it made me play my best. You give me good vibes."

"I'm glad, too," Lucy says, her mouth curling up in a sly smile. "Because I want to give you all the good vibes."

With that, she leans in close . . . so close I smell the gin on her breath, and some kind of tart lip balm.

I lean in, too. Shut my eyes.

Her lips press lightly against my chin. Just for a second, a flash.

I grin as I open my eyes, but Lucy's already darting off toward the SUV. She glances back as she opens the door, calling out, "Sleep tight, Rudy the Rockstar!"

A half-asleep Frank nearly topples to the ground before Lucy nudges him into the middle seat. The door closes, and the SUV drives away.

I'm left on the sidewalk, alone with a wad of cash. Still feeling that goddamn grandma peck, Lucy, warm on my chin.

I can still feel her hours later, keeping me awake as I toss and turn in bed.

Chapter 11

Lucy

The greenest of pastures, the fire, the ice.

I'm standing along the edge of Prospect Park Lake, observing what appears to be two voraciously mating turtles, when a tap on my shoulder startles me back to the human world.

"Lucy."

I spin around to see Rudy, and reach my arms out for a hug.

We hug in greeting now. That's a given. Which is great— I love a good hug, and Rudy is a Very Good Hugger. But the larger question today: do we continue to kiss chins? If so, Rudy may need to shave that orange scruff. My lips will get chafed.

It was quite a surprise, that almost-kiss—if that's what it was.

Not an altogether unpleasant one.

"Do we give each other those bird pecks to the chin again?" I say, because it's easier to make a joke than to think about why he stopped himself from kissing me that night.

He freezes just before giving me that hug, squinting as he furrows his brow. "Firstly, it was more of a grandma peck. Though shit, no, scratch that. Grandmas and birds seem equally unappealing. And secondly, I'm . . . sorry about that. It just happened?" His cheeks are pink, making his freckles look darker and more pronounced. The effect is oddly dazzling. "How about we try this instead?"

He leans in to kiss me on the cheek. Soft and lingering, with a little bit of a cheek-to-cheek nuzzle at the end. And then he follows it up with the hug, and it's just the right amount of tight and solid and warm.

The warmth feels extra good, because even though it's only the beginning of November, today feels wintry. Too wintry for the thin black-hooded sweatshirt Rudy's wearing. I'm in my winter parka, complete with matted faux fur along the hood. We're a strange contrast, the two of us, like we're coexisting in two wholly different seasons.

"Aren't you cold?" I ask when Rudy steps back, pulling my coat more tightly around me. I already miss his heat.

"Cold? Are you serious? This is *perfect* weather. I don't get cold until we hit freezing."

"It must be nice, to be so cold-blooded. Speaking of cold-blooded"—I point to the turtles—"I've discovered some rather amorous reptiles."

Rudy turns to observe the turtles, his jaw dropping. "Wow." He's an even more pronounced shade of pink now.

"Welcome to Prospect Park, and our grand day of Lucy's work-life adventure. You set a high bar with Ronny's show, so I had to be sure to deliver today." I turn away from the water, having seen enough scintillating *National Geographic* material for one day. "Are you quivering with anticipation?"

"I'm quivering, but more with anxiety than anticipation after our last Craigslist job."

"No dogs, don't worry." I wave him off as I start walking away from the lake. "Or at least not that I know of. Once you've done enough of these jobs, you can sort out the good from the bad from the very bad. I've only felt my life was at risk a handful of times."

"Oh, phew. Just a handful. We should be totally fine in that case."

"We're at Prospect Park! What could possibly be dangerous about a job here?"

"Please don't put that out into the universe."

"Nah. Elvira would have warned us. How could we find success if we die on—what is this, our sixth date? What are we counting as dates? Does grabbing a caffeinated beverage count?"

"Hmm. What differentiates hanging out versus dating versus working on the Great Elvira Challenge?"

"Well, kissing, for one. A proper steamy make-out. At minimum." As soon as I say this, my stomach flips. I glance over at Rudy, and his skin has gone from pink to an orchard apple red.

"Right," he says, his eyes fixed on the path. "A good make-out. There's that."

It shouldn't make us both so anxious, *making out*. We're thirty-somethings, for heaven's sake! My tongue has been deep down the throats of countless men whose names have been erased from memory (if I ever knew them at all), long-ago bar conquests, Saturday nights on the prowl with my now-defunct girl posse. My tongue has been everywhere, really. Too many places on too many people.

But kissing Rudy like that would be different.

Maybe because of the prophecy. Because we watched a woman *die* together.

Kissing Rudy—*really* kissing Rudy—feels like either an ending or a beginning.

Both options are equally terrifying.

"Well," I say, moving us along, "I don't think the exact count matters. I doubt the universe is taking score. What matters is the quality time, and today should definitely be quality."

I look at Rudy again, and this time, he's looking back at me, his skin returned to a more normal shade. He smiles. "When do I find out what this quality time is?"

I smile back. "Right now," I say, stopping in front of Lakeside, the park's compound of dining and recreation facilities. "You, my friend, are about to be back on set."

"On set?" His brows shoot up. "From a Craigslist ad? No auditions?"

"We're just extras, so our only job is to look good. Easy-peasy. It's a commercial for some local company, so I think the bar is low. No offense. You don't need a low bar, of course. They might sense your talent and give you the lead right on the spot."

He snorts. "Nah, no one cares about seeing me on screen these days, trust me. My last legitimate IMDB credit is fifteen years old."

"Oh, please. You're too modest." I wave him off as I look for signs of the shoot. The ad was fairly vague: *Extras needed for Lakeside Prospect Park commercial shoot. Local business. Dress for winter. $50 per hour, three-hour max.* I'd signed both of us up. Three hundred dollars! A good day in the office for me, and a job that felt specifically suited for Rudy to shine.

"There!" I say, pointing to a white tent surrounded by lights and cameras and frantic-looking people with clipboards and cellphones.

"At the rink? Are we ice skating?"

"God, no. The ad would have mentioned that. At least, I assume." I feel nauseous just at the thought. "I haven't skated since college, and that was a one-time thing. I used a kids' skate trainer at the Penn State rink and still managed to fall. I have the scar on my ankle to prove it."

"Hmm. Well. It kind of looks like there's skating involved."

I follow Rudy's gaze to the rink behind the tent, where a Zamboni is buffering the ice. There are overhead lights set up on each side of the rink, and several people dressed in all black, presumably crew, zipping around on the ice with cameras.

"Fuck."

"Maybe not every extra is on the rink."

I turn to face Rudy, and it appears he's trying very hard not to grin.

"This isn't funny. Can *you* skate?"

"Not to brag, but when I was nine, I just so happened to be in *Little Olympians*, the greatest kids' skating movie of all time. Maybe even the greatest kids' sports movie, period. They had a former gold-medal Olympian train us. And a few silver medalists doing backup."

"Um, okay, that's totally a humblebrag. And also, decades ago. Maybe you shouldn't be too cocky just yet."

I stomp toward the tent, hoping very fervently that Rudy is wrong. It never occurred to me, even knowing the location, that this job would involve ice skating. It's only *November*. Who goes skating in November?

Not me. I do not skate in November. Or in any other month.

When I reach one of the clipboard-wielding people at the tent—a young Southeast Asian woman who looks both frazzled and overcaffeinated—she immediately asks for my name and shoe size.

An ominous sign.

"I'm Lucy Minninger, a nine, but—"

"And you?" She cuts me off and looks back to Rudy.

"Rudy Ri—" He pauses.

"Minninger," I add in quickly. "My, er . . . husband." I'd thought it best to conceal the Riziero. Though in hindsight, perhaps using my last name was a bit much.

"Got it," she says, scribbling something down on her paper. "Shoe size?"

"Eleven."

She heads inside the tent to rummage through a pile of what is very clearly . . . boxes of ice skates.

Fuck me.

"Rudy Minninger?" he whispers in my ear. I jump, startled by the warmth of his breath against my neck. "I don't recall signing any marriage certificates."

"It wasn't my right to tell them they had an actual *celebrity* signing up. I wanted to preserve your anonymity."

"That was thoughtful," he says, and his smile tells me he means it. "Thank you. Even if they do think we're married."

"Of course." I hope any blush can be chalked up to the nip in the air. "Anyway, back to the larger issue here: I'm going to have to bail, clearly. I'll just watch my dear *husband* skate."

"Oh, no way, *wife*. You signed us up for this. We're in it together. How much money do we stand to make?"

"Three hundred total, if they use us for the full three hours."

"My going rate for any acting gig is fifteen hundred per day on set."

"Seriously?"

He nods.

"Great, even more reason to bail." I start to turn back, but he grabs me gently by the wrist. His fingers are a jolt of heat against my skin.

"I'll take a pay cut. It's for a good cause, after all. The Great Elvira Challenge." He's smiling at me as he says this, his lips and his eyes. The effect is just as warming as his hand.

"The ad said dress for winter, though," I say, my last attempt to avoid the ice. As much as I don't want to skate, I also don't want to be a quitter. I'd hate for that to be one of Rudy's early impressions of me. Lucy Minninger may be many things, but she is *not* a quitter. Other people quit on me, sure. Or they fire me. Either way, out of my hands. "I didn't think to remind you, because I assumed that was a given when I saw today's temp."

"This look totally says early winter to me." He drops my hand, spins around with outstretched arms to showcase his fuzzed and faded sweatshirt, making sure to emphasize the tiny holes on the cuffs with his protruding, wiggling thumbs.

"Nice. It looks like you've had that since your *Little Olympians* set days."

"Ouch. I do have other sweatshirts, for the record. This is just my favorite."

The woman returns with our skates, and as Rudy reaches out for the bigger pair, he asks, "Is my outfit acceptably wintry? My wife is concerned."

She squints at him, frowning. "It's not great, but we were prepared for some bozos to be underdressed and brought some coats and accessories. We knew what to expect from a *Craigslist* post." I'm almost offended by the way she says Craigslist, like it's a dirty word. Maybe it is, but it's *my* dirty word. She waves us off to a second smaller tent behind this one, and a short but overstuffed rack of puffy, shiny, furry outer garments.

"Perfect, thanks. I'll make sure my bozo looks impeccable, don't you worry." I grab my skates and loop arms with Rudy, tugging him toward the second tent. If I have to skate, I'll at least get to take pleasure in seeing Rudy encased in cheap faux fur.

"Bozo," Rudy says, chuckling. "And I thought your *Little Olympians* jab was harsh."

"Don't let it get to you. She's just bitter to be working a local commercial shoot. I'm sure she has her sights set on more glamorous jobs, like—oh, I don't know, maybe a movie with that overrated actor, what's his name . . . Rocco something? Rizzo? Rizzy? Razzy?"

Rudy stops walking, and I stop with him, our arms still linked. "Did you just call my brother overrated?" He's staring down at his Vans, his face unreadable.

"Shit. I did. It slipped out." *Nice, Lucy.* It's true, but still. Maybe a bit early to be casually insulting his sibling, no? "I mean . . . he's fine. I'm just more Nora Ephron than billion-dollar franchise. I'm sorry, though. I shouldn't have said it. Duh. That's your family."

"No, I'm really glad you did." Rudy looks up, beaming at me. "It's exhausting—and infuriating, if I'm being honest—hearing about how handsome and brilliant and genius he is all the time. Overrated is refreshing. Which I guess makes me a terrible brother, but . . ." He shrugs.

We leave it hanging on that *but* as we stand in front of the coat rack. I slip my arm free from Rudy's to flip through the fuzziest options, pulling out a few for him to try on. They're all a bit petite for his frame, but there's a fringed black-and-white-spotted fur bomber jacket that gives serious cow pelt vibes and would be utterly tragic to cast aside.

"This is terrible," he says, staring at himself through my phone's camera. "But I've worn worse. This beats the Polish folk costume I wore for a recent gig. And for the same pay."

"So, it's a winner?" I grin, rubbing his shoulder. It feels like a rabbit's rump.

"I wouldn't go so far as to ever call this winning, but I'll wear it."

"Perfect."

We're walking out of the tent, headed toward the ice—oh, God, *the ice*, I'd managed to avoid thinking about it while in wardrobe—when I hear someone call out:

"Lucy? Is that you?"

I spin around, and it takes a second to collect the separate pieces: Dimples. Cheekbones. Lips. That shiny, sculpted hair, sticking out from beneath a flannel fur-lined lumberman hat.

Hashtag. Disco. Douggy.

Universe, *WHY?*

Sarah-with-an-H at Rudy's show, and now this? We live in Brooklyn, for fuck's sake, not Greendale, PA! Highly unacceptable.

"Jesus Christ." I drop my skates on the grass. "What are you doing here?"

"Trying to build my résumé." He reaches up to smooth his curls, presumably forgetting he's wearing a ridiculous hat. His hand pets the fur instead. "My headshots are out with agents. I'll be booking legit jobs soon, but I figured I'd get a jump start."

"Ah. Great. Well . . ." I look over at Rudy, who's watching

this interaction with a bemused expression. "Best of luck. It was, er, nice to see you."

I'm already turning away, but Hashtag doesn't seem to understand this universal conversation ender. "What are you doing here?"

"Working. I do Craigslist jobs for a living." I cringe inwardly at my frankness, remembering how self-important I'd felt saying I was *not at liberty to say* more about my work. Fuck all. Who cares what Hashtag thinks?

"Oh. Um. Cool. Well, good to see—" He stops, his eyes landing somewhere next to me. "*Holy shit*. Rudy Riziero?"

Rudy looks around first, scouting the territory. Satisfied that we're adequately isolated, he gives a furtive nod. Poor Rudy, being recognized in that grizzled dairy cow jacket. This was a bad idea, being on set today. It wasn't fair to Rudy, making him *act* like this.

"I was such a fan," Hashtag blathers on, "*Black Hole Sons*, *Whiz of Riz*, movie bits. What are you doing *here*?" He glances around the humble set, the woman from the tent now barking orders into her cell. "I mean, you could still be in Hollywood, dude. Living the damn dream."

"Yeah. Well." Rudy goes to jam his hands in his sweatshirt pockets, remembering belatedly that he's in cowskin. He flinches as his fingers rub against the suspiciously authentic bristled fur. "I mostly left that scene behind when I graduated. I do a few random acting gigs here and there, but that life . . . wasn't for me." His face goes blank as he says this, and I wonder how true that really is—especially after his crack about IMDB. Maybe that wasn't just false modesty. I'm not sure *this* life is for him, either, the one he's living now.

I wonder what life *is* for him.

I hope more than ever that somehow, miraculously, we'll find it.

Together.

I hope that we don't go up in flames before we do.

"Forgive me," I say, taking the reins. "I didn't introduce you. Rudy, this is Hashtag Disco Douggy." I should win an award, for saying this out loud without laughing. Rudy's face shows a flash of confusion, but then just as quickly straightens out. The fan treatment. "We met on HeartThrobs, and had one unfortunate date, ending with me lighting his hair on fire." Rudy tries and fails to stifle his laughter—even he can't act his way through this one. I turn to Hashtag. "And this is, of course, Rudy, and we also met on HeartThrobs. Our unfortunate first date ended with a woman dying, practically on our laps. And yet, here we are." I grin. Hashtag is staring, mouth ajar.

It's satisfying, running into the twenty-three-year-old keyboard character in this way, flaunting my recent HeartThrobs success—if it can qualify as a *success*—with an idol of his.

"We better prep for the ice, get in character, all that jazz," I say, grabbing Rudy's hand and pulling him away. "You understand, of course, as an actor yourself."

Hashtag only manages a wobbly wave as we walk off.

"You went on a date with *him*? *Hashtag*? I mean, what the fuck is that about? And is he even out of college?"

If I'm not mistaken, Rudy sounds . . . *jealous.*

Jealous of a wannabe-DJ-hand-model who lives in his mother's basement.

"It wasn't one of my better HeartThrobs decisions. I missed the bio line about his name, or I'd have flipped down. I think." I shrug. "Anyway, probably for the best that I held the Flaming Zombie too close to his face. Maybe he'll reassess how much product he uses in his hair."

Rudy laughs so hard, he shakes all the way through his arm and his hand, which is still squeezed around mine. "I would say no, based on what I could see of that coif under his excessively wintry cap. But I guess I should feel lucky you only drenched me with water on our date. Water trumps flame, so thank you."

"You're welcome. Though I did drench him with water, too, I must confess."

We're at the rink then, where a disgruntled-looking middle-aged white man introduces himself as Darren, the *director*—a fancy word for what turns out to be a local artisanal (it's from Park Slope, so of course) hot chocolate company ad—and informs us that we'll be skating around in circles, smiling and laughing and "twinkling like goddamn snow angels." I'm tempted to point out that snow angels neither twinkle nor skate, but I don't sense Darren's the type who appreciates constructive critique.

"Don't fall, don't make too much noise, don't get too close to the head talent." With that, he walks off to convene with the *head talent*: two little girls and two older adults I assume are intended to be grandparents. We watch as they do some run-throughs on the ice, and *holy shit*, they're good. Or at least very decent. Full-fledged figure skaters by my low standards.

"Looks like these girls trained with Olympians, too," I whisper to Rudy. "And Gram and Pops could both skate circles around my bleeding body after I crack my head open on the ice."

Rudy chuckles. "Please no. Too soon for another dead body. Especially yours."

Especially mine.

Warped, but still flattering.

"I got your back," he says, wrapping an arm around my shoulders. "Don't worry."

And strangely enough, I *am* less worried. There's something about Rudy that makes him easy to believe. Easy to trust.

A kind of easiness that isn't nearly as boring as I might have anticipated. In fact, Rudy is . . . just about as far from boring as I could imagine. Huh.

When I finally have to pull on my skates and get on the ice, Rudy keeps his arm around my waist, moving in careful glides as I make tiny slices to propel my weight forward. He whispers a steady stream of tips and encouragement in my ear, insisting "you got this," even when I most assuredly do not *got* anything. But I feel stable with him there. Like maybe if I move slowly enough, I can make it through three hours without a concussion.

"You there," Darren calls out, clapping his hands. "The woman with the cow-man."

I look over at Rudy, then to the side of the rink, where Darren is red-faced and squinting at me. "Pick it up! You look like you're moving in slow motion."

"Can't she just play the part of a beginner?" Rudy yells over to him, frowning. "Every rink has one, right?"

"Not my rink," Darren says, already turning away, waving toward the camera person.

"Maybe the post could have been more specific about the required skating proficiency," I grumble. "But thanks for trying. That was sweet of you."

"We can just leave. No shame, really. You tried."

"No way, I don't give up on a job," I say, and with a sudden, fierce desire to prove this true, I push myself ahead wholeheartedly, Rudy's grip on me falling away.

"Lucy, what are—"

I tune him out and focus on the rhythm of each foot, long and steady strokes, slice, slide, glide, picking up momentum and speed. "I'm doing it, Rudy! *I'm doing it!*"

It occurs to me now, as I'm slicing, sliding, gliding, that we didn't make it to the point in the lesson about how to stop.

"Where the fuck are the brakes?" I shout, breaking one of Darren's golden rules. But it feels essential, as I'm about to break an even more important rule—the starring family is straight ahead, their backs to me.

"WHERE THE FUCK ARE THE BRAKES?!" I repeat, loudly enough for the family to turn toward me now, four pairs of wide eyes and dropped jaws, and then—

I'm shoved up against the side of the rink with a *whoosh*, the air knocked from my lungs. I bounce off from impact, crashing into another body behind me, pushing that body into a crumpled heap on the ice. A nice landing pad as I splat down fully on top of it, our two sets of flailing arms and legs twisting and tangling.

Ow.

I lift my head up, my cheek brushing against Rudy's chin scruff.

"Are you okay?" he gasps, clearly winded as he blinks up at me. He has very nice eyelashes, dark and curly and plentiful. His eyes are even more puddle-like this close up, a molten, bottomless brown topped by a few gold-flecked shimmers.

I nod, biting my lip. "Are you? Okay?"

"I'd say I probably need some ice on my head, but luckily, it's already right under me."

I snort, and then reach out to cup the side of his face. "Thank you for saving me." My fingers have a will of their own, the tips tracing down the stubbled edge of his jawline.

"Of course." He tilts his face, presses it against my palm. "I should have mentioned that skates don't have brakes."

"I broke all of Darren's rules, you know. I suspect we're about to be kicked off set."

"I suspect you're right."

We both smile. I tune out the steadily growing buzz of commotion around us. I focus instead on those neatly rimmed puddles. The constellation of freckles below that seem to lead me directly to his lips.

Rudy's eyes do a slow blink, then close.

I lean in, the tip of my nose brushing against his, and—

"Yeah, Lucy! You get it!"

Hashtag is suddenly there, smiling down with some kind of thoroughly gross approval. I can already hear him telling the story: *I went on a date with someone who's dating a Riziero . . .*

"I'm glad things didn't work out between us so you two could meet," he continues, lumping on additional grossness.

"Let's get a drink," I say, ignoring Hashtag as I sit upright, legs straddling Rudy's waist. "No Flaming Zombies. No Sex on the Beaches. Proper straight whiskey, the way God intended it to be drunk. My treat to make up for the three hundred dollars we most assuredly will not be collecting."

"Two for two in unpaid Craigslist jobs." He chuckles. "Maybe we've done enough career research? We can find other ways to work on the Great Elvira Challenge."

"Okay. Fair. So, what does that mean in terms of my invitation?"

"Yes. Of course. Anywhere with you, away from Pound Sign, sounds perfect."

"Great." I push myself up off the ice, Rudy steadying me as he stands, too.

"If we move fast," I whisper against his ear, "that glorious coat could be yours. What do you say?"

Darren is just behind us now, screaming for us to vacate his set.

Rudy looks down at the coat, considering. "I say . . . if you want to move fast, I need to carry you off this rink. Toss your skates, grab your shoes, *run*."

Without waiting for a reply, he swoops me up and over his shoulder.

And then the former Little Olympian whips us both away.

Chapter 12
Rudy

Seek out your friends wisely, forever play nice.

"And that's how I got the jacket. It's more of a trophy now," I say to Sheeraz and Matt, who look equal parts disgusted and disturbed by the sheer presence of this beastly coat.

Sheeraz turns away from me before he speaks. "Great story, now take it off? I've never felt so uncomfortable around a piece of outerwear before."

Matt laughs as he continues to study it. "This coat may have singlehandedly brought that wackadoo shit to Skinwalker Ranch, if you ask me. Summoned something evil from beyond."

While none of us will actually admit to believing in aliens—much like psychics—we've frequently obsessed over the possibility of them. We've spent many hungover Sundays debating the finer points of *Ancient Aliens*. A nice balance to Bourdain.

"My God, it's real cowskin!" Matt exclaims, wide-eyed as he gently pets my shoulders.

"Have you checked your email?" Sheeraz asks as he, too, steps up to poke the jacket. His curiosity won out. "Marguerite and I are trying to find a night to have a triple dinner date soon.

I sent some open dates. You may not call Lucy your girlfriend, but you've spent enough time together to introduce her to your nearest and dearest."

A suspect proposition—Sheeraz is notoriously pre-meditative. He never just *has* an idea. He's been brewing on something for a long time before a word is spoken or an email drafted.

Grinning, Matt immediately chimes in, "I got it, and Jules and I can make any of the nights work."

Awesome.

That leaves me in the precarious position of having to agree to at least one date out of . . . I flick through my phone and open the email. Seven suggested dates, which means there's no valid excuse. They know my schedule isn't that booked, not even on a good gig month. I'm not sure how to feel about this. On one hand, the pressure on me and Lucy has been relatively low thus far. To bring her to my roommates and their significant others, all together at a table to break bread, could push this casual-see-how-it-goes "relationship" to a new level.

Or stop it dead in its tracks. Whatever that might mean for our *destiny*.

Lucy's schedule is usually flexible, too, which only ups the unavoidability factor. I text her the dates with Sheeraz and Matt peering over my shoulder. Damn them.

She immediately responds.

Lucy: I can do any of those dates! I can't wait to meet the humans who willingly share their life with you.

Lucy: And their bathroom.

I turn to Sheeraz, resigned. "Let's make this Friday happen."

The faster, the better. I want to give Sheeraz the least amount of time to gather whatever he has in store for us.

Matt appears to be highly impressed by this. "Whoa, that

might be the fastest decision I've ever seen you make. Perhaps the El Flaco has left the building."

El Flaco . . . oh, how I despise that nickname.

It was given to me because I'm usually much less decisive. Flakey at best, and I've bailed on more occasions than I care to talk about. I'd love to ditch that name, though. It doesn't even make sense—it means "skinny" in Spanish, and I haven't ever really been "skinny" by anyone's definition, though LA and its vapid, surface level expectations about what it means to be attractive enough for showbiz initially kept me at what my old manager called first "chubby cute," and from there, "husky handsome." But I preferred the freshman fifteen and then some that's never come off. El Flaco came into being when I didn't show up to a Mexican restaurant for a big friend dinner once, and they wouldn't seat the group without the full party. That was . . . four years ago now. But the name lives on.

"For the record, I haven't flaked in a while. Mostly because we're all too busy to hang out these days, and there's nothing to skip. But also because I've made a conscious effort to keep promises and stick to plans."

"I know, dude, and we appreciate it." Sheeraz gives me another shoulder pat, clearly sensing that Matt's touched a nerve. "Anyway, I've got to go meet Margs. She's been trying to get in touch with the contractor of her dreams to redo the third floor of the brownstone. Maybe some touch-ups on the other floors, too. Expensive? Yes. Will it make her happy? Of course! So I must help her go over logistics . . . but I'm looking forward to Friday! It's going to be a *night*. Meeting your almost, sort-of girlfriend."

I choose to ignore the "contractor" piece, because that's way too much to unpack right now. "My 'sort-of girlfriend'? Are we in high school? She's not—"

Matt stands, too, cutting me off. "Yeah, Jules is teaching her first manga class tonight, and I said I'd sit in for moral support, so I have to run, too. But Friday will be fun."

Sheeraz is out the door first, and then I watch as Matt follows behind without checking to see if he has his keys. As I grab them off the table, the door shuts. I run to the window. "You forgot your keys, Matt!" He hops off the stoop, and I motion to toss them on the sidewalk.

"No worries," he says, "Jules has a spare, and I'm staying there tonight." He's off then, walking down the sidewalk with Sheeraz.

I drop the keys back on the table.

I guess I have the house to myself.

Again.

The American hibachi experience isn't really my bag.

It's shticky to the max—the onion volcano, the heart-shaped pile of rice arranged to look like Cupid's arrow has been cast through it. And really, who wants to catch shrimp in their mouth, just to risk the embarrassment of catching one in the face? Nope. Hard pass, for me, anyway. Give me a quiet stoop taco or bodega sandwich any day.

If I'd known the big dinner date would be here, I would've considered flaking out. El Flaco rides again. The only plus is that Lucy just so happens to be a massive fan of hibachi restaurants. We got here early to post up at the bar on her behest—more time to watch the chefs do their work. She was so jazzed, in fact, that she wore a thrifted Benihana T-shirt to celebrate.

I guess there *is* someone who genuinely likes the onion volcano and the heart rice and the tossed shrimp.

This someone sitting right next to me.

"It's like going to a concert and wearing a shirt from a band in the same genre," she says, laughing loudly as she takes a sip of her lychee martini.

A very . . . *special* someone.

"Anyway, I'm just excited to be meeting some of your friends," she says, "even if they're all commoners like me."

"Commoners?" I snort, almost spraying my sip of Sapporo.

"Well, you know, average people. No celebrities. Not to pry, or—fuck it, yes, to pry, but only because I'm curious, not because I have ulterior motives. Do you still talk to any of your old acting pals? I mean, you met everyone who was anyone back in the day, I'm sure. Any good ones who stuck around?"

I shrug. "Sure. A few. There are some genuinely good people who also just happen to be famous. We keep tabs on one another. We understand each other in a way no one else can."

I can tell I've piqued her curiosity, but Matt and Jules arrive then, approaching the bar with ridiculously large grins. They're the kind of couple that seems to dress alike the longer they're together, subconsciously at least, and tonight is no exception: denim jackets, black jeans, gray sweaters, New Balance sneakers.

"You must be Lucy!" Matt says. "A pleasure to meet you. I'm Matt, and this is my girlfriend, Julia."

"Call me Jules." She slides onto the stool next to Lucy, cozying right up. "Whoa, a Benihana shirt! I love that you dressed for the occasion."

Lucy gives me a smug I-told-you-so look. "Thank you very much. I'm so glad we can all chop it up together tonight." Lucy laughs at her own pun in the sincerest possible way. It makes all of us laugh, too.

"Already laughing, huh? I knew this was the right thing to do," Sheeraz says as he rolls through the door arm-in-arm with Marguerite. She's looking especially fancy tonight, even for her, wearing a long red dress and a white coat edged in fur I suspect isn't faux; she's always given me major Veronica Lodge vibes, in looks and in attitude, except with a born-and-raised Miami flair. Suits Sheeraz well, though, at least when it comes to style. He's looking extra shiny tonight, too. "Lucy! Damn glad to meet you! We're finally able to put a face to the name of the person Rudy's been spending more time with than, well . . . literally anyone else I know."

"And you must be Sheeraz, and Marguerite. So lovely to meet you, too!"

Marguerite gives Jules a hug, and then seems to hesitate, pausing before Lucy pulls her in for a squeeze, too.

Sheeraz sidebars me, leaning in close. "She does know there are people working here who probably failed out of Benihana, right? They better not spit in our food."

Lucy has the ears of a bat apparently, because she doesn't miss a beat: "Whoever cooks for us will know we mean business."

"An interesting approach," Sheeraz says, tilting his head as he seems to give this serious consideration. "I like the thought behind it—forcing a good meal by showing the cook your expertise."

Lucy smiles at Sheeraz, flashing her crossed fingers at him.

Our table is ready then, and we all settle in around the U-shaped entertainment station. Lucy and I in the middle, flanked by the two couples. I overhear Jules telling Lucy about the truths and mistruths of hibachi here in America, and her culinary experiences in Japan—her dad's side of the family lives there, and she visits every year. Lucy looks deeply invested. I make polite chitchat with Margs about the weather, then move on to Giants talk with Matt.

The sake flows.

The shtick is in full effect.

Lucy is, not surprisingly, the only one who catches shrimp in her mouth, and is also the only one egging on the chef to "go bigger!" with the onion volcano.

In between the clanging, banging, and knife tossing, there are a lot of general questions aimed in our direction. The overall effect is more of an interrogation—albeit a kind one without torture devices—than a conversation. Where Lucy lives, what she does, our meeting on HeartThrobs, the first date, and of course, that infamous last reading.

"I just can't believe she died on the table. *In front of you*," Marguerite says, loudly enough for the chef to hear.

He perks up, looking over at us while his fingers nimbly chop away at a piece of steak. "You had someone die at your table? At Benihana?"

Everyone has a question about our first date.

I take a long swig of my Sapporo tallboy.

Lucy shakes her head, looking wistful. "A French-Mexican restaurant. Our psychic died mid-reading. Not a fun way to go, for her or for us. But I suppose a Benihana death wouldn't be so bad, as far as death goes. At least it means your final meal was a delight."

The table laughs, and I laugh, too, though I can't help but feel more than a twinge of remorse for Elvira.

The chef finishes plating our food and takes off, much to Lucy's dismay. Sheeraz and Marguerite are on the veggie train, Matt and Jules are doing a surf-and-turf split, and Lucy and I both ordered chicken, separately. We're quiet for the first time this evening as we all dig into our heaping mountains of food.

"So," Sheeraz interjects after another round of drinks is served, "I wanted to bring you all here for more than some steamy food entertainment. We have an announcement to make."

Marguerite slips her hand out from under the table to reveal a gigantic engagement ring. "We're getting married!" she yells out to the table. To the whole restaurant, really. "Sheeraz proposed last night!"

I'm not surprised by the news, especially since he's been talking about "rings and things" for a while now. And that dream contractor anecdote. A quick glance at Matt tells me he's equally unfazed. We could hear this moment coming from Sheeraz's mouth for months. Tonight's mostly an opportunity for Margs to publicly present her new bling.

Lucy, however, is perhaps overly excited, even a little teary-eyed at the announcement. "Oh my goodness, that is so wonderful, you two!" She's out of her seat, rushing to their side of the table for hugs.

Matt and Jules are congratulating them, too, and suddenly we're all out of our chairs, hugging. I'm slapping Sheeraz on the back as I say—because I can't resist some light ribbing—"It's about time, my friend. I can't believe you kept her waiting this long while Matt and I got to hear you obsess about 'the right time.' Just kidding. Mostly. I was about to take you on a field trip to the jewelry store to get the ball rolling and make that 'rings and things' talk stop. Anything to make it stop . . ."

Sheeraz and Margs politely laugh it off as we all make our way back to our seats. I know Sheeraz well enough, though, to see that he's either a little upset about that comment, or has something else on his mind. Matt also seems . . . skittish. He's deflecting my attempts at eye contact, focused squarely on Jules and their clasped hands on the table. Are they about to announce their engagement, too? I do a quick check. No sparkly new ring on Jules's hand.

Jules takes a sip of her sake, and then aggressively clears her throat. "I don't want to take anything away from this hugely special news, but Matt and I also have a big life update. We're moving in together next month. We just signed a new lease in Queens."

Whoa.

Not that either of these announcements are necessarily a shock, but all in the same dinner? It's quite a . . . coincidence. This must have been more strategized than Sheeraz and Matt have let on. Thank God I have a whole stash of game faces in my arsenal.

"Wow. Nice, Matt! I never thought you had it in you to move out of Brooklyn."

"Just over the border. It's not Long Island or anything." Matt shudders.

"Technically, it's all Long Island," I dutifully point out.

I feel Lucy's eyes on me, taking it all in. My hands tapping on my thighs with gusto, sweat beading on my brow. I see where this is going, and we didn't need a triple-date hibachi night to make it happen. Engagement dinners are nice and all, and I'm happy to be a part of the celebration—I love Sheeraz, and Margs makes him happy. But this just feels like an ambush.

I've known all along that once Sheeraz got engaged, and certainly married, that I'd have to find another home. Hearing that Matt is leaving me alone with the newly engaged couple makes the inevitable seem more like tomorrow.

I'm not prepared for that.

Not mentally.

Definitely not financially.

Lucy reaches for my hand under the table. "I wish we had some sort of milestone to announce, but I guess we can say that we've had a few work dates—*dates*," she corrects herself, squeezing my hand—"and both managed to run into a former flame while we were out. Fortuitous? Perhaps." Lucy drops my hand and stretches her arms over the table, wiggling her fingers like she's casting an elaborate spell.

It's a valiant effort to change the course of our conversation. The group laughs politely, and from there, we cover innocuous topics until we're paid up and ready to leave.

I want the boys to tell me to my face that I'm out of a place to live—but on my own terms and turf, not while feeling bombarded from each side and right in front of Lucy.

"I'd love to take you all out for a nightcap to celebrate these big life moves," I say to everyone as we're walking out. "There's a solid bar just a few blocks down."

Matt gives a look to Jules indicating they probably had other plans, like puzzling with a boxed wine. Jules recognizes my gesture, though, and says, "Great idea, let's keep the celebration rolling!"

Sheeraz and Marguerite can't back out now, not after Jules's resounding yes. As we head down the street, the couples naturally disperse, the women gathering together in one cluster, and Sheeraz, Matt, and I staggering behind. There's a tension between us in the cold night air. It's like a mafia movie—that loaded moment when they're leading a "friend" to swim with the fishes.

No one says anything for the first block.

We wait on a corner for a red light that feels unusually long. The women are a block ahead now.

"I fully understand this means I'm out of the brownstone," I say, going for it, eyes firmly on the road in front of me. "You didn't have to plan an elaborate dinner so it could feel like a fun announcement rather than bummer news. I'm a big boy, I'll figure it out."

I glance up in time to catch Sheeraz looking at Matt knowingly, like I just uncovered their big plan. "Shit, dude," Sheeraz says, shaking his head. "I'm sorry. We didn't know how to tell you. Things seem to be going well for you, and neither of us wanted to add any negative vibes to your plate. And you just happened to pick the night after I was planning to propose for our group dinner, so . . . the stars kind of aligned. But I've been dropping those hints the last few months . . . 'rings and things' was supposed to be a way to get you thinking about my path without point-blank telling you that you'll have to bounce at some point. Perhaps you've rubbed off on me a little, Rudy, but I didn't want to deal with the potential conflict. I'm sorry for that."

Matt nods, giving me the same puppy-dog eyes he perfected in grade school. "We weren't trying to hide anything. We just . . . wanted to find the right time. We thought a triple date with Lucy would be that. Clearly, not a great plan. You deserved to find out more privately."

I know all this, and it's not like I can fault them. They're growing up, they're happy, and I want that for them. They're my best friends. Like brothers, really. More so than the one I'm related to by blood. It's been a good run—but most bachelor pads get the domestic upgrade eventually.

"I get it," I say, wrapping an arm around each of their shoulders and pulling them in, "and I'm glad we hashed that out so we can have a proper sendoff. I need a good reason to blow off some of this Ronny Boyd cash."

Our reconciliation is perfectly timed, as we finish up our slapping hugs and step into Moira's, one of the finest Irish watering holes in New York City.

"There's been a lot of intensive research accumulated over the years," I say, waving grandly toward the bar, "and I've determined this is the freshest Guinness in all of Brooklyn. I don't say that lightly."

I order six Guinness and six Powers Irish whiskies before anyone has a chance to decline. If this is my swan song with Matt and Sheeraz, at least as official roommates, I want to go out with a proper toast.

Lucy and I haven't spoken since dinner, so I make it a point to approach her at the bar, where she's posted up by herself a little ways down, looking like a total regular. Six Guinness pours will be all the time I need to get her up to speed.

"So, that's that," I say a few minutes later, having quietly hashed out the finer points of my talk with Matt and Sheeraz. "I'll look for a sublet, I guess, or maybe move farther south for a more affordable studio. I just wish they'd told me before the big event. I mean, they deliberated over how they were going to break it to me. Like I'm a child."

Lucy puts her hand on my back, rubs a slow circle between my shoulders. "I know tonight must have been hard. But change can be a good thing, right? You'll figure it out."

"Yeah. It'll be okay." I will figure it out. She's right. I have no choice.

"Nightcaps are here!" Marguerite yells to us from down the bar, holding up her clear liquor drink. "I can't do Guinness, Rudy, sorry. It's like eating another meal. That hibachi was enough to last me for a week."

"Actually," I say, not able to resist defending my beloved brew, "it's considered a light beer because of its low ABV and nitrogen bubbles. But I can certainly take it off your hands."

Once we all have our whiskey shots—except for Margs, with her tequila and soda—I raise my glass. "To old friends, beautiful relationships, and exciting new life adventures! Congratulations to all four of you, and I'm happy and honored to have been around to see the magic happen . . . wait, not *that* kind of magic happening . . . you know what I mean. Cheers!"

We clink and salute. Jules immediately launches into some questions about the wedding for Margs, Matt starts describing the new apartment to Sheeraz.

Out of absolutely nowhere, Lucy sets her glass down and bursts out with: "I have an extra room if you want to stay with me while you figure out next steps. More of an oversized closet. But it could fit an air mattress."

Uh.

Maybe she's just caught up in the overenthusiasm of the evening. Or it could be a pity invite. She looks and sounds sincere, though. Unnervingly earnest.

No matter the intentions, I'm completely floored. And by the looks of the other couples, they are, too. Four wide-eyed deer in excessively bright headlights.

There's a long pause. Too long.

Shit. I'm obligated to say something, aren't I?

"Er. That's very . . . kind of you, Lucy. I'll definitely consider the offer. I think I have a couple months at least, though, right?"

Margs gives a laser-eyed stare to Sheeraz.

Fuck. Pretty harsh, especially from a best friend.

"Ah, well," Sheeraz says, looking deeply uncomfortable. I give him a dead-eyed glare, not making the moment any easier for him. "We were thinking a month. Or . . . less if you can swing it? Margs met with that dream contractor, and he can only take us on if we get going right away. Which sucks, I know, but his work is really amazing. We want to give you time to look for a place, of course, though from the sounds of it, maybe you just found it . . . ?"

Damn him. This is so not the way I envisioned the conversation going. A month?

We all turn to our drinks. Matt and Jules are the first to finish. They grab their coats, barely say goodbye, and leave in a flash.

Now there were four.

Lucy is silent. Maybe because she realized, belatedly, her offer would have been a better one-on-one conversation, not to be discussed openly in front of the same people very much anticipating my departure.

It feels like this whole night has been paved—however poorly—with good intentions. Lucy stuck her neck out for me, and I mostly just brushed her off.

She deserves better.

We're in this together, aren't we? For Elvira, or for us, or for both. I'm not sure it matters.

Sheeraz and Margs start whispering now, clearly looking for an exit strategy. I make it easy for them. "You two look tired, you should bounce. This was great, and we're so happy for you."

It's a flurry of hugs, and then they're gone.

Just Lucy and me, at the bar.

A moment passes. We both take a long sip of Guinness.

"I want to thank you for tonight," I say, clearing my throat. "You were something special. You took care of me in a way that, if I'm being honest, I'm really not used to. When I felt uncomfortable at dinner, you got the conversation rolling on with your joke. Your spirit fingers."

Lucy has a light line of foam on her upper lip, and I'm tempted to brush it off with my thumb. But she licks it away before I have the chance.

We haven't talked about what happened at the rink. What almost happened, anyway.

Lucy, about to kiss me. And I closed my eyes, ready for it. Wanting it.

"You did it again here at the bar," I continue, "after I told you how my living situation was going to change, and . . ." I'm not sure how to finish that sentence. What to say about her offer.

Lucy shakes her head, frowning. "Don't be fake-polite to me about it. Telling me that it was *kind*, and you'll *consider it*. Fake-polite is my least favorite character trait, if I'm being honest. I'm not one of your fans. You don't have to yes me, or sugarcoat things. I don't want Rudy the entertainer when it comes to us. I want to hear how you really feel. Because that was probably weird and pushy of me, wasn't it? It just . . . slipped out. I was mostly trying to give you a positive distraction. Because I know they're your friends, but they sure didn't do such a great job at the whole friendship thing tonight, letting you know you're out like that. I really felt for you. And I . . . wanted to help. That's all."

"Shit. That means a lot, Lucy. Thank you. And you're right. I was being a little fake-polite, wasn't I? Not because I hated the idea. You just caught me off guard."

"Yeah?" The frown eases, slightly.

"Yeah. I mean, we haven't even kissed—aside from chins and cheeks, anyway—so how could I be worried about crashing with you?"

She snorts, which feels like a victory.

Maybe she wasn't going to kiss me on the ice.

Maybe I'm too in my head.

"This would be the easiest Craigslist shared space interview yet," I continue. "I know your favorite morning pick-me-up—matcha. Coffee is acceptable, too, but holds a firm second place in your heart. Shoes off at home is a rule that doesn't get broken, not even in a bathroom emergency. And I'm sure we can agree on some TV shows and movies—though I have my Nora Ephron limit—and I can make a pretty decent grilled cheese. So, everybody wins."

Uh. Wow.

That all just came out *so quickly*. Too quickly. A bit too much of the booze talking.

I have immediate regrets.

"On second thought," I say, clearing my throat, "let's sleep on it. With all that's happened tonight, it might be best—for both of us—to take the night to reflect."

Monetarily, moving in with Lucy makes sense. It's spontaneous, but temporary. I have no single friends left to share rent with at this point. It makes me nervous to think about jumping into a place with Lucy, but it makes me nervous to think about finding random Craigslist strangers to live with, too. As Sheeraz so kindly put it, ones that are half my age. I've only ever lived with trusted friends.

Here I am, though. With a ticking clock.

Lucy looks a little shook, her cheeks flushed under the bar lights.

Was making her wait the wrong idea?

Before I can give any awkward apologies, she nods and says, "I get it. You're right. We'll take the night. If I'm still feeling it, I'll write up the official Craigslist post for you to peruse. Apply if you'd like. Or don't. We'll be okay either way."

We'll be okay.

Will we, though?

I guess only time will tell.

Chapter 13

Lucy

The fruits of your labor, first sour now sweet.

I write up the post during my cab ride home from our night-cap, though I wait until the next morning to send it to Rudy—so I can at least pretend to be "taking the night."

Hypothetical-obsessed, wannabe writer with failed string of jobs seeking temporary roommate to occupy window-less, rodent-infested "guest bedroom" (i.e. storage closet). Ideal candidate must: readily answer hypotheticals, despite level of absurdity; track and kill rodents with a feline-esque tenacity; occasionally binge on poorly scripted reality TV, at the primary tenant's discretion. Must be willing to so-cialize with landlords, which may involve basement gin ex-perimentation. Rent may be paid in daily matcha and taco deliveries. Please, no superfan guests admitted after hours. (Or, strike that, any hours.) Any and all romantic inclina-tions will be painstakingly discussed and mutually con-sensual. Absolutely no broken hearts allowed. In lieu of a written contract, terms will be deemed official post whiskey toast.

I don't want to seem too eager. But . . . I *am*. I am eager. Despite Rudy's mixed bag of hot and cold reactions last night. It's a big decision. I get it.

I have doubts, too, of course. I probably know the nice old lady who runs the laundromat down the street better than I know my potential new roommate. And though Rudy's niceness usually seems authentic enough, at least with me—last night was an aberration I'll grant him, given the trying circumstances—I still can't tell if that niceness will light any fires for us.

Good fire, that is. Not the explosive, all-consuming fire that will ravage us if we fail at Elvira's prediction.

There's that fire to consider, too.

But it's not like it'll be a permanent arrangement. No one could permanently live in a glorified closet space. I've been alone for so many years, though, and there's something deeply appealing about fighting for bathroom time slots in the morning, or space on the love seat while we both stare like zombies at our various devices. Debating takeout options and sharing a feast of appetizers that might seem grotesque for one customer. Complaining about the weather, Tuesdays, overpriced salads. Whatever else it is that roommates do, because I forget, honestly, and even the bickering seems better than playing the part of the quintessential spinster day in and year out. I much prefer Rudy to a cat. I'm too allergic to cat dander to be a proper spinster.

I consider posting my note to Craigslist, just to take the joke full circle. But it could open the door for too many bizarre responses, even for my taste.

Rudy responds within an hour:

Would you rather live with a former 90s child star who isn't a great cook and has a somewhat unreliable stream of income (and maybe even more unreliable romantic history), but tries hard and means well and has no police record (mi-

nus that one weed incident after a Phish show) and will insist on paying half your rent (and throw in some spare change for rat poison, I know a guy with the goods)...OR... Spend the rest of your life wondering about Elvira's words, and what could have been?

I laugh, because a hypothetical was of course the best and only way to respond.

We're here because of a hypothetical.

Before I can reply, he texts again:

Actually, no. We can get to the bottom of what Elvira said either way. No ultimatum. But if you're still offering after sleeping on it more, my answer is yes. Let's try this. It's a weird enough situation already, right? Why not make it weirder?!

I look around my dark little home, this space that feels smaller by the day. A cave is supposed to be cozy, a refuge. This feels more like a cage.

It might be a disastrous idea. *Epically* disastrous. It could easily implode every good thing we've been building together. But in that case, maybe it would have always imploded, eventually, whether we lived together or not. Just like Sharlene told us. An extreme on either end, no in-between. Maybe we're just finding our answer, good or bad, sooner rather than later.

I wanted a story out of this, didn't I? And this—well, this is quite a story.

But maybe it's much more than that.

More than one extended comedy bit.

Because Rudy . . . he feels very real. And for once, I feel real, too.

I pick up my phone and text:

How soon can you pack your bags?

* * *

Very soon, it turns out.

Two days later, Rudy's standing in my doorway, three guitar cases, a rolling suitcase, a messenger bag, and a few overstuffed cardboard boxes balanced precariously in his arms or deposited on my doormat.

"I hope this is light enough," he says, eyeing his bags. "Margs was kind enough to store my amps and some other gear and clothes in the basement for now. Though I'm sure that time will come, too. It's probably destined to be a fine wine cellar or at-home theater room."

"Definitely light enough," I say, stepping outside to pick up a box of records. "Except—bad news. I don't have a record player."

Rudy grunts, picking up the two other boxes, somehow juggling them with all the other bags at once. Probably a trick he learned on the road. "I noticed. One should be coming in the mail tomorrow. My token of appreciation."

"Seriously?" I grin, almost dropping the box as I try to reach out to him for a clumsy one-armed hug. Rudy looks at the records, horror-struck at the idea of them falling onto the concrete stoop, and I pull back my hand. "That was sweet of you. Though that doesn't get you out of the rat poison, you know?"

"Ha-ha." He steps over the threshold, dropping the boxes and bags, and then lovingly removes all three guitar case straps from his back and leans them one after another against the wall. "I brought three of my babies. I hope that's okay, but I couldn't pick just one."

"Sure. Whatever you need to feel at home. For now," I tack on, a reminder to us both that this is just a transition period. No further expectations.

"My bass, my guitars, records, some black T-shirts, sweatshirts, jeans. My laptop and gear for recording and mixing." He shrugs. "I'm a simple man."

I give him space as he spends the next hour settling into his "bedroom." I hadn't ever used the closet for much—cardboard boxes filled with too many booties and statement necklaces from my twenty-something bar-crawling days, books by dead white men I haven't read since college, some barbells I used approximately once, a printer that hasn't worked properly in years. Most of it I either tossed or put out on the sidewalk, and the rest I convinced Frank and Estelle to store in their basement. They were very agreeable in helping with the cause, mostly because they were confident this foray would lead to great, hassle-free entertainment on their part.

I knock on the frame around the partially opened door to Rudy's room, not wanting to invade his private space unannounced.

"Come in," he says, and as I crack the door open wider, he gestures grandly, arms sweeping to showcase the fifty or so square feet of space filled to the brim with his belongings. He's wrangled a makeshift rack out of an old curtain rod and some hangers, inflated a tall, surprisingly luxurious-looking air mattress, and even hung up a few framed band posters and photos. It occurs to me now, seeing the simple scraps of Rudy's existence—more college dorm than Fifth Avenue—that we're both in our thirties, and both still scraping to get by.

If opposites attract, I should be with . . . I don't know, a banker or something financial-adjacent. A Wall Street guy. Which, admittedly, makes me queasy to imagine it, but what are we doing, me and Rudy?

How can we make it work together if we can barely make it work alone?

Are we just going to sink twice as fast? Double the weight?

"All set up," Rudy says, smiling at me, and I shove those thoughts down. I'm getting ahead of myself. Besides, that's the whole point of this experiment, right? Finding the success we both deserve. Improving our life circumstances. "I'll get the best sleep of my New York life in here—no streetlights or sirens, no testosterone-amped motorcyclists revving their engines in the middle of the night. It's perfect, really."

"I like what you've done with the place. Is that a signed poster of The Jam?" Rudy nods, looking slightly awed by my musical knowledge. *Thanks, Dad.* "Are you hungry? I was thinking we could get takeout for dinner. My treat."

"Of course. We need sustenance to go along with that contractual whiskey toast. I hope Scotch is okay, because I brought a mostly full bottle of Glenlivet. Eighteen year."

I whistle. Not well, scratchy and pitchy, but it gets the point across. "Damn. Eighteen. Was that courtesy of your Ronny money?"

Rudy winces hearing Ronny's name. "Nope. Courtesy of Margs. She bought it for the whole house last Christmas, and Sheeraz was stingy about what special occasions were deemed special enough. I snuck it into my suitcase on the way out. Since we won't have roommate moments to celebrate anymore, it only feels fair that as the one being unceremoniously kicked out, I get to keep the Scotch."

"That sounds perfectly reasonable to me."

"Thank you." He grins.

We spend the next hour debating the merits of burgers versus tacos versus dumplings. It's already everything I'd wanted from a roommate experience—though perhaps slightly less than ideal on an empty stomach.

"Have you tried the Suya place on Franklin?" I ask, my belly omitting an ominous growl.

Rudy shakes his head. "Suya?"

"Delicious Nigerian meat kebabs. End of discussion. My treat, my decision."

"Wow." Rudy squints at me as he rubs his thumb thoughtfully against his chin scruff. "That's how it's going to be around here, huh?"

"Yep." I wave him off as I jab in our delivery order—one

beef, one chicken, one shrimp kebab. Extra rice. Every additional topping—egg, avocado, plantain, kale. I'm about to ask for his preferred spice level when I decide not to open another conversational can and choose "extra spicy" for both of us.

Order complete, I toss my phone on the love seat cushion next to me and look up to see a round of Scotch waiting on the coffee table. "Phenomenal service. Thanks, roomie."

"You're welcome. *Roomie.*" He raises his glass, the amber liquid twinkling in the dying light filtering through my small front windows. "Here's to the next phase of the Great Elvira Challenge. We've canvassed the work side pretty thoroughly, with, er . . . limited success. And we've just barely survived our first big friend outing."

"Second," I say, lifting my glass next to his. "You've been exposed to the wonders of the dear Myrtles." I cast my eyes up to the ceiling. "Who would be very disappointed to be missing this inaugural moment. I told them you were moving in tomorrow."

Rudy chuckles. "Right, yes. The Myrtles. So, all in all, we've experienced quite a bit together in a record amount of time. At least for standard New York City dating protocols."

"May this next phase bring us fewer scrapes, fewer bites—"

"And fewer reminders of our past dating errors."

We clink our glasses together heartily—though still with great care, so as not to spill a single drop of the blessed brown nectar that is most definitely above my pay grade.

We each take small sips, savoring it. Even on Marguerite's dime, one can't rush their way through a bottle of eighteen-year Scotch.

"And so it is done," I say, leaning back against the love seat. "The deal is sealed. Welcome to the Spinster Cave."

"Maybe it's time for a new name?"

I shake my head. "Too soon. You just got here. Besides, Estelle and Frank spent way too much on that custom sign."

Rudy laughs, and we're quiet for a few minutes. I swirl the

rest of the Scotch in my glass in slow circles, watching the light from the window take its last gasp of breath for the day. Soon the orange glow from the streetlamps will trickle in, but for now, the cave is dark aside from a sliver of light spilling out from Rudy's room.

"It hasn't all been a failure. Right?" I ask, glancing over at Rudy.

He's already watching me.

"Of course not." Rudy smiles, and goddamn, it's such a *kind* smile. It makes me ache, the sheer kindness of it. The genuine goodness. Such a revelation, every time I see it. Everything hits me fully now, a tingly, electric wave:

Against all odds, this HeartThrobs novelty match is my *roommate.*

My friend.

A friend who is maybe, possibly, capable of being more.

Absolutely no broken hearts allowed.

Either we love fully, perfectly. Or we never love at all. No halfway. No casual. No flaming wreckage at the end of this.

Elvira, couldn't you at least have finished your fucking sentence?

I close my eyes and say a silent prayer, apologizing to the universe for cursing at a dead woman.

"I know we're not list people," I say, refocusing my thoughts, "but maybe it would help us to organize our next steps if we thought about what we've learned. Any recurring themes from our time together."

"That sounds like an excellent idea," Rudy says, taking the last swig of his drink and putting the glass down on the table. He pulls out his phone and opens a blank digital Post-it note. "One: we've discovered that we've both gone on dates with terrible humans. And the universe, cruel mistress that she is, likes to remind us of these poor decisions, despite living in a city with over eight million people. But"—he ticks a finger up in the air—"to acknowledge the silver lining here, it's been good fodder. Sarah-with-an-H and Hashtag are nothing if not tremendous characters for future comedic endeavors."

"Fair point. Perhaps the universe threw them in our paths on purpose. Maybe I was forced to witness Hashtag's overly coiffed hair again for a good cause." I grit my teeth and cringe at the thought of those shiny curls. Of Hashtag, period. In hindsight, I'm glad I set him on fire. What if I'd accidentally fucked him otherwise? "So, one solid positive. We also discovered our shared love of al pastor tacos. Maybe we're meant to co-own a taco truck?"

Rudy snorts as he shakes his head emphatically. "No way. I'm not about to get into the gringo taco business. I have far too much respect for authentic Mexican food to bastardize it. An Irish-Italian has no business in the taco industry."

"Okay. That's a hard no."

"Maybe," Rudy says, squinting at the very short list on his phone, "we focus on the things we shouldn't do to start? That's useful, too. For example: No taco truck. No skating rink. No dog walking start-up. No working with old misogynistic music gods."

I laugh. "We were decent at forgery. Clementine's publisher was very grateful for the signed pages. Not a peep about any grammatical wrongdoings."

"Ah, yes. Definite positive. Maybe we have an illustrious future ahead of us scamming checks? Or selling fake autographed headshots on eBay. You'd be shocked to know what some people are willing to pay at the cons I go to. I once saw a signed photo of the guy who voiced Howard the Duck go for eighteen hundred dollars. Partly because it included some of his cigar ash smudged on the picture. But still."

"That's more than my monthly rent. *Our* monthly rent," I correct, because it is temporarily a shared burden. It occurs to me now for the first time—I'll have *extra money* at the end of the month, a nearly unheard-of phenomenon in my bank account. There'll be no risk of overdrafting for something as pathetically inexpensive as a HeartThrobs Ultra subscription.

Which, it should be noted, hasn't been put into further use since meeting Rudy. Dating one person is complicated enough in the best of times. And especially so when that dating is fueled by the prediction of an old psychic who keeled over dead on your watch.

But Rudy . . . has *he* flipped?

Suddenly my fingers itch with the urge to log on, to see when Rudy was last active. But then if he checks, he'd think *I* was active. Quite the conundrum.

I suppose I could just . . . ask. I do excel at blunt questions.

But somehow, this feels too sensitive and precarious, even for me.

Mostly because I don't feel prepared to hear that he's still considering other options. We might not be defined. But that doesn't mean we're not *something*.

"Lucy?" Rudy nudges my elbow, leaning in close enough that I can smell his shampoo. Sharp and clean and simple. Castile soap. That feels very Rudy to me. No frills, multifunctional, gets the job done. Why use three products when you could use one? "Are you about to pass out from low blood sugar?"

I blink and shake my head. "You should know, though, as my roommate, that my hanger can be a dark and powerful thing. I can't be held accountable for the things I do while undernourished."

"I brought some peanut butter with me. Want me to spoon some in? A peanut butter lollipop—that's what my mom used to call it. Saved me and Rocco from mauling each other alive at least a hundred times."

It's strange, hearing Rudy casually name-drop an A-list celebrity this way. Knowing his *sibling* is maybe off on a red carpet somewhere, wearing a suit that costs as much as Rudy makes in a year. Rocco feels like nothing but a figment of star-dusted Hollywood imagination. The opposite of Rudy, who is flesh and blood, freckles and chin stubble, sweat and Castile.

"I can hold out for dinner," I say, "but I will, however, take a peanut butter pop every morning to start my day."

"I'll make note."

"Speaking of notes, where were we with our rather pathetic list?"

"Forgery. Item two on the positives column."

"Right. Maybe something like ghostwriting? Not that I've had much luck selling words."

"Hey. Not *yet*, you haven't."

Rudy winks at me, and it has an instantaneous warming effect on my entire body.

I don't know if it's something he picked up in his acting days or a natural God-given talent, but he has the smoothest wink I've ever seen. He could do a wink master class for extra funds.

I don't suggest this out loud.

"How about," he continues, seemingly unaware of the great power of his wink, "the fact that we reminded two awful exes how well-suited they were for one another? Bob has us to thank for reuniting his parents."

"Oh my God, yes!" I slap the arm of the love seat so hard, Rudy startles and nearly drops his phone. "And let us not forget how my deeply uncomfortable hypothetical brought Georgia and her overzealous customer together."

Rudy nods, looking thoughtful. "We're pretty much a pair of grown-up Cupids in the flesh. Whether or not those people are better off together, who's to say. But we helped make it happen, and without an app. Real-life meet cutes."

I stand up, partly to monitor the window for the delivery man, and partly because there's a rush of hot tingly energy rushing through my limbs. Like, as scrappy as this list may be, we're actually onto something. "Matchmaking. Terrible exes and dates that make for great stories. You're of course well-acquainted with spinning embarrassing or disappointing life moments into comedy gold. That's what *Eclipsed Too Soon* is all about, really. Using life's lemons to make some damn good lemonade. *Spiked* lemonade, if you will."

"You might not get paid to tell your stories, but I'd say you make some pretty fine spiked lemonade, too. It's the writer in you." He cuts me off before I can argue—I'm *not* a writer. I have the rejections archived in my inbox to prove it. "You take everything you see, everything you experience, and store it away in that wild brain of yours," he continues, reaching out for my hand as I pace by in front of him. I stop, keep my hand locked in his. "Sure, I might be the one who's done shows, but I see the way you make people laugh. Georgia. Carole at Little Zelda's, who's seen everyone who's anyone in the New York comedy scene, and you made her laugh more than I've ever personally witnessed."

"Stop. Carole? Really?"

"Yes. Really. You made my friends laugh, even in some horribly uncomfortable moments during our big night out. I've seen Frank laugh around you, and he strikes me as a tough nut to crack. And . . . you make me laugh. All the time. With the absolute weirdest shit I've ever heard in my life. But somehow, it works."

I'm not sure what to say. Because I don't want to *say* anything.

I want to fall into his lap, grab his face in my hands.

I want to kiss him. No more chin or cheek, no more halfway.

Whatever this is, whatever we are, it's never felt more real for me.

More inevitable.

Because Rudy isn't a story, a novelty, a feather in my dating cap; I couldn't care less that he was ever on TV, that his brother is a superstar. None of that matters.

He matters. That's it. Him. Us.

"Rudy, I need to tell—"

The doorbell rings.

"Oh, good, you won't have to faint," Rudy says, smiling as he drops my hand. Clueless. No sense whatsoever of what might have transpired had our Suya not appeared.

Am I imagining the chemistry?

Rudy is kind and warm and supportive, and I'm reading into that more than I should?

"How fortuitous," I mutter as I stumble over to the door. I sign the check in a daze, close the door, drop the brown bag on the table as I settle back in on the love seat. I leave an inch between us. Maybe it's for the best, the doorbell interrupting when it did. This is only night one of summer camp, and already I'm thinking about hurling myself onto Rudy's lap. I have to be more careful than that. *We* have to be more careful.

Pull yourself together.

We tear through the bag of kebab bowls and eat in a companionable silence. We divvy up the proteins as we go, both of us careful to make sure we're getting even splits of chicken and beef and shrimp. A mutual, nonverbal agreement.

I take my last perfect bite of spicy shrimp and sweet plantain and sit back.

"That was obscenely good," Rudy says, and then he pours another round of the Scotch. We clink glasses again, this time to Elvira. Because, as Rudy puts it, "Without her, I wouldn't be here with you, which means I might not have discovered Suya. And *that* would be a tragedy."

I laugh and take a small sip, and then I lean my head back, close my eyes.

Matchmaking.

Bad dates.

Storytelling.

Spiked lemonade.

I let the words swirl, shift, sink deep into my mind.

I take another sip, precariously, my head still back and my eyes still closed, and then—

"I have an idea," I say, the words popping out before I've even made sense of the flurry of thoughts snowballing together in my brain. But it's all there, a glimmering, golden knot nesting in the dark edges of my consciousness, and I yank at it, unspool it, latch on for dear life.

"We do a live comedy show," I start. "You and me. We have people get onstage to share their cringiest bad dates—maybe we act them out as they go—competing for the honor of the 'worst date.' Really the '*best* worst date' by our standards, because they'll take home all the praise and glory. We could even open with some of our own worst date stories. Monologues to warm them up, inspire them. Show them it's okay to share these awful stories. Better than okay. Cleansing, even, to put them out there in the wild and *laugh* about them. Hell, what a shining example we are—our worst date, a woman dying practically on our laps, brought us together."

Together.

Not quite. Almost. Maybe.

I rush past this one tiny but also somehow gargantuan word—far heavier than three short syllables have any right to be. I can't be distracted, not until I've finished.

"The audience," I continue, eyes still closed, "votes on the winner of the 'best worst date,' who then gets free drinks for the night, mingling and commiserating with the other contenders." I see it in front of me, the end of the radiant thread, all of it unfurled now in one neat line. "The event is for everyone, but with a special focus on singles—the potential to strike up matches after the show. People united by their shared worst date stories. We mingle, too. Help people feel at ease. Show them it's okay to have underwhelming dating experiences—maybe it's all for a greater good in the end. There's more out there for them."

Just like there was for us.

I take a gulp of air, lightheaded from everything that's shifted inside of me. Everything that's been purged.

Rudy's silent in response, and I lift the lid of my left eye just a fraction, peeking out at him. I'm terrified, suddenly, of what he might think. The idea exploded out so quickly, I can't tell if it's genius or dogshit or something murky and shapeless in between.

He's staring at me, those deep brown eyes bright with a new kind of intensity. Maybe he has some of that Irish witch in him, too, because I wouldn't be surprised if he's seeing through my skin right now. I feel . . . penetrated.

It's an incredibly pleasant feeling.

I keep going then, both eyes open, watching him watch me. "It's comedy, it's romance, it's a creative outlet for both of us in different ways, the culmination of things we've been working toward our entire lives—whether or not that work was intentional. We could start with a local show, maybe even at Little Zelda's? If it's a hit, we take it on the road. Maybe our *great destiny* isn't, you know, finding the cure for cancer or a solution for world peace, but making people laugh still feels pretty damn important. And starting up a comedy show about our mutual dating fails seems . . . especially appropriate for us, I'd say. It could be the beginning of a bigger brand—a podcast, a book—I don't know. But if nothing else, it's a start."

I stop.

Really and fully finished this time. Like I've sliced open the back of my head, given it a hearty shake, and drained myself of every drop of inspiration.

When Rudy still doesn't say anything, I down the rest of my Scotch. A sacrilege, but my racing nerves demand, and I obey.

"Say something. I beg you."

Rudy downs the rest of his Scotch, too.

"I'm glad that toast was to Elvira," he says, a grin slowly edging up the corners of his lips. It spreads wide, wider, widest across his cheeks, his freckles crinkling and shaping new, un-charted constellations. I want to trace every single one of them with my fingertip. "Because she would be proud right now. I can feel it."

"Really?" I whisper.

He nods, and leans in until our foreheads touch.

"Really. Because your idea?"

I take a breath, hold it, my lungs burning.

"It feels like our destiny."

Chapter 14
Rudy

A delicate union of skin, flesh, and meat.

I've never fancied myself a great graphics design person, but since yesterday when Lucy and I figured out what our "grand" purpose will be—or *might* be, temporarily, step one of what could be a lifelong journey—my brain's been firing on all cylinders.

Spiked Lemonade: A Best Worst Date Show.

Nobody here is trying to win a Nobel Prize with this destiny. But I do think there's something extremely cathartic about releasing these kinds of feelings in a room full of strangers—for us, and for them. That must count for something, right?

First up today, I took the Kool-Aid Man, turned his contents from red to yellow. Added some floating lemon wedges and turned the eyes into bottles of booze. The logo script is inspired by a local cider can they sell at Little Zelda's—a cursive font that starts large and gradually gets smaller as the word goes on. It's sharp, a little retro, and full of character. Anyone who sees this design should immediately expect a gimmicky show.

We are all about the gimmick. Within reason.

Lucy's words that seemed to explode out of nowhere—kind of like Elvira's, really—gave me everything I needed for a pitch:

Spiked Lemonade, hosted by Little Zelda's alum Rudy Riziero and bright newcomer Lucy Minninger—a live show where people share their cringiest bad dates with the hosts and the audience, competing for the honor of the "best worst date." Audience members tell their stories as the hosts act out some choice tidbits of the monologues. The audience votes on the winner of the "best worst date"—winner gets free drinks for the night, mingling and commiserating with other contenders. Maybe even finding a kindred spirit in the group. A possible love match.

I fire off a quick email to Marianne, the booker for Little Zelda's and a longtime friend, including the logo and pitch. Maybe I'm biased, but it feels like a phenomenal idea. An instant classic. I could send the pitch to other places, too, to up our chances, but I think Marianne will truly dig the concept. I've had a few conversations with her about some less-than-ideal first dates—common ground for most certified single New Yorkers. There's that, and the fact that my own show's been bleeding out people each month. *Eclipsed Too Soon* is on hiatus until after the holidays—too many special shows blocking up the calendar—but maybe a change of pace could help bring the numbers back up to snuff in the new year. Help keep my wallet padded.

Lucy is unaware that I've already made a logo—and reached out to a potential buyer. But I couldn't resist. It really is an ideal forum for both of us; she was spot-on about that. Lucy's natural ability to turn awkwardness into humor that puts people at ease, paired with my knowledge of producing a show and being able to improv and poke fun at embarrassing stories from my past. We're both shameless, at least for the right cause.

Seven minutes later, Marianne emails back: Yesss!!! This is awesome! It could be a great show to start the new year! I'll follow up with details and dates soon.

Damn.

That was fast.

A testament, I hope, to the kind of show we have on our hands.

I get up and head for the living room, where Lucy's been busy writing, sketching, Venn-diagramming the show. Her work ethic is really something to behold. It's shocking, honestly, that she can't keep a steady job, aside from Clementine.

It occurs to me now, watching her work, that maybe I should have clued her in before reaching out to Marianne. Maybe I broke the partner code, jumping the gun. Admittedly, I suck at the whole "partner" thing—it's been a long time.

I knock on the door frame to announce myself, and she jumps out of her chair, shrieking at the top of her lungs.

"You scared the shit out of me!"

Her reaction resembles that of the woman from *Psycho* in the infamous shower scene. Meaning: it's extreme. Extremely extreme. After taking a moment to let her compose herself, I say, "How can I avoid that next time? Apparently, a knock won't do, so . . . ?"

She gives a sheepish smile as she settles back down into her chair. "Sorry. I've been in this cave alone for so long, I need to get properly used to the idea of coexisting with another human. And I was just so in the zone, trying to work on the specifics of the show. But I was about to get you anyway, to ask for you to weigh in."

I walk over to where Lucy's sitting at her tiny desk, pushed up against the front wall with windows, the brightest spot in the apartment. I crouch down and stick my head over her shoulder, squint a little to start reading what she's got. It's substantial. Different bits for different situations. She has a list for every kind of date scenario and what props could be used to set the scene: tables, chairs, plates, glasses, candles. Concert dates, restaurant dates, outdoor picnic dates, movie dates, bar dates. You name the location, she has a scenario and what we might need to riff on the situation. I'm starting to see just how much experience Lucy really has with dating.

I don't have the heart to tell her we most likely won't be using Carrot Top prop stuff like this. Not the right moment— I want to build her confidence, not break it.

"This is a great start," I say, straightening and taking a step back. "And I, uh, have some news. I . . . made a logo and wrote up a short paragraph about what *Spiked Lemonade* could be, and sent it off to Marianne at Little Zelda's. She instantly bit!" I'm equal parts excited and terrified, saying this out loud. When Lucy doesn't respond, I keep talking: "She wants to run it right after the new year. We have a home for our show. Just like that! Er. If you want it, that is."

Lucy looks at me, blank-faced for a beat. But then she smiles, slowly, and that smile grows bigger, the biggest smile I've seen on her face to date. She stands, squealing with pure glee, and gives me a strong—organ-crushing strong—hug. Even still, all I feel is relief.

"What?" she yells. "Of course I want it! But how did you do that so fast? It hasn't even been twenty-four hours!"

I shrug, which is difficult in our tight hug. "I couldn't stop thinking about it last night. Got up this morning, started working on a logo, used your ideas for the pitch paragraph, and . . . sent it. I think I even forgot to put in a subject line. I was that guy. But it worked. Want to see the logo?" She nods, her chin bumping against my shoulder. I untangle our limbs and step back, grabbing my phone from my back pocket. I scroll through and then tilt the screen to show her my handiwork.

Another squeal. "Oh my God, Rudy! It's perfect! It reminds me of those delicious cider cans I see all over Brooklyn."

Lucy hugs me again. This time, though, it's less restrictive. It's softer, more affectionate. She grips my shoulders, her head nuzzled between my collarbones and neck. I reply in kind with my own nuzzle. Her skin smells like . . . a nice breeze. There's a gentle hint of her soap or perfume that reminds me of spring in Prospect Park. It's fresh, a bit sweet. Floral, but not in an obnoxious way.

I take a deep breath.

Pheromones are no joke. Her smell is even more intoxicating than the Glenlivet.

What is happening here?

Are we just blindly fulfilling the prophecy laid down by Elvira? Or is it more than that? A home, a show, a few near-kisses. All the pieces compile to make what, exactly?

A love story?

Love.

That might be going a little too far too soon, but either the Spinster Cave is luring me in with some kind of dark Venus flytrap–like magic, or there really is a genuine connection brewing here. Either way, getting romantic with your new roommate of a whole *day* feels out of bounds. Though . . . maybe we were never going to be just roommates. That was never in the cards for us, was it?

"We've been hugging for a long time, haven't we?" Lucy asks, cutting off my spiral.

I drop my arms and step back. I'm sure I have more than a little red forming on my cheeks, courtesy of that damn Irish blood. "Sorry. I got swept up in everything. Thinking about what a wild ride it's been. Wondering about what comes next."

Lucy reaches out for me again, her fingers gently skimming up and down my arms, wrist to bicep, bicep to wrist. She leaves a trail of goosebumps in her wake. "You have nothing to apologize for. I hugged you. It's just . . . a lot to process, isn't it? That this started on an app, and then we watched someone die on our *first date*. We dove right in, trying to figure out what Elvira meant about us being successful together. The dates, the show, the new living arrangement." She pauses and takes a breath, and I take one, too. "It actually feels," she says, "like we're a real couple, doesn't it?"

She said it first.

The deep-seated, stupidly patriarchal part of me is embarrassed that I didn't initiate this conversation. But the rest of me, the real and better me, feels straight-up joy.

Of course, I'm not eloquent or confident enough to express that feeling properly. "Well," I say, "just because we're living together and starting a comedy show together that revolves around dating doesn't mean we have to force being a couple."

Lucy looks shocked.

I'm shocked, too. I mean, *Jesus*. That was the absolute wrong way to respond.

Choose your words wisely, you thirty-four-year-old dumbass!

"What I'm trying to say, and totally butchering, is that I'd like to give it a chance, too." I lift her hand off my wrist, wrap my fingers around hers. "I just don't want us to feel like we *have to* because of all these other moving parts. I like you, Lucy. You're hilarious, smart, beautiful, and quite possibly the most unique person I've *ever* met. You wear your heart on your sleeve. You can be impulsive but also extremely calculated, and I don't know how you do both so well, but you—"

Before I can get another word out, we kiss.

Or Lucy kisses me, that is, crushing herself against me, a hot whirl of skin and lips and hair.

And I kiss back.

Of course I do.

I feel weightless, completely full and completely empty at the same time. I gasp and breathe in deep, breathe in Lucy— that spring breeze, mixed with milky green tea and strawberry jam—steadying myself against the sheer force of her.

Our bodies rearrange on instinct, mold against one another. Her arms wrap around my neck; mine find her waist. Her lips are delicate, like . . . butterfly wings. Which is maybe the goddamn sappiest thing I've ever thought in my entire life, but it's exactly how it feels. Delicate, but eager. There's no hesitation.

I'm not hesitating, either.

I stop for just a second, pull back an inch to take in everything that's happening. Lucy's parted lips as her eyelids flutter and then lift. She catches me staring and smiles. I smile back and kiss her again.

I've always analyzed, and overanalyzed, the difference between kisses. The lust-fueled kisses versus the loving ones, awkward or confident or overconfident, tipsy, sloppy, bitey, cutesy, slow burn, burnout, no burn at all. I'd thought I'd experienced every kind of kiss out there, but Lucy's feels different. Not easily categorized. Passionate and fierce, but with the honesty and openness of a "holy shit, this feels right" kind of kiss.

I can feel her heartbeat with each push and pull. Mine is pounding, too.

If this were a movie, the camera would pull up and do a 360-degree movement, circling around us. I can see it all, like I'm kissing her and watching us from above at the same time. Silver screen magic.

After a while—it's impossible to say how long, minutes, hours—we stop and hug again. Back to the shoulder and neck nuzzle. Silent for a moment. Just here, together.

"If I'm being totally honest," Lucy says then, quietly, tilting her gaze up to study me, "I've been wanting to kiss you for a while now. But I wasn't sure how you felt. Our unique situation made it even more . . . unpredictable."

It's not the first time someone's said something like this to me. Unlike Lucy, I have an incredibly solid poker face.

"Well, if *I'm* being totally honest, I've wanted to kiss you since my slip-up at the concert. The infamous awkward chin peck. Then we had that near-kiss at the rink, but after we agreed on being roommates . . . I didn't want to make things more complicated."

Lucy tugs on her earlobe, maybe a nervous habit I haven't seen before. There's still a lot of Lucy to learn. I want to, though. I want to learn everything. "This is all complicated. But right now, this moment with you, it felt . . . easy. Like it was the only right choice to make."

I lean my head down to kiss her forehead, a slow trail along her hairline. It feels like maybe the most intimate kiss yet. "I agree. And I'm glad we did it on our own terms, not completely driven by our shared hidden agenda of world domination."

Lucy crinkles her nose. "World domination, huh? You sure do dream big. I was just looking for some basic job security."

"That's a good goal, too." I laugh. "Are you hungry?" All the confessing—and kissing—has made me suddenly ravenous. "I can make a grilled cheese if you're interested? Maybe even open a can of tomato soup? Might be too ambitious to look through your utensil drawer for a can opener, but I would do it. For you."

Lucy grabs my hand and leads me toward the kitchen. "It's actually always on the table in plain sight. I go through a lot of soup and beans in this cave."

Lucy and I have been lounging on the couch, talking about the show for hours. Her legs are in my lap, and the rest of her is propped up by three pillows that can't seem to keep her comfortable. She adjusts them. Wriggles. Sighs. Readjusts. Wriggles. The easiest solution would be to change positions—which would involve taking her legs off of me—but she's clearly determined to be perched in this particular manner.

In the week since that first kiss (or more like full-on make-out session, but still, the first), the biggest shift has been in our personal space boundaries. As in—there are none. Hence, the current sitting arrangement.

It feels nice, though, being so close to someone at all times.

I forgot how much these little physical connections add up—what they do for your headspace and overall contentment level, that sense of security. It's been so long since I felt anything but the adrenaline rush of a satisfying hookup. I want that, too—the hookup. With Lucy. Obviously. But . . . slow and steady.

I give Lucy's ankle a soft squeeze and then put my mind back on the show.

"I have an idea for our ad campaign," I say. "How about: 'Think you've had the worst first date? Ours featured a freshly dead psychic. Come to *Spiked Lemonade* and share your story with us! Maybe you'll meet another worst first dater, and make the night your best first date!'"

Lucy takes a moment to contemplate. Her brow is furrowed, a look that's extra severe on her already sharp face. Sharp on the outside, soft on the inside. Softer than I would have guessed when we first met. "Hmm. I like it, but it's a little wordy. And we want to be sensitive when approaching Elvira's demise. It's a good launchpad, though. Maybe we can have a few different ads? What if we make postcard-size fliers with a brief description of some of our bad dates, and then have lines like: 'Can you top this?' Or 'What's your story?'"

A great idea. "For example," I say, "take your Hashtag story. We make a postcard with a tiki bar on it, maybe add some flames to top off the image. It could say, 'I set my date's hair on fire with a fun tropical drink. Does your worst first top this?'"

Lucy kicks her legs up with excitement, her feet narrowly missing my face. "Exactly like that! I can see the postcards scattered all around Little Zelda's, finding curious eyes. Other local spots, too. I don't want to be all digital in our approach. We should be building buzz on the streets. Retro promo."

"Yeah. I like that. More grassroots, and you can get right at the people who go to shows. No social media algorithm cutting into who sees them."

Lucy sits up and kisses me with so much gusto she ends up almost knocking both of us off the end of the love seat. Why the hell didn't she invest in a sofa? Who only buys a love seat? I grip the arm to keep us steady as we kiss some more, Lucy moving onto my lap as we go—our hands roaming, exploring, escalating to borderline too hot and heavy, considering our circumstances and consequences—and then we slowly pull apart to get back to the brainstorming. I stand up to cool off and head to the fridge for a seltzer. Polar, obviously. I sit down at the small kitchen table and take a few sips, trying to focus on my next line of questioning, but my mind keeps wandering. Lucy's lips. Her fingers running through the back of my hair while we kissed, tangling, hot, around my neck.

What comedy show are we writing again?

I can still feel her warm skin under my palms, the soft curve of her hips, and then her . . .

Wow, record time crushing a seltzer. I crunch the empty can in my fist just as my stomach emits a loud rumble. Lucy looks up at me with big eyes, inquisitive but smiling.

"Everything okay down there?"

I nod, patting my stomach. Welp, sometimes it just takes some awkward bodily function to get back on track.

Our show. Dating. Failures.

We haven't discussed the plan to act out these bad dates yet, but since I said we're going to improv on the audience's stories to Marianne, we have to follow through.

"Lucy," I start in slow, "have you ever done improv or anything in the acting world?"

Lucy looks slightly taken aback. "Improv? No. But I was in all the high school plays. Mostly in the chorus, but I had a few speaking lines in *Guys and Dolls* and *My Fair Lady*. I might not have been the main attraction, but I think I can retell a bad date story. We'll be fed all the gory details, and then we just try to make everyone laugh. Should be easy-peasy."

I want to choose my next words wisely. Because while basic natural talent doesn't need to be taught—it *can't* be taught, you either have it or you don't—the ability does have to be harnessed. I'm not an expert, but I had enough Comedy 101 lessons as a kid to understand that much, at least. "Performing in front of an audience, especially your peers, is awesome experience to have under your belt. I'd choose a room of strangers over friends and family any day. And you're right about the stories being a good inspiration well, meaning we don't have to create something out of nothing. But there *are* some basic rules so we don't get stuck onstage."

Lucy stands and walks slowly over to the kitchen table, settling down across from me.

"Okay then, so should we practice?" she asks in a matter-of-fact way that gives me the impression she genuinely wants to learn.

"That's a great idea! Let's run through a few rules first. I promise they'll help you shine—enhance your already amazing natural ability to crack people up, just being you."

Lucy beams, her dimples on full display.

Damn. That smile. I see it all day, every day now, and it still doesn't get old.

"Well then, Professor Riziero, paint—I mean, *teach*—me like one of your French girls."

"Ahh, excellent *Titanic* reference . . . see? You're hopping on the nostalgia train already. Always a wise move, especially with the Little Zelda's crowd. So, improv. I was taught by a master, and essentially it boils down to some basic rules. Ready?"

Lucy nods and pulls her cell phone out of her pocket to take notes.

"Okay, here it goes. First rule: Always go with the flow. Go along with whatever we start with, no matter what, staying the course. Never say no. Second rule: Add to the story that's being presented. Keep the original story moving with statements and gestures that build the version of the story we're creating on the spot."

Lucy continues to take notes, head down and focused on her screen. Despite her supposed lack of organization skills, right now she looks very much the part of an overachieving straight-A student.

"Third and final rule: There are no mistakes, only opportunities to make more jokes."

Lucy looks up and laughs. "That's it? That's how my friends and I have been telling stories our entire lives. At least I have been, anyway. They always get longer, spinning out with more additions. It's about taking an old story and making it new. We do say no, though, and cut each other off, but we've never had an audience. I got it covered, trust me."

She's right. I didn't need to give her this pep talk. I should trust the process. Trust her.

I stand up from the table. "You're right. You have a natural talent, and you should always trust that. Honestly, we might not need to do that much if these stories are as terrible as some of ours. The props might not even be necessary. But we'll feel it out as we go. Follow our instincts. Full disclosure . . . the 'master class' I took in improv came from reading Tina Fey's book *Bossypants,* so not a traditional class, per se. But c'mon, it's Tina Fey."

Lucy stands, too, and comes around to my side of the table. "I think," she says, "you're a great teacher, even if you don't have a degree."

"You did seem to be taking copious notes."

"Notes? I wasn't taking notes. I got it all, though. Always agree, add to the story, and there are no mistakes. Grace and Susie were texting about meeting up over Thanksgiving."

I give her a raised eyebrow, like an angry disciplinarian. She grins in response. "Well, I'm glad you were paying at least some attention to me. But here I was, thinking you were taking serious notes like some former straight-A student over there."

"I was actually the salutatorian of my very small high school. No big deal, just a brainiac flexing over here. I barely even had to study." She crinkles her whole forehead and somehow also pulses her ears up and down. Like she's literally flexing her brain.

It's ridiculous. I love it.

She stops flexing and reaches out for my hands. "I know this is really new and all, but they were asking if you'd be coming back to PA. Not on Thanksgiving proper, but that weekend. I said I'd ask."

Without a tinge of hesitation, I hear myself say: "That'd be fun. I'd love to meet the people who gave you such fine improv skills. And to watch you slay with your quick-witted retorts."

Lucy looks shocked.

Did I fail this test? Was I supposed to balk a little?

I don't think we're playing games. I hope not, at least.

Lucy's quiet for a minute—sixty seconds longer than usual—and then she lets go of my hands, grabbing me tight around the waist instead.

"You're very cool, you know that? I was afraid to ask and have it be weird."

I squeeze her back. "Well, I think it's very cool that you asked. Lifelong friends seem like the toughest crowd, so I'm flattered you think I can handle it. And also terrified that I could screw it up. I mean, as a former *celebrity*, I know there are many assumptions that come with the territory when dating a dear friend."

Lucy stares at me straight on. Those deep green eyes. How could I have possibly said no to those eyes? I mean, it should have been easy, in theory. We're early in, and this is a full-on hometown tour.

But it felt good to say yes.

"I'm not worried. You make me happy, and my friends will see that, even if one may have had a crush on you or your brother. Or if someone read a Reddit rumor about you doing illicit things in the bathroom during middle school. Or saw in the tabloids way back that you once hated on Philly so bad, you were banned from the city limits."

I gasp. "*What?* Excuse me? Firstly, if there was a crush, I hope they ended up with a ginger. Unless it was Rocco they were after. Then I just pity them. And yes, there was a rumor in middle school that involved someone catching me being intimate with myself, but it was JUST A RUMOR! Everyone in public school was looking to rip on the kid from TV! And okay, I'm a Giants fan, and I watched a guy in Philly get his Giants hat ripped from his head and *set on fire* because he cheered for a touchdown. It's brutal down there! I like the people and the food, just not the sports. I was kicked out of the stadium, not the city itself, thank you. I'm hoping your friends can move past that, or this might never work."

"I assure you, my friends don't give a shit about Philly sports. Or your middle school masturbation habits."

"Great! Then we should get along swimmingly."

"Great." Lucy grins.

It's set then. I've made my bed.

I'm going to meet the parents.

Chapter 15

Lucy

Under the stars, become one with the moon.

Thanksgiving at the Minninger house proves to be just like always: frenzied, grumbly, haphazard, and—ultimately—delicious, against all odds.

My parents bicker, in what feels like a scripted piece of annual tradition, about the logistics of getting the obscenely oversized turkeys on the grill—my mother's patented way of cooking the birds—and when to put the sausage stuffing in the oven, the various dairy-drenched casseroles, rolls, pies. The color-coded time sheet that looked so foolproof at eight in the morning is a scribbled-over incoherent mess by noon. Aunts and uncles and cousins descend upon our home at four, and they drink cranberry old-fashioneds—my most significant contribution to the day, other than a well-scrubbed toilet—while waiting for the dinner that is, predictably, two hours late.

My mother's telling everyone who asks—and everyone who doesn't ask—about Rudy, and we all stuff in our desserts with a side of clips from *Black Hole Sons* and *The Whiz of Riz*, everyone on their phones, pulling up every last Rudy tidbit they can find. Hopefully, his weed arrest is hard intel to come by.

I've decided not to mention *Spiked Lemonade*, as much as I'm itching to brag about our idea. I want to have a successful show under my belt before I open myself up to the family's pride and excitement. I've had enough public disappointments as it is.

Letting Rudy slip away would be disappointment enough, show or no show.

"He's coming tomorrow, you know, to our *house*," my mom says, approximately the tenth time this evening, as she sips the dregs of her first and only old-fashioned. Her tolerance for liquor is always amusingly low. Less amusing tonight. "He's meeting us first, and then some of Lucy's girlfriends will be joining in. That seems serious, doesn't it? Childhood friends and parents?"

"It's about time, isn't it?" my mom's younger sister says, glancing smugly at my twenty-five-year-old cousin at the end of the table, already married and pregnant (*twins*, no less, always an overachiever), and a freshly minted homeowner of a house not five minutes away from my aunt and uncle. The Holy Trinity of filial success.

My phone vibrates on my lap, and I look down, eager for distraction.

Rudy: You better be saving some grilled bird. My dad's sending me down with a gallon of his Italian wedding soup. Is your family asking about me as much as mine's asking about you?

I laugh so loudly, everyone else stops talking. Fifteen pairs of sharp bird eyes, all on me.

"Is that *him*?" my mom says, moony-eyed and swaying. Perhaps partly from the old-fashioned. But not exclusively.

"Is Rocco there, too?" Aunt.

"Does he still talk to Piper?" Cousin.

"What's his net worth?" Uncle.

"Should we FaceTime him to wish him a happy Thanksgiving?" Mom.

My dad, posted up quietly by the record player, gives me a pained, sympathetic look.

Ignoring everyone, I turn back to my phone.

Lucy: Oh I can guarantee you that my family is winning the contest.

Lucy: Landslide victory.

Lucy: Are you scared for tomorrow?

Rudy: Just a little. You?

Lucy: Just a little.

Lucy: More excited, though.

Rudy: Yeah. Me, too.

I almost type *I miss you*, but I have the common sense to dial it back. Too soon. Too overzealous. I'm about to put my phone down when another text comes in.

Rudy: This might sound weird, but . . .

Rudy: I miss you.

"Your backyard is literally a cornfield. And your front yard is literally the woods. And holy shit, is that a *barn*?" Rudy's spinning around in circles, open-mouthed, like we're standing in the middle of the Grand Canyon and not my parents' driveway.

I smile as I softly tap his chin closed with my palm. "I didn't realize Jersey suburbia had made you such a city slicker. Yes, that's an *actual* barn. We won't be yanking any dangly cow udders for creamer in the morning, though, sorry to say. It's just extra storage space, because apparently in the suburbs, even a basement and attic are not adequate."

It's only been two days since I said goodbye to Rudy in Brooklyn, but I'm happier than I expected to be, seeing him here. This place that still feels like home, even after so many years in the city. These woods, the fields, that *barn*. He's a piece of it all now, too.

I take a step forward to grab those ginger-stubbled cheeks for a kiss.

Rudy leans into it, nuzzling my palm.

My eyes are fluttering shut—just as the front door opens with a loud *whoosh*.

We turn to see my mother, grinning and waving like an overly caffeinated game show contestant as she *prances* down the walkway. I'd politely asked her to give us a minute—hoping for, you know, a more figurative minute. She must have set the egg timer.

"Rudy! Hello!" She closes in, and then promptly freezes in front of Rudy, a veritable snowwoman, her face looking deeply uncertain: a handshake or, dare she do it, *hug*.

"Pleasure to meet you, Mrs. Minninger," Rudy says, lips pulled tight as he bites down a grin. He lifts his arms, moving in for a proper full-on hug.

My mother is clearly delighted by this turn of events, melting as she nestles in against his chest. "I assure you," she says, her words muffled against his black sweatshirt (of course), "the pleasure is all mine. And please, call me Margaret. We want you to feel at home."

"Er. Of course, Margaret. Thank you."

She pulls away, though she keeps her palms pressed against his upper arms. "It's wonderful to meet the person who's been keeping my daughter so busy up in the big city. Not a single visit to Greendale since September! You would think we're an ocean apart." She side-eyes me, lips pursed in a tight line. And then, one second later, maybe half, looks back to Rudy with what can only be described as a rabid shit-eating grin. "But I suppose her time away from us was for a very good cause."

Cause, defined here as: marriage. A home in the suburbs, preferably in Greendale. Grandkids. Hell, maybe an in-law suite down the road.

I grab Rudy's bags and we make our way inside, my mother still latched onto his arm. She has the quintessential Eastern PA spread laid out on the living room table: three types of ring bologna arranged with cubes of cheese in varying shades of yellow and orange, a jar of grainy mustard, a dish of pick-led vegetables, deviled eggs, tomato pie, shoofly pie, *and* funny cake.

"Just a light snack," she says, handing Rudy a paper plate with a colorful cartoon turkey saying: *Let's get gobbling!* "I'm making a pot roast and mashed potatoes for when Susie and Grace come over." She turns to me then, like she's just remembered my existence. "Do you know if the kids are coming? The spouses? I need to know how many potatoes to peel."

I shake my head, slipping my phone from my pocket. "They couldn't give me a straight answer about the family units. It usually seems like a game-time decision. But I'll ask now."

"Rest assured, I can help out by eating any excess mashed potatoes," Rudy says, smiling at my mom as he tentatively picks up a few pieces of ring bologna, one of each variety. Light pink, solid dark purple, dark purple with chunky white flecks. His brows furrow as he studies the flecks.

Mom is off to the kitchen then, shouting up the stairs for Dad to come down.

"It's surprisingly good," I say, dropping my phone onto the table. "Like a sweet, cold sausage. Just don't ask about the ingredients. And use a generous dollop of mustard. Hopefully, you can learn to appreciate it, because it's an essential part of any proper PA Dutch gathering."

"So it's a rite of passage?"

"Pretty much, yes. The first round, at least. Scrapple is the second." I grin at him. "But you can load it up with apple butter if you don't like the taste."

"Huh. It's bizarre that I grew up two hours north of you, but somehow it feels like my rental car transported me into a whole different universe. I don't even recognize those pies."

"Aren't you a seasoned traveling performer? How have you not experienced such delicacies before?"

Before Rudy can respond, my phone pings. Grace. I pick it up and swipe through to read her response.

Grace: Lucy! Omg SO SORRY. The kids have been demons today, and Gwen scheduled a brewery night with her work crew without telling me. UGH. GWEN. Things are pure chaos here, and I think we have to raincheck. Can we try again over Christmas??? Dying to meet Rudy! (Or maybe we'll actually make it up to see the big tree this year! I know we say it every year, but one of these times it'll happen! LOL!) We'll have to catch up this week to hear all about Rudy meeting Margaret and Owen!

"What is it?" Rudy asks, his first piece of ring bologna suspended in his fingers midair, hovering near his lips.

"Eh. It's nothing." It's not *nothing*. It's a whole lot of disappointing something. But I press on a smile anyway. I won't let this ruin Rudy's first glimpse of Greendale. "Grace can't make it, sadly. The kids are acting up, and—"

Ping. Susie.

Susie: Is Mercury in retrograde?!? Mine are being terrors today, too, and Ollie is snotty, and now I'm starting to feel

snotty, so ah! We'll need that raincheck, too. But I second the idea of trying for Christmas! Maybe dinner at our place? (Or the tree! Yes! Remember when we did Santa Con and Lucy made out with a stranger carrying mistletoe on a fishing pole by the tree? Didn't she bring him back to the apartment? Ha ha! That's our girl!) XOXO

Welp. Smiling is impossible now.

I throw the phone down on the table, narrowly missing the vat of pickled carrots and green beans. Tears prickle along the edges of my eyes, and I try my damnedest to blink them away.

Rudy puts down his plate. "Hey. Talk to me."

"No one is coming," I mumble, not able to look him in the eyes.

His bushy brows furrow deeply. "What do you mean?"

"Susie and Grace are too busy momming."

"I'm sorry." He takes a step closer, his hand grazing my wrist. "Does this . . . happen with them a lot?"

I shrug. Sniffle. Try to cover it with a light, pathetic cough.

"I get it," he says, his fingers weaving around mine. "Remember when hometown friends used to hang out at local dives and drink way too much on Thanksgiving Eve? I spent the night with my mom on the couch, drinking Chardonnay and watching *Real Housewives of New Jersey*. My first time, for the record. My mom claims she only watches because my little cousin goes to parties at one of the star's McMansions, so she likes to keep tabs."

I laugh. Swipe at a rogue tear. "We were texting Wednesday night, but somehow you failed to mention that particular detail."

"Yes, well. I wanted to preserve some dignity. But it felt perhaps *useful* to tell you now."

"So we can mutually feel like losers?"

He nods. "Exactly. The last standing childless singletons of our hometown crews."

"I'm sorry you came all the way down to Greendale for them to ditch."

"Don't be sorry. I still get to meet your parents. And see you."

"You see me every day."

"But not like this. Not here."

I smile. *Here.*

This sacred place where no one I've dated has stood before. The magic-hour light is filtering through the living room windows, leaving Rudy doused in a warm, butter-yellow glow.

He smiles back.

I'm glad he's the first.

I'm glad it's him standing here now.

"I found him," my mother says, clomping back into the room, tugging my dad along by his sweater sleeve. "Upstairs in bed, napping off his lunch. I told him to go easy on the leftovers, but I swear his turkey sandwich was six inches tall!"

"Four inches at most," he says, smiling pleasantly. My father is as pleasant as they come. The epitome of it, really. Much like Rudy, now that I think of it. "Welcome, Rudy."

"Great to meet you, Mr. Minninger."

"Please. Owen."

Rudy nods. "Owen."

There's a slight pause, and then: "Hug already," my mom commands, putting a hand on each of their shoulders as she nudges them close. "When Rudy's in our home, he's family." Her eyes go glassy at the word. *Family.* She's no doubt seeing visions of diapered grandbabies dancing in her head.

My dad shrugs and leans in, giving Rudy a few gentle pats on the back. "Oh, ring bologna!" he exclaims, pulling back from the hug. "Three varieties. The red-carpet treatment of bologna." He grabs a plate and proceeds to build a stacked tower of bologna.

"The girls aren't coming," I say, turning to my mom.

"They aren't coming?" She frowns. "Why not?"

I reach for the cheese spread, pretend to intensely analyze the different varietals: pale yellow, bright yellow, medium orange. "Rough day with the kids. Busy spouses."

"Oh." My mom is quiet for a moment. I decide on all three kinds of cheese, stuffing each cube into my mouth in quick succession.

"Maybe it's a good thing," Rudy says, brushing his hand against the small of my back. "More quality time with all of you. I'll meet them next time I visit."

Next time.

I bite my lip as my mom instantly brightens. *Susie and Grace who?*

"Yes! You're exactly right. And I'll send you home with mashed potatoes for the rest of the week. I know my daughter isn't good for much in the kitchen. No offense," she adds, smiling over at me before she bustles back into the kitchen.

This would be a convenient moment to add that Rudy and I actually *share* a kitchen. And a living room. Bathroom. Front door. But that feels like a step too far. A step from which there is no return.

Plus, they'll assume we're having sex.

Which we're not.

But we could be.

If Rudy wants that. If I want that.

I glance over at Rudy, who is now talking to my dad over by the floor-to-ceiling shelves of records. I miss whatever Rudy says, but I see the look of deep respect on my dad's face.

Fuck.

Of course I want that.

I want that very, very much.

I shove more cheese into my mouth and follow my mom into the kitchen.

* * *

Dinner is late (true of all meals at home, not just holidays—*European chic*, as my mom says knowingly, though she's never stepped foot in Europe), loud, and wine-soaked, courtesy of the three bottles of red Rudy got yesterday from an uncle in the Italian wine business.

I've never seen my dad have more than a modest glass, not even at weddings. But he's on his third. Fourth, maybe? I've lost count. The glasses refill too quickly.

Speaking of weddings, my mother has uttered the *W* word on three separate occasions, all non-sequiturs, said with twinkly eyes in Rudy's direction. If Rudy cares, or even notices, he doesn't let on. He's laughing and joking and looking as comfortable as I've ever seen him.

Which, unfortunately, only makes me think about sex, *with him*, even more.

It's not as if the thought hasn't crossed my mind before—crossed *every* inch of my body, really. After all those long, meandering kisses. Pressed up tight against each other. Hands greedily exploring. In our tiny apartment, just the two of us. It's been impossibly long since the last time anyone scratched that particular itch.

I shouldn't be having the thought *now*, though, not while getting drunk at my childhood home with my parents.

But his comfort, *my* comfort, too, the total ease in this situation that could feel completely and utterly weird, is maybe one of the sexiest things I've ever encountered in real life. Far sexier than six-packs and biceps. This deep sense of normalcy, sitting here, in this two-hundred-year-old drafty room where I did everything for eighteen years, studied for tests and made dioramas and ate homemade pizza religiously every Friday night. With Rudy.

Rudy.

I shake my head, attempt to tune back into the table scene playing out around me.

My dad is telling a rambling story—a man who never rambles—about a time at the old hunting cabin with his buddies when he had too many cigars and rum and Cokes, and some epic adventure that involved Def Leppard and aerosol and a raging campfire. I'm waiting for the punchline when my mother leans in so close to me, her lips bump against my neck as she hisses into my ear:

"He's the real deal, isn't he? I feel it in my old bones. You and him."

I give a lovely fake little laugh. "Way too soon, Mother."

"Mm. I don't think so. But we'll see."

Rudy looks over at me, just for a beat, before turning back to my dad. Like he's checking in on me, saying a quick hello. It's so warm and familiar and—

Double fuck.

It's not way too soon.

Not for me.

"What next? Are you tired?" Rudy asks as he hangs the dish towel up, the last dinner plate cleaned and dried and put away in the cabinet. I washed and he dried after we'd sent my parents off to bed, full glasses of water in their hands, and with assurances that Rudy would be delighted to try scrapple for breakfast.

I shake my head, drying my hands against my jeans. "Not really. Are you?"

"No. Red wine makes some people sleepy"—he smiles up at the ceiling, my parents—"but it has the opposite effect on me. Maybe it's the sugar. I'm all hyped up."

"Want to go for a stroll outside?"

I'm hyped, too, and not just from the wine sugars.

I could use the cold air.

Especially before *bedtime*, and sleeping in my old bed. *Together*. Me. Rudy. One full-sized mattress. My mom had assumed, even without the roommate intel, that would be the arrangement, and it had felt too awkward to correct her. It was supposed to be the other way around—her telling me he needed a separate sleeping space, not me chastely insisting he take the office futon.

"Sure. I'd love a tour of the grounds."

He leans in, and—thank God, we're going to kiss, finally, here where my mother stands every night washing dishes, but that's fine, because—

Oh. He's reaching for the last bottle of wine, still half-full. "For added warmth," he says, eyes sparkling as he takes a swig.

Those goddamn twinkly puddle eyes, they do too much to me.

Make me feel too much.

He passes me the bottle, and I take a sip.

We put on our shoes and jackets then—well, Rudy puts on his sweatshirt—and step outside onto the porch. It's a mild November night. Even I could probably survive in a sweatshirt with only minimal grumbles.

"Almost a full moon," I say as we stroll down the path toward the wide-open expanse of yard before the field. I'm suddenly acutely aware of how dark it is otherwise. How alone we are.

"So many stars," he says, almost a whisper. I glance over at him, and he's looking up at the sky reverently. "You're lucky you grew up in the middle of what could be a national park."

"I didn't really appreciate it," I say, leading him into the grass. I'm not sure where we're going. The field. The woods on either side of us. The barn at the edge of the yard. "It's all relative, I guess. When you see the same thing every day, it stops feeling special. I didn't realize how good I had it until I came back on college breaks. And especially after moving to the city."

"I could get used to this, I think."

"Yeah?" It shocks me, the idea of Rudy not being in a city. We've never talked about this—where we want to end up—but

I assumed he was a New York City lifer. The comedy, the music. The possibilities.

"Maybe. I don't mind driving to get to the city."

I'm not sure what we're explicitly talking about—him living here, or him living anywhere outside city limits. He doesn't elaborate, and I don't ask.

We're slowly passing by the barn, and I don't know why, but I stop walking and reach out for his hand. "Want to go in?"

He looks over at me, and it's too dark to see what exactly is in his eyes, but he nods, lacing his fingers through mine. His hair is lit up by the moon, looking more reddish than usual, more like it used to as a kid on my TV screen, coppery in the light. I want to run my fingers through it. I want to tug it, feel it rub against my cheeks.

I turn and pull him along behind me, our shoes crunching through leaves as we veer off the bricks. I push through the squeaky old barn door, Rudy right behind me, and reach to flick on the light. I stop myself, though. There's enough moonlight filtering in from the windows at either end of the barn.

We stop in the middle of the floor, wedged between stacks of Rubbermaid bins and cardboard boxes, a few pieces of assorted furniture.

I want to kiss him.

I want to kiss him more than I've ever wanted to kiss him. Kiss anybody, for that matter.

Instead, I say, "I'm sorry my friends didn't come. I know that was part of the reason for your trip. But I hope you still had a good night. Even if my mom, er . . . comes on a bit strong."

Rudy laughs, rumbly and throaty, and takes a step closer to me. So close I can feel the heat coming off his chest. "Your mom's great. Your dad, too. You have nothing to apologize for." He looks down at the ground, opens his mouth, stops himself. Starts again. "It's maybe not my business, but . . . these friends? It feels like you deserve better. I know they were your best friends from the early days. But . . . people grow up. Grow apart. That's life."

I think about it, then. How long it's been since I really, genuinely talked to Susie or Grace. About anything besides potty training or bad dates. Mostly potty training. Which is fine. I'm happy they've built families. But when's the last time they honestly cared about my life?

"I don't know," I say, looking down, too. "It's hard, with so much past. And it's not like I have lots of other friends for present-day Lucy. New York City has been a revolving door, and I'm not built to be a loner."

Rudy's fingers graze my chin, tilt my face up so I'm looking straight at him.

"You have the Myrtles."

I laugh. "True."

"And you have me."

"Yeah?" I feel a rush of heat through my veins, a swooping, dizzying sensation.

He nods. "Of course you do."

A pause, and then I let go of his hands and reach up for his face, his warm cheeks, and press my lips against his. He moans, or I moan, or we both do, and I'm falling into his arms, tangling myself around him.

We're kissing until I'm breathless, pulling away, gasping, looking up at those eyes. Eyes as wide as mine feel, as surprised, as awed—and then we're kissing again.

"The old sofa," I say, pushing him over to the couch that's been in here for the last year or two, covered no doubt in barn debris that I don't care about at the moment. I'm pulling him by the zipper of his sweatshirt, unzipping it, tugging it down his arms. I grab for his T-shirt next, pulling at it as we drop, him first, me on top of him, onto the sofa.

"Lucy?" he asks, and then glances toward the door. "Your parents? Are you . . . sure?"

"My parents will be sleeping for twelve hours, and"—I take a breath—"yes. I am."

"What about the roommate rules?"

"I'm giving my consent."

"And you have mine. Don't get me wrong. But what about the other rule?"

No broken hearts.

I don't answer him. Instead, I pull his shirt all the way up and over his head, tossing it in the air, where it catches on an old fake Christmas tree.

He reaches for my jacket, and I help him, pushing it off behind me. My sweater is next, joining the jacket on the dusty barn floor, and I lean in for another kiss, my skin pressing against his as he reaches behind me and unclasps my bra.

"Presumably"—I force myself to sit back, grinding my hips hard into his—"you travel prepared?" *For nights out, superfans, women before me,* I don't say.

"Not that this kind of thing happens a lot," he says, breathing heavily, grinning at me, "but yes. In my wallet. Which is conveniently still in my back pocket."

"Thank God," I say, already unbuttoning his jeans.

We rearrange ourselves quickly, bumping and elbowing and laughing. I end up lying on my back on the sofa, every last scrap of clothing gone. But somehow, cold is the last thing I feel, even if it is November.

We kiss again for a long time, our hands everywhere, my fingers finding every inch of soft freckled skin usually covered by black cotton and black denim. His fingers touch every last bit of me, too, pressing and exploring and rubbing, fingers that I can tell have plucked strings for most of his life—fingers that know *exactly* what they're doing.

And then, when I beg for it, he pushes himself inside of me, and maybe it's because we're at my parents' house, where everything is steeped in my nostalgia, but goddamn if the song

"2 Become 1" doesn't play in my brain, and nothing has ever felt so cliché and so utterly, ridiculously perfect.

We *are* one—breathing, panting, shaking, painted together in the snow-white moonlight splashing in from the windows.

"I can't believe we're doing this in my parents' barn," I say, gasping for air.

"I'm disappointed there's no actual hay," Rudy says, gasping along with me, "because a literal roll in the hay for our first time would have made for the ultimate story to never tell our grandkids."

"You're thinking about our grandkids right now?"

"Good point. How about some cock-crowing puns instead?" We laugh and grasp one another even more tightly, Rudy's palms against my cheeks, my thighs wrapped snugly around his back. And then he's rocking and thrusting, and the stars suddenly seem to shine brighter—the stars high above the barn window, and the stars inside my head.

Bright, white, exploding stars.

We fall like that, together, into the swirling, twirling Greendale night sky.

"Question," Rudy says, squeezing me. We're cuddling on the sofa, wrapped up in a blanket of questionable cleanliness that I pulled from a Rubbermaid. "No judgment. I'm just curious. Was the barn your sex kingdom growing up?"

"My *sex kingdom*? Please elaborate."

"You know, like your go-to place. Instead of cheap hotel rooms or basements."

"No."

"Really?"

"You're my first roll in the non-literal hay of my parents' barn, I promise."

"Wow. That feels like an honor."

"I was a virgin until college," I say, because this night—

this moonlit barn, Rudy's warm arms wrapped around my shoulders—has me feeling deeply open and honest. "I didn't really date in high school. And by really, I mean not at all. I had a lot of girlfriends, but I was . . . I don't know, *too much* for the guys, maybe. My crushes were never reciprocated."

"Huh."

"I know, it must seem strange to you, seeing as you dated a hot co-star and no doubt had plenty of other girls tossing panties at you on the school bus."

He laughs. "Please. I didn't ride the bus."

I pinch the underside of his bicep. "You know what I mean. I'm sure you had plenty of girlfriends."

"I guess. Only one serious girlfriend. But I dated a decent amount."

"So what was your sex kingdom?"

"My parents' pool house. My Jeep. Cheap hotel rooms. Sometimes not so cheap."

"Wow."

"What?"

"We lived very different teenage years."

He shrugs, tightening his hold on me. "Maybe. But we're in the same place now, aren't we?" He lifts his head up, looks around the barn. "And it's a pretty sweet place, if you ask me. Ten out of ten would recommend an old family barn for spontaneous lovemaking."

"You did not just call it *lovemaking*," I say, pursing my lips in mock disgust. "That's how they say it in the soap operas my mom still insists on watching. Very nineties of her."

"*Lovemaking*," he says again, louder this time. "LOVE-MAKING!"

"Stop!" I stifle a giggle as I pull back, yanking the blanket off of him as I scramble to the other end of the sofa. "Stop, or it won't happen again. I can't abide by that terminology."

"Oh yeah?" he says, pushing himself up and crawling over

toward me, his brilliant naked body practically glowing in the moonlight. The sight is somehow brand new and achingly familiar, like it's the first time and the thousandth time we've been together this way.

"Yeah," my mouth says, but my body is already responding, reaching for him, pressing him up against my chest. The blanket drops to the floor.

Lovemaking, fornicating, screwing, fucking—it's happening again, whatever the term.

It's all of them, it's none of them, it's *everything.*

Chapter 16
Rudy

As gravity tugs you from Earth oh so soon.

After a brisk walk to get cappuccinos—I've convinced Lucy they're almost as good as matcha, at least from the right place— and croissants from a newly discovered local French truck, we return to the Spinster Cave. A box is waiting for us at the doorstep.

"The show fliers!" Lucy scoops up the box. "I'm so excited to see how these came out." She glances back at me as she jabs a key in the door. "Which reminds me, I forgot to get the mail yesterday. Would you mind checking?"

She tosses me her keys, and I head to the mailbox. It's chockfull of shit. Christmas cards from Lucy's friends back home. Too many menus, a tax lien letter for a previous tenant, and a check from my union. Residuals.

Ahh yes, the extra pick-me-up cash I'm always grateful to see, except for when they turn out to be in the nickels-and-dimes category. I was on TV so long ago that some stuff pays pennies. Literally. *Pennies.* I've received far too many one-cent checks in my life. Such a weird waste of money, time, resources. I mean, it's fifty-four more cents just to stamp the damn envelope, not to mention the ink and paper, the manual labor.

I used to track what was coming in on the union app, but I forgot my password and have been too lazy to figure it out. Besides, this way, it's a fun surprise.

"Want to play the lottery today?" I ask Lucy, waving the envelope grandly as I step inside the cave.

She looks confused. Sad, even. Not the reaction I anticipated. "Eh. I'm not a big fan of the lottery. Don't get me wrong, I've played a Powerball game or two whenever it gets ridiculously high, because who can resist? But I can't help but think of the desperate people who blow all their money looking for that big payout. Makes my heart hurt."

Oof. I should have used a better analogy.

"Not the real lottery, don't worry. My own personal lottery, and it always pays out." I toss the rest of the mail onto the kitchen table, and grab for my wallet. I rifle through cards and bills to find a finely folded check—my first-ever one-cent payment. A funny piece of fodder for my *Eclipsed Too Soon* after-show Q&A. Truth be told, also a potential flirting tactic.

I hand the check to Lucy. She squints to read it, the ink faded into the folded ridges.

"Does this say one cent? They really send you that?"

I laugh. "They really do, yes. Aggravating, but also kind of hilarious. Therein lies the 'lottery' analogy. Will this check in my hand now"—I wave it again for emphasis—"be a dinner-and-drinks-date kind of check? A solo bodega lunch? Pennies on the dollar? Or, lastly, the rarest, most prized of them all, a rent-and-groceries-for-a-month kind of check? Maybe even with that dinner-and-drinks date on top."

Lucy is fully onboard now, and has moved to stand right in front of me. More accurately, she's crouched down on the ground to then pop up between me and the table, giving herself an unparalleled front seat. "This *is* a fun lottery. Ah! I'm nervous for you!"

"I'm only nervous when it's been a slow month and I'm counting on a big check. Which is . . . kind of the case now. Want to do the honors?"

I realize as I say this that I'm about to disclose some financials to my . . . girlfriend? We haven't said the words yet, but c'mon. I haven't slept in my bed since we got back from PA. My room's become the second office.

I've always had a hard time trying to transition between the physical and emotional sides of dating, but with Lucy, it's so easy. We don't have to try. It just happens. Like I've finally broken the cycle of bad dating situations post Piper, that fear of putting much—or any—of myself out there. For all the fruitless searches, I'm happy to see that some good internal work could change my outlook on things. Or then again . . . maybe it's just Lucy.

Maybe it only ever would have been this easy with her.

Lucy extends her hand out for the envelope, bringing me back. "It'd be my honor to bestow money onto you, whether said money is a penny or a few grand. Preference for the latter. But either way, this is much better than watching people in the corner of a Wawa scratching their hearts out."

I interject quickly, "Please don't scratch the check."

Lucy grins and rips the top of the envelope open, pulling out a check for . . . "Six-hundred-and-seventy-three dollars and thirty-nine cents," she announces with an auctioneer flourish.

"Seriously?"

"Yep. I would happily take this check randomly in my mail!" She smiles and grabs my face, planting an overblown, intentionally slapsticky kiss. "We can have a nice dinner, and then do with the rest whatever you please."

She kisses me again, for real this time. Slower. Softer.

There's nothing funny about this kiss.

I'm tempted to sweep her straight into the bedroom, but Lucy pulls away. "The box," she whispers against my cheek, breathing heavily. "Let's open it."

"Mmm," I mumble against her hair, and then I head over to the kitchen drawers to find a cutting tool. Butter knife secured, I grab the box from the counter and get to work on the tape. "You seem to have the magic touch today, so why don't you check the fliers first, too?"

Lucy steps up next to me and reaches into the box, then turns her back to give a covert first look. She squeals. At a very high frequency. And then spins back toward me. Her face has become too small for her smile—her lips are just about touching her ears.

"Rudy! They're incredible! Perfectly sized cards that totally encapsulate the vibe of the show! Our show! That's less than a month away! Can you believe it?"

I'm not sure I've ever heard so many exclamation points in one breath.

But yes, I *can* believe it.

It's been a time vortex since we got back from PA. December usually goes that way, but this year, it feels especially true. *Spiked Lemonade* is already at fifty-percent tickets sold, and fliering other Little Zelda's shows with these postcards will help the cause even more. There's a great show tonight, *Sordid Lives of Single People*, with strong crossover appeal.

We continue through the day as we now typically do when neither of us has gigs, and Clementine isn't sending Lucy on errands—some TV with show brainstorming on the side, an order of tacos or dumplings for lunch. A record goes on, and then we're back in bed, though definitely not sleeping. More show talk after. Somehow, just like that, we've stretched the day all the way to an hour before the show.

We head out, fliers in tow.

Lucy, who's effusively excited to both flier and to tell people about the show, is walking down the street in front of me, talking to herself and pretending to shake hands. I can't tell if she's kidding or not, but I want her to feel comfortable, so I don't question her process. After a few minutes of quiet observation, I speed up until I'm close enough to reach for her.

I give her hand a squeeze. She squeezes back. "Don't worry. I've done this hundreds of times. People either grab the flier and make no eye contact, they're friendly and take it happily, or they ignore you altogether. Even the worst case isn't that bad. Our idea is solid. We know it. Little Zelda's knows it. That's what matters."

Lucy stops walking and gives me an intense wide-eyed stare. I'm a deer in her headlights. Then she leans in and gently kisses my lips.

"How do you always know the right things to say? Was it that obvious I was running scenarios in my head?"

Uh. Yes. Incredibly obvious.

"Well," I say, gently, "you were . . . mumbling to yourself. And I might have seen you go in for an imaginary handshake. You do you, though. Whatever works."

We laugh and start walking again, Lucy seeming looser and lighter.

It's a weird thing, going to hawk your own show. A show you've poured dozens of hours into already, hammering out the details. The reward for shows is a long con, a waiting game. It's hard to grasp how well you're actually doing in the moment. Before it all begins.

But I have faith.

I believe in Lucy.

Another morning waking up between Lucy's sheets.

It took some easing in, but we've moved to a new relationship level:

I'm officially . . . comfortable sleeping naked.

Lucy, too.

It's always been my preference, but I was withholding that particular information during the beginning of our roommate days. We weren't having sex yet and, in my personal experience, sleeping naked with someone else around usually leads to sex. I can't confirm that it's scientific fact, though my research is convincing. But soon after our trip to PA, I let it happen, and now, like a virus—a good virus, a great one—it's spread to Lucy. My research continues, and still corroborates my previous investigations: sleeping naked leads to sex. Every morning and every night since we've been back. Afternoon lunch dates, too.

Currently, our legs are tangled together, and I have my arm over her shoulder. *Big spooning*, I think, is the correct term. We're sleeping in, because the late-night show talk—mining all of our own personal bad dates for fodder—turned into a *Golden Girls* marathon that ended around sunrise.

I slowly rub my leg up and down her thigh. Her skin is so soft, like a perfectly made blanket of cashmere. It sounds cliché—or maybe creepy, in a Hannibal Lecter kind of way—but it's an accurate description. I nuzzle against her back and trace my fingers along her stomach. I can't help myself.

I go in for a big belly button poke.

Lucy screams.

She slaps my hand away and rolls over to give me an intensely dramatic—and adorable—fake scowl. "My belly button, my rules! And that rule is no belly button poking. Ever."

And then, like a switch flips in that strange, wonderful brain of hers, she reaches out to cup my cheeks, her eyes as serious as I've ever seen them. Her tongue is on my mouth first, then her teeth, tugging gently, then not so gently, before her lips press into mine. I roll on top of her, pinning her against the sheets, then pull my mouth from her lips to her long neck, her sharp collarbones. Skipping past her stomach altogether, I edge lower, settling in between her thighs. She's warm and wet and—

The buzzer rings.

Lucy shoots up, knocking her knee into my nose.

A second of flashing pain, and then . . . blood running down my face and onto the bed.

"Oh my God, are you okay? Fuck. Fuck. Fuck," Lucy yells as she's scouring the room for clothes. She tosses my black T-shirt at me to use as a blood stopper.

"It's probably a delivery," I say, muffled by the cotton pressed to my face. "The Myrtles will handle it."

Lucy is desperately trying to put her jeans on, but one leg is inside-out, causing a jam-up in the middle. She falls to the ground in a messy heap. I jump out of bed to help her.

"It's Clementine! Shocking she'd come to me, I know, but she had a coffee meeting around the corner, and she has stuff to drop off before going to LA for her big glamorous movie shoot"—she rolls her eyes—"and she said she'd bring it by between eleven and noon, depending on how her meeting went. It's . . . eleven-oh-five." With one hand on my face, still holding the shirt tight, I grab her inside-out leg and force it back right-side in. I even grab her socks with one hand.

"I'd go to the door for you, but she might see the blood and assume I offed you." I tug on my boxers and grab Lucy's bathrobe for additional coverage.

"Probably a good call."

Lucy, now fully dressed, runs to the door and yanks it open. She's right. I do a quick peek to confirm. Clementine is standing on the other side, one hand clutching a stack of papers, the other hand on her hip, looking displeased. But that might be her resting face.

"Are you . . . okay?" she asks, squinting as she tries to look past Lucy into the darkness of the cave. "I heard a lot of commotion."

"Oh, yeah. I was having trouble with a, er, jean drawer that was jammed. I unstuck it, but I ended up flying into the bed from pulling so hard."

A semi-decent lie, especially on the fly.

I need fresh clothes first and foremost. I do a quick check of my nostrils—the bleeding seems to have stopped. One more swipe of the T-shirt, and then I edge out of Lucy's door on tiptoes. Just one tight turn away from my room.

Creak. Creeeak.

Damn these old parquet floors.

I chance a quick glance back toward the front door. Clementine is staring straight at me.

"Uh. Sorry, Lucy. Was this a bad time?"

I pull the robe tighter around me.

Lucy glances back at me, looking unusually sheepish. "That's my new roommate. The person I'm . . . dating. Rudy. I mentioned him?"

Clementine's the one looking sheepish now. I guess like most bosses—not that I know from personal experience, since I've never technically had one—she only listens when it's about her.

"Oh, right. The musician, right?" She gives a stiff wave. "Well, I'll make it quick. Just a few bills and other boring filing things to handle ASAP. And also: You go, gurl!" Gross. I can hear that "u." Nothing worse than someone trying to right the ship with a colloquialism that's inappropriate for a twenty-something white girl living in New York City. As a writer, no less.

I refuse to formally meet Lucy's boss in a faded terry cloth robe, so I slip away into my room while they talk business, throw on an unbloodied shirt and some jeans, put a little pomade in my hair, give it a quick comb through. It's been a long time since I felt the urge to clean up my appearance for anyone other than me. For Lucy, though, I want to.

I give myself a quick final check and head out of the closet.

I'm halfway to the door when Clementine does one of the most ultimate double takes I've ever seen in my life. And I've seen a lot of them. If there were a camera on her, it'd be the meme of the year.

"Rudy Riziero! Holy shit! I'm a huge fan!" She spins from me, to Lucy, back to me, looking breathless in her overenthusiasm. "Lucy, you didn't specify it was THAT Rudy! Oh my God, I'm so embarrassed. Hi, I'm Clementine! Lucy's my assistant."

She seems to stand a little straighter with that assistant line. A subconscious dig? Or . . . totally conscious?

I take a few steps closer, until I'm standing right next to Lucy. I brush up against her shoulder and stay there. "Nice to meet you, Clementine. I've heard a lot about you." I glance over at Lucy, who looks like she's stuck between two mental places. She clearly heard *assistant* loud and clear, but she also seems amused by how awkward Clementine's acting. Bias aside, I'd say the point goes to Lucy.

"Thanks for bringing these over," she says, a thin smile on her lips. "I know you're really busy. With the big LA trip and all."

Clementine takes a second to respond, finally seeming to notice just how hard she's been staring at me. "Sure, sure. No problem whatsoever. I was in the hood and actually had some plans fall through for later today, if you guys were up for a hang? We could get brunch? Lunch?"

This is my time to shine.

Clementine's teed up one of the best ways to both make Lucy feel good and to get out of this train wreck of a stop-and-chat.

"That's a great idea," I say, putting an arm around Lucy's shoulder. "But maybe another time? I was going to take Lucy out for a surprise trip to another Brooklyn neighborhood. A nice little staycation date, exploring a new spot together."

Clementine is stunned. I said "take Lucy out" and "date," and now she's fully processing that her "assistant"—which feels too generous a word, like calling a babysitter a nanny—is dating me. I can practically smell burning hair, her brain is working so hard. She takes a moment to compose herself. "Ah, that sounds so great! You have fun now, wow, that's like, so fun! Cool, cool. Talk to you soon, Lucy, and thanks for all you do." She about-faces, walks off our stoop, then out of the gate and out of our lives. At least for the day.

Lucy grins up at me. "Thanks for laying it on so thick. You really twisted her up."

"I wasn't planning on showing off as your arm candy today, but I thought, why the hell not? Seemed like a good cause."

"Did you really want to do that today? Have a staycation?"

I pause to consider. "In the moment, it just seemed like a good excuse to bow out. But now? Oh, yeah! Let's see the ocean. Grab a hot dog. I love Coney this time of year. Mostly dead, but it still has enough rations for a day trip. There's Nathan's, the place next to Nathan's that serves shitty beer, the ocean, the pier. It's perfect. We should, er, finish what we started, and then head out."

Lucy starts slowly pushing me back towards her room. "You had me at hot dogs," she whispers—hisses, really, *dogsss*. "The ocean view and shitty adult beverage are just icing."

Her words are so breathy and high pitched that I'm tensing up, shivers shooting down my spine. She continues as we move through her doorway: "It all sounds . . . *delicioso*!"

It's by far the weirdest, most visceral word that's ever been whispered into my ears. Pure torture, and Lucy knows it. I back away as fast as I can, but Lucy's faster.

She laughs and pushes me onto the bed, hopping up to straddle me. "It's all fun and games until I say *delic*—"

I pull her down with me, kissing her so she can't speak anymore. And also because, well, she just threw me onto the bed. I think that's a sign, right?

We stay in bed for hours, then order takeout. Rain check on the December beach hang.

We have all the time in the world for Coney.

* * *

The next day, I get a friend request from Clementine. A message, too:

Rudy, it was so nice meeting you! Sorry I was being totally weird, but my older sister and I watched Black Hole Sons religiously. She'd dubbed all the shows onto VHS and sucked me in, too. Anyway, the show meant a lot to me, and so did you. I'm sure you get that all the time, but I thought it was worth mentioning. ALSO! I don't know if Lucy told you, but I'm heading to LA to shoot the movie for my first book in January. As fate would have it, the actor picked to play a (young! hip!) dad dropped off last minute. I've spoken to casting, and they're eager to watch if you'd put yourself on tape? If you're interested (please please!), I'll send the script and sides for your self-tape. You'd be perfect for the role! Take care! -CC

Well, that was . . . unexpected.

On one hand, I'd get to be in a legit movie. But as a dad? Sheesh. I guess I have been gone a long time. A slip-up early on could've landed me in the teen dad department easily, so it makes sense.

I could always read it and say it's not for me. Politely, since she's Lucy's boss.

Though . . . what's the harm in saying yes if it works out? I've been trying to find the right acting gig, haven't I? And LA is always much nicer than New York City in January.

Fuck. January.

The show.

Don't get ahead of yourself.

I can't do that to Lucy. Bail on our first show. Of course I can't.

Though it sure would feel nice to stick it to my A-list

brother. Show him I could come and go from Hollywood as I pleased, while he's forced to keep making movie after movie for the sake of staying relevant. Show my family, too. Show everyone. That I have what it takes, even if I don't typically get handed roles these days . . . unless you're talking about the web series business of having someone who used to be famous onboard, just to garner more attention. A novelty name for the credits. Problem is, with nowhere for the shows to be greenlit, they just sit around on the Internet as trailers. Useless content for the perpetually unhoused project.

We were equals once, Rocco and me. He's not better—he just gets more breaks for continuing his entertainment journey, never taking a step back. Maybe he wasn't totally wrong about that part. But I could still do just as well, if I were given some of the same resources and opportunities. And sure, his abs would help, too.

This movie could be my best chance. A viable opportunity that could actually work out.

But . . . nope.

Won't do it.

Because of Lucy and *Spiked Lemonade* and her relationship with Clementine. And because I shouldn't have to prove myself, not to Rocco, not to anyone.

Do I want to prove it to myself, though? Do I want this purely for *me*?

Shit. No. Can't even go there. No matter why I might want it, I can't. Not this role.

My fingers shake over the phone as I try to come up with the right words.

Hey, Clementine, thanks for reaching out! I truly appreciate how much that show meant to you. It meant a lot to me, too. Anyway, I haven't really been pursuing a lot of on-camera gigs these days. That being said, I'd be happy to read

and see how it makes me feel. Thanks for thinking of me! Best, RR

I press Send, put the phone away, and hope that maybe my hesitation was enough for Clementine to not send it after all, so I don't even have to entertain the thought.

Chapter 17
Lucy

A family rift swallows all who are near.

"Is this sweater too much?" I ask, tugging at a glittery gold pom-pom stitched onto the vintage technicolor Christmas tree sweater I'd unearthed from deep inside the bowels of my dresser. "And are you sure," I ramble on, not waiting for Rudy to respond, "your parents are okay with me being here tonight? I could keep driving to PA. Drop off the rental car a day early."

"Not too much," Rudy says, a cloud of white puffing out from his lips in the cold. Even he's wearing a proper winter jacket tonight. "And yes. One-hundred-percent sure. My mother nearly blasted my eardrum with the delighted squeal that ripped out when I told her the news."

"Really? That loud?"

"Really."

"She sounds like my kind of girl."

"She's *absolutely* your kind of girl."

"Okay, then," I say, fortified with this news, starting up the sidewalk that cuts through his parents' bedazzled front yard. Flashing multicolored icicle lights, a life-sized wooden manger lit with two massive spotlights, a waving inflatable Frosty that's double my height. "Let's do this."

This being Christmas Eve at the Riziero home.

With both the Italian and the Irish sides present. According to Rudy, his family takes the holiday Very Seriously. Not Seven Fishes style, but Rudy assured me it's a plentiful buffet of expensive booze and cheese-filled pasta and a homemade sausage bread that's been passed down through the generations.

It'd been a last-minute invite, after a night of karaoke upstairs with Estelle and Frank. A "landlord-tenant holiday mixer," they'd called it. Basement gin may have played a marginal role. But Rudy asked again the next morning. And my mother was all too thrilled to push back my arrival until Christmas Day. Oh no, she said, they wouldn't miss me *at all*.

The wreath on their front door is so large I could easily use it as a hula hoop. In fact, Rudy and I both could use it as a hula hoop.

I reach my hand out to ring the doorbell.

"We don't have to buzz in," Rudy says, chuckling. "I grew up in this house."

I laugh, too, though it comes out as more of a nervous screech. I've never met the parents of a boyfriend before. And not just parents in this case, oh no: aunts and uncles and cousins, even a ninety-three-year-old great uncle, for fuck's sake. Rudy's side of the wedding aisle. Sweat is pooling under my effusively festive sweater. "You can take the boy out of Jersey, but you can't take Jersey out of the boy."

"Emphasis on *northern* Jersey," he says, stepping past me to reach for the doorknob. "There's a very big dif—"

He cuts off abruptly as the door swings open. I see Rudy's face first. The wide eyes, illuminated by flashing Christmas lights. The smile that puckers instantly into a tight line.

I look toward the open door to see the source of the displeasure, and . . .

Holy.

Shit.

The holiest of shits.

And not because it's the eve of dear Jesus' birth.

But because it's Him.

Rocco Riziero.

Just a few inches away from me. Breathing the same Jersey air as I am. *Rocco.* A face I've seen on too many screens and pages to count. Here, now, in the flesh. He seems to tower above both of us—partly because the door is a step above, partly because the genetic gods doled out a good six inches extra to the elder Riziero brother.

Somehow, impossibly, he's even more handsome than he is on screen. Huh. I would have expected the opposite, for him to look dimmer, more regular Jersey Joe without the flashy pyrotechnics of movie magic. But no, his dark hair is a perfect tangly swoop, and his skin looks *naturally* suntanned on December 24, like he was just out picking some fresh olives in a grove alongside the Mediterranean. Rocco, it would seem, skipped the Irish DNA altogether. He's wearing a soft-looking green sweater and dark jeans that both fit like a second skin and are undoubtedly more expensive than everything in my wardrobe, combined.

"Hey, little bro," he says, and when he smiles, his teeth are brighter than the white twinkly lights hung around the eaves of the porch. I resist the urge to shield myself.

When Rudy doesn't seem to have the capacity for words, I step forward, extending a hand. "Er. Merry Christmas! I'm Lucy. Your brother's . . ." I shoot a panicked look at Rudy, who doesn't notice, because his eyes are exclusively fixed on his brother. Oh, hell. "Girlfriend."

"I've heard, and it's a pleasure to meet my little brother's partner. It's been a while since he's brought anyone around," Rocco says, still smiling, and—holiest, holiest shit of all—he reaches his arms out wide and pulls me in for a hug. It's a quick one, five seconds tops, all hard lines and rigid angles. It's got nothing on Rudy's hugs. "Welcome to the Riziero Christmas Eve, Lucy. I'm digging that tree sweater."

"Really?" *Lord, I know you're busy tonight, but please do not let my cheeks flush. Amen.*

He nods. "Makes your eyes pop. Though I imagine they pop no matter what you wear, because they're the most incredible shade of green."

Uh. That was sweet, I guess? But maybe a little too sweet, because Rudy's entire face is a festive shade of red.

When I don't immediately respond, Rocco continues, breezily, "I hope you're prepared to consume your weight in cured meats and fine cheeses."

"Oh, I'm most definitely prepared. I've been eating extra cheese all week to up my body's natural capacity for lactose."

Neither brother laughs, and I'm about to launch into Chocolate Week because I'm not sure what else the hell to say and Rudy is incapable of contributing, when, thank God, a woman with red flowy hair who looks to be Rudy's twin twenty-five years removed appears behind Rocco and cuts in.

"Rudy!" She flings herself into his arms, and luckily, he snaps back to life quickly enough that they don't both topple into the bushes. "I'm sad I missed the big surprise! Can you believe it? Your big brother, home for Christmas? I can't remember the last time he wasn't off on location for the holidays!"

"More like jetting off to some exotic paradise with his supermodel du jour," Rudy says, very matter-of-factly, as he pats his mom on the back.

Rocco shrugs, not denying it. He leans against the doorframe in what could only be described as the most artful lean of all time. He's taken a course on it in Hollywood, surely. I've never understood why people—or every woman in a rom-com, anyway—find leaning to be so sexy, but one would have to be completely coldblooded to deny the primitive appeal of Rocco's lean right now, his perfect fucking body and perfect fucking face glowing under the twinkle lights. It's unfair, really.

"That might be somewhat true," he says, glancing at me, and I immediately look away, cursing myself for being caught openly staring. The last thing I want is to bolster his ego. Or for Rudy to catch me. Which, damn it, he did, because he's staring at me now, a question in his gaze. "But I always offer to send Mom and Dad to paradise, too, for the holidays, and they never take me up on it."

"I would never miss Christmas with the family! Here. At home. Where most people celebrate holidays." Mrs. Riziero almost sounds annoyed when she says this, but her words are still thick with adoration and affection.

She turns to me then, remembering there is someone in this world other than her two glorious sons. "Lucy!" There it is, the squeal. It's a good one. "I'm Eunice. Rudy's mom," she tacks on, as if anyone with sight wouldn't immediately make this connection. "It's so wonderful to meet you." We're hugging then, and it's soft and warm and laced with the scent of cinnamon and Chardonnay. "I was just saying to Rudy's father, can you remember the last time Rudy brought someone home to meet us?"

"A recurring theme," Rudy says, rolling his eyes. Behind his mother's back, of course. I doubt even thirty-four-year-old Rudy would dare roll his eyes straight to his mother's face.

But then again, her sixth sense. "That's not a criticism, my love," she says sweetly, pulling back from our hug and rolling her own eyes for my benefit.

"I think we all remember too well the last girlfriend I brought home," Rudy says, calmly. Too calmly, like there is a very dark, swirly storm not far off in the distance. I start to reach for his hand, but stop myself, my fingers dangling limply midair. Because he's thinking about her. Piper. "Or should I say *we* brought home, because didn't Rocco bring her the year after we broke up? I wouldn't remember. I spent that one alone. Drinking Jim Beam at a shitty cabin upstate. Because that was better than being here." His eyes are daggers on Rocco. Those puddles have frozen into pointy icicles.

Rocco takes a step back. I do, too.

Eunice spins around to cup Rudy's chin firmly in her palms. "We are *not* talking about her tonight. This is Christmas Eve, and we're here with family, all together, for the first time in years. No dwelling in the past. You boys were kids. Do Lucy and I a favor, please, and act like the mature thirty-something humans I know you to be." With that, she turns and grabs my hand, marches me wordlessly across the threshold and down the hallway that leads to a bright and noisy kitchen, packed in with bodies of all shapes and sizes cutting, cooking, eating foods.

I blink, trying to process the transition from the porch to here, Rudy and Rocco, Piper. It's been so many years. It hadn't even occurred to me that he wasn't properly over her. That he hadn't at the very least made some kind of peace with Rocco.

"Wine or cocktail, my dear?" Eunice asks, smiling at me with Rudy's smile, nothing like Rocco's clinical perfection. "Perhaps a cocktail to start, after that first round of introductions?"

I nod numbly and she turns and disappears into the crowd, leaving me alone in the corner of a room filled with strangers, everyone eyeing me curiously over their cutting boards and casserole dishes.

"I'm sorry," Rudy whispers, suddenly next to me again. Smiling at me in a shy and uncertain way that would ordinarily be rather sexy. "That was . . . embarrassing, and I feel like an ass. My mom was right. I was acting like a kid. It's just—Rocco. He does that to me. Every time. Like, I see him, and suddenly I'm time travelling in a fucking pod, until we're snarky little punks again, always trying to one-up one another, to be better. The best."

"I understand," I say automatically, even if I don't, not at all, because I never had a sibling. I was never a celebrity. And I was also never betrayed by the person I trusted more than anyone in the world. But I'm not sure what else to say in the moment, not without risking an outburst of ugly tears in front of the whole Riziero family. Because *of course* Rudy would never be completely over Piper fucking Bell. Who could be?

Like a merry red-haired Christmas angel, Eunice materializes in front of me, carrying a snowflake-covered tumbler filled to the brim with a dark red drink that reeks of whiskey and cranberry. "Take a few gulps," she says, "and then Rudy can introduce you to the rest of the family. They're all eager to meet you, I can assure you of that. It's no insult that Rudy doesn't often bring dates home. It's a compliment to you."

From the corner of my eye, I see Rocco slip into the kitchen, the crowd of adoring family parting for him neatly as he passes through, slapping his back, angling their bodies toward him like he's their radiant sun. He stops in front of a makeshift bar, a long row of wine bottles and liquors and a massive punch bowl filled with the blood-red drink in my hand.

As instructed, I take a few healthy gulps to fortify myself. I swallow, take a deep breath. It smells like holiday heaven in here, fresh bread and sugary treats and melting cheese. The drink tastes like holiday heaven, too, fruity but not too sweet, a little bit spicy, a lot bit boozy.

"Okay," I say, reaching for Rudy's hand. If he's not dwelling, I won't, either. Just because he can't forgive Rocco doesn't mean he's still in love with her. It doesn't mean what he feels for me is less real. Besides, it's Christmas Eve, and I refuse to ruin my appetite. "Ready."

It's a full-fledged parade then, through the kitchen and past the dining table, the bar, into the living room, handshakes and hugs, a sprinkling of pleasantries and (hopefully, on my part) appropriate anecdotes and questions. A new drink is pressed into my hand as soon as I've finished the first, and somewhere along the route, I'm also delivered an enormous plate of cheeses and prosciutto and bresaola, a delectable, cured beef I've been missing out on for three decades. Sausage bread, too, hot and steaming, fresh from the oven.

"Rudy has a girlfriend! Our very own Christmas miracle!"

"Who would have thunk it? Little Rudy bringing a real woman home! How much is he paying you, Luce?"

"What a delightful surprise! Oh, Eunice must be so thrilled. It's been so long! Hasn't it been so long?"

There's a consensus, at least. Young and old alike.

No one, especially not ninety-three-year-old Uncle Freddy, thought they'd live to see the day Rudy brought a special lady friend home again. Uncle Freddy, a shriveled, liver-spotted darling of a man, informs me—discreetly, when Rudy pops out for a bathroom break—that there's an alarming dearth of Riziero progeny, and it's squarely on Rocco's and Rudy's shoulders to make sure the name lives on. "Though I suppose," he stage whispers, leaning in from his place of honor on the family recliner, next to my metal folding chair, "for all we know, Mr. Hollywood has a few bambinos running around out there, but none with the Riziero name."

I'm mid-sip as he says it, and almost spit out a spray of cocktail.

Rudy's dad sweeps in then, arms reaching out for me as he crosses the living room. I can tell right away who he is—unlike Eunice, he's a perfect balance of both Rudy and Rocco. It's like in the lottery of life, his features were divvied up into two separate buckets, no mixing between the two. It's the first I've seen of him all night. He's been outside, grilling an assortment of meats, not one to be scared off by the frigid air, apparently. Father like son. He's not even wearing a jacket, just a striped red sweater.

I stand, brushing parmesan flecks and breadcrumbs from my pants, and we hug with no preamble. He's a good hugger, like Rudy and Eunice. One would think the millionaire actor in the family would give the best hugs, all those on-screen embraces in his repertoire, but no.

"Remo," he says, pulling away, smiling at me with blue eyes identical to Rocco's. They suit Remo better. The blue is icy ocean water on Rocco, warm summer sky on Remo. "Welcome to the family."

I almost say that I'm not actually a member of the family—sure, I'm having sex, lots of sex, with his son, and so far, he hasn't tired of my stories or my questions, and we're managing to live together without fighting over the TV or dirty dishes or monthly bills. We have a show together, a real show, opening in just a few weeks. Yes, yes, yes, all of those things. We're all of that. But family means a ring. A more certain kind of future.

Family means *I love you.*

Though I do, don't I?

I love Rudy.

It hits me here, in his childhood living room, with an electric jolt. The certainty.

I've loved him since our night in the barn, haven't I? No. Before that. Forging Clementine's signature? Ice skating? The day he moved in?

Rudy is back then, and I smile like I'm not burning up from the inside out, because it's too soon to feel this way, and much too soon to say it out loud. We're chatting some more, aunts and uncles and cousins flitting into the conversation. We're talking about *Spiked Lemonade* then, and a handful of people whip out their phones to look at the event page.

"It says 'low ticket count remaining' here on the Internet!" an elderly aunt exclaims, looking up at both of us with too much surprise. "That seems good. Is it a small venue?"

"It's Brooklyn's premiere comedy space," I say, hopefully not too defensively, looping my arm through Rudy's. "Only the best acts in the city perform there. Your nephew paved the way for us with his own excellent show. Which he's still doing, too, later in the month. Because he's so in demand."

"Very good," she says, smiling at Rudy with a newfound sense of pride. I'm not especially keen on this particular aunt. Rudy's kind to her, and to everyone here—because of course he is, it's Rudy—and I take his lead, but it's no easy feat to bite my tongue. "We knew you'd find your way, sweetie," she continues. "It can't be easy. What with an older brother like yours, the *amazing* work he's doing. And the childhood you had, the expectations and—"

Fortunately, Eunice chooses this moment to declare dinner ready, saving me from having to swoop in and tell an elderly woman to shut the hell up on Christmas Eve. Her timing is a gift to us all, truly.

Dinner is a seemingly impossible arrangement, roughly forty people crammed in around the dining room table and the collection of circular folding tables and TV trays set along the sides of the room. Shoulders, elbows, knees bumping as we locate our name cards and settle in our benchlike rows of chairs.

I'm at the table proper, Rudy on my right, Uncle Freddy my left, and I'm just tucking into the largest manicotti shell I've ever seen when the vacant seat across from us is claimed.

Rocco.

Oh, Eunice. Surely this wasn't the best plan?

The brothers are quiet for a few minutes, hyper-focused on cutting and chewing, and I start to relax. I savor every bite of perfect, creamy ricotta.

Until, "I heard about your big new show," Rocco says, taking a swill of red. "I'm perpetually impressed by how you keep thinking up new gig ideas. Keep finding fans. It's all very . . . inventive. Seriously—it's quite a feat. I wish I had that kind of ingenuity."

Well, that was . . . surprisingly kind? *Inventive* could maybe go either way based on tone and delivery, but Rocco's use of it sounded genuine enough. Like he's actually trying for some peaceful brotherly dialogue for the holiday. I take a sip of my drink, feeling cautiously optimistic about the dining experience ahead.

"I know this is hard for you to comprehend," Rudy says

between gritted teeth, his utensils clenched in a death grip—clearly choosing to *not* take *inventive* as a compliment—"because you're content just reading poorly written lines from a script, but I actually like to write and create and shape my shows around live reactions. I *like* to meet the people who got the shows we did, who get my shows now. I'm not trying to hide from fans behind Gucci shades and tinted limo windows."

Rocco shakes his head, chuckling amiably, despite Rudy's jabs. I'm actually kind of impressed by his decency. "Hey, now, I wish I could engage with my fans the way you do. But our experiences are . . . different these days. Have you had people breaking into your property, trying to crawl inside through a dog door? I did. Last month. Or how—"

"No pissing contests," Remo says from the end of the table, because it appears everyone is now fully listening to the two brothers warring. "Not on Christmas Eve. Not ever. At least not under this roof."

"Sorry, Dad," Rudy says, nodding dutifully. I hope this is the end, and we can all tidily finish the night and Rocco can hop on a plane again to somewhere far, far away, but then Rudy continues, "I should say, though, while I have everyone's attention, that I'm not only doing my live gigs. I don't mind dipping into the old acting thing once in a while, not for the right reason. The right script."

"Oh?" Rocco asks, those perfect eyebrows of his that he surely has threaded on a weekly basis lifting high in surprise.

"Yep," Rudy says, crossing his arms over his chest. He looks oddly puffed up, larger than life, almost. A Rudy that is far more like the one I anticipated meeting after that flip up on HeartThrobs. "I got asked to try out for a movie shooting in LA at the beginning of January. It's an awesome story, based on a YA novel. Lucy actually works with the author. Huge best-seller."

I'm hearing the words—it's the quietest the house has been

all night, I could very literally hear a pin drop—but none of them are making sense. The drinks were stiff, but not stiff enough to addle my mind.

"Clementine's movie?" I ask slowly, shaking my head, trying the words out loud to see if they make any more sense. No. Not at all. "You? January? But—" *Spiked Lemonade*. Our first show. The Great Elvira. Us. Everything.

Rudy glances at me, eyes barely meeting mine, before turning back to Rocco. "I got the part. I was on the fence, because I have so much good stuff going in Brooklyn. But it's a brilliant script. Smart, funny, *original*." He shrugs. "A no-brainer, really."

A no-brainer.

It wasn't even a difficult decision.

All it took was one better offer.

The crowd erupts in loud cheers and toasts. Rudy finds my hand under the table and squeezes, but I slip my stiff fingers out of his grasp and push my plate away.

It's not until the dinner is cleared, and the crowd has moved into the living room for dessert and limoncello, that Rudy looks at me again. Really looks at me.

"It wasn't a no-brainer," he says quietly. "Clementine reached out after we met. Sent the script. I was planning on saying no. It wasn't a formal audition, but I went ahead with it to be polite, for your sake, too. That was part of it, at least. It all just . . . came together so fast. I didn't give them an answer yet. I wanted to talk to you first, but I also didn't want to ruin the holiday. Then Rocco was here, and . . . he makes me so angry. And bitter. And shit, I'll admit it—he makes me *jealous*. I felt like I had to be the big man with the big Hollywood job. I suck, and I'm sorry. I don't have to say yes if you don't want me to. I'll tell my family it fell through." He shrugs, looking so deeply . . . sad.

I hate that he's sad, but also—fuck his sadness.

Fuck his politeness, too.

"This is what I feared most about dating you. That extreme politeness, the kind of polite you've been trained to be your whole life."

Rudy puts his hands up, pleading or defensive, I can't tell. "Lucy, I—"

"No. Let me finish. I get that you're an entertainer. You have to act a certain way to appease people. Maybe that's part of the job. But you don't get to do that in real life, too. Not with me. Not *for* me, either. You didn't have to suck up to Clementine for my sake. You don't get to use that as an excuse."

"She's your boss."

"So?"

"So, you're not real with her either, are you? You bitch about her every day, but you grin and bear it when you hand over her twenty-dollar green juice. That's how the world works. We don't always get to let it all hang out."

I try to think of a comeback, but damn it, he's not completely wrong. I'm not my real self with Clementine, not by a long shot. And I hate it. "You're right. Maybe I should quit."

"It's your one steady gig. Sometimes you have to just suck it up, Lucy. That's how people keep a job. That's how people have a consistent income."

"Oh, like you know about that? With your *lottery* checks?"

Rudy flinches, and I feel both the wrath and the sympathy deep in my bones. "No. I don't. But maybe this movie will help. Maybe it's a good thing. For both of us. Do you want to keep on scraping by?"

"You want to do it, then? The movie?" My voice is so cool, so measured, I barely recognize it as my own.

Rudy stares at me for a long moment, looking so deeply into my eyes, the effect is dizzying. Not a good dizzy. He sighs. "Maybe? I wasn't lying. The script really is brilliant. It would feel nice to . . . act again. To have a role that means something. I don't think I've been totally honest with myself all these years—about just how much I do miss acting. I've auditioned here and there, but nothing big ever panned out. Then this came along, just kind of fell into my lap, and maybe . . . it's a sign?"

"A *sign*? Right. I see. So what about our show, then? The *signs* that led us there? That all means something, too, I thought. And what about your show?"

"Maybe we can postpone," he says, looking down at the table.

"No. It's less than two weeks away, and too many tickets have sold. They might not give us another shot. So . . . I'll do it. The show. Don't tell Marianne—or at least, don't tell her until it's so close to showtime, she might not cancel." The words come out before I consider them fully, but I'm surprised to realize how much I mean them. "I've failed for so long at the writing thing, and maybe that's because romance isn't my specialty. I mean, clearly." I laugh, loudly, and it's the only thing that holds back the sob that threatens to tear me in two. "But working on this show? Focusing on the comedy instead? It's maybe the first good decision I've made about my career in a long time. Maybe ever. I want this, Rudy."

No. I *need* this.

"But . . ." *They're paying for me*, he doesn't have to say. He's looking at me again, eyes brimming with pity, and it's this more than anything that clinches it.

"*Please.*"

It's completely absurd, I know it is, the idea of doing my first live show alone. But what if this is the one chance for me to do *something* besides serving Clementine lattes and green juice for all of eternity? I don't want that chance to slip away. Fuck Clementine and her brilliance. I wasn't lying; I do want to quit. But I need to find other ways to make money first.

This show might be a start.

And I would rather try and fail than let this whole experiment go down the drain.

We met the Great Elvira for a reason. I feel it deep in my gut.

Rudy nods slowly. "Okay. I won't tell her. Not until the morning of the show. She'll hate me for it, but these things happen, and Marianne and I go way back. She might want to pull the plug, but I'll do my best to convince her. No promises, though."

"Thank you." And then, because apparently I'm hell-bent on totally ruining my holiday, I ask: "Is this battle with Rocco because of Piper? Do you still have feelings for her?"

"*No.*" He practically yells it, and then seems to remember his family is a wall or two away. He takes a deep breath, steadies himself. "Not her. It's about Rocco, and how he betrayed me. We were best friends, and sometimes it feels like he died. That best friend. That Rocco, dead and buried. The big hot-shot star who flies around the world with supermodels, who puts in no effort with his family but gets all the praise, while I get all the pity? I don't know him. And I can't stand that we're related."

I'm relieved about Piper, not that it improves our situation now. "You should work on that. Talk to him. Talk to somebody. It's not healthy, carrying that baggage. Letting it dictate your life. And maybe I'm just naïve, but I thought he was making a genuine effort to connect with you tonight. And you seem to take any opportunity to twist what he says into a negative."

Rudy sighs, looking up at the ornate crystal chandelier dangling over our heads. It'll probably crash down on us, our *destiny* steadily on the decline. Everything may soon be crashing down around us, just like Sharlene warned us it might. "Can we talk about us? Because I hope you know, this doesn't mean we—"

I stand up, cutting him off. "Let's not right now. You should be with your family. I should be with mine. I think I'll head down tonight. Surprise my parents. Maybe stay with them for a few extra days."

"Are you sure?"
I nod, swallowing back a cry, because it's a lie.
I'm not sure. About tonight. Him. Us.
There's only one thing I'm sure about:
The show must go on.

Chapter 18
Rudy

Beware a clean slate when there's nothing to clear.

When I was a senior in high school, I spent my New Year's Eve seeing Billy Joel in a network VIP box at MSG. I had to fly to LA early New Year's Day for the last season of *The Whiz of Riz*, but that didn't stop me from getting exceptionally drunk on free booze in the suite, and then puking in the middle of the Lincoln Tunnel on my limo ride home. The next morning, I survived my first, but certainly not last, hungover plane ride. It was awful, sure. But there was also a badge of honor in it.

This New Year's Eve flight to LA is similar, minus any badge. There's no honor this time. I feel drained and shamed. My gut is twisting, from guilt instead of booze.

The whole Rocco and Piper nightmare started on a New Year's Eve, too. It's never been my favorite holiday, so this year seems to be on trend.

Despite the blowup on Christmas Eve, Lucy and I have still been talking. A little. Lucy decided to stay in PA the week between Christmas and New Year's Eve, and I hunkered down in our place. It felt weird to be alone there with all her stuff, while she was most definitely talking shit about me to her folks. Well deserved, but still stings.

I've initiated most of the texts so far. Her responses are somehow pleasant and pointed—it's an art, really, to pull that blend off. The work of a true wordsmithstress.

I decide to text her now to see how she's doing, back in her Spinster Cave for the holiday.

Rudy: I hope you're having a good last night of 2015! I miss you. So much.

When she doesn't immediately respond, I send another message.

Rudy: Are you having fun?

One minute. Five. Ten. I contemplate a third text, when my phone vibrates.

Lucy: Sure. Another New Year's Eve drinking basement gin with the Myrtles. Not exactly how I anticipated ending this year.

I reply immediately. Because when you're stuck on an airplane for hours, paying the outrageous fee for Wi-Fi, you get to be extra attentive about texts.

Rudy: I'm sorry I'm not there. I can't believe they're making me come out to get fitted on New Year's fucking Day to start shooting on the second. I feel really bad, but I know it'll work out.

Rudy: WE will work out.

Rudy: This is just a blip. I'm not disappearing.

Rudy: Promise.

Damn, dude, laying it on a little thick, huh?

I keep hearing her voice in my head, though, telling me about my extreme politeness. How my need to appease people extends beyond the job.

Me. An appeaser? Fuck, that hurts. Probably because it's true.

I stare at my phone for a while, waiting.

When Lucy doesn't give me anything back, I'm not sure what else to add except for *"Happy New Year!!!"* at the stroke of midnight on the East Coast. There's nothing happy about any of this, though.

I broke Elvira's prophecy.

I decided that hopping on a plane to make a film for my girlfriend's nemesis boss was the best thing to do. A film that would prove to Rocco—and to everyone, myself included—I still had the star power to land a flashy Hollywood job. I picked *this* over a great show I spent a lot of time working on, a show shared with someone so unique and funny and beautiful and . . .

Shit. I'm ready to get off this plane.

Too much time alone, thirty thousand feet above ground, to overanalyze and spiral. I should've had a couple of doubles before I left and slept it off. There's nothing useful to be done now. No one to talk to, no one who really gets what—

Sharlene.

Her name strikes me like a lightning bolt through the clouds next to my window.

I never followed up with her. I wanted to, wanted to ask more questions, but when I dipped back in to get my credit card, she wasn't working. Life moved on. But I need to get in touch with her. Now.

So I do what twenty-something Rudy would have done— creep online to make contact. A somewhat embarrassing strategy, but it did work on occasion.

Francois Santos's Instagram account is fairly up-to-date. Plenty of food pics, but very few of the waitstaff. I keep scrolling and . . . finally! There she is, Sharlene, in that same glowing crystal ball tee, holding a plate of merguez tacos. Tagged and everything.

I make it a point to all-caps who I am in the first sentence, so she doesn't immediately dismiss me:

ELVIRA'S LAST COUPLE NEEDS YOUR HELP!

Hey Sharlene,

I know this is really damn personal, so I totally understand if you ignore me, but I'm desperate for any help I can get. I'd love to know how your destined relationship exploded, and if you had any solid "hindsight is 20/20" pointers. I maybe screwed it up, royally. I hopped on a plane, left her and a project we were working on together. We tried to listen to what Elvira, and you, said. We created something great, and I decided to pause it—or maybe blow it up for good— because of a selfish impulse . . . what a dumb shit, right? Anyway. I guess I'm looking for a silver lining or an Elvira cheat code to get us back on track.

Thanks,
Rudy

Send.

Judging by her Instagram posting frequency, I'm not sure I'll get a response before my imaginary son's fifth birthday, but it was a Hail Mary for me.

I can't change being in the sky, on my way to do what I've been doing since I was my imaginary son's age.

Maybe it's already far too late to change my path.

* * *

I arrive at LAX around 10:30 p.m. and hop on a shuttle to the hotel.

By choice, I'm staying at the Hilton by the airport. I don't care about the long commute or how much the rental car costs—if I have to spend any real amount of time in LA, I'm staying by the beach. At the very least, I can catch some sun and maybe a swim in the Pacific, staying the hell away from "Brooklyn West," as I like to call it. It's where ninety percent of my LA acquaintances live. Silver Lake, Echo Park, etc. Everyone wants to see you, but if you're on the west side, it's a sure way of getting ghosted or worse. The "worse" is the game where you have no intention of hanging out, but you string someone along all day until something better inevitably pops up. LA folks are upper crust when it comes to stringing people along.

Thinking of it now reminds me of just how much I love New York.

The Hilton screams "New Year's Eve Party Central!," but there are just a handful of people wandering the lobby, most of them staff. There's no way I'm going to spend my second midnight with strangers at the hotel bar. The curse of leaving Lucy on New Year's Eve has been written: two chances to celebrate, both miserable and alone. I get up to the room, and thankfully, there's a stocked fridge, so I decide to host a one-man pity party.

And oh, what a pity party it is. Me and my eleven-dollar mini Budweiser, trying not to cry into my kid-sized bag of Cool Ranch Doritos.

I turn on the TV to catch the Pacific Time New Year, even though it feels less than, being here, not celebrating on Big Apple time. But when the countdown to midnight ticks to zero, I text Lucy. Even if it's three in the morning for her, and the ball is squarely not in my court.

Rudy: Happy New Year times two, Lucy. I'm sorry. I can't say that enough.

I stare at the screen for a few minutes, just in case she happens to be up and inclined to chat. But no. Not even any lingering ellipses. I toss the phone onto the nightstand.

I need to finish this beer and get to sleep. Tomorrow is a big day.

But it's hard to relax when all I can think about is how Lucy's the reason I'm here—her boss sweeping in, taking me away from everything Lucy and I had going together.

She didn't really do that, though, did she? Take me away. Clementine probably doesn't even know about our show.

I took myself out. I did it.

Me. My decision.

Lucy, Elvira, the last few months, it all brought me here. A place where it could actually be possible to recharge my acting career. For years now, I've used Rocco's career as the shining example of a path I never wanted to take—but then a role would come up, an opportunity, and that old switch turned on. Some deep-seated instinct. The fear of failure, it muddled things. But maybe there's a reason I could never really shake the acting bug. A reason I couldn't even say no to all those web series pilots.

Is this what Elvira was trying to get across to me?

Is that what I want? Is that why we met?

Or did I blow our chance to fulfill the worst best date ever because of a selfish and unhealthy motivation to prove something out of spite?

I turn the lights off and lay in bed, the TV still on.

Wondering if this was quite possibly the worst decision of my life.

I wake up to a slew of texts from Clementine:

CC: HNY! So . . . fitting is postponed.

CC: I can't believe they went around my back. I'm so sorry, but I still believe all will work out. Deep breaths!

CC: They're going to screen test you against their replacement pick at the end of the week. At least they're still paying for a hotel and per diem! More soon. Enjoy LA in the meantime!

Fuck me.

I thought this was a done deal. Not a competition.

This is why they flew me all the way out here?

For a last-minute audition to determine my fate?

I keep typing and deleting my response. I want to get my point across that it's pretty messed up to send someone out here on a whim. But . . . Lucy's still my girlfriend—at least I hope she still considers herself to be my girlfriend—and I don't want to add to the shit pile I've already made by pissing off her boss.

Rudy: Oh man, that was unexpected. Took all last week to prepare, so I'm not worried about a screen test. Thanks for the heads up. And happy new year!

Nicer than I would have liked.

But at least I can have my own little vacation day, visiting some favorite spots. First stop on the nostalgia train: La Fiesta Brava and the best fish taco on the west side. Close to where I lived my last year out here.

I get to the restaurant, delighted to find it's not only open, but I have the place to myself, probably because everyone else has actual plans for the holiday. Five minutes after ordering, my food arrives, looking as amazing as I remembered. The tilapia is plated on top of my tacos, showcasing the full fillet of fish. I smell the lime marinade on top, always the perfect amount of citrus and heat. Truly, the ultimate taco. I snap a pic and send it to Lucy with the caption:

Rudy: Best fish taco in LA, wish I could share it with you. Miss you. Hope your first day of 2016 is a good one.

After four tacos and chips and salsa and no response from Lucy, I head up the PCH. My favorite ride as a teenager. I'd drive up to Zuma Beach to get my head right if I was missing the East Coast, or if I had a stressful day on set. It's a drive I made with Piper in the passenger seat countless times, too, day trips to the beach, fancy dinners on the water. Speaking of, I pass by Moonshadows, the epitome of early-eighties Malibu money restaurants. It started out as a joke, us going there together, but ended up becoming a monthly ritual. Amazing ocean views inside and out. Interesting clientele, too, so Piper and I would stargaze, watch the tide, and laugh at all the spiffily dressed well-to-dos and wannabes.

I wonder if Piper made Rocco take her to Moonshadows, too. If so, I can take solace in knowing that he would have hated it there. Rocco prefers less-flashy places, despite being a celebrity.

Or at least that used to be true, back when I knew anything about him.

As I continue along the PCH, I'm reminded of the last time I was at Zuma, with Piper. Saying our goodbyes before my flight east for school. A more permanent goodbye than our usual, back when I was always flying back and forth between Cali and Jersey. In the moment—and for years after—it'd felt like one of the worst days of my life.

But here, now, those negative feelings are gone. Every last one of them.

My ability to go after what I want, and to listen to that little voice in my head—even when it's telling me to take the hard way out, like leaving Hollywood and putting three thousand miles between me and my girlfriend—paved the way for everything I've accomplished in New York. I might not be rich, but I've managed to do what I feel passionate about. If I'd stayed out here, I would've never been able to follow my creative dreams. As much as that day stung, it helped build me back up. It was a new beginning.

I pull over and park in an empty lot.

New Year's Day at Zuma Beach. A real cleansing moment.

I'm not the most spiritual person, much to my mother's chagrin, but as I walk down to the water, I start talking to the ether anyway. Can't hurt.

"I know it's been a while since the last time I was here, but I want to thank you for the days of calm and perseverance you gave me all those years ago. This beach means a lot to me. And . . . I need some of that calm again now. I'm worried I messed up, leaving Lucy the way I did, all for one Hollywood gig. Because there's never been someone like her in my life. She, like you—um, Zuma—has helped me become a better person. I hope I know what I'm doing being out here. Risking everything."

I've been in my own little trance, and look up to see a couple staring at me like I'm on drugs. Admittedly, it for sure looks like that. A grown man speaking to the ocean, thanking it for its presence and its powers. Actually, that sounds pretty damn cool, if you ask me. I start yelling gibberish and waving my arms with clenched fists towards the sky, "Squeeble squabble rain rain go away snook grimble!"

As suspected, unlike the great people of New York City, who can be casual and ignore these kinds of rants, the LAers freak out and start quickly moving away from me.

Rocco and I used to have this joke where we would start normal conversations and then escalate them into ridiculous nonsense babble, until we could only identify what we were saying through body language. A tripped-out version of charades. It always got us laughing.

We had a lot of great brother moments like that, on and off set.

A random memory comes to me now—Rocco and I, breaking into a Sea World parking lot, driving the people movers around until the security guards chased us. Because Rocco was older, in better shape, and faster, he was able to get security to target him while my shorter, stubbier legs got me up and over the chain-link fence first—then Rocco left them in the dust to follow me. A real big brother move, and without cameras. Just brothers taking care of each other.

Fuck, I miss that.

After a few more minutes of ocean gazing, I trudge back up the beach to my car.

I keep driving.

The next few days in LA are like a strange kind of purgatory.

An extended beach and food tour with occasional stops to grab some vinyl. I even go to the Valley and cruise around my old stomping grounds, the place where I learned to drive and get my bearings straight in this sprawling city that felt like a second home. I haven't let a single person know I'm out here. No social media posts. Nothing. It's actually quite nice, this alone time. Though it would be better if Lucy were here. Our texts are drying up, more so every day.

I miss her. Constantly.

Clementine asked to meet up today—two days before the screen test. She's the first person who's not a bartender I'll talk to face-to-face. I requested the Venice Ale House, the home of good beers and an ahi tuna sandwich I dream about every couple of months. She's running late, because it's LA and everyone runs late, so she texts me her order. I've passed it on to the waitress, a T(empeh)-L-T and tea, and am halfway through my first beer when I see her walk in. I almost miss her at first glance, because she looks completely different than she did in Brooklyn. She's fully embodied LA hipster chic, complete with flared bell-bottoms and a big yellow hat, a vibrant tie-dye shirt rolled up at the corner of her left hip.

That was fast.

"So," she says, launching right in as she takes a seat across from me, "I hope you've been having a good time. Not too good of a time, though. I want to make sure you're ready to woo Rad—the director."

"Ha, yeah, I may have gotten a little more color than normal on my first day here, but today the red's more of a tan. As tan as an Irishman gets, anyway. By tomorrow, it'll be perfect. And don't worry about me. I'm a professional. I know my lines. And I already looked up Rad. I didn't see any of his past work, but he seems to really know the YA space."

Clementine appears to be both shocked and troubled by this admission. "Rad is *amazing*, Rudy, and you need to watch one of his films tonight so you can talk about that with him. He would really appreciate you knowing some of his work."

Ugh. Yet another frustrating point about this town and · industry. Can't I just respect someone without having to kiss their ass and fluff their ego? Can't we just assume the roles, you tell me what to do, and I do it?

Clearly, Clementine doesn't catch that I'm completely checked out of this conversation, as she starts to rapidly scroll on her phone, still talking. "*Prom Witch* is on Netflix. You can watch tonight! It's so good. You'll see what I'm talking about. Rad is really, well, *rad*." She laughs in a way that wholly captures the essence of LOL. It's disturbing. "I've been talking you up a lot, of course, and he said he kind of remembered *Black Hole Sons*. I told him to watch a few episodes, too, and I'm sure he did. He listens to me."

Honestly, this couldn't get any worse. I'm trying so hard to focus on the sandwich coming and praying we can sit in silence while we eat. Low odds.

I order another beer when our food arrives.

"I've never had tempeh before," Clementine says, eying her plate, "but I've been around so many health-conscious people since I got here, I figured I'd try out the whole vegan thing. When in Rome, right?"

I raise my beer to her iced tea for a cheers. I mostly just feel bad for her now. To get so immediately swallowed whole by a new place that would rather see you conform than break out and be yourself.

"Here's to you, Clementine. What a cool experience, to have your pages turned into frames. I hope you enjoy all LA has to offer, but . . . make sure you keep some of yourself out here, too, okay? There's plenty of room for all types, and you deserve to show everyone your true self."

Whoa, spoken like a real sage. An unwanted, unsolicited kind of sage, but still. In true Clementine fashion, she doesn't seem to have heard more than the accolade at the top of the toast, but that's fine, too. Maybe she is *exactly* LA and just needed to come here to realize it. Maybe she'll never come back, and Lucy will be officially out of the one stable gig she's got going.

Miraculously, she lets me eat the entire sandwich in peace. I'm grateful for her twitchy phone fingers. As we're finishing up, she stands abruptly, saying her Airbnb host has a pipe issue, and her things—Pinky included—are in danger of getting soaked. She rushes out with barely a goodbye.

Thank God for that pipe.

As I'm sitting at the table alone, I take a good look down the Venice boardwalk. There's the usual riffraff running around, saying things like, "My bowl has a hole in it, can you fill it with some bud?" and "I know you got some dough, bro, could you Venmo me a five spot?" A shirtless guy in a banana hammock roller-skates in circles, a snake wrapped around his shoulders. He's a staple on this boardwalk. I remember him—or someone just like him, at least—from my LA days. After he passes by, I notice a table across from me with a crystal ball set on top, purple fabric engulfing the ball like a bird's nest. A sloppily written sign hangs from the table: "Thirty bucks gets you all the info on your future. You down for your destiny?"

There's nobody by the table to put a face to the sign, so my mind automatically conjures up Elvira. Though she wouldn't be caught, well, *dead* working a table like that. My eyes move back to the scrawl.

Destiny.

Destined.

Sharlene.

I haven't checked my Instagram inbox in a few days, and I can't keep up with notifications. Too many weird fan messages to track.

I take out my phone and scroll through my inbox.

There: *Sharatthebar73.*

She actually responded.

I skim through her message quickly. Then I read it again, slower this time.

Hey Rudy, I was wondering about you 2 . . .

Sorry to hear you might be ending up on the same shit end stick that I'm on. There's plenty of room for you. I don't have any cheat codes or much wisdom on the subject. We started to fizzle, me and Claudio. Let our carte blanche from Elvira carry us and it wasn't meant for that. Relationships are normally worked on. Full of give and takes. We relied on the word "destined" and forgot that some real work and barrier wall demolition was still a part of the deal. We'd used all our savings, went in on a restaurant together—he liked to cook, I didn't want to be a forever waitress—and just kept doubling down. Ignored our problems. Then a couple days before the soft opening, there was a gas leak explosion that destroyed the whole restaurant. We were lucky to make it out alive. You'd think an event of that magnitude would bring us closer together, but it just turned into pointing fingers. Quickly followed by releasing all the relationship shortcomings we'd held in on account of our "destined" status. It literally and figuratively exploded us.

We were perfect for each other, I do believe that, but we were too damn stubborn to make it work. All I can say to you is to follow what you really feel in your heart. Selfishness doesn't reside there, it's only in your brain and dick. Keep me posted, I'd love to hear a sweet redemption story.

–Shar

I finish my beer, thinking about what I just read.

Jesus. Poor Sharlene and Claudio.

Epic building fire aside, her wisdom resonates not only for Lucy, but for my brother, too. I still carry that "fuck you, Rocco" card that's gotten me to where I am today: resentful, jealous, and full of hate towards my own blood.

Sharlene is right. Lucy was, too, when she called me out on Christmas Eve.

Why be out here and not see my brother?

Well, I guess there are a multitude of reasons.

Or there *were*, at least.

But right now, they all seem to be old news. Not part of my life anymore. What's the point in resenting him? I like my life. The gigs. The people.

I feel strangely calm, connecting these dots.

Maybe I had to get back to LA to really see what's important. To put the parts of life that matter most in perspective. The parts I can control right now, at least. Like seeing Rocco.

I type out the text and hit Send before I can change my mind.

Rudy: Hey, I'm in town. For that gig. Wanna meet up tomorrow?

Our last exchange before Rocco's unanswered Outlaws text was from the summer, me saying: *Happy birthday, hope it's not terrible.* Mom was nagging me all day to reach out. To his credit, he still thanked me straightaway.

His response now is instant, too:

Rocco: I'm not working until February, so I'm just at home hanging out. Come by whenever. Glad you made it out here.

Is he really glad? Was Lucy right—and maybe he is genuinely trying to reconnect?

I guess we'll find out.

I sit on the patio, watching a guy shove a CD in every person's face that walks by. That's a Venice tradition I'm glad to see still exists in the times of download cards. Some things, at least, never change.

Rocco's house is outrageous.

Mom's gushed about it, tried to show me photos, but I tuned it out. It's all brand new to me today.

The house sits atop a hill in the Santa Monica mountains, overlooking the Pacific. Very large, but I discover on our tour that, in true Rocco fashion, half of the house is bare. He's a creature of habit and mostly lives in five rooms—bedroom, living room, kitchen, two shitters—leaving the other twenty or so to collect dust.

"So, this is home," he says, wrapping up the tour in his living room. There's a long wall of floor-to-ceiling windows showcasing the private beach down below. What would it be like to wake up to this every morning? It's night and day, Lucy's cave and this house. "You know me, it was about the view and outdoor space more than the house itself. I live alone. Why put stuff in all those other rooms?"

"You sound as curmudgeonly as Dad, always keeping the

thermostat off unless it was literally below freezing." Rocco laughs, a real one. A sound from my distant past.

We're quiet again for a minute, looking out at the ocean.

What did I come here to say?

What do Rocco and I have to talk about?

I scramble to think of another memory, a Dad joke. Something even halfway relevant. Even the first was a stretch. But then Rocco says, "You finally came back. I know you've been here before for music and comedy stuff—not that you called me up then—but I mean *back* back. Acting. I'm proud of you, little bro. I know it must not be easy, getting in the game again. And I . . . want to apologize."

I haven't been here for more than ten minutes, and already I'm getting into some serious talk that *Rocco* initiates?

Unexpected. Very.

"You don't have to apologize," I say, turning away from the window to face him. He's already watching me with those intense blue eyes of his, just like Dad's. "I've done a lot of thinking these last few days, and I've arrived at a good place. That's why I reached out."

He nods. "Is it the project making you happy?"

I take a few steps, sit down on his long leather couch. Damn. It's the softest couch my ass has ever touched. I shake my head at Rocco. "Not the project, no. Actually, that's having the opposite effect. I'm in a good place because I finally realized the things I've been mad about for so many years aren't relevant anymore. I mean, sure, you getting together with Piper was pretty low. The lowest of the low. We were still trying to figure things out long distance—which you knew, of course, because you knew everything, always—but then that New Year's Eve came around, you and her . . . definitely the nail in the coffin. But yeah, that was so many years ago. She's not in either of our lives anymore. I have someone great in Brooklyn who has my back. Someone I think I might be in love with."

I hadn't planned on saying that part.

Love.

But it came out, and I don't hate the sound of it. It doesn't feel wrong.

Rocco refuses to make eye contact. He keeps staring down at the remote on the couch. Classic Rocco move. When we would get yelled at by our parents growing up, I'd always listen and look them in the eye, and Rocco would fidget with stuff and avoid their scowls at all cost. You'd think the most successful actor in the family would have more confidence.

Maybe it's a good thing, though. That this hasn't changed. He's not too smooth.

"I know it wasn't a cool thing to do, but it just kind of . . . happened with Piper. The three of us spent so much time together, and once you left, it was just the two of us. Maybe we were missing the trio vibe, and that made it easier to transition into life here without you. But that's also bullshit, I know. I always had a crush—not that I would've admitted it, not even to myself. And once you two were struggling with the distance, that relationship status up in the air . . . I saw my shot. Swooped in. It was all me, you should know that. Never her, not in the beginning. She took time to get there."

He pauses, clears his throat. Eyes still on that damn remote, like it's the most interesting piece of tech in the world. Though to be fair, it *is* the most high-tech remote I've ever seen. Elon Musk probably has the same one.

"Like you said," he starts up again, "it's long over now, and she isn't in either of our lives. The truth is, I'm fucking lonely out here. No one likes me for me. No one knows me. Wah wah, right? Such a sob story, I know. But honestly, little bro, I'm jealous of what you have."

Jealous.

Rocco is jealous—of me.

"I'm happy for you, too, though," he continues. "I thought Lucy was great, for what it's worth." He finally looks up at me. "Her and Mom hit it off. That's a plus, right?"

Another classic Rocco move. Just as he finally acknowledges what he did, he moves the conversation along—brings Lucy into things before I can dwell in the past. Time to move on.

It is, though. It's time. He's right about that.

"She is great, and I just hope I didn't mess everything up flying out here. On New Year's Eve. And our show was supposed to start this week—still is, but without me if I stick around here. Which could blow up in my face if it sucks, and would end my relationship with the venue. I'd be out two shows. The booker would tell other bookers, snuffing me out of the scene, at least in New York. I risked all that. And honestly? A big part of this trip was proving to you that I could step away from the business and come back on my own terms. Come back to be a dad in a film that, upon further review . . . I didn't actually book yet."

"What do you mean? They flew you out and put you up all week just as a maybe?"

I shrug. "I don't know. Lucy's author boss said someone dropped out last minute, and she wanted me in the role. I sent in a self-tape. They told me I got it. After I landed, though, I found out it wasn't a done deal. I have a screen test tomorrow."

He grimaces. "Oof. That sucks."

"Yeah, well, it was stupid of me to fixate on you and what you'd said to me about college. 'If you leave, you won't be able to come back. You step out of the spotlight, the spotlight moves on.' I believed that for a long time. And used it as a mantra to push what I wanted to do. Away from here." *Away from you, too.* A life on my own terms.

Rocco looks genuinely hurt.

Like he'd forgotten what he'd said to me all those years ago. It was a real piece of shit thing to tell someone who only wanted to get an education, to not miss out on a quintessential life experience that felt so . . . normal. Rocco didn't care about "normal." He didn't want to learn how to live below his means to pursue other kinds of creative dreams.

He picked *this*.

For better and for worse.

"I don't remember saying that, but I wouldn't put it past me. I was trying to make you feel guilty about leaving because I selfishly wanted you to stay. I wanted you to be like me. I wasn't a musician or a comedian. Just an actor. That's it. You have so much more inside than I do, and honestly? I was jealous then, too—jealous of your talents—and I wanted to keep us as similar as possible. The Riziero brothers, always a package deal. And I'm so sorry for that. Looking back, that's the worst kind of brother to be. Trying to make you less than yourself."

Finally.

The genuine apology I've needed for so many years. The confession I wanted, but never expected.

"You're an incredible actor, and don't sell yourself short as a comedian. But . . ." I shake my head, grinning. "You're a shit musician, probably the most tone-deaf singer I've ever heard in my life. So don't quit your day job, not if you want all this luxury." I stand and twirl around, pointing at all the space in this ginormous house.

Rocco starts laughing again.

It cuts off in a heartbeat, though, and he pushes me down on his fancy-schmancy couch.

"Let's go back, little bro. You upended your perfect do-what-you-want-when-you-want life to spite me by taking a role you're not sure you actually want, and that you now don't even have secured? Shit. You must really hate me. Why would you do that? Aside from the money? You just told me you might be in love with the person you ditched on a cool new project. And on top of that, you ditched her on *New Year's Eve*?" He gives me his old-school big-brother glare, a look of judgment I haven't been burned by since I was nineteen. And it burns hotter than hell right now. "I know we have our problems, but bringing that baggage along to Lucy is deeply shitty, I have to say."

Now I'm the one who can't meet his eyes. "It's been eating at me since I stepped on the plane. The money is good, the inevitable 'I told you I could do it' to your face even better. It gets old, you know, being the struggling Riziero brother. You're not the only one who gets jealous. But I also wanted to do it for myself because, even after everything, I miss parts of this life. I miss acting. It just took me some time to realize that. Because you, Piper, LA. All of it put this incredible chip on my shoulder for so long, made me believe it was the whole industry I was running from—when really it was my relationships with you, with this place and its standards and expectations. My rationale was clouded, and Lucy took the hit for it. But you're right, it's not cool. It's low. And selfish. It makes me no better than anyone else who turns their back on someone for their own personal gain. Present company included."

Rocco smacks me on the back. Hard.

I start coughing, caught mid-swallow by the hit. Rocco tries to help by grabbing my shoulders and shaking me, like he's emptying a big bag of grains. Up and down, side to side, until every last grain is out. It's silly and stupid and perfect, and neither of us can stop laughing. There might even be a few tears.

Finally, Rocco lets me go, and we both go in for a hug. A real one.

I'm hugging my *brother.*

I take it all in, the wave of relief. A whole tsunami of it.

Rocco lets go of me after a good minute or three, and then immediately gets back to playing the serious older brother.

"As I see it, you have two options: You use this time as a much needed 'get your mind right' trip, and haul ass back to Brooklyn to salvage your relationship and show. Or you go nail the screen test and see if the life you left is the life you want again now. You could stay here. Hell, I'll even order more furniture. But just know, even if Lucy didn't break up with you yet, choosing to stay here means it's the end. Are you okay with walking away?"

I shake my head. "But like you said, we *didn't* break up."

Rocco gives me a pointed look that suggests I'm a first-class asshole for saying that.

"Read the room, Rudy! The clock is ticking. And that clock will run out, especially if you do this movie. Take it from your older, more experienced, done-all-the-dumb-shit-with-women, lonely brother. If you care about her, you know what you should do." He pauses to give me a second to absorb his great wisdom. Then does another one-eighty-degree turn: "Want to play some Madden on the big screen? I have a theater in the basement. Skipped that part of the tour—didn't want to make you too jealous."

"We both can't be the Giants, though," I say emphatically.

"No shit! My house, my rules. You can be the Jets."

"Fuck that! I'll whip your ass with the Eagles, and it'll sting that much worse."

As we descend the stairs into his sleek black-leathered man cave, the world at least feels right again with my brother.

We'll play a little Madden.

And then I'll figure out the rest.

Chapter 19

Lucy

A beginning, an ending, may be one and the same.

"What do you think, should we wear matching outfits tomorrow?" Estelle asks, rifling through my wardrobe with a deeply disapproving look on her face. "It's not too late for a trip to Saks, you know. Or maybe Bergdorf? They have such a divine high tea on the top floor. I'd kill for a good tea sandwich. *Kill.*" She glances pointedly at Frank, but he's too busy jotting down ideas in his notebook to take notice.

"Did I ever tell you two," he says eagerly, "about the time I took a girl to the zoo on a date? I laughed watching a monkey take a gigantic poo off a treetop, and she said I was disgusting and childish. Broke it off with me right then and there, left me all alone with my ice-cream cone at the monkey cage. Mint chocolate chip, I'll never forget. That's a good one, right? Pretty brutal?" He looks up at me, eyes lit with pride.

"That story sucks, Frank." Estelle has slammed my wardrobe doors shut and is now pulling out my dresser drawers. She tosses one shirt after another into a heap on the bed, shaking her head. I can only be mildly offended, because half of them came from Forever 21 sales racks half a decade ago. "If that's one of the best worst date stories you can think of, Lucy would be better off asking a rat in the gutter to join her onstage. That would at least keep people awake."

Frank looks crestfallen, and I resist the urge to laugh.

It's a positive sign, though, feeling even the temptation to laugh.

I haven't laughed about much of anything since the holidays—Rudy leaving me and the show and the whole Great Elvira Challenge in the dust trail behind his plane to LA.

I shouldn't be this surprised.

It's *hilarious*, really, my extreme naïveté. I've got nothing on the legions of celebrities Rudy's met in his day. Sure, Elvira keeling over on us mid-prophecy made things interesting for a little while. But nothing stays interesting forever, does it?

Maybe he got all the fodder he needed from me. Maybe the bit ran its course.

He's barely texted for the last few days. "Good morning." "Good night." Maybe a weak "how's your day?" somewhere in between. Some LA taco pics. There've been a few missed calls, a round of phone tag no one seems intent on winning.

Or maybe what I said about the *lottery*, about Rocco, cut too deep. Maybe Rudy thinks I went too far.

I don't regret it, being honest, but I wish I could have said it more gently.

I wish the conversation had been more of a comma, not a period.

Maybe it could still be an ellipsis.

Maybe it's not up to us to decide.

"I have a much better one, come to think of it," Frank says, flashing me a sharp, toothy grin, pulling me back to the task at hand. "I took a woman out to a classy joint in the Village, and after devouring a dish of what she thought was, quote, 'the most perfect corn in the world,' and then realizing it was *ant larvae,* she chucked all over her very expensive sea bass tacos. I tell you, Luce, there wasn't a vomit-free table by the time we were escorted out. Small place, intimate. Not a human in there could avoid the noxious stench."

"Holy shit," I say, nodding, genuinely impressed. Frank has upped his game. This story has definite stage potential. Thank God, too, because I've been very much doubting my grand idea to bring them up onstage with me. But they're warm bodies, which makes me feel less alone. Bickering warm bodies with a fondness for storytelling and warped perspectives on love. "How could anyone confuse corn and larvae? Where did you find this woman?"

Estelle clears her throat, loudly, reminiscent of a garbage truck compactor. "It was *very delicious* larvae, that's how," she says through gritted teeth. "Heavily seasoned." She's abandoned the pile of unsatisfactory clothes and is now giving Frank what may be her deadliest glare yet. She would absolutely kill, no question about it, with or without the incentive of a cucumber-cream-cheese petit fours.

"That was *you*?" I do it now, no holding back. I laugh, and it feels so damn good.

I laugh so hard that my stomach, twisted in an ugly knot since the holidays, starts to unravel. A little bit, at least. I feel looser. Lighter.

Frank, as Frank does, guffaws. Estelle holds off for a solid ten seconds, lips pursed in an increasingly wiggly line, before she breaks, too. Gives a good titter.

I miss Rudy.

I miss my roommate. My prophecy co-conspirator.

I miss the wild adventure of the last few months, the dizzying rush of it all—the strangely certain sensation that I was going *somewhere,* with *someone,* instead of standing still. Alone. Writing. Failing. Working as Clementine's errand girl, scraping by as a Craigslist extraordinaire (if you call odd jobs like clipping parakeet claws and an old woman's toenails back-to-back with no scrapes *extraordinary*).

This show might very well be a disaster, I realize that.

But I'm hoping with everything in me it's not.

I'm hoping this is the change I need. Not another rejection on the pile.

If I do go down, though, the Myrtles are willing to go down with me. That's friendship. True, bone-and-sinew–deep friendship. They're much more than warm bodies.

And at the very least, we'll have what I hoped for at the beginning of this—a story to tell. Not the story I expected. Not the one I may want.

But nonetheless—one for the ages.

Who would have thought there were so many ways to text someone goodnight?

Fifteen at least, by my count.

I've typed and texted them all in the last ten minutes. *Night.* (Too abrupt, seems passive-aggressive. Which I am, obviously, but more subtly, I hope.) *Sweet dreams.* (Too kind, and fake, which I refuse to be.) *Night night.* (Too cutesy. Am I a fucking toddler? Get it together, Lucy.) *Sleep tight.* (Does anyone really like to be tight when they sleep? Rudy certainly doesn't, given his penchant for sleep nudity. That seems like *sleeping loose.*)

I land on *Sleep good, Rudy*, which makes me feel both noble and generous. Before I can press Send, dots appear on Rudy's message screen. He's typing. Not typing. Typing.

Shit.

Ten minutes down the drain. My carefully crafted message will require revisions based on his text. Maybe he'll ask me about my day. Ask me something. Anything.

Dots disappear again. Reappear.

Okay, then. *I'll* lead.

And I won't wait for a response. I need to sleep. Or, more likely, to toss and turn in the dark with my eyes closed, wondering what Marianne will say to Rudy in the morning when she realizes he's no longer on our coast. I need to at least make an attempt at rest.

Because (hopefully) I have a debut comedy show tomorrow night in *New York City*, the crown jewel of the comedy world, a show that was supposed to be hosted by a duo, a couple so epic there was an actual *fatal* prophecy about their greatness. But no, now it's all on me and my two well-meaning assistants. Because of Rudy. Because our dream wasn't big enough for him. This success could never be enough. How could it be, when he grew up on red carpets? The floor at Little Zelda's is sticky with cheap beer and hipster sweat.

I press Send on my message, and then I silence my phone and toss it on the nightstand.

I manage a few hours of sleep, at least.

I'm sipping black coffee number one of the day when Marianne emails us with the final ticket numbers. Bright and early and eager. Loads of exclamation points. An average of three for every sentence, to be precise.

For good reason: *Spiked Lemonade* is sold out, except for a handful of tickets they leave available at the door. Better numbers than any *Eclipsed Too Soon* show, Marianne makes sure to note.

In a parallel universe where Rudy hadn't flaked, I would be delighted by this update. Sold out! Our first show! My first show! However, we're in a universe where Rudy most definitely *did* flake, and so now this particular update only makes me want to vomit. A room filled to capacity with people who don't give any fucks whatsoever about little old Lucy Minninger from small-town PA.

It hits me now, the full weight of our lie.

Or not a *lie*, necessarily, but the absence of truth. Questionable ethics at best. And I asked for this. It was all me. I asked Rudy to withhold this vital information from Marianne until the final hours. What if she holds a permanent grudge? What if this loses him a future of performing at Little Zelda's? No *Spiked Lemonade*, no *Eclipsed Too Soon*, no any show, ever again. What if Marianne knows other venues and comedy bookers, too, and spreads the word about Rudy?

Why am I only worrying about this *today*?

I stare at the screen, refreshing every two minutes, waiting for Rudy to respond, before I remember that he's three hours behind.

I drink another cup of coffee. Recommence staring at the screen.

Ten rolls around, and I decide that given the dire circumstances, it's an acceptable time on the West Coast. I skip past his uninspired text from the night before—*Hope you had a good day, Lucy*—and dive right into the emergency at hand.

Lucy: Holy shit, did you see Marianne's email?!

Dots appear within seconds. He must have an early call time. I think about him, on set, doing something so big and important, and I feel resentful. But I also feel a stab of pride. He deserves a shot, doesn't he? He deserves every shot.

But so did we.

So do I.

Rudy: I saw it. No worries. Show's still on.

Oh my God. *Show's still on.*

It's still happening.

Marianne knows, and it's still happening.

I'm equal parts relieved and horrified.

Lucy: Really???

Rudy: Really.

I want to ask more—how he broke it to Marianne, how enraged she is, the odds of her slicing my throat open when I walk off stage—but maybe it's better for my mental state to not have all the details. This day is already enough. So I keep it simple.

Lucy: Thank you.

I wait a few minutes, expecting something more. Hoping. Nothing comes, though. I could say more, too, but I don't.

I do one final run-through of inventory.

Scene-setting odds and ends, potential date wear accessories. Rudy had worried that props might be over the top, and maybe he was right, because what do I know about hosting a comedy show? He's the expert. But props make me feel prepared. I'll cling to whatever life raft I can find.

Right now, that raft is an overstuffed cardboard box: candles (battery-operated, no risk of inadvertently setting an audience member on fire); wine and rocks glasses (plastic, no risk of slicing open an audience member); plates and cutlery (paper, plastic); picnic basket and blanket (no inherent risk factors); wigs, hats, glasses, scarves, a sparkly gold boa for good measure. And shoved in at the top, after much debate, Rudy's cowhide monstrosity of a coat. An unsavory reminder of him and the Great Elvira Challenge, but also too dynamite of a prop to allow my stupid feelings to get in the way.

One final glance in the mirror—red lips, thick cat-eyes, loose curls, black leather jacket over a vintage green Peter Pan-style dress, collared in white around the sleeves and neckline. A surprise delivery, courtesy of Estelle, that landed on my doorstep earlier today. The dress has a sexy, swingy, sophisticated 1950s housewife vibe—a housewife who can make a perfect Jell-O mold one minute, and down a double shot of Scotch the next. Projecting an unflappable confidence I don't actually feel, despite the ticked-off checklist and neatly packed prop box.

A loud knock pulls me away from the mirror. The reflection of eyes that are far too mopey and sad, especially considering it's maybe the smoothest eyeliner job of my life, despite the coffee jitters. Shame.

"Your chariot has arrived," Frank yells out, and then makes a loud, trumpetlike hoot.

I open the door, propping it with my foot as I hoist the box into my arms. "Oh good, you called the cab already?"

He shakes his head. "Much better."

"Please, darling." Estelle appears at his shoulder, shaking her salon-fresh nest of what can only be described as neon-blond platinum curls. I can't see their full outfits beneath their jackets, but I see snippets of sparkles (Estelle) and leather (Frank), and of course, velvet (both). "Yes, darling, we're going to *host a show*. My God, it would be positively plebian to take a cab. A *cab!*" She chuckles airily, and Frank joins in.

They're in good spirits, at least.

"Oh-kay, so how . . ." I hear the chorus of honking first, and then I see it—the glossy stretch limo that's double-parked along the street, causing an eastbound gridlock. "Ah. I see."

Frank beams. "Only the best for our Luce on her big debut night!"

"*Our* big debut night," Estelle says. "Lest we forget I've agreed to share the escamol story. A grand sacrifice for the greater cause."

"Ant pupae," Frank corrects her.

Estelle looks down her nose at him, despite being shorter by a foot. "*Escamol.* It's referred to as escamol, Frank. Are you determined to be plebian after all?"

"We'll iron out the terminology in the car," I say, shifting the weight of the box in my arms. "Could one of you hold this while I lock up?"

Estelle looks mildly affronted by the ask, but Frank obliges, holding the box out in front of him as if the cardboard might leave something unsavory on his jacket. He goes above and beyond, carrying it all the way to the limo. It's maybe the most manual labor I've ever seen him do, unless one would categorize mashing juniper berries as "labor."

The limo is the most lux of my life—only my second limo, to be fair, the first being a podunk PA rental split ten ways for senior prom. Not that I can savor the plush leather seats, or the double magnum bottle of Moet on ice that Frank and Estelle pop and pour out as the car starts moving and they begin to hash out the finer details of Estelle's pupae puke.

There's a crystal flute filled to the rim in my hand, but I barely take one sip.

Too much riding on tonight, as tempting as a gentle buzz may be.

I check my phone—no good-luck text from Rudy. Maybe my thank-you was our last exchange of the day. He went out on a limb for me, after all. That might be the final kindness coming my way. I asked for authenticity, didn't I? I shouldn't need niceties now.

After too little time, the limo stops in front of Little Zelda's, and—*oh, what the hell*—I down my flute of champagne. Maybe it's okay to have the *gentlest* buzz. We have ninety minutes before the show, plenty of time for the counterbalance of adrenaline and water and more coffee, if they have it.

"Let's finish this up," Frank says, putting the bottle in my free hand. "The driver is ours all night long, you're welcome, and I have a bottle of sixteen-year-old single malt waiting for us on the other end. Figure we may need it."

Again, *oh, what the hell*, as I lift the bottle to my lips and take a swig. Just one. "That's enough for now," I say, putting the rest of the bottle back on ice, tilting it away from Estelle's grabby fingers. "We're cut off until after the show. We're professionals."

"Er, Lucy," Frank says, eyeing the Moet longingly, "I hate to remind you, but none of us are actual professionals. We're barely even amateurs."

"We're seasoned storytellers. That's what matters." I hope. Oh hell, how I hope.

I push open the limo door. One leg out, then the other, heels on the sidewalk, feeling a bit like an old Hollywood starlet stepping onto the red carpet. Minus a carpet, red or otherwise. Or cameras. Or fans.

Though, shit. No.

There actually *are* a few fans.

Audience members starting to form a short line. Fans of Rudy. Not fans of mine, of course. Bundled up, waiting for the doors to open in an hour. True dedication, especially in January. There's a proper Brooklyn mound of exhaust-blackened, trash-speckled snow lining the sidewalk by the entrance.

Did Marianne send out an e-blast this morning, letting people know it's just me?

Did they come anyway?

Or will Rudy's absence be a surprise, and not the happy kind? No one will hear the news and say, "That's okay, we still get to see *Lucy Minninger*!"

I feel instantly, overwhelmingly nauseous, staring at that line. Beads of sweat prickle at the back of my neck.

This was idiotic of me. How did I think I could pull this off without my co-star? The real star. Rudy's Polaris, and I'm some inconsequential star on a constellation no one cares to know by name. Or no, I don't even have a constellation—I'm all on my own, shining dimly and blandly, a loner with no solar community.

Fuck, maybe I'm not even a star. Just a few flecks of asteroid dust.

Sure, I have some incredibly awful first-date stories in my arsenal. And sure, I can spin them into entertaining stories for friends. I can make people laugh. If there's one thing I can do, that I've *always* been able to do, it's humor. I believe in that—in myself. But there's probably something more to being an actual comedian people pay good money to see onstage—especially discerning critics like these hale and hearty Carhartt- and flannel-bedecked Brooklynites lined up in front of me.

How do I know if I have that *something*?

And even if I do, will people give me a chance to prove it before they walk out?

"Uh, Lucy?" Estelle calls from the open door behind me. "Hello?"

I ignore her, noticing now the humongous, brightly lit marquee above my head:

SPIKED LEMONADE, FEATURING RUDY RIZIERO
AND LUCY MINNINGER

Seeing my name up there, our names together, makes me want to cry.

"Could you kindly move your ass so I can get out?" Estelle asks, shoving the cardboard box against said ass to nudge me along.

"Luce? Don't tell me you're having second thoughts," Frank says, coming around from the other side of the limo.

I turn to Frank, dragging my pitiful eyes off that foot-high *Rudy and Lucy*, and am stunned by the look of extreme concern on his face. Frank always cares about my well-being, in his own gruff Frank way, but it's maybe the most openly emotional expression I've ever seen his features pull off in tandem, eyes and lips and cheeks all asking the same question: *Are you okay?*

No, Frank. I'm not. At all.

"Second thoughts?" Estelle crows loudly, pushing the box against me with such vigor that it does the trick this time, pushing me far enough into the sidewalk that she can exit the limo. "I won't allow it."

"You won't allow it?" I ask, pulling my jacket around me more tightly to fight off the cold night.

"Absolutely not," Estelle says, and where her face lacks Frank's concern, she makes up for it with her equally authentic indignation. "We—*you*, I mean—have done far too much work. Besides, you can make anyone laugh. I've seen it a thousand times. Bartenders, waiters, delivery people, that cranky pharmacist on the corner who barely acknowledges me when he hands over my laxa— *Pills.* You make me and Frank laugh, and otherwise, the only things we laugh about are each other. At, not with."

It's an exceptionally high compliment, coming from her. "I really appreciate the pep—"

"Yeah yeah, so let's get this show going, shall we?" She shoves the box in my hands and then, noticing the line of fans, snaps into a rigid posture-perfect stance, eyes hungrily roaming the sidewalk for paparazzi.

Of which there is, of course, none.

But she's right, it's time to get the show going, and that means first meeting Marianne. Who may or may not want to slip arsenic in my water at the end of the night.

I'm only just pushing open the door, the scent of stale hops and bar nachos hitting me in a thick wave, when I hear a woman say, with a surprising degree of pleasantness, "Ah, there they are! You must be Lucy. I'm Marianne."

Marianne looks exactly as I suspected a Brooklyn comedy booker would: blunt black bangs, clear-frame glasses, hot fuchsia lips. Lips that are, against all odds, smiling at me.

Why the hell is she smiling at me?

"Where's Rudy?" She's looking past me toward the door, where the Myrtles have stalled, still staring doe-eyed at the fans. "I was just about to text him for an ETA. I was getting nervous." She laughs, eyes still on the entrance.

Marianne doesn't know.

She.

Doesn't.

Know.

Why doesn't she know?

No worries, Rudy said. No worries!

Oh, I have so many worries right now. So many. A swarm of worries has infested my entire body. I may black out.

"Uh, er," I manage to say, which is softer and more succinct than the "WHAT THE HELL IS SHE TALKING ABOUT?" flashing through my brain in hot neon.

Marianne's gaze snaps back to me. Those fuchsia lips are no longer smiling. She's caught a whiff of that worry. The air is drenched with it. "Is something wrong?"

The way she asks this question, it's clear there is only one way I'm supposed to answer: *Of course not! Rudy's right around the corner, talking to a fan!*

"Kind of?" I mumble.

"Please elaborate."

"Well, so Rudy, I thought he told you, but ah . . . he's in LA. He got a role in a big movie, super last-minute, and he couldn't turn it down, so—"

"Last-minute? Exactly how last-minute? Ten minutes ago?"

"Uh, er," I say again, ever so eloquently. "I'm not sure exactly?" To be fair, I don't know the exact minute the offer came in. I wasn't privy to all of the details, either.

"You're not sure," she deadpans. "Your partner up and left for LA, and you're not sure when that happened. Isn't he your boyfriend? Or was that just a shtick to sell tickets?"

Ouch. That one lands especially hard. "He was supposed to tell you," I say quietly. "I thought you knew."

"You thought he told me, and I was just letting the show go on like nothing happened? Without even bothering to discuss what it would look like without Rudy? The *star*? The reason we have a sold-out room tonight?"

Estelle and Frank are suddenly flanking me on either side. A Myrtle wall of defense.

"Lucy is much funnier than Rudy," Estelle says.

"Much," Frank confirms.

"And she has worse dating stories than him," Estelle adds. "Truly pitiful. Lucy has the worst dating luck."

Frank nods. "Abysmal."

"Who are *they*?" Marianne asks, squinting at them through her oversized glasses. I wonder, briefly, if they're even prescription.

"Um. My friends. They were going to help out onstage."

"I see. Help out. And are your friends comedians?"

"Not technically speaking, no."

"And you personally have also never done a show?"

I shake my head. "Do you want us to leave?"

"I want that, yes. Very much so. But . . ." Marianne sighs, throwing her hands up in the air. "It's too late to cancel. There are people waiting already."

"So, we're still on then?" Estelle asks, cheerily.

Marianne glowers at her. Estelle doesn't blanch. Estelle never blanches.

"Yes. But only because I'm desperate. Or out of my mind, I don't know. Fuck." She closes her eyes for a few seconds, probably fantasizing about me and Rudy dead and bloodied, our organs strung from the stage lights. "Let's go to the green room, and you can walk me through the show. I want to hear your plans. And I want to drink whiskey. A lot of whiskey."

She turns toward the empty bar and stomps away.

I'm left clutching the box of props, without a clue about where to find the green room. Without a clue about how this could have gotten so confused.

"Didn't you say Rudy told her?" Frank asks.

"That's what he led me to believe, yes."

Why?

If *Spiked Lemonade* isn't a smashing success, his entire Little Zelda's career is over.

I can't dwell, though. There will be plenty of free, jobless time to dissect later if tonight doesn't go well.

Right now, I have a show to put on.

And hopefully, for all our sakes, it's a damn good one.

Chapter 20
Rudy

Long will you prosper if you treasure my name.

It's always faster flying back to New York from Los Angeles.

The jet stream has your back, pushing the plane through the air. Mother Nature herself providing comfort and safety from the City of Angels, shepherding you back to the greatest city in the world. This certainly feels true today for my own exit. Like I'm back on the right path.

The path nature—the *universe*—intended.

After my talk with Rocco, his words about losing Lucy wouldn't stop reverberating through my brain. I couldn't do that. I couldn't lose her. No movie, no matter what. Even though the actor I was up against found a better role and ditched Clementine's project the morning of the screen test. So they re-offered me the job, officially. And I refused. Explained that the extra days gave me more clarity about my path, and this film wasn't part of it. Clementine wasn't thrilled, to put it mildly. But she did at least assure me Lucy's job was safe.

I packed my bags and rebooked a plane home for bright and early the next morning.

Today, the day of the show.

My plane should easily land a few hours before showtime. No need to tell Marianne anything's gone awry. My plan is to walk into Little Zelda's with plenty of time before curtains go up, explain my dumbassery and profusely apologize, and hopefully not get dumped before entertaining a sold-out crowd of people as I make some sort of gesture to show my love and support for the woman I abandoned.

This plan needs some serious Elvira flare, though. Because me showing up and saying I'm sorry isn't enough. Not after what I've done.

If the smattering of rom-coms I've watched in my life has taught me anything, it's that the Grand Gesture is key.

Upon landing at JFK, the pilot informs us they're having trouble with the gate, and we'll have to sit on the tarmac until they figure it out. Well, shit, good thing I have some padded time. I listen to the Ramones to pump me up while I wait. Too many songs.

All in all, I'm down an hour by the time we de-plane. I get a rideshare to Party City for some special Elvira gear, but traffic is unkind—burning me for another thirty minutes. Down to ninety minutes before showtime.

I can still do this. I *have* to do this.

Luckily, the universe starts to work in my favor, because the store has exactly what I need: a cheesy fortune teller getup, a long white wig, and a Magic 8 Ball for some extra pop. Lucy had said she'd "pick that over a psychic anytime." Her first HeartThrobs message to me. The best callback I can think of, at least with a ticking clock. This has to work, right? The homage to our first exchange, reviving Elvira one last time to make my final stand. It's all I got.

The traffic outside looks to be a nightmare, a bumper-to-bumper gridlock. So, the subway it is. A straight shot down Fourth Ave. Shouldn't take more than twenty minutes. I could text Lucy that I'm on my way . . . but I don't. I'm an entertainer at heart, what can I say, and I want the big entrance. The "Surprise!" effect. My sneaky drop-in is either going down as the best move I've ever made, or one I'll regret for a long time to come. Forever, maybe. Fifty-fifty odds.

The train's making good time . . . until a few minutes in, when we slow to a crawl and then eventually stop mid-tunnel. The train operator's voice squawks over the speaker, breaking up with static but still clear enough to make out: "Delayed due to police activity ahead. Thank you for your patience."

Fuck me. *Of course* this is happening.

I'm just a guy trying to take a piss, and the universe is a giant gust of wind, blowing it right back on me. I get it. Took me a moment, I suppose. Too many moments. I did have the common sense to bag the gig and head back to where my heart belongs. At what cost, though? And to what end? To make a Grand Gesture? To be a hero to redeem my own villainy? Me, me, me, and not enough about Lucy. If there's any hope for this relationship, I need to correct my selfish behavior.

Starting now.

I grab my phone, but of course, we're in a spot with no service. How ironic, right? Just when I finally decide to do the right thing, it becomes impossible. Marianne must be so pissed. The heat Lucy's undoubtedly facing . . .

Please, train, universe, can we get going?

I pause, holding my breath.

The train and the universe both seem to ignore my plea.

The subway car is getting increasingly sketchy with the wait. One person on the emergency call button screaming that she needs to get off the train to pick up her kid from daycare. Another who's started stretching out and doing squats on their seat, too close to a young college-aged kid who's desperately trying to avoid eye contact while reading a book called *The Truth about Confidence and Submission*. Though normally this is the kind of scenario fit for me to pillage for future witty banter, I can only stare at my phone, watching the minutes tick off, until we're ten away from showtime.

The speaker clicks back on: "Thank you for your patience. We'll be moving again, stopping at the next station, and then this train will be running express."

Double fuck . . . not nearly as close to Little Zelda's if we're skipping local stops.

I get off at the next station anyway, a stop above where I want to be, and decide to run the rest of the way. At least I feel like I'm actively trying. And getting sweaty. Very sweaty. Another callback that, in this moment, feels cathartic and cleansing.

This is my one chance to make things right. Before we explode like Sharlene and Claudio did—whatever form our own explosion might take. I don't want to find out.

I cross the final block, and I'm there, at Little Zelda's, and Marianne's working the door.

She, rightfully so, gives me a pointed *What the hell?* glare before launching in. "Wow, what a *lovely* surprise. I thought you had some fancy business to attend to on the other coast? Listen, I don't know what game you're playing, but next time you want to break a deal, could you at least give me a heads-up instead of having your partner tell me night-fucking-of that she's got a new crew? It's a train wreck up there. Lucy's pretty damn funny, I'll give you that, but the older couple, yikes. She would've been better off alone. We've already had a handful of refund requests because you didn't show, and I'm sure there will be more."

Her words sting, especially *train wreck*. Lucy's show. Our show. And it's all my fault.

I'm not sure a shitty Party City costume is enough to right my wrongs.

I lean in closer to the door to get a sense of the vibe onstage, and immediately hear a lot of talking over one another. Frank yells something animatedly.

"I'm sorry," I say, turning back to Marianne. "I had the chance to go do a movie that I last-minute decided wasn't for me. I messed up. With you. With Lucy. But I'm here now. And I'm going to turn this around, M, I swear. This idea has legs, and could be a great show. I just left it in the dust because I was being a dumbfuck."

She sighs, then purses her intensely pink lips. "At least you recognize your dumbfuckery. That's a start. Now please, go fix the show!"

"Will do. Er. Just one quick question." Marianne's looking increasingly annoyed that I'm still standing here. I talk faster. "Have they said anything yet about our first date with a dead psychic? The Great Elvira?"

"I don't know! Do you hear them up there, just stepping all over one another? The old couple's been telling a lot of stories from New York in the eighties, bumming people out. 'Back in the old days' this, 'don't make 'em like they used to' that. It's not helping their cause, that's for sure."

"Got it, thanks," I say, "I won't let you down." Marianne gives me a clipped nod, and I head inside. Maybe a few people have bailed, but it's still a packed house. All eyes on Lucy and the Myrtles.

The first course of action is to put this damn costume on. I run into the box office and get assembled. Flowy, sparkly, heinous perfection. Next step is to direct Lucy with some anonymous notes, taking a cue from a club I used to play in Philly many years ago. The owner of the club passed notes mid-set— "cut the Dead jams," "no more falsetto." Only a real dick does that to a band. And I definitely wasn't singing falsetto. That was a low blow.

My notes will be kinder and more constructive. I want to help Lucy—and pave the way for my big reveal. I grab some napkins from the bar and jot down a few suggestions, then hand them discreetly to JoJo, the stage manager, who's standing by the soundboard, watching the show. I ask him to slip the notes to Lucy.

The first note says: *Tell Estelle and Frank to stop speaking over one another.*

I watch as Lucy reads it, flips it over to see if there's more. She glances up at the audience for a few seconds, looking confused, before turning to the second napkin.

Tell one of YOUR worst first date experiences. It's why we're all here.

Lucy slips both napkins into her pocket, and I swear she stands up a little straighter. She cuts off Estelle and Frank with a loud throat clear.

"While I appreciate their take on dating in the twentieth century, I know why we're all here." She claps her hands, like a kindergarten teacher demanding attention. "How many of you have set your date's hair on fire with a tropical tiki drink?"

The crowd erupts. No hands are raised.

"Ah, just as I suspected. So yes, I did that. Our first date. *Only* date, obviously. His chosen name was Hashtag, by the way—you heard me correctly, a pound sign, a powerful symbol of his *brand*—and as if that wasn't ghastly enough, he discussed his toes and their aptitude for foot modeling at great length. Perhaps he deserved his coif to go up in flames?"

More laughter. It's working.

Lucy's getting the show back on track, and she still has no idea I'm here. The story continues—Chocolate Week, the burning pineapple, the fire, the water in the face—and the audience is there for the ride, eating it up. It might be her first time onstage like this, but Lucy's a natural, totally working the room. When the crowd laughs, she finds ways to keep hitting that joke for more laughs. It's special to watch, and my heart is beating too fast. I don't think a woman could be sexier to me than Lucy is right now. Owning that stage, being true to herself.

I'm so damn proud of her.

And so damn mad at myself for putting all of this at risk.

Lucy wraps up the Hashtag bit and calls up an audience participant: a woman who starts telling an intense story about a first date who came straight from a house fire—completely unwashed from the incident, soot on his nose, reeking of smoke. He said his ferret started the fire, chewed through a power cord and electrocuted itself. Burned the whole house down to the ground. His ninety-year-old grandmother got carted off in an ambulance. He didn't want to bail on the date, though.

Sheesh. Well, alright. That's more depressing than funny. The audience has been mostly silent, except for the ferret bit . . . poor ferret. I make a mental note that ferret jokes are apparently a hit, no matter how grisly.

Lucy seems to be quietly considering next steps. She gave up early on in trying to act this one out. A house burning down isn't exactly great comedic fodder. Though I suppose there's a *National Lampoon's Christmas Vacation* vibe. Frank and Estelle are arguing off mic, loudly, and picking up steam— Frank wants to jump in on the ferret bit, and Estelle's trying to restrain him.

Frank is the victor, grabbing at the mic and going for it: "My college roommate had a ferret named Shwingnuts because he was off-the-walls nutty, but was also not neutered, so . . ."

The audience pity-laughs and groans at the same time.

This feels like my cue.

I send up a silent prayer to Elvira: "I'm sorry I messed up, and this is the only way I can think of to fix it. Please know I'm not making fun of you; I'm invoking your spirit to make your last words ring true. To honor your final prophecy."

No response, but lightning doesn't immediately strike me down. A positive sign?

I wait one more beat, and then I stand up in front of the soundboard, my full costume on display. I cut off Frank's collegiate ferret experience, proclaiming in an Elvira-esque old-timey brogue: "Sometimes first dates are destined for failure, and that's okay! Not every first date is a match for the ages!"

Lucy looks like she's seen a ghost—which means the costume achieved the desired effect. Good or bad, jury's still out.

I slowly walk to the stage and clamber up as an old woman might do, with a few botched attempts and a roll to get myself up and over. The crowd seems amused. And confused.

I grab a mic from Frank. "I am the Great Elvira, and I have witnessed many first dates during my time as a shticky restaurant psychic. But none were as special as the first date I was reading when I tragically died at the hands of Father Time. Shall I tell you about it?"

The crowd obliges with a nice round of applause.

Lucy interjects, her eyes pinned on me. "Hmm. This sounds familiar. If I remember correctly, the night began with my date arriving thirty minutes late, soaked in his own sweat—drowning in it, really—and he wiped his face with his flannel shirt to dry off. And yet, I stayed . . ." Her face is unreadable, a careful stage mask, as she turns to the audience. "What can I say, I have a thing for men who get the nervous sweats. It's easier to tell when they're lying. Or so I thought." She gives an exaggerated shrug, and the audience continues to eat out of her palm.

"I was only trying . . . I mean"—I clear my throat and return to my Elvira accent—"*he* was only trying to be the least amount of late possible, running from the subway, and that flannel was coming off regardless, because it was an unseasonably warm October day, and, well"—back to my voice—"you do have those big green eyes that made it hard to think about anything else. The sweat was from nerves, too. You made me nervous." For someone who just turned down a Hollywood job, I suck at staying in this character. Hopefully, I still get an A for effort.

Lucy appears to consider this. "It's one thing to open up with a psychic hypothetical on a dating app—more creative than 'what up, cutie'—but it's another thing altogether to have an actual reading on a first date. My suitor either used this trick a lot, or it was fate how things panned out. I'm not sure I believe in fate, so . . . ?"

"Well," I jump back in, "as the Great Elvira, I can assure you this suitor had never been read by me before. I wouldn't forget a chronic over-sweater like that. And wasn't he on TV as a child? Who could forget that cherubic little face," I say, grinning.

"Mmm, right, so Elvira, what brings you here, then? To Earth. And this show, specifically. Are you back to get revenge? Curse me? Murder me? If this is my last night alive, my stage companions here have a killer basement full of bathtub gin that's . . . semi-drinkable. Maybe we could do it there?"

Excellent. Lucy and I are riffing now. And I'm not one to pass up a chance to make some jokes and keep the improv train moving.

"My darling Lucy, I wouldn't ever want to get revenge on you. This is just a pit stop to say hello because I heard about this brilliant show of yours. No, I'm here on Earth because of my great-grandson—I've been haunting that little shit ever since I died. He was on a real scare tear that last week, juvenile shit like hiding behind chairs and drapes. No originality, nothing bloodcurdling, just repetitive, and I guess my poor old heart couldn't take it anymore. It's alright, though, I have the rest of his life to screw up . . . I mean, to 'scare' him. Lovingly, of course."

Lucy laughs out loud. The first crack. "Elvira, you'd started to say that together we would succeed in . . . something. Have we failed the final prophecy you couldn't quite finish? Failed one another?"

Lucy is baiting me in front of the audience. Does she want me to grovel?

If so, fine by me. Happy to grovel away. There are far worse penances.

"Ah yes, the prophecy that tipped me over onto the other side of the veil. Let me see, it was about . . . well . . . I can't remember *exactly* what it was—I was a busy working psychic, my dear, thousands of clients with all kinds of destinies and desires. But if my wispy ghost brain is correct, I believe it was about discovering the best paths together. And this show was supposed to be the beginning of that, right? But your suitor bailed?" I drop the accent again. The shtick has gone as far as it can. "I would say he's terrified that he ruined the prophecy, and that it eats at him every breathing moment. Because he can't imagine a world where he imploded something this good. But he also hopes that a true prophecy can't be unturned. That maybe even the lows are all part of the journey. He wants to be real with you, always, and he's sorry, Lucy, so sorry, and he's come to his senses. Hopefully, not too late." I pull off the wig and the dress, neatly place them both on a barstool at the side of the stage.

I wait for the verdict as the fans' eyes pinball from me to Lucy, back to me.

It's excruciating.

"What a psychic she was, that Elvira," Lucy says after a moment, her voice somber. She's actively not looking in my direction. "May she rest in peace, truly. We mean no disrespect bringing her into the show tonight. Elvira met two awkward strangers on a first date and, intentionally or not, she sent them on a grand quest. I'll always be grateful to her for that." She clears her throat, and if I'm not mistaken, she's fighting off tears.

I am, too. There's moisture on my face, and it's not sweat this time.

Lucy closes her eyes, composing herself. When she looks up again, she's staring at me with a fire in her eyes. A very hot fire.

"And you, Rudy Riziero, almost ruined everything by bailing on that path, bailing on me and all the good people here tonight." Lucy turns to the audience, shaking her head. "Who'd like to treat Rudy with a little *Game of Thrones* reference he's sure not to get, because I know for a fact he's never watched a single episode?"

My mouth drops open. A pillow-talk reveal. Lucy went for the jugular. "Telling people I haven't watched *Game of Thrones* is too far! That was one of my biggest secrets, and—"

Lucy cuts me off. "Alright everyone, let's give Rudy some proper shame, and then we'll move on and get back to the reason we're here tonight: hilariously horrible first dates. *Other* hilariously horrible first dates, that is. I think we've adequately covered ours. So, shall we?"

Lucy, Estelle, Frank, and the entire audience point and chant as one, all eyes narrowed on me: "Shame! Shame! Shame!"

I might not get the reference, but no matter—I'll take whatever form shame takes. As long as Lucy forgives me.

Lucy stops chanting first. Everyone gradually takes her cue, the shouts trickling away.

I take a step closer to her. She looks so beautiful tonight, wearing a green dress I've never seen before, a color that makes her eyes blaze brighter than ever. Her lips are so red—so full and pouty and mischievous and perfect.

Lucy reaches for me.

Our palms meet first, then our arms, and suddenly, I'm pressed against every warm, welcoming inch of her. I'm not sure who kisses who, but we are—kissing, completely tangled up together—and the whole audience is watching.

It's the most PDA I've ever had in real life, off-screen. Too many cameras around in my formative teen years with Piper. I never shook that off, even when the cameras stopped rolling.

Right now, though, I don't care who's watching. Don't care that those red lips must be leaving tracks all over my face.

It feels too good.

At some point, Frank and Estelle clear their throats, in sync for once in their lives, and we pull apart and get back to it. The four of us this time.

Not the way we originally envisioned it, but that turns out to be okay. The Myrtles, with some hand-holding and a little restraint, are actually a great add to the show, providing some multi-generational overlap that makes things interesting. Lucy gets even better and sharper as she goes, and creates a catch-phrase along the way: "And that's not all, is it?" People seem to love that. As we wrap up, top honors go to a woman whose date was getting served by his soon-to-be-ex outside his apartment, and when he refused to open the door, she went up the fire escape and crawled through the window, just as our contestant was orgasming. Classic.

All in all, solid show. Minus the "train wreck" of a beginning. But no one seems to be complaining at the after party. The mingling is a hit—I overhear more than a few attendees chatting about their mutual laughably horrendous dating encounters.

Lucy and I have been glued at the hip. People keep coming up to us, congratulating us, as if we're holding court at our wedding reception. I'm not sure if it's more about the show or our romantic reunion, but either way, it feels nice.

As we're standing by the bar, wrapping up a conversation with some fans, I see my old plus-twos with their current plus-twos approaching. Matt, Jules, Sheeraz, and Marguerite were at the show. That's . . . unexpected. We've barely talked since the move.

Sheeraz speaks first, jabbing his finger sharply in the soft spot between my arm and shoulder. "You sonofabitch! You didn't tell me you got a gig in LA! I mean, we aren't roommates anymore, but still . . . an update would've been nice. Anyway, glad you didn't bail. I was beginning to think our heart-to-hearts were for nothing." He grins at me, then turns to Lucy. "Really fun evening. You stole the show."

Lucy blushes and looks to Marguerite, who's nodding in agreement. "Holy shit, you're so funny, Luce!"

"Wow, thank you. It was a . . . nerve-racking day, thinking Rudy wouldn't show. I'm glad you stayed after those first fifteen minutes."

Julia comes in for a big hug with Lucy. "You're hugely brave for plowing ahead. That took a lot of strength. Irreverence, too. Just the job for Lucy Minninger."

Matt leans in next to me and says, quietly, "I might've lost a bet that you weren't going to show up. A small price to pay for your happiness."

I laugh and pat him on the back. "I don't blame you. I'm even surprising myself these days. Must be the company I keep." I glance over at Lucy, deep in conversation with Julia. "Clearing the air with Rocco helped, too."

Matt looks shocked. "Seriously, and you didn't tell me?"

"I know, I know, but it was recent. Like forty-eight hours recent. Maybe we can find a time to catch up? A proper old roommates' night out feels long overdue."

As I say this, I grab Sheeraz's hand and pull him in. "I'm trying to practice more gratitude. I appreciate and respect both of you for coming tonight, but more importantly, for being my friends. Our beautiful life milestones should never be reasons to tear us apart—they should be causes for celebration. So, thank you. Consider this my audition for the best man speech. For either or both. Sheeraz, you're first up. Don't act like you haven't thought about it . . ." They laugh. It feels good to be around these humans, key players in a life era I'll always cherish.

I miss them.

I'm happy for them.

When they clear out after another round—along with a

pleasantly buzzed Frank and Estelle, safely tucked in their homeward bound limo—Lucy and I post up at the bar. Alone for the first time. Silently sipping our drinks, letting the night sink in as the club empties around us.

I lean into her, my lips brushing against the tip of her earlobe. "*You* made this whole night happen. For what it's worth—not much, probably—I thought I would be here with plenty of time to talk to you before the show. But first it was airport troubles, then traffic, then a stalled train underground with no Wi-Fi for a message to go through . . . all excuses, though. The point is: I fucked up, and you persevered. Made it a hit. You were amazing out there, a total natural. You had the audience eating out of your hands, all while keeping the Myrtles from stomping over one another. And *that* was no small feat."

She laughs. "The beginning was a challenge. They meant well, though, and they got it together once you were there to help lay down the law. They were so . . . proud of me, though. Like, real 'parent' proud. And honestly? I'm pretty damn proud of myself, too. So proud, as a matter of fact, that I'm officially going to quit my job with Clementine. I need to move past my resentment. Focus on what makes me happy. And this?" She spins in her stool to take in Little Zelda's. "Making people laugh makes me *very* happy."

"A big decision. But the right one, I think."

"Thank you." She turns to face me, pressing her knees against mine. "You did fuck up, for the record. Big time. I love Christmas, and you ruined mine. And I was looking forward to kissing my boyfriend on New Year's Eve, and you ruined that, too." Lucy is nose to nose with me, staring me down. "Strike three would have been not sweeping in to save the show we worked so hard to create together." She leans back, but she has a smile on her face.

I missed that smile.

I've never missed a smile so much.

"But you did come back," she says, "even if you were late to the party. You called it at two strikes, thank God. So all's forgiven, but don't you dare do anything like this again, got it? We're a *team*. We'll only make it with good communication and honesty. Don't pull any fancy actor shit on me, okay? And no more secret sibling vendettas. It's not fair to an only child like me. We'll figure out the rest as we go. Money. Stability. Adulthood. Tonight gives me faith."

I nod. "So much faith. I'll never fail to have your back again, I promise you that. And you should know . . . I talked to Rocco in LA. Partly because of what you said."

"Yeah?"

"Yeah. And it helped me. A lot. So thank you."

She grins. "I'll always be there to lay down the truth for you. No matter how harsh."

I grin back. "I don't doubt it."

We kiss then.

Long and lingering enough that it inspires a few catcalls from stragglers by the bar.

And from Marianne, whom I haven't seen since my dramatic entrance. Walking over to us with an envelope in hand, our earnings for the night.

"Aren't you two *cute*," she says, smirking, but not altogether unpleasantly. "Well, that was something . . . really. Next time you encounter a scheduling problem like that, Rudy, please let me know right away. We'll work it out. We lost a few early in, so you technically didn't sell out. But we came close. And it was all uphill after the rocky start."

Lucy cringes. "I'm so sorry about—"

"Lucy, no," Marianne cuts in, "not your fault at all. You were great, the funniest one up there. Sorry, Rudy." She shrugs.

I'm not one to argue with that. She *was* the funniest. Honest, natural, and so smart.

"See?" I say, wrapping an arm around Lucy's shoulders.

"Everyone felt that way! M, I am truly sorry. I didn't want to mess up either relationship, and I almost destroyed both. I made some terrible life decisions, and I understand if you cut me from the roster. But I sincerely hope we can do more shows together."

Marianne looks at me and, after a pause surely meant to torture, smiles. "You've groveled enough, I suppose. I'll let it slide. This time. I'm glad you came to your senses, you dipshit. Lucy seems like a keeper. Don't fuck this one up. I'll see you both in February for the next round—a nice Valentine's treat." And with that, she pats me on the back and walks away.

"Firstly, we have another show next month," Lucy says. "Secondly, she's fantastic. I hope we can be friends."

"I had a feeling you two would get along."

I reach for my bag to slip the envelope away, knocking it against the bar with a thud.

"Uh," Lucy says, looking down at the bag. "Do you have a bowling ball in there?"

Oh, right. The ultimate callback. I completely forgot to use it onstage. "It was supposed to be my sweet finish before I got shamed onstage. A Magic Eight Ball."

She gasps. "An homage to our very first exchange! I'm impressed. Really. I might've forgone the shaming had I known."

I laugh. "No way. You absolutely still would've shamed me."

"Yeah. You're probably right."

I pull the Magic 8 Ball from the bag and place it between us on the bar. "What should we ask it?" I say in my best Elvira voice. Okay, *that* was the last time. "How about, 'Did we make Elvira proud for trying to fulfill her prophecy?' Does that sound good?"

Lucy winks—both awkward and endearing, as is her way—and gives a thumbs-up.

We both grab for the ball and shake together, the tips of our fingers touching.

We pause. Flip it. Wait.

As the bubbles settle, an answer is revealed on the inner triangle:

It is decidedly so.

I wrap my arms around Lucy, and we kiss again. Less steamy bar make-out this time, more of a "sealed with a kiss" close on these last few months. I don't care if it is a stupid toy, the 8 Ball says we did good, and that counts for something. Tonight's not an ending, though.

It's only the beginning.

Lucy and I say goodbye to Carole—who's *gushing* with praise, totally unprecedented—and a few last remaining fans, and then we make our exit.

As we turn up Fifth Ave, I spot a graffiti-covered food truck I've never seen around here before. We walk closer, and I realize it's not just any old food truck—it's a *taco* truck.

And here I thought this night couldn't get any better.

Lucy runs ahead and puts in an order before I even make it to the truck. I'm content to plunk down on a nearby bench, to wait and reflect on how it's all fallen so neatly into place. Pieces I didn't even know I was looking for.

"We're lucky, last customers of the night," Lucy says, returning with her hands full. "One of each taco, a grand total of seven. I hope you're hungry." She sits beside me and nuzzles into my shoulder.

"I'm hungry, and I'm happy," I say, nuzzling back. "Lucy, I love you."

"That's excellent news," she whispers against my neck. "Because I love you, too."

I look up toward the sky, the stars seeming especially bright and shiny for Brooklyn. The night sky here is usually so dim. Muted.

Nothing is dim or muted about tonight.

Thank you, Elvira. For this experience. For leading us here.

My little prayer sent into the universe, I turn back to Lucy and the tacos, which smell exceptionally delicious.

We're going bite for bite on the carnitas taco when the truck's idle engine rumbles into gear. I glance up as it's slowly easing away from the curb. A low-lying fluorescent sign on the truck's side reads: MYSTIC TACOS.

A very good name.

As the truck turns the corner, a nearby streetlamp flashes on the graffitied bumper. There's a strand of tall, swirly gold letters, almost seeming to glimmer in the light:

Elvira wuz here

The truck turns the corner and disappears into the night.

Lucy

GASP

Nine months later . . .

"**Y**ou really know how to treat a lady for an anniversary," I say, stumbling and nearly tripping over a flat, crumbling gravestone marker obscured by the grass, "taking her out for a cemetery picnic to celebrate."

"*Green-Wood* Cemetery," Rudy says, smiling at me from where he stands atop a small hill, next to an imposing mausoleum that reads: STEINWAY. I mean, of course they had the bucks for such finery in the afterlife. "I wouldn't take you to any run-of-the-mill plot of graves on such a special day. But this place?" He spreads his arms out wide, taking in the whole of Green-Wood, which, according to the brochure I picked up at the gate, encompasses a whopping 478 acres. "This is more like a stunning park that just so happens to have a lot of dead bodies tucked away underground. And aboveground in mini palaces, like this one right here," he says, tapping his fingers lightly against the stone slab siding of the crypt. "You think the Myrtles will spend eternity together in something fancy like this?"

I laugh, huffing out a breath as I finish the climb and stop beside him. "You better believe they've already bought themselves a prime plot of dirt. Somewhere in Queens, though, since that's where they're from, and because it's practically a necropolis, there's so much coffin real estate up there. Still fighting over the details, though, last I heard. Frank wants one of those phallic pillars, Estelle wants to have statues of them made—carved from marble, obviously."

"Hmm. Why not both? One phallic tower, one marble Estelle?"

"You'll have to suggest that to them. Or, no. Maybe don't. They have me on the will for the house, you know. Don't want them to suspect we're overthinking their demise or anything."

Rudy laughs, and then he takes my hand, leading me past the Steinways and into a thicket of trees, past a wrought-iron fenced-in family plot, and onto an overlook that juts out over sprawling hills of tombstones and trees and flowers. There's a pond below us, circled by a row of fancy mausoleums, a small village inhabited by absurdly rich corpses.

"This is an interesting place," I say, spinning around to take it all in as Rudy pulls an old quilt from his bag and spreads it out over the ground. "Memorable. I'll give you that."

"I can't believe you've lived in Brooklyn for so many years and never came here."

"I can't believe you keep talking, when the tacos tucked in your bag are supposedly the best in all of Brooklyn, and you're just letting them get cold and soggy." I plop down onto the blanket, reaching my arms up to demand sustenance.

Rudy obediently takes out the brown bag and settles in next to me, spreading out a feast of tacos and tamales and chips and sauces. Enough to feed a family of four. We'll devour every last morsel.

We don't talk for at least ten minutes, we're too occupied with tasting each taco—splitting each meticulously down the middle as we go, one bite for him, one for me, back and forth until we finish, then moving onto the next.

"You've been holding out on me for the last year," I say, closing my eyes as I savor the last bite of a mushroom taco so divine, it can't possibly consist solely of fungi. It's some kind of culinary miracle.

"Can you believe it's been a whole year since we met?" he asks, and when I open my eyes, he's smiling at me with so much radiant joy, those freckled cheeks of his crinkled and dimpled, I can't stop myself from leaning in for a kiss. He tastes like peppers and corn and hot sauce, and it is total perfection—*he* is total perfection, and I don't want any other lips but these for the rest of my life.

"It feels like it's been a week," I say. "But it also feels like it's been a lifetime."

He nods thoughtfully, reaching for the last taco—al pastor, of course. We always save the best for last. One of at least a thousand things we agree on. "I feel you. It's like we've known each other forever, but every day still feels new. Because there's always more to learn about Lucy Minninger. I could never get bored. Not with you."

"Better not," I say, leaning in as he holds out the taco for me to take a bite. Sweet and spicy and so outrageously delicious, I let out a loud moan. "Again. Why have we known each other for three hundred and sixty-five days, and I'm just now trying these tacos?"

He shrugs as he takes a bite, too. "We've been busy eating other delicious tacos. Busy all around, really. Busy loving one another. Busy with music, busy with writing, busy with working on our totally badass show that, let me remind you, we're taking to LA next week."

We *have* been busy—busy in all the best ways, together and apart.

Step one for me: bidding farewell to Clementine and Pinky. Then getting a part-time job at the cute new bookshop that'd popped up a few blocks away from our cave—nameless now, the Spinster Cave sign happily retired. Starting to write again, a little every day, because suddenly, maybe thanks to a certain handsome ginger I know, I felt equal parts inspired by comedy *and* romance. The rom doesn't feel so impossible to grasp. No seven- (or five-, or one-) figure book deals yet, but after months of querying something new, I signed with a literary agent. I'm not just a writer these days—I'm a writer *with an agent.* That's not everything, but it's a start. A much better start than cleaning up Pinky's shit from the sidewalk.

And step one for Rudy: getting hired by a popular New York City band to play bass on their latest album, and then go off and on the road for six months. Still finding time for his show.

Still finding time for our show. Always.

He hasn't been late for any others, thankfully. Perfectly punctual.

Marianne wasn't thrilled when we told her we were taking a few months off from Little Zelda's—a few months for a comedy residency in LA, a few months for Rudy to tour me around all the places that made him who he is today. To spend some time with Rocco. To eat all the best tacos the West Coast has to offer.

We finish our chips and pack up, and Rudy takes my hand. "Let's stroll it off," he says, tugging me away from where we parked the Myrtles' shiny new BMW. "You know, this place was built just as much for the living as the dead. It was here before Prospect Park—before Central Park, too. A place to enjoy nature, and to reflect on the circle of life."

I have to admit, as we stroll past a hilly mound of wildflowers and a row of trees with perfect October orange leaves, it really is gorgeous here. And peaceful—maybe the most peaceful place in all of Brooklyn. We haven't passed by another living and breathing soul since we got here. It's an unconventional place to celebrate a year of life together, but what about us has been conventional?

"Can you hold my phone for a minute," Rudy says abruptly, dropping my hand as he stops beside a newer line of graves. He clears his throat. "I want you to take a video of me."

"What are you planning to do?" I ask as I grab the phone

and flick the camera open. "Have we been watching too many *Ghost Adventures*? Are you trying to capture some paranormal activity?"

He shakes his head, clearing his throat again.

"You okay? Did you get some hot sauce down the wrong pipe?"

"Lucy."

"Rudy."

"Camera's rolling?"

"Yep."

It happens in slow motion then. One minute, he's standing in front of me, and the next—

He's down on one knee.

He's down on one knee, and there's a small green velvet box in his hands.

I gasp.

A full-body gasp that leaves me with no air left in my lungs.

I put a hand on the closest gravestone to steady myself.

"Lucy, you've made this last year the best and brightest of my life. Every moment with you is an adventure, and it's an adventure I never want to end. I've been on this planet long enough to know—to know that this is it for me. *You*, Lucy Minninger, are it for me. There's no one else like you. An understatement, really. You're my forever partner, in all things life and love and comedy, if you'll have me. For all the days we have here on this green earth together, and"—he glances around the rows of stones, radiating outward in every direction—"for whatever comes after that, too. Because I won't stop loving you at death do us part. Our love is more cosmic than that. So, will you—"

I squeal, the phone slipping through my fingers, falling onto the grass. "YES!"

"—marry me?" he finishes, and by then, I'm already down on my knees in front of him.

"A million times yes, for all eternity," I say, cupping his cheeks in my hands.

"Really?" He's grinning, and if I thought he was radiant before, he is brighter than the sun now—he *is* my sun. The brightest star in any solar system.

"Really."

"Do you want me to, you know, show you the ring first?"

"It could be a mood ring from a gumball machine, and my answer would still be yes."

He laughs as he pops open the box, and set inside the cream-colored satin, there's a thin diamond-studded gold band with a large oval emerald nested delicately in the filigree setting.

"I know a big diamond is more traditional, but this one reminded me of your eyes," he says. I don't have words as I extend my finger, and he slips it on. A perfect fit. Estelle must have helped him. "And I've never seen eyes as blindingly beautiful as yours."

"I already said yes," I say, choking back a sob. "You don't have to keep buttering me up."

"I'll never stop," he says. And then he tilts his chin pointedly at the gravestone next to us, the one that held me up during the proposal.

I look at it for the first time. A sleek dark gray. Freshly carved, not faded like so many of the other markers we've seen. Letters that I read, quickly at first, and then more slowly, two, three, four times:

ELVIRA GRAY

in big, bold caps at the top, and then, in a more delicate script below:

Oldest Psychic in New York.

And today's date, one year past.

The day she died.

The day we met.

"Holy shit. Did you—"

Rudy nods. "I planned it. Yep. Nothing woo-woo about this particular twist. Came here to scout it out a few weeks back. It only felt right. She brought us together, didn't she? Who knows what would have happened if we'd had any other first date? Neither of us were much good at second dates."

"No, we weren't, were we?"

Rudy reaches into his back pocket, pulls out a flask. "To Elvira," he says, uncapping it and letting a drop of whiskey splash against the fresh grass above her grave.

"To Elvira," I repeat, taking a small sip after he hands me the flask.

It's only then I remember my phone, bending over to pick it up from the ground. "I'm glad we have this moment captured forever. Obnoxious squeal and all. Very clever of you."

"I thought so, too."

"I'll have to scour the footage to see if Elvira made her presence known."

"Oh, she's here. I can feel it. Maybe my mom's not the only Irish witch in the family."

He wraps an arm around my shoulders, and we stand there for a few minutes, staring at Elvira's gravestone in silence.

Until—

"Yoo-hoo!"

"Way to go, kiddos!"

"Would you believe we rode in a *yellow cab* to be here with you?"

"A taxicab! That's how much we love you!"

I glance up to see the Myrtles, waving and grinning, as they pick their way between the stones to reach us.

"I take it you told them?" I say, turning back to Rudy.

"It only felt right—asking both sets of your parents. Though in hindsight, maybe I shouldn't have given them the specifics."

"It's okay. We'll have plenty of alone time in LA to celebrate properly."

"And to plan."

"Speaking of planning," Estelle says, huffing as she closes in on us, "I was already thinking that the Botanic Garden could be a spectacular venue, on us of course, or maybe . . ."

I bob my head, smiling through a flurry of hugs and kisses and unsolicited wedding advice, turning back to glance at Elvira's final resting place once more before I'm swept away, back toward the car.

Rudy takes my hand in his as we walk, squeezing tight.

I lean in and whisper, "Can we have a cemetery picnic every year?"

He nods. "I wouldn't have it any other way."

We step back onto the road, side by side. Ready to go.

Ready for all of the weird and wonderful adventures of Lucy and Rudy still to come.

Authors' Note
The (True) Story Behind the Story

Saturday, May 1, 1999: Los Angeles, California

Seventeen-year-old Danny took the stage at the Nickelodeon Kids' Choice Awards, accepting an award as cast member on the Best TV Show of the year, *All That.* It was a good day—live performances by TLC and Britney Spears and NSYNC (who once penned up the backseat of Danny's Chevy Tahoe, but that's a story for another day); a star-studded afterparty, where a certain A-list teen actress was desperately trying to woo him. He met a young female Olympian that evening, too—an Olympian he'd soon take out for a few dates. At the end of the night, he went home to his family's apartment in Burbank, to rest up for another week on set.

Saturday, May 1, 1999: Green Lane, Pennsylvania

While thirteen-year-old Kate's life was woefully undocumented by media outlets, and her whereabouts can't be as precisely pinned, she can guesstimate with reasonable accuracy how she spent this particular Saturday night: May 1 was the birthday of her best friends, twins she'd met at the local Little League field back before kindergarten. They'd probably have been celebrating with a sleepover—attempting French braids, playing Truth or Dare, choreographing dance moves to Britney Spears's songs, eating too many Cheetos, and most likely watching the Kids' Choice Awards on TV. (In absolute agreement that Jonathan Taylor Thomas very much deserved to be added to the Hall of Fame.)

So yes, one could say Danny and Kate had . . . rather different formative years.

Danny debuted on the screen at the tender age of six, after first being spotted by a talent manager at a mall in New Jersey. Early jobs doing commercials and a soap opera soon led to bigger roles—such as playing larger-than-life kid brother "Little Pete" on Nickelodeon's *The Adventures of Pete & Pete*, and then later becoming a celebrity panelist on the game show *Figure It Out* and a cast member of aforementioned sketch comedy show *All That*. He dabbled in non-Nickelodeon shows and films, too: *The Baby-Sitters Club*, *The Magic School Bus*, and *The Mighty Ducks* are some career highlights. He walked red carpets, regularly did charity events with superstars, went on tour with 98 Degrees. And he also went to public school in New Jersey, at least when he wasn't being tutored on set in California. He worked at the local bagel store, too—not because he needed the money, but because his parents wanted him to keep his head on straight. (It mostly worked.)

Kate loved putting on shows, too. For her parents' friends, subjecting them to live musical theater and comedy shows and sermons from her humble living room stage. She tried out for every play the high school drama club put on, and never got more than Party Guest #5. She even took a community college acting class in her tween years; she nearly threw up having to do improv. So it seemed she wasn't destined for life as an actress after all—but where she failed onstage, she excelled in the classroom, especially in her English and literature courses. She studied and devoured books every night and every weekend, and became valedictorian of her small high school in Pennsylvania.

Danny left LA and acting after high school; he wanted college on the East Coast, he wanted freedom, he wanted "normal." He attended Hampshire College (bonus: no grades!) in Massachusetts and studied music, with a focus on the upright bass. After graduation, he moved to New York City to start the next phase of life; he'd grown up in its shadow, and had always known it was meant to be his home. His work ventures were many and varied, whatever it took to pay the bills each month—delivering wine in a box truck to restaurants all over the city for a family distribution business; performing with his longtime band (first formed in high school), Jounce, at festivals and music venues across the country; writing and shooting with his sketch comedy troupe, ManBoobs Comedy. He did some acting and voiceover jobs here and there, including a character for the popular video game, *Grand Theft Auto V*.

Kate chose Penn State University when it came time for college; she wanted to be driving distance from her family home, from the friends she grew up with. She wanted something new, but not too new. She majored in English with a focus on creative writing and women's studies; she knew she wanted to work with words, because words were what made her happiest— what made the most sense. By the time she graduated, she was set on publishing and bringing stories to life, so she said farewell to the security of Pennsylvania and everything/one she knew, and moved to New York City. A place she'd only been approximately three times in her life (for Times Square and Broadway and the Statue of Liberty). A place that terrified her—the size, the noise, the strangeness of it all—but the best and brightest place in the world for books. After attending the Columbia Publishing Course, she found a marketing job at Macmillan; after two years, she left to work at a literary agency. She had found her home.

Danny and his band Jounce became staples on the Lower East Side rock scene, playing regularly at the many venues in the neighborhood. On and off stage, he discovered his power of inducing nostalgia for other older millennials—anyone who'd been a kid in the glorious era of nineties pop culture. He never had to initiate conversations and "meet and greets" with women; he relied on fans approaching him for most of his dating at the time. A convenient strategy . . . though also fraught with problems. Plenty of awkward interactions, and too many superfans knowing where he lived. As Danny got older (and at least slightly wiser), he moved to Brooklyn and attempted to become more of the monogamous type. Pursuing relationships with more adulting: shared vacations, holidays, friend groups. But despite his best efforts, Danny's transient work schedule with band tours and acting work would always end up in the way. Time and time again, relationships imploded before they ever fully took off.

While Kate was flourishing on the career side—steadily building a list of brilliant writer clients, getting her own book deal as an author, two YA novels sold to Viking—her social life left quite a bit to be desired. Especially her dating life, which consisted mostly of one terrible first date after another, courtesy of Match and OkCupid and Coffee Meets Bagel and really every app that had been designed to engineer twenty-first century meet cutes. She'd only had one boyfriend, a passing college relationship; anything beyond date three was mostly uncharted territory. New York City dating was . . . a challenge. The only plus to all the failed dating attempts were the stories. Oh, the stories! So many stories. They were fodder for all her friends still in Pennsylvania, friends who were busily getting married, buying houses, birthing babies. The single-in-the-city life seemed destined never to end.

Until Danny and Kate both came across one of the more questionable apps of the era: Tinder. Danny mostly for "comedic fodder" (or so he liked to say), and Kate for actual proper dating (unlike the majority of fellow swipers, it would seem).

Kate came across Danny's profile during a marathon swiping session, background to the latest episode of *The Bachelorette*—but she was swiping left so quickly, so many disappointing candidates on the offer, one exotic animal on display after another, that she swiped left on rote. Only to realize a split second after the fact that the *Daniel* she'd just rejected was *Danny Tamberelli*, the red-headed boy from her TV screen as a kid, currently an active part of the Brooklyn comedy circuit (a pro-tip she learned from a fan on a recent date). With no options to backtrack and a strange, niggling compulsion to match with Danny, Kate deleted Tinder, started from scratch, and swiped furiously for days (a fact she wouldn't admit for months to come) until she came across his profile a second time—carefully swiping right this time around. Only it wasn't a match. The hours of swiping had been for naught.

Or so it seemed. Because a few days later, Danny came across Kate, too. He was torn (if he's being honest); she seemed "chill" in some pictures, reading at Central Park, looking reflective at the Met. But then she was all "dolled up" in others, looking—as he put it—supremely "high maintenance." But . . . he took a chance. She liked tacos and whiskey, after all; she couldn't be all bad. He swiped right.

They matched, the heavens erupted in song, and while Kate spent hours upon hours agonizing over an appropriately witty and decidedly un-creepy message (not wanting to come across as a superfan, obviously), Danny went for his template cut-and-paste greeting:

When I want to test a psychic, I barge in unannounced and if they look frightened I just say, "weren't you expecting me?" and walk out. Otherwise, if they're cool about the whole thing, I'll stick around. How bout you?

Kate was underground on a train when the message came in, and though the MTA claims that Wi-Fi is an actual thing, it most definitely was not; she had to wait until the train came to a station, so she could fly up the stairs and read his cryptic hypothetical while standing outside her favorite Brooklyn bodega. After hours of deliberation, she replied:

Nah, I wouldn't even bother with the testing in the first place. When I was 18, I paid 50 bucks for a tarot reading and the lady ate Doritos and watched TV the whole time she predicted my future. I'd pick an 8 ball every time. ✨ 🎱 ✨

And from here is where Danny and Kate's love story diverges fully from this book—their first date was standard fare, a few drinks at a dive bar in Prospect Heights. (Though in hindsight, a visit to a psychic would have been a very appropriate first meeting! A death mid-reading, though, less than ideal.) Things went smoothly from there—two chronically inept daters found dating to suddenly feel bizarrely easy; one date became two, ten, twenty, one hundred. Next up: an apartment together in Crown Heights, an engagement on a wintry beach in Montauk, a wedding in an old steel mill in Bethlehem, a baby boy thirteen months after that.

They worked from their Brooklyn apartment, every day, always together. Kate agenting and writing YA novels; Danny working on his various shows, podcasting with his former TV brother "Big Pete," making music. Raising a tiny, feral, outrageously amazing human. The pandemic came, and their work-from-home life became a mandate, not a choice. They decided it might be fun to create together for once—to write a story steeped in their truths, the highs and lows of life and love in their beautiful city, and the twisty paths that brought them together, to Tinder, to a dive bar in Brooklyn on one unseasonably warm October night. A story that also left plenty of room for creativity—and a sprinkling of magic: *The First Date Prophecy.*

Acknowledgments

We've talked about collaborating and creating together for years now—it's always been the dream, sharing our hearts and minds and very different creative processes in that way—and once we had this idea, the "what if" inspired by our first Tinder conversations (preserved in screenshots that will live on forever, thanks to Kate's incredible foresight to document before deleting the app for good!), we knew we'd found "the one."

We'd collectively had a very long, sometimes hilarious, sometimes heartbreaking romantic journey to find one another; there was certainly no shortage of fodder when it came to depicting New York City dating misadventures. So we decided to take the leap and jump all in with this concept, bleeding so much of ourselves and our experiences out on the page—writing a love letter to one another and to our city, and to all of our readers who have faced a similarly tumultuous road to finding their person. A reminder that love comes on its own clock, in its own surprising and mysterious ways. Working on this novel together, chapter by chapter, was a bright light through the pandemic, the isolation, and the uncertainty; Lucy and Rudy and their world became our safe space, our inspiration, and our hope.

This book came to be because of so many special people—those we know and love now, and those who made brief but valuable cameos somewhere along the way.

Eternal gratitude to our brilliant literary agent, Jill Grinberg, for her unwavering encouragement and enthusiasm from our very first pitch—the tiny, insecure baby seed of this idea—and her sharp insights throughout each and every step of the process. And to Denise Page, as always, for her exceptionally wise takes and invaluable support. We are endlessly appreciative of the JGLM dream team.

So many, many thanks to our amazing editor, Elizabeth Trout, for loving Lucy and Rudy as much as we do, for your keen editorial insights and championing in-house, for your warmth and steadfast positivity. We are so thrilled to be on this adventure with you and with the Kensington team; special thanks to Steve Zacharius, Adam Zacharius, Lynn Cully, Jackie Dinas, Jane Nutter, Lauren Jernigan, Alexandra Nicolajsen, Barbara Brown, and Carly Sommerstein.

To those who helped pave Danny's path in the entertainment world, from *The Adventures of Pete & Pete* to *The Mighty Ducks* and *All That* and beyond, the creators and writers, comedians, and musicians who trusted and inspired him—and to the fans who continue to celebrate that work: Thank you, always. You have helped to shape Danny and his world, his vision and perspective, in the most meaningful ways.

To our friends who rallied and cheered for us throughout our romantic trials and tribulations—and who continue to do so now, supporting us through life's domestic and writing adventures: You are part of our forever families, and your unconditional love throughout the journey helped make all things possible.

To the Detweilers and the Tamberellis, our families who

have seen it all, done it all by our sides, and who have loved us so well and so generously from day one: Thank you for raising two passionate dreamers, giving us the encouragement and trust to fly freely, and the strength and confidence to always find our way back to the ground. You are our hearts and our home, our constants, wherever else life may take us. Thank you, too, to our mothers for their early reads and the praise that helped us push through to the end; apologies if you had to cover your eyes for any of the more *romantic* scenes . . . ! (It's not us! It's Lucy and Rudy!)

And lastly, our dearest Alfred and Penelope. Thank you for letting Mommy and Daddy hide away sometimes to frantically jot down words. You are our brightest joy, our greatest hope, and the most important reason for everything we do. We hope you discover your own unique fairy tales, whatever wacky/wild/wonderful shapes those paths might take.

Visit our website at
KensingtonBooks.com
to sign up for our newsletters, read
more from your favorite authors, see
books by series, view reading group
guides, and more!

Become a Part of Our
Between the Chapters Book Club
Community and Join the Conversation